WITHDRAWAL
AT THE MEMORY BANK

"Feel any pressure inside your head?"

"No."

"How about your eyes? See any spots or flashes in front of them?"

"No!" snapped Jordan.

"Take it easy," said the man from Intelligence. "This is my business."

"Sorry."

"That's all right. It's just that if there's anything wrong with you or the bank I want to know it." He rose from the rewind spool, which was now industriously gathering in the loose tape; and unclipping a pressure-torch from his belt, began resealing the aperture. "It's just that occasionally new officers have been hearing too many stories about the banks in Training School, and they're inclined to be jumpy."

"Stories?" said Jordan.

"Haven't you heard them?" answered the Intelligence man. "Stories of memory domination—stationmen driven insane by the memories of the men who had the Station before them. Catatonics whose minds have got lost in the past history of the bank, or cases of memory replacement . . ."

"Oh, those," said Jordan. "Are they true?"

"Some," he said bluntly.

—from "Steel Brother"
by Gordon R. Dickson

ROBOT WARRIORS

INTRODUCTION BY GORDON R. DICKSON

WITH CHARLES G. WAUGH
AND MARTIN HARRY
GREENBERG, EDITORS

ACE BOOKS, NEW YORK

ROBOT WARRIORS

An Ace Book / published by arrangement with
the editors

PRINTING HISTORY
Ace edition / October 1991

ISBN: 0-441-53166-0

Ace Books are published by The Berkley Publishing Group,
200 Madison Avenue, New York, New York 10016.
The name "ACE" and the "A" logo
are trademarks belonging to Charter Communications, Inc.

PRINTED IN THE UNITED STATES OF AMERICA

10 9 8 7 6 5 4 3 2 1

Contents

Introduction

When I was very young I had a toy robot some eleven inches high, fashioned and painted to look as if he was made of steel. He could be wound up; and once this was done, he would whir internally and walk slowly, arms swinging. I used to half close my eyes, and imagine him as ten feet high, moving ponderously and purposefully to some task beyond human strength.

Nowadays we live with robots. They are buried in our microwave ovens and cars and a hundred other useful places. But they are not a part of our imagination anymore—and perhaps that is our loss.

The emergence of the robot into imagination and reality is more recent than many people think. In fact, only since Karel Čapek, the Czechoslovakian satirist, introduced the concept and the word in his play *R.U.R.*, in 1920, little more than a decade before my toy robot was built. But robots caught the literary imagination immediately.

One reason for this, and possibly the strongest reason, was that the idea of the robot carried with it an implication of something created by man; but showing, individually at least, some of the abilities of living humanity. Something, also, that could get out of humanity's control and become a threat. The fascination of it, consequently, was like that which lies at the root of Mary Shelley's *Frankenstein*, in which the Frankenstein monster offers the same sort of wonder and appeal.

When it came to the flowering of robotics in the science fiction literary areas, however, a couple of special, but separate, factors were at work.

In the stories of this volume, the earlier writers, particularly, like Poul Anderson and Christopher Anvil, were heavily influenced not only by latter-day technology but by the forecasting of this same technology in fiction form, in the magazine *Astounding* (now *Analog*). This was the magazine that led the science fiction field under the aegis of an editor, John Campbell, who was himself a physics graduate and a hard-science writer. John Campbell preferred hard-science stories; and robot stories, by definition, could not be anything else.

Campbell indeed made no secret of the fact that his inclinations lay in the hard-science direction. They were, in fact, so powerful that one of the interesting spin-offs of his attitude was that he at least once advertised, in the magazine itself, for technologically qualified, but otherwise amateur, writers. In the advertisement, he emphasized that he was interested in those who knew the hardware they were writing about—in a hands-on sense—as a first requirement, with writerly ability as only a secondary requirement.

His ideas in general made for a popular and successful magazine that found fertile grounds at the time in the minds of many of his writers; and some who have come into science fiction since his death. That was the first, strong influence on science fiction's robotics literature.

The second was that during the Campbell period and after, books would periodically appear on the shelves of booksellers which were anthologies of hitherto unpublished novelettes or novellas, each by a different writer. All of the stories might start from the same assumption, or be built around the same idea; but invariably they would be very different in the final forms that individually resulted.

The publishing idea behind such volumes was hopefully that the reader, on encountering this variety of stories all written from a single concept or story idea, would be moved to say (or at least feel) *"how different!"*—in that no one story approached any of the others in its finished form; and that therefore the reader would be filled with wonder at the ingenuity of writers who could come up with such unlike pieces of fiction from the same idea.

But the actual fact was, it was a wonder that the stories bore even as much resemblance to each other as they did. This, because a writer, by nature, cannot help being creative as he or she works; and therefore instinctively uses any idea merely as a springboard to build something that is uniquely his or her own. Moreover, since all people—and that includes writers—vary remarkably from one to the other with their own personal attitudes and inventiveness, the stories are also bound to vary accordingly.

Under these and other influences, between the late twenties and the mid-fifties there were published some hundreds of science fiction stories in which robots or some aspect of them entered, but with no two stories alike. Inevitably, in that large number, they fell into subclasses; and one of the more interesting subclasses was that of robots designed to be of use in war—whether present or futuristic.

So it should not be surprising that the stories in this volume, although they are all concerned with robotics in warfare, show the rich variation they do. Keith Laumer's *A Relic of War* is a deeply touching story. Christopher Anvil's story is a rollicking example of fictional humor. Poul Anderson's *Kings Who Die* is as grand and somber as its title implies; and behind them all, I can see my old friend, the tin robot—heavily striding, striding.

Perhaps you will see him there too. . . .

ROBOT WARRIORS

KINGS WHO DIE

Poul Anderson

Luckily, Diaz was facing the other way when the missile exploded. It was too far off to blind him permanently, but the retinal burns would have taken a week or more to heal. He saw the glare reflected in his view lenses. As a ground soldier he would have hit the rock and tried to claw himself a hole. But there was no ground here, no up or down, concealment or shelter, on a slice of spaceship orbiting through the darkness beyond Mars.

Diaz went loose in his armor. Countdown: brow, jaw, neck, shoulders, back, chest, belly . . . No blast came, to slam him against the end of his lifeline and break any bones whose muscles were not relaxed. So it had not been a shaped-charge shell, firing a cone of atomic-powered concussion through space. Or if it was, he had not been caught in the danger zone. As for radiation, he needn't worry much about that. Whatever particles and gamma photons he got at this distance should not be too big a dose for the anti-X in his body to handle the effects.

He was alive.

He drew a breath which was a good deal shakier than the Academy satorist would have approved of. ("If your nerves twitch, cadet-san, then you know yourself alive and they need not twitch. Correct?" To hell with that, except as a technique.) Slowly, he hauled himself in until his boots made magnetic contact and he stood, so to speak, upon his raft.

Then he turned about for a look.

"*Nombre de Dios,*" he murmured, a hollow noise in the helmet. Forgotten habit came back, with a moment's recollection of his mother's face. He crossed himself.

Against blackness and a million wintry stars, a gas cloud expanded. It glowed in many soft hues, the center still bright, edges fading into vacuum. Shaped explosions did not behave like that, thought the calculator part of Diaz; this had been a standard fireball type. But the cloud was nonspherical. Hence a ship had been hit. A big ship. But whose?

Most of him stood in wonder. A few years ago he'd spent a furlough at Antarctic Lodge. He and some girl had taken a snowcat out to watch the aurora, thinking it would make a romantic background. But then they saw the sky and forgot about each other for a long time. There was only the aurora.

The same awesome silence was here, as that incandescence which had been a ship and her crew swelled and vanished into space.

The calculator in his head proceeded with its business. Of those American vessels near the *Argonne* when first contact was made with the enemy, only the *Washington* was sufficiently massive to go out in a blast of yonder size and shape. If that was what had happened, Captain Martin Diaz of the United States Astromilitary Corps was a dead man. The other ships of the line were too distant, traveling on vectors too unlike his own, for their scout-boats to come anywhere close to where he was.

On the other hand, it might well have been a Unasian battlewagon. Diaz had small information on the dispositions of the enemy fleet. He'd had his brain full just directing the torp launchers under his immediate command. If that had indeed been a hostile dreadnaught which got clobbered, surely none but the *Washington* could have delivered the blow, and its boats would be near—

There!

For half a second Diaz was too stiffened by the sight to react. The boat ran black across waning clouds, accelerating on a streak of its own fire. The wings and sharp shape that were needed in atmosphere made him think of a marlin he had once hooked off Florida, blue lightning under the sun . . . Then a flare was in his hand, he squeezed the igniter and radiance blossomed.

Just an attention-getting device, he thought, and laughed unevenly as he and Bernie Sternthal had done, acting out the standard irreverences of high school students toward the psych course. But Bernie had left his bones on Ganymede, three years ago, and in this hour Diaz's throat was constricted and his nostrils full of his own stench.

He skyhooked the flare and hunkered in its harsh illumination by his radio transmitter. Clumsy in their gauntlets, his fingers adjusted controls, set the revolving beams on SOS. If he had been noticed, and if it was physically possible to make the velocity changes required, a boat would come for him. The Corps looked after its own.

Presently the flare guttered out. The pyre cloud faded to nothing.

The raft deck was between Diaz and the shrunken sun, but the stars that crowded on every side gave ample soft light. He allowed his gullet, which felt like sandpaper, a suck from his one water flask. Otherwise he had several air bottles, an oxygen reclaim unit and a ridiculously large box of Q rations. His raft was a section of inner plating, torn off when the *Argonne* encountered the ball storm. She was only a pursuit cruiser, unarmored against such weapons. At thirty miles per second, relative, the little steel spheres tossed in her path by some Unasian gun had not left much but junk and corpses. Diaz had found no other survivors. He'd lashed what he could salvage onto this raft, including a shaped torp charge that rocketed him clear of the ruins. This far spaceward, he didn't need screen fields against solar-particle radiation. So he had had a small hope of rescue. Maybe bigger than small, now.

Unless an enemy craft spotted him first.

His scalp crawled with that thought. His right arm, where the thing lay buried which he might use in the event of capture, began to itch.

But no, he told himself, don't be sillier than regulations require. That scoutboat was positively American. The probability of a hostile vessel being in detection range of his flare and radio—or able to change vectors fast enough—or giving a damn about him in any event—approached so close to zero as made no difference.

"Wish I'd found our bottle in the wreckage," he said aloud. He was talking to Carl Bailey, who'd helped him smuggle the Scotch aboard at Shepard Field when the fleet was alerted for departure. The steel balls had chewed Carl to pieces, some of which Diaz had seen. "It gripes me not to empty that bottle. On behalf of us both, I mean. Maybe," his voice wandered on, "a million years hence, it'll drift into another planetary system and owl-eyed critters will pick it up in boneless fingers, eh, Carl, and put it in a museum."

He realized what he was doing and snapped his mouth shut. But his mind continued. *The trouble is, those critters won't know about Carl Bailey, who collected antique jazz tapes, and played a rough game of poker, and had a D.S.M. and a gimpy leg from rescuing three boys whose patroller crashed on Venus, and went on the town with Martin Diaz one evening not so long ago when—What did happen that evening, anyhow?*

He dreamed . . .

There was a joint down in the Mexican section of San Diego which Diaz remembered was fun. So they caught a giro outside the Hotel Kennedy, where the spacemen were staying—they could afford swank, and felt they owed it to the Corps—and where they had bought their girls dinner. Diaz punched the cantina's name. The autopilot searched its directory and swung the cab onto the Embarcadero-Balboa skyrail.

Sharon sighed and snuggled into the curve of his arm. "How beautiful," she said. "How nice of you to show me this." He felt she meant a little more than polite banality. The view through the bubble really was great tonight. The city winked and blazed, a god's hoard of jewels, from horizon to horizon. Only in one direction was there anything but light: westward, where the ocean lay aglow. A nearly full moon stood high in the sky. He pointed out a tiny distant glitter on its dark edge.

"Vladimir Base."

"Ugh," said Sharon. "Unasians." She stiffened a trifle.

"Oh, they're decent fellows," Bailey said from the rear seat.

"How do you know?" asked his own date, Naomi, a serious-looking girl and quick on the uptake.

"I've been there a time or two." He shrugged.

"What?" Sharon exclaimed. "When we're at *war*?"

"Why not?" Diaz said. "The Ambassador of United Asia gave a party for our President just yesterday. I watched on the news screen. Big social event."

"But that's different," Sharon protested. "The war goes on in space, not on Earth, and—"

"We don't blow up each other's lunar bases either," Bailey said. "Too close to home. So once in a while we have occasion to, uh, parley is the official word. Actually, the last time I went over—couple years ago now—it was to return a craterbug we'd borrowed and bring some algablight antibiotic they needed. They poured me full of very excellent vodka."

"I'm surprised you admit this so openly," said Naomi.

"No secret, my dear," purred Diaz in his best grandee manner, twirling an imaginary mustache. "The news screens simply don't mention it. Wouldn't be popular, I suppose."

"Oh, people wouldn't care, seeing it was the Corps," Sharon said.

"That's right," Naomi smiled. "The Corps can do no wrong."

"Why, thankee kindly." Diaz grinned at Sharon, chucked her under the chin and kissed her. She held back an instant, having met him only this afternoon. But of course she knew what a date with a Corpsman usually meant, and he knew she knew, and she knew he knew, so before long she relaxed and enjoyed it.

The giro stopped those proceedings by descending to the street and rolling three blocks to the cantina. They entered a low, noisy room hung with bullfight posters and dense with smoke. Diaz threw a glance around and wrinkled his nose. *"Sanabiche!"* he muttered. "The tourists have discovered this place."

"Uh-huh," Bailey answered in the same disappointed *sotta voce*. "Loud tunics, lard faces, 3V and a juke wall. But let's have a couple drinks, at least, seeing we're here."

"That's the trouble with being in space two or three years at a time," Diaz said. "You lose track. Well—" They found a booth.

The waiter recognized him, even after so long a lapse, and called the proprietor. The old man bowed nearly to the floor and begged they accept tequila from his private stock. *"No, no, señor Capitan, conserva el dinero, por favor."* The girls were delighted. Picturesqueness seemed harder to come by each time Diaz made Earthfall. The evening was off to a good start in spite of everything.

But then someone paid the juke.

The wall came awake with a scrawny blond fourteen-year-old, the latest fashion in sex queens, wearing a grass skirt and three times life size:

> *Bingle-jingle-jungle-bang-POW!*
> *Bingle-jingle-jangle-bang-UGH!*
> *Uh'm uh red-hot Congo gal an' Uh'm lookin' fuh a pal*
> *Tuh share muh bingle-jingle-bangle-jungle-ugh-YOW!*

"What did you say?" Sharon called through the saxophones.

"Never mind," Diaz grunted. "They wouldn't've included it in your school Spanish anyway."

"Those things make me almost wish World War Four would start," Naomi said bitterly.

Bailey's mouth tightened. "Don't talk like that," he said. "Wasn't Number Three close enough call for the race? Without even accomplishing its aims, for either side. I've seen . . . Any war is too big."

Lest they become serious, Diaz said thoughtfully above the racket: "You know, it should be possible to do something about those Kallikak walls. Like, maybe, an oscillator. They've got oscillators these days which'll even goof a solid-state apparatus at close range."

"The F.C.C. wouldn't allow that," Bailey said. "Especially since it'd interfere with local 3V reception."

"That's bad? Besides, you could miniaturize the oscillator so it'd be hard to find. Make it small enough to carry in your pocket. Or even in your body, if you could locate a doctor who'd, uh, perform an illegal operation. I've seen uplousing units no bigger than—"

"You could strew 'em around town," Bailey said, getting interested. "Hide 'em in obscure corners and—"

"*Ugga-wugga-wugga, hugga me, do!*"

"I *wish* it would stop," Naomi said. "I came here to get to know you, Carl, not that thing."

Bailey sat straight. One hand, lying on the table, shaped a fist. "Why not?" he said.

"Eh?" Diaz asked.

Bailey rose. "Excuse me a minute." He bowed to the girls and made his way through the dancers to the wall control. There he switched the record off.

Silence fell like a meteor. For a moment, voices were stilled too. Then a large tourist came barreling off his bar stool and yelled, "Hey, wha'd'you think you're—"

"I'll refund your money, sir," Bailey said mildly. "But the noise bothers the lady I'm with."

"Huh? Hey, who d'yuh think yuh are, you—"

The proprietor came from around the bar. "If the lady weeshes it off," he declared, "off it stays."

"What kinda discrimination is this?" roared the tourist. Several other people growled with him.

Diaz prepared to go help, in case things got rough. But his companion pulled up the sleeve of his mufti tunic. The ID bracelet gleamed into view. "First Lieutenant Carl H. Bailey, United States Astromilitary Corps, at your service," he said; and a circular wave of quietness expanded around him. "Please forgive my action. I'll gladly stand the house a round."

But that wasn't necessary. The tourist fell all over himself apologizing and begged to buy the drinks. Then someone else bought them, and someone after him. Nobody ventured near the booth, where the spacemen obviously wanted privacy. But from time to time, when Diaz glanced out, he got many smiles and a few shy waves. It was almost embarrassing.

"I was afraid for a minute we'd have a fight," he said.

"N-no," Bailey answered. "I've watched our prestige develop exponentially, being Stateside while my leg healed. I doubt if there's an American alive who'd lift a finger against a Corpsman these days. But I admit I was afraid of a scene. That wouldn't've done the name of the Corps any good. As things worked out, though—"

"We came off too bloody well," Diaz finished. "Now there's not even any pseudolife in this place. Let's haul mass. We can catch the transpolar shuttle to Paris if we hurry."

But at that moment the proprietor's friends and relations, who also remembered him, began to arrive. They must have been phoned the great news. Pablo was there, Manuel, Carmen with her castanets, Juan with his guitar. Tío Rico waving a bottle in each enormous fist; and they welcomed Diaz back with embraces, and soon there was song and dancing, and the fiesta ended in the rear courtyard watching the moon set before dawn, and everything was just like the old days, for Señor Capitan Diaz's sake.

That had been a hell of a good furlough . . .

II

Another jet splashed fire across the Milky Way. Closer this time, and obviously reducing relative speed.

Diaz croaked out a cheer. He had spent weary hours waiting. The hugeness and aloneness had eaten further into his defenses than he wished to realize. He had begun to understand what some people told him, that it disturbed them to see the stars on a clear mountain night. (Where wind went soughing through pines whose bark smelled like vanilla if you laid your head close, and a river flowed cold and loud over stones—oh, Christ, how beautiful Earth was!) He shoved such matters aside and reactivated his transmitter.

The streak winked out and the stars crowded back into his eyes. But that was all right. It meant the boat had decelerated as much as necessary, and soon there would be a scooter homing on his beam, and water and food and sleep, and a new ship and eventually certain letters to write. That would be the worst part.

But not for months or years yet, not till one side or the other conceded the present phase of the war. Diaz found himself wishing most for a cigarette.

He hadn't seen the boat's hull this time, of course; there had been no rosy cloud to silhouette its blackness. Nor did he see the scooter until it was almost upon him. That jet was very thin, since it need only drive a few hundred pounds of mass on which two spacesuited men sat. They were little more than a highlight and a shadow. Diaz's pulse filled the silence. "Hallo!" he called in his helmet mike. "Hallo, there!"

They didn't answer. The scooter matched velocities a few yards off. One man tossed a line with a luminous bulb at the end. Diaz caught it and made fast. The line was drawn taut. Scooter and raft bumped together and began gently rotating.

Diaz recognized those helmets.

He snatched for a sidearm he didn't have. A Unasian sprang to one side, lifeline unreeling. His companion stayed mounted, a chucker gun cradled in his arms. The sun rose blindingly over the raft edge.

There was nothing to be done. Yet. Diaz fought down a physical nausea of defeat, "raised" his hands and let them hang free. The other man came behind him and deftly wired his wrists together. Both Unasians spent a few minutes inspecting the raft. The man with the gun tuned in on the American band.

"You make very clever salvage, sir," he said.

"Thank you," Diaz whispered, helpless and stunned.

"Come, please." He was lashed to the carrier rack. Weight tugged at him as the scooter accelerated.

They took an hour or more to rendezvous. Diaz had time to adjust his emotions. The first horror passed into numbness; then there was a sneaking relief, that he would get a reasonably comfortable vacation from war until the next prisoner exchange; and then he remembered the new doctrine, which applied to all commissioned officers whom there had been time to operate on.

I may never get the chance, he thought frantically. *They told me not to waste myself on anything less than a cruiser; my chromosomes and several million dollars spent in training me make me that valuable to the country, at least. I may go straight to Pallas, or wherever their handiest prison base is, in a lousy scoutboat or cargo ship.*

But I may get a chance to strike a blow that'll hurt. Have I got

*the guts? I hope so. No, I don't even know if I hope it. This is a
cold place to die.*

The feeling passed. Emotional control, drilled into him at the
Academy and practiced at every refresher course, took over. It
was essentially psychosomatic, a matter of using conditioned
reflexes to bring muscles and nerves and glands back toward
normal. If the fear symptoms—tension, tachycardia, sweat, de-
creased salivation and the rest—were alleviated, then fear itself
was. Far down under the surface, a four-year-old named Martin
woke from nightmare and screamed for his mother, who did not
come; but Diaz grew able to ignore him.

The boat became visible, black across star clouds. No, not a
boat. A small ship . . . abnormally large jets and light guns, a
modified *Panyushkin* . . . what had the enemy been up to in his
asteroid shipyards? Some kind of courier vessel, maybe. Recog-
nition signals must be flashing back and forth. The scooter passed
smoothly through a lock that closed again behind. Air was
pumped in. Diaz went blind as frost condensed on his helmet.
Several men assisted him out of the armor. They hadn't quite
finished when an alarm rang, engines droned and weight came
back. The ship was starting off at about half a gee.

Short bodies in green uniforms surrounded Diaz. Their immac-
ulate appearance reminded him of his own unshaven filthiness,
how much he ached and how sandy his brain felt. "Well," he
mumbled, "where's your interrogation officer?"

"You go more high, Captain," answered a man with colonel's
insignia. "Forgive us we do not attend your needs at once, but he
says very important."

Diaz bowed to the courtesy, remembering what had been
planted in his arm and feeling rather a bastard. Though it looked
as if he wouldn't have occasion to use the thing. Dazed by relief
and weariness, he let himself be escorted along corridors and
tubes, until he stood before a door marked with great black
Cyrillic warnings and guarded by two soldiers. Which was almost
unheard of aboard a spaceship, he thought joltingly.

There was a teleye above the door. Diaz barely glanced at it.
Whoever sat within the cabin must be staring through it, at him.
He tried to straighten his shoulders. "Martin Diaz," he husked,
"Captain, U.S.A.C., serial number—"

Someone yelled from the loudspeaker beside the pickup. Diaz
half understood. He whirled about. His will gathered itself and
surged. He began to think the impulses that would destroy the

ship. A guard tackled him. A rifle butt came down on his head. And that was that.

They told him forty-eight hours passed while he was in sickbay. "I wouldn't know," he said dully. "Nor care." But he was again in good physical shape. Only a bandage sheathing his lower right arm, beneath the insigneless uniform given him, revealed that surgeons had been at work. His mind was sharply aware of its environment—muscle play beneath his own skin, pastel bulkheads and cold fluorescence, faint machine-quiver underfoot, gusts from ventilator grilles, odors of foreign cooking. And always the men, with alien faces and carefully expressionless voices, who had caught him.

At least there was no abuse. They might have been justified in resenting his attempt to kill them. Some would call it treacherous. But they gave him the treatment due an officer and, except for supplying his needs, left him alone in his tiny bunk cubicle. Which in some respects was worse than punishment. Diaz was actually glad when he was at last summoned for an interview.

They brought him to the guarded door and gestured him through. It closed behind him.

For a moment Diaz noticed only the suite itself. Even a fleet commander didn't get this much space and comfort. The ship had long ceased accelerating, but spin provided a reasonable weight. The suite was constructed within a rotatable shell, so that the same deck was "down" as when the jets were in operation. Diaz stood on a Persian carpet, looking past low-legged furniture to a pair of arched doorways. One revealed a bedroom, lined with micropools—ye gods, there must be ten thousand volumes! The other showed part of an office, a desk and a great enigmatic control panel and—

The man seated beneath the Monet reproduction got up and made a slight bow. He was tall for a Unasian, with a lean mobile face whose eyes were startlingly blue against a skin as white as a Swedish girl's. His undress uniform was neat but carelessly worn. No rank insignia were visible, for a gray hood, almost a coif, covered his head and fell over the shoulders.

"Good day, Captain Diaz," he said, speaking English with little accent. "Permit me to introduce myself: General Leo Ilyitch Rostock, Cosmonautical Service of the People of United Asia."

Diaz went through the rituals automatically. Most of him was preoccupied with how quiet this place was. How very quiet. But the layout was serene. Rostock must be fantastically important if his comfort rated this much mass. Diaz's gaze flickered to the other man's waist. Rostock bore a sidearm. More to the point, though, one loud holler would doubtless be picked up by the teleye mike and bring in the guards outside.

Diaz tried to relax. *If they haven't kicked my teeth in so far, they don't plan to. I'm going to live.* But he couldn't believe that. Not here, in the presence of this hooded man. Even more so, in his drawing room. Its existence beyond Mars was too eerie. "No, sir, I have no complaints," he heard himself saying. "You run a good ship. My compliments."

"Thank you." Rostock had a charming, almost boyish smile. "Although this is not my ship, actually. Colonel Sumoro commands the *Ho Chi Minh*. I shall convey your appreciation to him."

"You may not be called the captain," Diaz said bluntly, "but the vessel is obviously your instrument."

Rostock shrugged. "Will you not sit down?" he invited, and resumed his own place on the couch. Diaz took a chair across the table from him, feeling knobby and awkward. Rostock pushed a box forward. "Cigarettes?"

"Thank you." Diaz struck and inhaled hungrily.

"I hope your arm does not bother you."

Diaz's belly muscles tightened. "No. It's all right."

"The surgeons left the metal ulnar bone in place, as well as its nervous and muscular connections. Complete replacement would have required more hospital equipment than a spaceship can readily carry. We did not want to cripple you by removing the bone. After all, we were only interested in the cartridge."

Diaz gathered courage and snapped: "The more I see of you, General, the sorrier I am that it didn't work. You're big game."

Rostock chuckled. "Perhaps. I wonder, though, if you are as sorry as you would like to feel you are. You would have died too, you realize."

"Uh-huh."

"Do you know what the weapon embedded in you was?"

"Yes. *We* tell our people such things. A charge of isotopic explosive, with a trigger activated by a particular series of motor nerve pulses. Equivalent to about ten tons of TNT." Diaz gripped the chair arms, leaned forward and said harshly: "I'm not blabbing anything you don't now know. I daresay you consider it a violation of the customs of war. Not me! I gave no parole—"

"Certainly, certainly." Rostock waved a deprecating hand.

"There are—what is your idiom?—no hard feelings. The device was ingenious. We have already dispatched a warning to our Central, whence the word can go out through the fleet, so your effort, the entire project, has gone for nothing. But it was a rather gallant attempt."

He leaned back, crossed one leg over the other, and regarded the American candidly. "Of course, as you implied, we would have proceeded somewhat differently," he said. "Our men would not have known what they carried, and the explosion would have been triggered posthypnotically, by some given class of situations, rather than consciously. In that way, there would be less chance of betrayal."

"How did you know, anyway?" Diaz sighed.

Rostock gave him an impish grin. "As the villain of this particular little drama, I shall only say that I have my methods." Suddenly he was grave. "One reason we made such an effort to pick you up before your own rescue party arrived, was to gather data on what you have been doing, you people. You know how comparatively rare it is to get a prisoner in space warfare; and how hard to get spies into an organization of high morale which maintains its own laboratories and factories off Earth. Divergent developments can go far these days, before the other side is aware of them. The miniaturization involved in your own weapon, for example, astonished our engineers."

"I can't tell you anything else," Diaz said.

"Oh, you could," Rostock answered gently. "You know as well as I what can be done with a shot of babble juice. Not to mention other techniques—nothing melodramatic, nothing painful or disabling, merely applied neurology—in which I believe Unasia is ahead of the Western countries. But don't worry, Captain. I shall not permit any such breach of military custom.

"However, I do want you to understand how much trouble we went to, to get you. When combat began, I reasoned that the ships auxiliary to a dreadnaught would be the likeliest to suffer destruction of the type which leaves a few survivors. From the pattern of action in the first day, I deduced the approximate orbits and positions of several American capital ships. Unasian tactics throughout the second day were developed with two purposes: to inflict damage, of course, but also to get the *Ho* so placed that we would be likely to detect any distress signals. This cost us the *Genghis*—a calculated risk which did not pay off—I am not omniscient. But we did hear your call.

"You are quite right about the importance of this ship here. My superiors will be horrified at my action. But of necessity, they have given me *carte blanche*. And since the *Ho* itself takes no direct part in any engagement, if we can avoid it, the probability of our being detected and attacked was small."

Rostock's eyes held Diaz's. He tapped the table, softly and repeatedly, with one fingernail. "Do you appreciate what all this means, Captain?" he asked. "Do you see how badly you were wanted?"

Diaz could only wet his lips and nod.

"Partly," Rostock said, smiling again, "there was the desire I have mentioned, to—er—check up on American activities during the last cease-fire period. But partly, too, there was a wish to bring you up to date on what we have been doing."

"Huh?" Diaz half scrambled from his chair, sagged back and gaped.

"The choice is yours, Captain," Rostock said. "You can be transferred to a cargo ship when we can arrange it, and so to an asteroid camp, and in general receive the normal treatment of a war prisoner. Or you may elect to hear what I would like to discuss with you. In the latter event, I can guarantee nothing. Obviously I can't let you go home in a routine prisoner exchange with a prime military secret of ours. You will have to wait until it is no longer a secret. Until American intelligence has learned the truth, and we know that they have. That may take years. It may take forever: because I have some hope that the knowledge will change certain of your own attitudes.

"No, no, don't answer now. Think it over. I will see you again tomorrow. In twenty-four hours, that is to say."

Rostock's eyes shifted past Diaz, as if to look through the bulkheads. His tone dropped suddenly to a whisper. "Have you ever wondered, like me, why we carry Earth's rotation period to space with us? Habit; practicality; but is there not also an element of magical thinking? A hope that somehow we can create our own sunrises? The sky is very black out there. We need all the magic we can invent. Do we not?"

III

Some hours later, alarms sounded, voices barked over the intercoms, spin was halted but weight came quickly back as the ship accelerated.

Diaz knew just enough Mandarin to understand from what he overheard that radar contact had been made with American units and combat would soon resume. The guard who brought him dinner in his cubicle confirmed it, with many a bow and hissing smile. Diaz had gained enormous face by his audience with the man in the suite.

He couldn't sleep, though the racket soon settled down to a purposeful murmur with few loud interruptions. Restless in his bunk harness, he tried to reconstruct a total picture from what clues he had. The primary American objective was the asteroid base system of the enemy. But astromilitary tactics were too complicated for one brain to grasp. A battle might go on for months, flaring up whenever hostile units came near enough in their enormous orbitings to exchange fire. Eventually, Diaz knew, if everything went well—that is, didn't go too badly haywire—Americans would land on the Unasian worldlets. That would be the rough part. He remembered ground operations on Mars and Ganymede much too well.

As for the immediate situation, though, he could only make an educated guess. The leisurely pace at which the engagement was developing indicated that ships of dreadnaught mass were involved. Therefore no mere squadron was out there, but an important segment of the American fleet, perhaps the task force headed by the *Alaska*. But if this was true, then the *Ho Chi Minh* must be directing a flotilla of comparable size.

Which wasn't possible! Flotillas and subfleets were bossed from dreadnaughts. A combat computer and its human staff were just too big and delicate to be housed in anything less. And the *Ho* was not even as large as the *Argonne* had been.

Yet what the hell was this but a command ship? Rostock had hinted as much. The activity aboard was characteristic, the repeated sound of courier boats coming and going, intercom calls, technicians hurrying along the corridors, but no shooting.

Nevertheless—

Voices jabbered beyond the cell door. Their note was triumphant. Probably they related a hit on an American vessel. Diaz recalled brushing aside chunks of space-frozen meat that had been his Corps brothers. Sammy Yoshida was in the *Utah Beach*, which was with the *Alaska*—Sammy who'd covered for him back at the Academy when he crawled in dead drunk hours after taps, and some years later had dragged him from a shell-struck foxhole on Mars and shared oxygen till a rescue squad happened by. Had the

Utah Beach been hit? Was that what they were giggling about out there?

Prisoner exchange, in a year or two or three, will get me back for the next round of the war, Diaz thought in darkness. *But I'm only one man. And I've goofed somehow, spilled a scheme which might've cost the Unies several ships before they tumbled. It's hardly conceivable I could smuggle out whatever information Rostock wants to give me. But there'd be some tiny probability that I could, somehow, sometime. Wouldn't there?*

I don't want to. Dios mío, how I don't want! Let me rest a while, and then be swapped, and go back for a long furlough on Earth, where anything I ask for is mine and mainly I ask for sunlight and ocean and flowering trees. But Carl liked those things too, didn't he? Liked them and lost them forever.

There came a lull in the battle. The fleets had passed each other, decelerating as they fired. They would take many hours to turn around and get back within combat range. A great quietness descended on the *Ho*. Walking down the passageways, which thrummed with rockblast, Diaz saw how the technicians slumped at their posts. The demands on them were as hard as those on a pilot or gunner or missile chief. Evolution designed men to fight with their hands, not with computations and pushbuttons. Maybe ground combat wasn't the worst kind.

The sentries admitted Diaz through the door of the warning. Rostock sat at a table again. His coifed features looked equally drained, and his smile was automatic. A samovar and two teacups stood before him.

"Be seated, Captain," he said tonelessly. "Pardon me if I do not rise. This has been an exhausting time."

Diaz accepted a chair and a cup. Rostock drank noisily, eyes closed and forehead puckered. There might have been an extra stimulant in his tea, for before long he appeared more human. He refilled the cups, passed out cigarettes and leaned back on his couch with a sigh.

"You may be pleased to know," he said, "that the third pass will be the final one. We shall refuse further combat and proceed instead to join forces with another flotilla near Pallas."

"Because that suits your purposes better," Diaz said.

"Well, naturally. I compute a higher likelihood of ultimate success if we follow a strategy of—No matter now."

Diaz leaned forward. His heart slammed. "So this *is* a command ship," he exclaimed. "I thought so."

The blue eyes weighed him with care. "If I give you any further information," Rostock said—softly, but the muscles tightened along his jaw—"you must accept the conditions I set forth."

"I do," Diaz got out.

"I realize that you do so in the hope of passing on the secret to your countrymen," Rostock said. "You may as well forget about that. You won't get the chance."

"Then why do you want to tell me? You won't make a Unie out of me, General." The words sounded too stuck up, Diaz decided. "That is, I respect your people and, and so forth, but, uh, my loyalties lie elsewhere."

"Agreed. I don't hope or plan to change them. At least, not in an easterly direction." Rostock drew hard on his cigarette, let smoke stream from his nostrils and squinted through it. "The microphone is turned down," he remarked. "We cannot be overheard unless we shout. I must warn you, if you make any attempt to reveal what I am about to say to you to any of my own people, I shall not only deny it but order you sent out the airlock. It is that important."

Diaz rubbed his hands on his trousers. The palms were wet. "Okay," he said.

"Not that I mean to browbeat you, Captain," said Rostock hastily. "What I offer is friendship. In the end, maybe, peace." He sat a while longer looking at the wall, before his glance shifted back to Diaz's. "Suppose you begin the discussion. Ask me what you like."

"Uh—" Diaz floundered about, as if he'd been leaning on a door that was thrown open. "Uh . . . well, was I right? Is this a command ship?"

"Yes. It performs every function of a flag dreadnaught, except that it seldom engages in direct combat. The tactical advantages are obvious. A smaller, lighter vessel can get about much more readily, hence be a correspondingly more effective directrix. Furthermore, if due caution is exercised, we are not likely to be detected and fired at. The massive armament of a dreadnaught is chiefly to stave off the missiles which can annihilate the command post within. Ships of this class avoid that whole problem by avoiding attack in the first place."

"But your computer! You, uh, you must have developed a

combat computer as . . . small and rugged as an autopilot—I thought miniaturization was our specialty."

Rostock laughed.

"And you'd still need a large human staff," Diaz protested. "Bigger than the whole crew of this ship!

"Wouldn't you?" he finished weakly.

Rostock shook his head. "No." His smiled faded. "Not under this new system. I am the computer."

"What?"

"Look." Rostock pulled off his hood.

The head beneath was hairless, not shaved but depilated. A dozen silvery plates were set into it, flush with the scalp; there were outlets in them. Rostock pointed toward the office. "The rest of me is in there," he said. "I need only plug the jacks into the appropriate points of myself, and I become—no, not part of the computer. It becomes part of me."

He fell silent again, gazing now at the floor. Diaz hardly dared move, until his cigarette burned his fingers and he must stub it out. The ship pulsed around them. Monet's picture of sunlight caught in young leaves was like something seen at the far end of a tunnel.

"Consider the problem," Rostock said at last, low. "In spite of much loose talk about giant brains, computers do not think, except perhaps on an idiot level. They merely perform logical operations, symbol-shuffling, according to instructions given them. It was shown long ago that there are infinite classes of problems which no computer can solve: the classes dealt with in Godel's theorem, that can only be solved by the nonlogical process of creating a metalanguage. Creativity is not logical and computers do not create.

"In addition, as you know, the larger a computer becomes, the more staff it requires, to perform such operations as data coding, programming, retranslation of the solutions into practical terms, and adjustment of the artificial answer to the actual problem. Yet your own brain does this sort of thing constantly . . . because it is creative. Moreover, the advanced computers are heavy, bulky, fragile things. They use cryogenics and all the other tricks, but that involves elaborate ancillary apparatus. Your brain weighs a kilogram or so, is very adequately protected in the skull and needs less than a hundred kilos of outside equipment—your body.

"I am not being mystical. There is no reason why creativity cannot someday be duplicated in an artificial structure. But I think that structure will look very much like a living organism; will, indeed, be one. Life has had a billion years to develop these techniques.

"Now if the brain has so many advantages, why use a computer at all? Obviously, to do the uncreative work, for which the brain is not specifically designed. The brain visualizes a problem of say, orbits, masses and tactics, and formulates it as a set of matrix equations. Then the computer goes swiftly through the millions of idiot counting operations needed to produce a numerical solution. What we have developed here, we Unasians, is nothing but a direct approach. We eliminate the middle man, as you Americans would say.

"In yonder office is a highly specialized computer. It is built from solid-state units, analogous to neurones, but in spite of being able to treat astromilitary problems, it is a comparatively small, simple and sturdy device. Why? Because it is used in connection with my brain, which directs it. The normal computer must have its operational patterns built in. Mine develops synapse pathways as needed, just as a man's lower brain can develop skills under·the direction of the cerebral cortex. And these pathways are modifiable by experience; the system is continually restructuring itself. The normal computer must have elaborate failure detection systems and arrangements for re-routing. I in the hookup here sense any trouble directly, and am no more disturbed by the temporary disability of some region than you are disturbed by the fact that most of your brain cells at any given time are resting.

"The human staff becomes superfluous here. My technicians bring me the data, which need not be reduced to standardized format. I link myself to the machine and—think about it—there are no words. The answer is worked out in no more time than any other computer would require. But it comes to my consciousness not as a set of figures, but in practical terms, decisions about what to do. Furthermore, the solution is modified by my human awareness of those factors too complex to go into physical condition of men and equipment, morale, long-range questions of logistics and strategy and ultimate goals. You might say this is a computer system with common sense. Do you understand, Captain?"

Diaz sat still for a long time before he said, "Yes. I think I do."

Rostock had gotten a little hoarse. He poured himself a fresh cup of tea and drank half, struck another cigarette and said earnestly: "The military value is obvious. Were that all, I would never have revealed this much to you. But something else developed as I practiced and increased my command of the system. Something quite unforseen. I wonder if you will comprehend." He finished his cup. "That repeated experience changed me. I am no longer human. Not really."

IV

The ship whispered, driving through darkness.

"I suppose a hookup like that would affect the emotions," Diaz ventured. "How does it feel?"

"There are no words," Rostock repeated, "except those I have made for myself." He rose and walked restlessly across the subdued rainbows in the carpet, hands behind his back, eyes focused on nothing Diaz could see. "As a matter of fact, the only emotional effect may be a simple intensification. Although . . . there are myths about mortals who become gods. How did it feel to them? I think they hardly noticed the palaces and music and feasting on Olympus. What mattered was how, piece by piece, as he mastered his new capacities, the new god won a god's understanding. His perception, involvement, detachment, totalness . . . there *are* no words."

Back and forth he paced, feet noiseless but metal and energies humming beneath his low and somehow troubled voice. "My cerebrum directs the computer," he said, "and the relationship becomes reciprocal. True, the computer part has no creativity of its own but it endows mine with a speed and sureness you cannot imagine. After all, a great part of original thought consists merely in proposing trial solutions. The scientist hypothesizes, the artist draws a charcoal line, the poet scribbles a phrase. Then they test them to see if they work. By now, to me, this mechanical aspect of imagination is back down on the subconscious level where it belongs. What my awareness senses is the final answer, springing to life almost simultaneously with the question, and yet with a felt reality to it such as comes only from having pondered and tested the issue for thousands of times.

"Also, the amount of sense data I can handle is fantastic. Oh, I am blind and deaf and numb away from my machine half! So you will realize that over the months I have tended to spend more and more time in the linked state. When there was no immediate command problem to solve, I would sit and savor it."

In a practical tone: "That is how I perceived that you were about to sabotage us, Captain. Your posture alone betrayed you. I guessed the means at once and ordered the guards to knock you unconscious. I think, also, that I detected in you the potential I need. But that demands closer examination. Which is easily given. When I am linked, you cannot lie to me. The least insincerity is written across your whole organism."

He paused, to stand a little slumped, looking at the bulkhead. For a moment Diaz's legs tensed. *Three jumps and I can be there and get his gun!* But no, Rostock wasn't any brain-heavy dwarf. The body in that green uniform was young and trained. Diaz took another cigarette. "Okay," he said. "What do you propose?"

"First," Rostock said, turning about—and his eyes kindled—"I want you to understand what you and I are. What the spacemen of both factions are."

"Professional soldiers," Diaz grunted uneasily. Rostock waited. Diaz puffed hard and plowed on, since he was plainly expected to: "The only soldiers left. You can't count those ornamental regiments on Earth, nor the guys sitting by the big missiles. Those missiles will never be fired. World War Three was a large enough dose of nucleonics. Civilization was lucky to survive. Terrestrial life would be lucky to survive, next time around. So war has moved into space. Uh . . . professionalism . . . the old traditions of mutual respect and so forth have naturally revived." He made himself look up. "What more clichés need I repeat?"

"Suppose your side completely annihilated our ships," Rostock said. "What would happen?"

"Why . . . that's been discussed theoretically . . . by damn near every political scientist, hasn't it? The total command of space would not mean total command of Earth. We could destroy the whole eastern hemisphere without being touched. But we wouldn't because Unasia would fire its cobalt weapons while dying, and there'd be no western hemisphere to come home to either. Not that that situation will ever arise. Space is too big. There are too many ships and fortresses scattered around; combat is too slow a process. Neither fleet can wipe out the other."

"Since we have this perpetual stalemate, then," Rostock pursued, "why is there perpetual war?"

"Well, uh, partial victories are possible. Like our capture of Mars, or your destruction of three dreadnaughts in one month, on different occasions. The balance of power shifts. Rather than let its strength continue being whittled down, the side which is losing asks for a parley. There are negotiations, which end to the relative advantage of the stronger side. Meanwhile the arms race continues. Pretty soon a new dispute arises, the cease-fire ends, and maybe the other side is lucky that time."

"Is this situation expected to be eternal?"

"No!" Diaz stopped, thought a minute, and grinned with one corner of his mouth. "That is, they keep talking about an effective international organization. Trouble is, the two cultures are too far apart by now. They can't live together."

"I used to believe that myself," Rostock said. "Lately I have not been sure. A world federalism could be devised which would let both civilizations keep their identities. There have in fact been many such proposals, as you know. None has gotten beyond the talking stage. None ever will. Because you see, what maintains the war is not the difference between our two cultures, but their similarity."

"Whoa, there!" Diaz bristled. "I resent that."

"Please," Rostock said. "I pass no moral judgments. For the sake of argument, at least, I can concede you the moral superiority, remarking only in parenthesis that Earth holds billions of people who not only fail to comprehend what you mean by freedom but would not like it if you gave it to them. The similarity I am talking about is technological. Both civilizations are based on the machine, with all the high organization and dynamism which this implies."

"So?"

"So war is a necessity— Wait! I am not talking about 'merchants of death,' or 'dictators needing an outside enemy,' or whatever the current propaganda lines are. I mean that conflict is built into the culture. There *must* be an outlet for the destructive emotions generated in the mass of the people by the type of life they lead. A type of life for which evolution never designed them.

"Have you ever heard about L. F. Richardson? No? He was an Englishman in the last century, a Quaker, who hated war but, being a scientist, realized the phenomenon must be understood clinically before it can be eliminated. He performed some brilliant theoretical and statistical analyses which showed, for example, that the rate of deadly quarrels was very nearly constant over the decades. There could be many small clashes or a few major ones, but the result was the same. Why were the United States and the Chinese Empire so peaceful during the nineteenth century? The answer is that they were not. They had their Civil War and Taiping Rebellion, which devastated them as much as required. I need not multiply examples. We can discuss this later in detail. I have carried Richardson's work a good deal further and more rigorously. I say to you now only that civilized societies must have a certain rate of immolations."

Diaz listened to silence for a minute before he said: "Well, I've sometimes thought the same. I suppose you mean we spacemen are the goats these days?"

"Exactly. War fought out here does not menace the planet. By our deaths we keep Earth alive."

Rostock sighed. His mouth drooped. "Magic works, you know," he said, "works on the emotions of the people who practice it. If a primitive witch doctor told a storm to go away, the storm did not hear, but the tribe did and took heart. The ancient analogy to us, though, is the sacrificial king in the early agricultural societies: a god in mortal form, who was regularly slain that the fields might bear fruit. This was not mere superstition. You must realize that. It worked—on the people. The rite was essential to the operation of their culture, to their sanity and hence to their survival.

"Today the machine age has developed its own sacrificial kings. We are the chosen of the race. The best it can offer. None gainsays us. We may have what we choose, pleasure, luxury, women, adulation—only not the simple pleasures of wife and child and home, for we must die that the people may live."

Again silence, until: "Do you seriously mean that's why the war goes on?" Diaz breathed.

Rostock nodded.

"But nobody—I mean, people wouldn't—"

"They do not reason these things out, of course. Traditions develop blindly. The ancient peasant did not elaborate logical reasons why the king must die. He merely knew this was so, and left the syllogism for modern anthropologists to expound. I did not see the process going on today until I had had the chance to . . . to become more perceptive than I had been," Rostock said humbly.

Diaz couldn't endure sitting down any longer. He jumped to his feet. "Assuming you're right," he snapped, "and you may be, what of it? What can be done?"

"Much," Rostock said. Calm descended on his face like a mask. "I am not being mystical about this, either. The sacrificial king has reappeared as the end product of a long chain of cause and effect. There is no reason inherent in natural law why this must be. Richardson was right in his basic hope, that when war becomes understood, as a phenomenon, it can be eliminated. This would naturally involve restructuring the entire terrestrial culture. Gradually, subtly. Remember—" His hand shot out, seized Diaz's shoulder and gripped painfully hard. "There is a new element in history today. Us. The kings. We are not like those who spend their lives under Earth's sky. In some ways we are more, in other ways less, but always we are different. You and I are more akin to each other than to our planet-dwelling countrymen. Are we not?

"In the time and loneliness granted me, I have used all my new powers to think about this. Not only think; this is so much more than cold reason. I have tried to feel. To love what is, as the Buddhists say. I believe a nucleus of spacemen like us, slowly and secretly gathered, wishing the good of everyone on Earth and the harm of none, gifted with powers and insights they cannot really imagine at home—I believe we may accomplish something. If not us, then our sons. Men ought not to kill each other, when the stars are waiting."

He let go, turned away and looked at the deck. "Of course," he mumbled, "I, in my peculiar situation, must first destroy a number of your brothers."

They had given Diaz a whole pack of cigarettes, an enormous treasure out here, before they locked him into his cubicle for the duration of the second engagement. He lay in harness, hearing clang and shout and engine roar through the vibrating bulkheads, stared at blackness and smoked until his tongue was foul. Sometimes the *Ho* accelerated, mostly it ran free and he floated. Once a tremor went through the entire hull, near miss by a shaped charge. Doubtless gamma rays, ignoring the magnetic force screens, sleeted through the men and knocked another several months off their life expectancies. Not that that mattered. Spacemen rarely lived long enough to worry about degenerative diseases. Diaz hardly noticed.

He's not lying, Rostock. Why should he? What could he gain? He may be a nut, of course. But he doesn't act like a nut either. He wants me to study his statistics and equations, satisfy myself that he's right. And he must be damn sure I will be convinced, to tell me as much as he has.

How many are there like him? Only a very few, I'm sure. The man-machine symbiosis is obviously new, or we'd've had some inkling ourselves. This is the first field trial of the system. I wonder if the others have reached the same conclusions as Rostock. No, he said he doubts that. Their psychology impressed him as being more deeply channeled than his. He's a lucky accident.

Lucky? Now how can I tell? I'm only a man. I've never experienced an IQ of 1,000, or whatever the figure may be. A god's purposes aren't necessarily what a man would elect.

The eventual end to war? Well, other institutions had been ended, at least in the Western countries; judicial torture, chattel slavery, human sacrifice— No, wait, according to Rostock human sacrifice had been revived.

"But is our casualty rate high enough to fit your equations?" Diaz had argued. "Space forces aren't as big as old-time armies. No country could afford that."

"Other elements than death must be taken into account," Rostock answered. "The enormous expense is one factor. Taxpaying is a form of symbolic self-mutilation. It also tends to direct civilian resentments and aggressions against their own governments, thus taking some pressure off international relations.

"Chiefly, though, there is the matter of emotional intensity. A spaceman not only dies, he usually dies horribly; and that moment is the culmination of a long period under grisly conditions. His grounding brothers, administrative and service personnel, suffer vicariously: 'sweat it out,' as your idiom so well expresses the feeling. His kinfolk, friends, women, are likewise racked. When Adonis dies—or Osiris, Tammuz, Baldur, Christ, Tlaloc, whichever of his hundred names you choose—the people must in some degree share his agony. That is part of the sacrifice."

Diaz had never thought about it just that way. Like most Corpsmen, he had held the average civilian in thinly disguised contempt. But . . . from time to time, he remembered, he'd been glad his mother died before he enlisted. And why did his sister hit the bottle so hard? Then there had been Lois, she of the fire-colored hair and violet eyes, who wept as if she would never stop weeping when he left for duty. He'd promised to get in touch with her on his return, but of course he knew better.

Which did not erase memories of men whose breath and blood came exploding from burst helmets; who shuddered and vomited and defecated in the last stages of radiation sickness; who stared without immediate comprehension at a red spurt which a second ago had been an arm or a leg; who went insane and must be gassed because psychoneurosis is catching on a six months' orbit beyond Saturn; who— Yeah, Carl had been lucky.

You could talk as much as you wished about Corps brotherhood, honor, tradition, and gallantry. It remained sentimental guff . . .

No, that was unjust. The Corps had saved the people, their lives and liberties. There could be no higher achievement—for the Corps. But knighthood had once been a noble thing, too. Then, lingering after its day, it became a yoke and eventually a farce. The warrior virtues were not ends in themselves. If the warrior could be made obsolete—

Could he? How much could one man, even powered by a machine, hope to do? How much could he even hope to understand?

The moment came upon Diaz. He lay as if blinded by shellburst radiance.

As consciousness returned, he knew first, irrelevantly, what it meant to get religion.

"By God," he told the universe, "we're going to try!"

V

The battle would resume very shortly. At any moment, in fact, some scoutship leading the American force might fire a missile. But when Diaz told his guard he wanted to speak with General Rostock, he was taken there within minutes.

The door closed behind him. The living room lay empty, altogether still except for the machine throb, which was not loud since the *Ho* was running free. Because acceleration might be needful on short notice, there was no spin. Diaz hung weightless as fog. And the Monet flung into his eyes all Earth's sunlight and summer forests.

"Rostock?" he called uncertainly.

"Come," said a voice, almost too low to hear. Diaz gave a shove with his foot and flew toward the office.

He stopped himself by grasping the doorjamb. A semicircular room lay before him, the entire side taken up by controls and meters. Lights blinked, needles wavered on dials, buttons and switches and knobs reached across black paneling. But none of that was important. Only the man at the desk mattered, who free-sat with wires running from his head to the wall.

Rostock seemed to have lost weight. Or was that an illusion? The skin was drawn taut across his high cheekbones and gone a dead, glistening white. His nostrils were flared and the colorless lips held tense. Diaz looked into his eyes, once, and then away again. He could not meet them. He could not even think about them. He drew a shaken breath and waited.

"You made your decision quickly," Rostock whispered. "I had not awaited you until after the engagement."

"I . . . I didn't think you would see me till then."

"This is more important." Diaz felt as it he were being probed with knives. He could not altogether believe it was his imagination. He stared desperately at the paneled instruments. Their nonhumanness was like a comforting hand. *They must only be for the benefit of maintenance techs,* he thought in a very distant part of himself. *The brain doesn't need them.*

"You are convinced," Rostock said in frank surprise.

"Yes," Diaz answered.

"I had not expected that. I only hoped for your reluctant agreement to study my work." Rostock regarded him for a still century. "You were ripe for a new faith," he decided. "I had not taken you for the type. But then, the mind can only use what data are given it, and I have hitherto had little opportunity to meet Americans. Never since I became what I am. You have another psyche from ours."

"I need to understand your findings, sir," Diaz said. "Right now I can only believe. That isn't enough, is it?"

Slowly, Rostock's mouth drew into a smile of quite human warmth. "Correct. But given the faith, intellectual comprehension should be swift."

"I . . . I shouldn't be taking your time . . . now, sir," Diaz stammered. "How should I begin? Should I take some books back with me?"

"No." Acceptance had been reached. Rostock spoke resonantly, a master to his trusted servant. "I need your help here. Strap into yonder harness. Our first necessity is to survive the battle upon us. You realize that this means sacrificing many of your comrades. I know how much that will hurt you. Afterward we shall spend our lives repaying our people—both our peoples. But today I shall ask you questions about your fleet. Any information is valuable, especially details of construction and armament which our intelligence has not been able to learn."

Doña mía. Diaz let go the door, covered his face and fell free, endlessly. *Help me.*

"It is not betrayal," said the superman. "It is the ultimate loyalty you can offer."

Diaz made himself look at the cabin again. He shoved against the bulkhead and stopped by the harness near the desk.

"You cannot lie to me," said Rostock. "Do not deny how much pain I am giving you." Diaz glimpsed his fists clamping together. "Each time I look at you, I share what you feel."

Diaz clung to his harness. There went an explosion through him.

NO, BY GOD!

Rostock screamed.

"Don't," Diaz sobbed. "I don't want—" But wave after wave ripped outward. Rostock flopped about in his harness and shrieked. The scene came back, ramming home like a bayonet.

"We like to put an extra string on our bow," the psych officer said. Lunar sunlight, scarcely softened by the dome, blazed off his bronze eagles, wings and beaks. "You know that your right ulna will be replaced with a metal section in which there is a nerve-triggered nuclear cartridge. But that may not be all, gentlemen."

He bridged his fingers. The young men seated on the other side of his desk stirred uneasily. "In this country," the psych officer said, "we don't believe humans should be turned into puppets. Therefore you will have voluntary control of your bombs; no posthypnosis, Pavlov reflex or any such insult. However, those of you who are willing will receive a rather special extra treatment, and that fact will be buried from the consciousness of all of you.

"Our reasoning is that if and when the Unasians learn about the prisoner weapon, they'll remove the cartridge by surgery but leave the prosthetic bone in place. And they will, we hope, not examine it in microscopic detail. Therefore they won't know that it contains an oscillator, integrated with the crystal structure. Nor will you; because what you don't know, you can't babble under anesthesia.

"The opportunity may come, if you are captured and lose your bomb, to inflict damage by this reserve means. You may find yourself near a crucial electronic device, for example a space-ship's autopilot. At short range, the oscillator will do an excellent job of bollixing it. Which will at least discomfit the enemy, and may even give you a chance to escape.

"The posthypnotic command will be such that you'll remember about this oscillator when conditions seem right for using it. Not before. Of course, the human mind is a damned queer thing, that twists and turns and bites its own tail. In order to make an opportunity to strike this blow, your subconscious may lead you down strange paths. It may even have you seriously contemplating treason, if treason seems the only way of getting access to what you can wreck. Don't let that bother you afterward, gentlemen. Your superiors will know what happened.

"Nevertheless, the experience may be painful. And posthypnosis is, at best, humiliating to a free man. So this aspect of the program is strictly volunteer. Does anybody want to go for broke?"

The door flung open. The guards burst in. Diaz was already behind the desk, next to Rostock. He yanked out the general's sidearm and fired at the soldiers. Free fall recoil sent him back against the computer panel. He braced himself, fired again and used his left elbow to smash the nearest meter face.

Rostock clawed at the wires in his head. For a moment Diaz guessed what it must be like to have random oscillations in your brain, amplified by an electronic engine that was part of you. He laid the pistol to the screaming man's temple and fired once more.

Now to get out! He shoved hard, arrowing past the sentries, who rolled through the air in a crimson galaxy of blood globules. Confusion boiled in the corridor beyond. Someone snatched at him. He knocked the fellow aside and dove along a tubeway. Somewhere hereabouts should be a scooter locker—there, and nobody around!

He didn't have time to get on a spacesuit, even if a Unasian one would have fitted, but he slipped on an air dome over the scooter. That, with the heater unit and oxy reclaim, would serve. He didn't want to get off anywhere en route; not before he'd steered the machine through an American hatch.

With luck, he'd do that. Their command computer gone, the enemy were going to get smeared. American ships would close in as the slaughter progressed. Eventually one should come within range of the scooter's little radio.

He set the minilock controls, mounted the saddle, dogged the air dome and waited for ejection. It came none too soon. Three soldiers had just appeared down the passageway. Diaz applied full thrust and jetted away from the *Ho.* Its blackness was soon lost among the star clouds.

Battle commenced. The first Unasian ship to be destroyed must have been less than fifty miles distant. Luckily, Diaz was facing the other way when the missile exploded.

SECOND VARIETY

Philip K. Dick

The Russian soldier made his way nervously up the ragged side of the hill, holding his gun ready. He glanced around him, licking his dry lips, his face set. From time to time he reached up a gloved hand and wiped perspiration from his neck, pushing down his coat collar.

Eric turned to Corporal Leone. "Want him? Or can I have him?" He adjusted the view sight so the Russian's features squarely filled the glass, the lines cutting across his hard, somber features.

Leone considered. The Russian was close, moving rapidly, almost running. "Don't fire. Wait." Leone tensed. "I don't think we're needed."

The Russian increased his pace, kicking ash and piles of debris out of his way. He reached the top of the hill and stopped, panting, staring around him. The sky was overcast, with drifting clouds of gray particles. Bare trunks of trees jutted up occasionally; the ground was level and bare, rubble-strewn, with the ruins of buildings standing out here and there like yellowing skulls.

The Russian was uneasy. He knew something was wrong. He started down the hill. Now he was only a few paces from the bunker. Eric was getting fidgety. He played with his pistol, glancing at Leone.

"Don't worry," Leone said. "He won't get here. They'll take care of him."

"Are you sure? He's got damn far."

"They hang around close to the bunker. He's getting into the bad part. Get set!"

The Russian began to hurry, sliding down the hill, his boots sinking into the heaps of gray ash, trying to keep his gun up. He stopped for a moment, lifting his field glasses to his face.

"He's looking right at us," Eric said.

The Russian came on. They could see his eyes, like two blue stones. His mouth was open a little. He needed a shave; his chin was stubbled. On one bony cheek was a square of tape, showing blue at the edge. A fungoid spot. His coat was muddy and torn. One glove was missing. As he ran, his belt counter bounced up and down against him.

Leone touched Eric's arm. "Here one comes."

Across the ground something small and metallic came, flashing in the dull sunlight of midday. A metal sphere. It raced up the hill after the Russian, its treads flying. It was small, one of the baby ones. Its claws were out, two razor projections spinning in a blur of white steel. The Russian heard it. He turned instantly, firing. The sphere dissolved into particles. But already a second had emerged and was following the first. The Russian fired again.

A third sphere leaped up the Russian's leg, clicking and whirring. It jumped to the shoulder. The spinning blades disappeared into the Russian's throat.

Eric relaxed. "Well, that's that. God, those damn things give me the creeps. Sometimes I think we were better off before."

"If we hadn't invented them, they would have." Leone lit a cigarette shakily. "I wonder why a Russian would come all this way alone. I didn't see anyone covering him."

Lieutenant Scott came slipping up the tunnel, into the bunker. "What happened? Something entered the screen."

"An Ivan."

"Just one?"

Eric brought the viewscreen around. Scott peered into it. Now there were numerous metal spheres crawling over the prostrate body, dull metal globes clicking and whirring, sawing up the Russian into small parts to be carried away.

"What a lot of claws," Scott murmured.

"They come like flies. Not much game for them any more."

Scott pushed the sight away, disgusted. "Like flies. I wonder why he was out there. They know we have claws all around."

A larger robot had joined the smaller spheres. A long blunt tube with projecting eyepieces, it was directing operations. There was not much left of the soldier. What remained was being brought down the hillside by the host of claws.

"Sir," Leone said. "If it's all right, I'd like to go out there and take a look at him."

"Why?"

"Maybe he came with something."

Scott considered. He shrugged. "All right. But be careful."

"I have my tab." Leone patted the metal band at his wrist. "I'll be out of bounds."

He picked up his rifle and stepped carefully up to the mouth of the bunker, making his way between blocks of concrete and steel prongs, twisted and bent. The air was cold at the top. He crossed over the ground toward the remains of the soldier, striding across the soft ash. A wind blew around him, swirling gray particles up in his face. He squinted and pushed on.

The claws retreated as he came close, some of them stiffening into immobility. He touched his tab. The Ivan would have given something for that! Short hard radiation emitted from the tab neutralized the claws, put them out of commission. Even the big robot with its two waving eyestalks retreated respectfully as he approached.

He bent down over the remains of the soldier. The gloved hand was closed tightly. There was something in it. Leone pried the fingers apart. A sealed container, aluminum. Still shiny.

He put it in his pocket and made his way back to the bunker. Behind him the claws came back to life, moving into operation again. The procession resumed, metal spheres moving through the gray ash with their loads. He could hear their treads scrabbling against the ground. He shuddered.

Scott watched intently as he brought the shiny tube out of his pocket. "He had that?"

"In his hand." Leone unscrewed the top. "Maybe you should look at it, sir."

Scott took it. He emptied the contents out in the palm of his hand. A small piece of silk paper, carefully folded. He sat down by the light and unfolded it.

"What's it say, sir?" Eric said. Several officers came up the tunnel. Major Hendricks appeared.

"Major," Scott said. "Look at this."

Hendricks read the slip. "This just come?"

"A single runner. Just now."

"Where is he?" Hendricks asked sharply.

"The claws got him."

Major Hendricks grunted. "Here." He passed it to his companions. "I think this is what we've been waiting for. They certainly took their time about it."

"So they want to talk terms," Scott said. "Are we going along with them?"

"That's not for us to decide." Hendricks sat down. "Where's the communications officer? I want the Moon Base."

Leone pondered as the communications officer raised the outside antenna cautiously, scanning the sky above the bunker for any sign of a watching Russian ship.

"Sir," Scott said to Hendricks. "It's sure strange they suddenly came around. We've been using the claws for almost a year. Now all of a sudden they start to fold."

"Maybe claws have been getting down in their bunkers."

"One of the big ones, the kind with stalks, got into an Ivan bunker last week," Eric said. "It got a whole platoon of them before they got their lid shut."

"How do you know?"

"A buddy told me. The thing came back with—with remains."

"Moon Base, sir," the communications officer said.

On the screen the face of the lunar monitor appeared. His crisp uniform contrasted to the uniforms in the bunker. And he was cleanshaven. "Moon Base."

"This is forward command L-Whistle. On Terra. Let me have General Thompson."

The monitor faded. Presently General Thompson's heavy features came into focus. "What is it, Major?"

"Our claws got a single Russian runner with a message. We don't know whether to act on it—there have been tricks like this in the past."

"What's the message?"

"The Russians want us to send a single officer on policy level over to their lines. For a conference. They don't state the nature of the conference. They say that matters of—" He consulted the slip: "—matters of grave urgency make it advisable that discussion be opened between a representative of the UN forces and themselves."

He held the message up to the screen for the general to scan. Thompson's eyes moved.

"What should we do?" Hendricks said.

"Send a man out."

"You don't think it's a trap?"

"It might be. But the location they give for their forward command is correct. It's worth a try, at any rate."

"I'll send an officer out. And report the results to you as soon as he returns."

"All right, Major." Thompson broke the connection. The screen died. Up above, the antenna came slowly down.

Hendricks rolled up the paper, deep in thought.

"I'll go," Leone said.

"They want somebody at policy level." Hendricks rubbed his jaw. "Policy level. I haven't been outside in months. Maybe I could use a little air."

"Don't you think it's risky?"

Hendricks lifted the view sight and gazed into it. The remains of the Russian were gone. Only a single claw was in sight. It was folding itself back, disappearing into the ash, like a crab. Like some hideous metal crab . . . "That's the only thing that bothers me." Hendricks rubbed his wrist. "I know I'm safe as long as I have this on me. But there's something about them. I hate the damn things. I wish we'd never invented them. There's something wrong with them. Relentless little—"

"If we hadn't invented them, the Ivans would have."

Hendricks pushed the sight back. "Anyhow, it seems to be winning the war. I guess that's good."

"Sounds like you're getting the same jitters as the Ivans."

Hendricks examined his wristwatch. "I guess I had better get started, if I want to be there before dark."

He took a deep breath and then stepped out onto the gray rubbled ground. After a minute he lit a cigarette and stood gazing around him. The landscape was dead. Nothing stirred. He could see for miles, endless ash and slag, ruins of buildings. A few trees without leaves or branches, only the trunks. Above him the eternal rolling clouds of gray, drifting between Terra and the sun.

Major Hendricks went on. Off to the right something scuttled, something round and metallic. A claw, going lickety-split after something. Probably after a small animal, a rat. They got rats, too. As a sort of sideline.

He came to the top of the little hill and lifted his field glasses. The Russian lines were a few miles ahead of him. They had a forward command post there. The runner had come from it.

A squat robot with undulating arms passed by him, its arms weaving inquiringly. The robot went on its way, disappearing under some debris. Hendricks watched it go. He had never seen that type before. There were getting to be more and more types he had never seen, new varieties and sizes coming up from the underground factories.

Hendricks put out his cigarette and hurried on. It was interesting, the use of artificial forms in warfare. How had they got started? Necessity. The Soviet Union had gained great initial success, usual with the side that got the war going. Most of North America had been blasted off the map. Retaliation was quick in coming, of course. The sky was full of circling diskbombers long before the war began; they had been up there for years. The disks began sailing down all over Russia within hours after Washington got it.

But that hadn't helped Washington.

The American bloc governments moved to the Moon Base the first year. There was not much else to do. Europe was gone, a slag heap with dark weeds growing from the ashes and bones. Most of North America was useless; nothing could be planted, no one could live. A few million people kept going up in Canada and down in South America. But during the second year Soviet parachutists began to drop, a few at first, then more and more. They wore the first really effective anti-radiation equipment; what was left of American production moved to the Moon along with the governments.

All but the troops. The remaining troops stayed behind as best they could, a few thousand here, a platoon there. No one knew exactly where they were; they stayed where they could, moving around at night, hiding in ruins, in sewers, cellars, with the rats and snakes. It looked as if the Soviet Union had the war almost won. Except for a handful of projectiles fired off from the Moon daily, there was almost no weapon in use against them. They came and went as they pleased. The war, for all practical purposes, was over. Nothing effective opposed them.

And then the first claws appeared. And overnight the complexion of the war changed.

The claws were awkward, at first. Slow. The Ivans knocked them off almost as fast as they crawled out of their underground tunnels. But then they got better, faster and more cunning. Factories, all on Terra, turned them out. Factories a long way underground, behind the Soviet lines, factories that had once made atomic projectiles, now almost forgotten.

The claws got faster, and they got bigger. New types appeared, some with feelers, some that flew. There were a few jumping kinds. The best technicians on the Moon were working on designs, making them more and more intricate, more flexible. They became uncanny; the Ivans were having a lot of trouble with them. Some of the little claws were learning to hide themselves, burrowing down into the ash, lying in wait.

And then they started getting into the Russian bunkers, slipping down when the lids were raised for air and a look around. One claw inside a bunker, a churning sphere of blades and metal—that was enough. And when one got in others followed. With a weapon like that the war couldn't go on much longer.

Maybe it was already over.

Maybe he was going to hear the news. Maybe the Politburo had decided to throw in the sponge. Too bad it had taken so long. Six years. A long time for war like that, the way they had waged it. The automatic retaliation disks, spinning down all over Russia, hundreds of thousands of them. Bacteria crystals. The Soviet guided missiles, whistling through the air. The chain bombs. And now this, the robots, the claws—

The claws weren't like other weapons. They were *alive*, from any practical standpoint, whether the Governments wanted to admit it or not. They were not machines. They were living things, spinning, creeping, shaking themselves up suddenly from the gray ash and darting toward a man, climbing up him, rushing for his throat. And that was what they had been designed to do. Their job.

They did their job well. Especially later, with the new designs coming up. Now they repaired themselves. They were on their own. Radiation tabs protected the UN troops, but if a man lost his tab he was fair game for the claws, no matter what his uniform. Down below the surface automatic machinery stamped them out. Human beings stayed a long way off. It was too risky; nobody wanted to be around them. They were left to themselves. And they seemed to be doing all right. The new designs were faster, more complex. More efficient.

Apparently they had won the war.

Major Hendricks lit a second cigarette. The landscape depressed him. Nothing but ash and ruins. He seemed to be alone, the only living thing in the whole world. To the right the ruins of a town rose up, a few walls and heaps of debris. He tossed the dead match away, increasing his pace. Suddenly he stopped, jerking up his gun, his body tense. For a minute it looked like—

From behind the shell of a ruined building a figure came, walking slowly toward him, walking hesitantly.

Hendricks blinked. "Stop!"

The boy stopped. Hendricks lowered his gun. The boy stood silently, looking at him. He was small, not very old. Perhaps eight. But it was hard to tell. Most of the kids who remained were stunted. He wore a faded blue sweater, ragged with dirt, and short pants. His hair was long and matted. Brown hair. It hung over his face and around his ears. He held something in his arms.

"What's that you have?" Hendricks said sharply.

The boy held it out. It was a toy, a bear. A teddy bear. The boy's eyes were large, but without expression.

Hendricks relaxed. "I don't want it. Keep it."

The boy hugged the bear again.

"Where do you live?" Hendricks said.

"In there."

"The ruins?"

"Yes."

"Underground?"

"Yes."

"How many are there?"

"How—how many?"

"How many of you. How big's your settlement?"

The boy did not answer.

Hendricks frowned. "You're not all by yourself, are you?"

The boy nodded.

"How do you stay alive?"

"There's food."

"What kind of food?"

"Different."

Hendricks studied him. "How old are you?"

"Thirteen."

It wasn't possible. Or was it? The boy was thin, stunted. And probably sterile. Radiation exposure, years straight. No wonder he was so small. His arms and legs were like pipe cleaners, knobby and thin. Hendricks touched the boy's arm. His skin was dry and rough; radiation skin. He bent down, looking into the boy's face. There was no expression. Big eyes, big and dark.

"Are you blind?" Hendricks said.

"No. I can see some."

"How do you get away from the claws?"

"The claws?"

"The round things. That run and burrow."

"I don't understand."

Maybe there weren't any claws around. A lot of areas were free. They collected mostly around bunkers, where there were people. The claws had been designed to sense warmth, warmth of living things.

"You're lucky." Hendricks straightened up. "Well? Which way are you going? Back—back there?"

"Can I come with you?"

"With *me*?" Hendricks folded his arms. "I'm going a long way. Miles. I have to hurry." He looked at his watch. "I have to get there by nightfall."

"I want to come."

Hendricks fumbled in his pack. "It isn't worth it. Here." He tossed down the food cans he had with him. "You take these and go back. Okay?"

The boy said nothing.

"I'll be coming back this way. In a day or so. If you're around here when I come back you can come along with me. All right?"

"I want to go with you now."

"It's a long walk."

"I can walk."

Hendricks shifted uneasily. It made too good a target, two people walking alone. And the boy would slow him down. But he might not come back this way. And if the boy were really all alone—

"Okay. Come along."

The boy fell in beside him. Hendricks strode along. The boy walked silently, clutching his teddy bear.

"What's your name?" Hendricks said, after a time.

"David Edward Derring."

"David? What—what happened to your mother and father?"

"They died."

"How?"

"In the blast."

"How long ago?"

"Six years ago."

Hendricks slowed down. "You've been alone six years?"

"No. There were other people for a while. They went away."

"And you've been alone since?"

"Yes."

Hendricks glanced down. The boy was strange, saying very little. Withdrawn. But that was the way they were, the children who had survived. Quiet, Stoic. A strange kind of fatalism gripped them. Nothing came as a surprise. They accepted anything that came along. There was no longer any *normal*, any natural course of things, moral or physical, for them to expect. Custom, habit, all the determining forces of learning were gone; only brute experience remained.

"Am I walking too fast?" Hendricks said.

"No."

"How did you happen to see me?"

"I was waiting."

"Waiting?" Hendricks was puzzled. "What were you waiting for?"

"To catch things."

"What kind of things?"

"Things to eat."

"Oh." Hendricks set his lips grimly. A thirteen-year-old boy, living on rats and gophers and half-rotten canned food. Down in a hole under the ruins of a town. With radiation pools and claws, and Russian dive-mines up above, coasting around in the sky.

"Where are we going?" David asked.

"To the Russian lines."

"Russian?"

"The enemy. The people who started the war. They dropped the first radiation bombs. They began all this."

The boy nodded. His face showed no expression.

"I'm an American," Hendricks said.

There was no comment. On they went, the two of them, Hendricks walked a little ahead, David trailing behind him, hugging his dirty teddy bear against his chest.

About four in the afternoon they stopped to eat. Hendricks built a fire in a hollow between some slabs of concrete. He cleared the weeds away and heaped up bits of wood. The Russians' lines were not very far ahead. Around him was what had once been a long valley, acres of fruit trees and grapes. Nothing remained now but a few bleak stumps and the mountains that stretched across the horizon at the far end. And the clouds of rolling ash that blew and drifted with the wind, settling over the weeds and remains of buildings, walls here and there, once in a while what had been a road.

Hendricks made coffee, and heated up some boiled mutton and bread. "Here." He handed bread and mutton to David. David squatted by the edge of the fire, his knees knobby and white. He examined the food and then passed it back, shaking his head.

"No."

"No? Don't you want any?"

"No."

Hendricks shrugged. Maybe the boy was a mutant, used to special food. It didn't matter. When he was hungry he would find something to eat. The boy was strange. But there were many strange changes coming over the world. Life was not the same anymore. It would never be the same again. The human race was going to have to realize that.

"Suit yourself," Hendricks said. He ate the bread and mutton by himself, washing it down with coffee. He ate slowly, finding the food hard to digest. When he was done he got to his feet and stamped the fire out.

David rose slowly, watching him with his young-old eyes.

"We're going," Hendricks said.

"All right."

Hendricks walked along, his gun in his arms. They were close; he was tense, ready for anything. The Russians should be expecting a runner, an answer to their own runner, but they were tricky. There was always the possibility of a slip-up. He scanned the landscape around him. Nothing but slag and ash, a few hills, charred trees. Concrete walls. But some place ahead was the first bunker of the Russian lines, the forward command. Underground, buried deep, with only a periscope showing, a few gun muzzles. Maybe an antenna.

"Will we be there soon?" David asked.

"Yes. Getting tired?"

"No."

"Why, then?"

David did not answer. He plodded carefully along behind, picking his way over the ash. His legs and shoes were gray with dust. His pinched face was streaked, lines of gray ash in riverlets down the pale white of his skin. There was no color to his face. Typical of the new children, growing up in cellars and sewers and underground shelters.

Hendricks slowed down. He lifted his field glasses and studied the ground ahead of him. Were they there, some place, waiting for him? Watching him, the way his men had watched the Russian runner? A chill went up his back. Maybe they were getting their guns ready, preparing to fire, the way his men had prepared, made ready to kill.

Hendricks stopped, wiping perspiration from his face.

"Damn." It made him uneasy. But he should be expected. The situation was different.

He strode over the ash, holding his gun tightly with both hands. Behind him came David. Hendricks peered around, tight-lipped. Any second it might happen. A burst of white light, a blast, carefully aimed from inside a deep concrete bunker.

He raised his arm and waved it around in a circle.

Nothing moved. To the right a long ridge ran, topped with dead tree trunks. A few wild vines had grown up around the trees, remains of arbors. And the eternal dark weeds. Hendricks studied the ridge. Was anything up there? Perfect place for a lookout. He approached the ridge warily, David coming silently behind. If it were his command he'd have a sentry up there, watching for troops trying to infiltrate into the command area. Of course, if it were his command there would be the claws around the area for full protection.

He stopped, feet apart, hands on his hips.

"Are we there?" David asked.

"Almost."

"Why have we stopped?"

"I don't want to take any chances." Hendricks advanced slowly. Now the ridge lay directly beside him, along his right. Overlooking him. His uneasy feeling increased. If an Ivan were up there he wouldn't have a chance. He waved his arm again. They should be expecting someone in the UN uniform, in response to the note capsule. Unless the whole thing was a trap.

"Keep up with me." He turned toward David. "Don't drop behind."

"With you?"

"Up beside me! We're close. We can't take any chances. Come on."

"I'll be all right." David remained behind him, in the rear, a few paces away, still clutching his teddy bear.

"Have it your way." Hendricks raised his glasses again, suddenly tense. For a moment—had something moved? He scanned the ridge carefully. Everything was silent. Dead. No life up there, only tree trunks and ash. Maybe a few rats. The big black rats that had survived the claws. Mutants—built their own shelters out of saliva and ash. Some kind of plaster. Adaptation. He started forward again.

A tall figure came out on the ridge above him, cloak flapping.

Gray-green. A Russian. Behind him a second soldier appeared, another Russian. Both lifted their guns, aiming.

Hendricks froze. He opened his mouth. The soldiers were kneeling, sighting down the side of the slope. A third figure had joined them on the ridge top, a smaller figure in gray-green. A woman. She stood behind the other two.

Hendricks found his voice. "Stop!" He waved up at them frantically. "I'm—"

The two Russians fired. Behind Hendricks there was a faint *pop*. Waves of heat lapped against him, throwing him to the ground. Ash tore at his face, grinding into his eyes and nose. Choking, he pulled himself to his knees. It was all a trap. He was finished. He had come to be killed, like a steer. The soldiers and the woman were coming down the side of the ridge toward him, sliding down through the soft ash. Hendricks was numb. His head throbbed. Awkwardly, he got his rifle up and took aim. It weighed a thousand tons; he could hardly hold it. His nose and cheeks stung. The air was full of the blast smell, a bitter acid stench.

"Don't fire," the first Russian said, in heavily accented English.

The three of them came up to him, surrounding him. "Put down your rifle, Yank," the other said.

Hendricks was dazed. Everything had happened so fast. He had been caught. And they had blasted the boy. He turned his head. David was gone. What remained of him was strewn across the ground.

The three Russians studied him curiously. Hendricks sat, wiping blood from his nose, picking out bits of ash. He shook his head, trying to clear it. "Why did you do it?" he murmured thickly. "The boy."

"Why?" One of the soldiers helped him roughly to his feet. He turned Hendricks around. "Look."

Hendricks closed his eyes.

"Look!" The two Russians pulled him forward. "See. Hurry up. There isn't much time to spare, Yank!"

Hendricks looked. And gasped.

"See now? Now do you understand?"

From the remains of David a metal wheel rolled. Relays, glinting metal. Parts, wiring. One of the Russians kicked at the heap of remains. Parts popped out, rolling away, wheels and springs and rods. A plastic section fell in, half charred. Hendricks bent shakily down. The front of the head had come off. He could make out the intricate brain, wires and relays, tiny tubes and switches, thousands of minute studs—

"A robot," the soldier holding his arm said. "We watched it tagging you."

"Tagging me?"

"That's their way. They tag along with you. Into the bunker. That's how they get in."

Hendricks blinked, dazed. "But—"

"Come on." They led him toward the ridge. "We can't stay here. It isn't safe. There must be hundreds of them all around here."

The three of them pulled him up the side of the ridge, sliding and slipping on the ash. The woman reached the top and stood waiting for them.

"The forward command," Hendricks muttered. "I came to negotiate with the Soviet—"

"There is no more forward command. *They* got in. We'll explain." They reached the top of the ridge. "We're all that's left. The three of us. The rest were down in the bunker."

"This way. Down this way." The woman unscrewed a lid, a gray manhole cover set in the ground. "Get in."

Hendricks lowered himself. The two soldiers and the woman came behind him, following him down the ladder. The woman closed the lid after them, bolting it tightly into place.

"Good thing we saw you," one of the two soldiers grunted. "It had tagged you about as far as it was going to."

"Give me one of your cigarettes," the woman said. "I haven't had an American cigarette for weeks."

Hendricks pushed the pack to her. She took a cigarette and passed the pack to the two soldiers. In the corner of the small room the lamp gleamed fitfully. The room was low-ceilinged, cramped. The four of them sat around a small wood table. A few dirty dishes were stacked to one side. Behind a ragged curtain a second room was partly visible. Hendricks saw the corner of a coat, some blankets, clothes hung on a hook.

"We were here," the soldier beside him said. He took off his helmet, pushing his blond hair back. "I'm Corporal Rudi Maxer. Polish. Impressed in the Soviet Army two years ago." He held out his hand.

Hendricks hesitated and then shook. "Major Joseph Hendricks."

"Klaus Epstein." The other soldier shook with him, a small

dark man with thinning hair. Epstein plucked nervously at his ear. "Austrian. Impressed God knows when. I don't remember. The three of us were here, Rudi and I, with Tasso." He indicated the woman. "That's how we escaped. All the rest were down in the bunker."

"And—and *they* got in?"

Epstein lit a cigarette. "First just one of them. The kind that tagged you. Then it let others in."

Hendricks became alert. "The *kind*? Are there more than one kind?"

"The little boy. David. David holding his teddy bear. That's Variety Three. The most effective."

"What are the other types?"

Epstein reached into his coat. "Here." He tossed a packet of photographs onto the table, tied with a string. "Look for yourself."

Hendricks untied the string.

"You see," Rudi Maxer said, "that was why we wanted to talk terms. The Russians, I mean. We found out about a week ago. Found out that your claws were beginning to make up new designs on their own. New types of their own. Better types. Down in your underground factories behind our lines. You let them stamp themselves, repair themselves. Made them more and more intricate. It's your fault this happened."

Hendricks examined the photos. They had been snapped hurriedly; they were blurred and indistinct. The first few showed—David. David walking along a road, by himself. David and another David. Three Davids. All exactly alike. Each with a ragged teddy bear.

All pathetic.

"Look at the others," Tasso said.

The next pictures, taken at a great distance, showed a towering wounded soldier sitting by the side of a path, his arm in a sling, the stump of one leg extended, a crude crutch on his lap. Then two wounded soldiers, both the same, standing side by side.

"That's Variety One. The Wounded Soldier." Klaus reached out and took the pictures. "You see, the claws were designed to get to human beings. To find them. Each kind was better than the last. They got farther, closer, past most of our defenses, into our lines. But as long as they were merely *machines*, metal spheres with claws and horns, feelers, they could be picked off like any other object. They could be detected as lethal robots as soon as they were seen. Once we caught sight of them—"

"Variety One subverted our whole north wing," Rudi said. "It was a long time before anyone caught on. Then it was too late. They came in, wounded soldiers, knocking and begging to be let in. So we let them in. And as soon as they were in they took over. We were watching out for machines . . ."

"At that time it was thought there was only the one type," Klaus Epstein said. "No one suspected there were other types. The pictures were flashed to us. When the runner was sent to you, we knew of just one type. Variety One. The big Wounded Soldier. We thought that was all."

"Your line fell to—"

"To Variety Three. David and his bear. That worked even better." Klaus smiled bitterly. "Soldiers are suckers for children. We brought them in and tried to feed them. We found out the hard way what they were after. At least, those who were in the bunker."

"The three of us were lucky," Rudi said. "Klaus and I were—were visiting Tasso when it happened. This is her place." He waved a big hand around. "This little cellar. We finished and climbed the ladder to start back. From the ridge we saw that they were all around the bunker. Fighting was still going on. David and his bear. Hundreds of them. Klaus took the pictures."

Klaus tied up the photographs again.

"And it's going on all along your line?" Hendricks said.

"Yes."

"How about *our* lines?" Without thinking, he touched the tab on his arm. "Can they—"

"They're not bothered by your radiation tabs. It makes no difference to them, Russian, American, Pole, German. It's all the same. They're doing what they were designed to do. Carrying out the original idea. They track down life, wherever they find it."

"They go by warmth," Klaus said. "That was the way you constructed them from the very start. Of course, those you designed were kept back by the radiation tabs you wear. Now they've got around that. These new varieties are lead-lined."

"What's the other variety?" Hendricks asked. "The David type, the Wounded Soldier—what's the other?"

"We don't know." Klaus pointed up at the wall. On the wall were two metal plates, ragged at the edges. Hendricks got up and studied them. They were bent and dented.

"The one on the left came off a Wounded Soldier," Rudi said. "We got one of them. It was going along toward our old bunker. We got it from the ridge, the same way we got the David tagging you."

The plate was stamped: *I-V*. Hendricks touched the other plate. "And this came from the David type?"

"Yes." The plate was stamped: *III-V*.

Klaus took a look at them, leaning over Hendricks's broad shoulder. "You can see what we're up against. There's another type. Maybe it was abandoned. Maybe it didn't work. But there must be a Second Variety. There's One and Three."

"You were lucky," Rudi said. "The David tagged you all the way here and never touched you. Probably thought you'd get it into a bunker, somewhere."

"One gets in and it's all over," Klaus said. "They move fast. One lets all the rest inside. They're inflexible. Machines with one purpose. They were built for only one thing." He rubbed sweat from his lip. "We saw."

They were silent.

"Let me have another cigarette, Yank," Tasso said. "They are good. I almost forgot how they were."

It was night. The sky was black. No stars were visible through the rolling clouds of ash. Klaus lifted the lid cautiously so that Hendricks could look out.

Rudi pointed into the darkness. "Over that way are the bunkers. Where we used to be. Not over half a mile from us. It was just chance Klaus and I were not there when it happened. Weakness. Saved by our lusts."

"All the rest must be dead," Klaus said in a low voice. "It came quickly. This morning the Politburo reached their decision. They notified us—forward command. Our runner was sent out at once. We saw him start toward the direction of your lines. We covered him until he was out of sight."

"Alex Radrivsky. We both knew him. He disappeared about six o'clock. The sun had just come up. About noon Klaus and I had an hour relief. We crept off, away from the bunkers. No one was watching. We came here. There used to be a town here, a few houses, a street. This cellar was part of a big farmhouse. We knew Tasso would be here, hiding down in her little place. We had come here before. Others from the bunkers came here. Today happened to be our turn."

"So we were saved," Klaus said. "Chance. It might have been others. We—we finished, and then we came up to the surface and started back along the ridge. That was when we saw them, the Davids. We understood right away. We had seen the photos of the First Variety, the Wounded Soldier. Our Commissar distributed them to us with an explanation. If we had gone another step they would have seen us. As it was we had to blast two Davids before we got back. There were hundreds of them, all around. Like ants. We took pictures and slipped back here, bolting the lid tight."

"They're not so much when you catch them alone. We moved faster than they did. But they're inexorable. Not like living things. They came right at us. And we blasted them."

Major Hendricks rested against the edge of the lid, adjusting his eyes to the darkness. "Is it safe to have the lid up at all?"

"If we're careful. How else can you operate your transmitter?"

Hendricks lifted the small belt transmitter slowly. He pressed it against his ear. The metal was cold and damp. He blew against the mike, raising up the short antenna. A faint hum sounded in his ear. "That's true, I suppose."

But he still hesitated.

"We'll pull you under if anything happens," Klaus said.

"Thanks." Hendricks waited a moment, resting the transmitter against his shoulder. "Interesting, isn't it?"

"What?"

"This, the new types. The new varieties of claws. We're completely at their mercy, aren't we? By now they've probably gotten into the UN lines, too. It makes me wonder if we're not seeing the beginning of a new species. *The* new species. Evolution. The race to come after man."

Rudi grunted. "There is no race after man."

"No? Why not? Maybe we're seeing it now, the end of human beings, the beginning of the new society."

"They're not a race. They're mechanical killers. You made them to destroy. That's all they can do. They're machines with a job."

"So it seems now. But how about later on? After the war is over. Maybe, when there aren't any humans to destroy, their real potentialities will begin to show."

"You talk as if they were alive!"

"Aren't they?"

There was silence. "They're machines," Rudi said. "They look like people, but they're machines."

"Use your transmitter, Major," Klaus said. "We can't stay up here forever."

Holding the transmitter tightly, Hendricks called the code of the command bunker. He waited, listening. No response. Only silence. He checked the leads carefully. Everything was in place.

"Scott!" he said into the mike. "Can you hear me?"

Silence. He raised the gain up full and tried again. Only static.

"I don't get anything. They may hear me but they may not want to answer."

"Tell them it's an emergency."

"They'll think I'm being forced to call. Under your direction." He tried again, outlining briefly what he had learned. But still the phone was silent, except for the faint static.

"Radiation pools kill most transmission," Klaus said, after awhile. "Maybe that's it."

Hendricks shut the transmitter up. "No use. No answer. Radiation pools? Maybe. Or they hear me, but won't answer. Frankly, that's what I would do, if a runner tried to call from the Soviet lines. They have no reason to believe such a story. They may hear everything I say—"

"Or maybe it's too late."

Hendricks nodded.

"We better get the lid down," Rudi said nervously. "We don't want to take unnecessary chances."

They climbed slowly back down the tunnel. Klaus bolted the lid carefully into place. They descended into the kitchen. The air was heavy and close around them.

"Could they work that fast?" Hendricks said. "I left the bunker this noon. Ten hours ago. How could they move so quickly?"

"It doesn't take them long. Not after the first one gets in. It goes wild. You know what the little claws can do. Even *one* of these is beyond belief. Razors, each finger. Maniacal."

"All right." Hendricks moved away impatiently. He stood with his back to them.

"What's the matter?" Rudi said.

"The Moon Base. God, if they've gotten there—"

"The Moon Base?"

Hendricks turned around. "They couldn't have got to the Moon Base. How would they get there? It isn't possible. I can't believe it."

"What is this Moon Base? We've heard rumors, but nothing definite. What is the actual situation? You seem concerned."

"We're supplied from the Moon. The governments are there, under the lunar surface. All our people and industries. That's what keeps us going. If they should find some way of getting off Terra, onto the Moon—"

"It only takes one of them. Once the first one gets in it admits the others. Hundreds of them, all alike. You should have seen them. Identical. Like ants."

"Perfect socialism," Tasso said. "The idea of the communist state. All citizens interchangeable."

Klaus grunted angrily. "That's enough. Well? What next?"

Hendricks paced back and forth, around the small room. The air was full of smells of food and perspiration. The others watched him. Presently Tasso pushed through the curtain, into the other room. "I'm going to take a nap."

The curtain closed behind her. Rudi and Klaus sat down at the table, still watching Hendricks. "It's up to you," Klaus said. "We don't know your situation."

Hendricks nodded.

"It's a problem." Rudi drank some coffee, filling his cup from a rusty pot. "We're safe here for a while, but we can't stay here forever. Not enough food or supplies."

"But if we go outside—"

"If we go outside they'll get us. Or probably they'll get us. We couldn't go very far. How far is your command bunker, Major?"

"Three or four miles."

"We might make it. The four of us. Four of us could watch all sides. They couldn't slip up behind us and start tagging us. We have three rifles, three blast rifles. Tasso can have my pistol." Rudi tapped his belt. "In the Soviet army we didn't have shoes always, but we had guns. With all four of us armed one of us might get to your command bunker. Preferably you, Major."

"What if they're already there?" Klaus said.

Rudi shrugged. "Well, then we come back here."

Hendricks stopped pacing. "What do you think the chances are they're already in the American lines?"

"Hard to say. Fairly good. They're organized. They know exactly what they're doing. Once they start they go like a horde of locusts. They have to keep moving, and fast. It's secrecy and speed they depend on. Surprise. They push their way in before anyone has any idea."

"I see," Hendricks murmured.

From the other room Tasso stirred. "Major?"

Hendricks pushed the curtain back. "What?"

Tasso looked up at him lazily from the cot. "Have you any more American cigarettes left?"

Hendricks went into the room and sat down across from her, on a wood stool. He felt in his pockets. "No. All gone."

"Too bad."

"What nationality are you?" Hendricks asked after a while.

"Russian."

"How did you get here?"

"Here?"

"This used to be France. This was part of Normandy. Did you come with the Soviet army?"

"Why?"

"Just curious." He studied her. She had taken off her coat, tossing it over the end of the cot. She was young, about twenty. Slim. Her long hair stretched out over the pillow. She was staring at him silently, her eyes dark and large.

"What's on your mind?" Tasso said.

"Nothing. How old are you?"

"Eighteen." She continued to watch him, unblinking, her arms behind her head. She had on Russian army pants and shirt. Gray-green. Thick leather belt with counter and cartridges. Medicine kit.

"You're in the Soviet army?"

"No."

"Where did you get the uniform?"

She shrugged. "It was given to me," she told him.

"How—how old were you when you came here?"

"Sixteen."

"That young?"

Her eyes narrowed. "What do you mean?"

Hendricks rubbed his jaw. "Your life would have been a lot different if there had been no war. Sixteen. You came here at sixteen. To live this way."

"I had to survive."

"I'm not moralizing."

"Your life would have been different, too," Tasso murmured. She reached down and unfastened one of her boots. She kicked the boot off, onto the floor, "Major, do you want to go in the other room? I'm sleepy."

"It's going to be a problem, the four of us here. It's going to be hard to live in these quarters. Are there just the two rooms?"

"Yes."

"How big was the cellar originally? Was it larger than this? Are there other rooms filled up with debris? We might be able to open one of them."

"Perhaps. I really don't know." Tasso loosened her belt. She made herself comfortable on the cot, unbuttoning her shirt. "You're sure you have no more cigarettes?"

"I had only the one pack."

"Too bad. Maybe if we get back to your bunker we can find some." The other boot fell. Tasso reached up for the light cord. "Good night."

"You're going to sleep?"

"That's right."

The room plunged into darkness. Hendricks got up and made his way past the curtain, into the kitchen. And stopped, rigid.

Rudi stood against the wall, his face white and gleaming. His mouth opened and closed but no sounds came. Klaus stood in front of him, the muzzle of his pistol in Rudi's stomach. Neither of them moved. Klaus, his hand tight around his gun, his features set. Rudi, pale and silent, spread-eagled against the wall.

"What—" Hendricks muttered, but Klaus cut him off.

"Be quiet, Major. Come over here. Your gun. Get out your gun."

Hendricks drew his pistol. "What is it?"

"Cover him." Klaus motioned him forward. "Beside me. Hurry!"

Rudi moved a little, lowering his arms. He turned to Hendricks, licking his lips. The whites of his eyes shone wildly. Sweat dripped from his forehead, down his cheeks. He fixed his gaze on Hendricks. "Major, he's gone insane. Stop him." Rudi's voice was thin and hoarse, almost inaudible.

"What's going on?" Hendricks demanded.

Without lowering his pistol Klaus answered. "Major, remember our discussion? The Three Varieties? We knew about One and Three. But we didn't know about Two. At least, we didn't know before." Klaus's fingers tightened around the gun butt. "We didn't know before, but we know now."

He pressed the trigger. A burst of white heat rolled out of the gun, licking around Rudi.

"Major, this is the Second Variety."

Tasso swept the curtain aside. "Klaus! What did you do?"

Klaus turned from the charred form, gradually sinking down the wall onto the floor. "The Second Variety, Tasso. Now we know. We have all three types identified. The danger is less. I—"

Tasso stared past him at the remains of Rudi, at the blackened, smoldering fragments and bits of cloth. "You killed him."

"Him? *It*, you mean. I was watching. I had a feeling, but I wasn't sure. At least, I wasn't sure before. But this evening I was certain." Klaus rubbed his pistol butt nervously. "We're lucky. Don't you understand? Another hour and it might–"

"You were *certain?*" Tasso pushed past him and bent down, over the steaming remains on the floor. Her face became hard. "Major, see for yourself. Bones, Flesh."

Hendricks bent down beside her. The remains were human remains. Seared flesh, charred bone fragments, part of a skull. Ligaments, viscera, blood. Blood forming a pool against the wall.

"No wheels," Tasso said calmly. She straightened up. "No wheels, no parts, no relays. Not a claw. Not the Second Variety." She folded her arms. "You're going to have to be able to explain this."

Klaus sat down at the table, all the color drained suddenly from his face. He put his head in his hands and rocked back and forth.

"Snap out of it." Tasso's fingers closed over his shoulder. "Why did you do it? Why did you kill him?"

"He was frightened," Hendricks said. "All this, the whole thing, building up around us."

"Maybe."

"What, then? What do you think?"

"I think he may have had a reason for killing Rudi. A good reason."

"What reason?"

"Maybe Rudi learned something."

Hendricks studied her bleak face. "About what?" he asked.

"About him. About Klaus."

Klaus looked up quickly. "You can see what she's trying to say. She thinks I'm the Second Variety. Don't you see, Major? Now she wants you to believe I killed him on purpose. That I'm—"

"Why did you kill him, then?" Tasso said.

"I told you." Klaus shook his head wearily. "I thought he was a claw. I thought I knew."

"Why?"

"I had been watching him. I was suspicious."

"Why?"

"I thought I had seen something. Heard something. I thought I—" He stopped.

"Go on."

"We were sitting at the table. Playing cards. You two were in the other room. It was silent. I thought I heard him—*whirr*."

There was silence.

"Do you believe that?" Tasso said to Hendricks.

"Yes. I believe what he says."

"I don't. I think he killed Rudi for a good purpose." Tasso touched the rifle, resting in the corner of the room. "Major—"

"No." Hendricks shook his head. "Let's stop it right now. One is enough. We're afraid, the way he was. If we kill him we'll be doing what he did to Rudi."

Klaus looked gratefully up at him. "Thanks. I was afraid. You understand, don't you? Now she's afraid, the way I was. She wants to kill me."

"No more killing." Hendricks moved toward the end of the ladder. "I'm going above and try the transmitter once more. If I can't get them we're moving back toward my lines tomorrow morning."

Klaus rose quickly. "I'll come up with you and give you a hand."

The night air was cold. The earth was cooling off. Klaus took a deep breath, filling his lungs. He and Hendricks stepped onto the ground, out of the tunnel. Klaus planted his feet wide apart, the rifle up, watching and listening. Hendricks crouched by the tunnel mouth, tuning the small transmitter.

"Any luck?" Klaus asked presently.

"Not yet."

"Keep trying. Tell them what happened."

Hendricks kept trying. Without success. Finally he lowered the antenna. "It's useless. They can't hear me. Or they hear me and won't answer. Or—"

"Or they don't exist."

"I'll try once more." Hendricks raised the antenna. "Scott, can you hear me? Come in!"

He listened. There was only static. Then, still very faintly—

"This is Scott."

His fingers tightened. "Scott! Is it you?"

"This is Scott."

Klaus squatted down. "It is your command?"

"Scott, listen. Do you understand? About them, the claws. Did you get my message? Did you hear me?"

"Yes." Faintly. Almost inaudible. He could hardly make out the word.

"You got my message? Is everything all right at the bunker? None of them have got in?"

"Everything is all right."

"Have they tried to get in?"

The voice was weaker.

"No."

Hendricks turned to Klaus. "They're all right."

"Have they been attacked?"

"No." Hendricks pressed the phone tighter to his ear. "Scott, I can hardly hear you. Have you notified the Moon Base? Do they know? Are they alerted?"

No answer.

"Scott! Can you hear me?"

Silence.

Hendricks relaxed, sagging. "Faded out. Must be radiation pools."

Hendricks and Klaus looked at each other. Neither of them said anything. After a time Klaus said, "Did it sound like any of your men? Could you identify the voice?"

"It was too faint."

"You couldn't be certain?"

"No."

"Then it could have been—"

"I don't know. Now I'm not sure. Let's go back down and get the lid closed."

They climbed back down the ladder slowly, into the warm cellar. Klaus bolted the lid behind them. Tasso waited for them, her face expressionless.

"Any luck?" she asked.

Neither of them answered. "Well?" Klaus said at last. "What do you think, Major? Was it your officer, or was it one of *them*?"

"I don't know."

"Then we're just where we were before."

Hendricks stared down at the floor, his jaw set. "We'll have to go. To be sure."

"Anyhow, we have food here for only a few weeks. We'd have to go up after that, in any case."

"Apparently so."

"What's wrong?" Tasso demanded. "Did you get across to your bunker? What's the matter?"

"It may have been one of my men," Hendricks said slowly. "Or it may have been one of *them*. But we'll never know standing here." He examined his watch. "Let's turn in and get some sleep. We want to be up early tomorrow."

"Early?"

"Our best chance to get through the claws should be early in the morning," Hendricks said.

The morning was crisp and clear. Major Hendricks studied the countryside through his field glasses.

"See anything?" Klaus said.

"No."

"Can you make out our bunkers?"

"Which way?"

"Here." Klaus took the glasses and adjusted them. "I know where to look." He looked a long time, silently.

Tasso came to the top of the tunnel and stepped up onto the ground. "Anything?"

"No." Klaus passed the glasses back to Hendricks. "They're out of sight. Come on. Let's not stay here."

The three of them made their way down the side of the ridge, sliding in the soft ash. Across a flat rock a lizard scuttled. They stopped instantly, rigid.

"What was it?" Klaus muttered.

"A lizard."

The lizard ran on, hurrying through the ash. It was exactly the same color as the ash.

"Perfect adaptation," Klaus said. "Proves we were right. Lysenko, I mean."

They reached the bottom of the ridge and stopped, standing close together, looking around them.

"Let's go." Hendricks started off. "It's a good long trip, on foot."

Klaus fell in beside him. Tasso walked behind, her pistol held alertly. "Major, I've been meaning to ask you something," Klaus said. "How did you run across the David? The one that was tagging you."

"I met it along the way. In some ruins."

"What did it say?"

"Not much. It said it was alone. By itself."

"You couldn't tell it was a machine? It talked like a living person? You never suspected?"

"It didn't say much. I noticed nothing unusual."

"It's strange, machines so much like people that you can be fooled. Almost alive. I wonder where it'll end."

"They're doing what you Yanks designed them to do," Tasso said. "You designed them to hunt out life and destroy. Human life. Wherever they find it."

Hendricks was watching Klaus intently. "Why did you ask me? What's on your mind?"

"Nothing," Klaus answered.

"Klaus thinks you're the Second Variety," Tasso said calmly, from behind them. "Now he's got his eye on you."

Klaus flushed. "Why not? We sent a runner to the Yank lines and *he* comes back. Maybe he thought he'd find some good game here."

Hendricks laughed harshly. "I came from the UN bunkers. There were human beings all around me."

"Maybe you saw an opportunity to get into the Soviet lines. Maybe you saw your chance. Maybe you—"

"The Soviet lines had already been taken over. Your lines had been invaded before I left my command bunker. Don't forget that."

Tasso came up beside him. "That proves nothing at all, Major."

"Why not?"

"There appears to be little communication between the varieties. Each is made in a different factory. They don't seem to work together. You might have started for the Soviet lines without knowing anything about the work of the other varieties. Or even what the other varieties were like."

"How do you know so much about the claws?" Hendricks said.

"I've seen them. I've observed them take over the Soviet bunkers."

"You know quite a lot," Klaus said. "Actually, you saw very little. Strange that you should have been such an acute observer."

Tasso laughed. "Do you suspect me, now?"

"Forget it," Hendricks said. They walked on in silence.

"Are we going the whole way on foot?" Tasso said, after awhile. "I'm not used to walking." She gazed around at the plain of ash, stretching out on all sides of them, as far as they could see. "How dreary."

"It's like this all the way," Klaus said.

"In a way I wish you had been in your bunker when the attack came."

"Somebody else would have been with you, if not me," Klaus muttered.

Tasso laughed, putting her hands in her pockets. "I suppose so."

They walked on, keeping their eyes on the vast plain of silent ash around them.

The sun was setting. Hendricks made his way forward slowly, waving Tasso and Klaus back. Klaus squatted down, resting his gun butt against the ground.

Tasso found a concrete slab and sat down with a sigh. "It's good to rest."

"Be quiet," Klaus said sharply.

Hendricks pushed up to the top of the rise ahead of them. The same rise the Russian runner had come up, the day before. Hendricks dropped down, stretching himself out, peering through his glasses at what lay beyond.

Nothing was visible. Only ash and occasional trees. But there, not more than fifty yards ahead, was the entrance of the forward command bunker. The bunker from which he had come. Hendricks watched silently. No motion. No sign of life. Nothing stirred.

Klaus slithered up beside him. "Where is it?"

"Down there." Hendricks passed him the glasses. Clouds of ash rolled across the evening sky. The world was darkening. They had a couple of hours of light left, at the most. Probably not that much.

"I don't see anything," Klaus said.

"That tree there. The stump. By the pile of bricks. The entrance is to the right of the bricks."

"I'll have to take your word for it."

"You and Tasso cover me from here. You'll be able to sight all the way to the bunker entrance."

"You're going down alone?"

"With my wrist tab I'll be safe. The ground around the bunker is a living field of claws. They collect down in the ash. Like crabs. Without tabs you wouldn't have a chance."

"Maybe you're right."

"I'll walk slowly all the way. As soon as I know for certain—"

"If they're down inside the bunker you won't be able to get back up here. They go fast. You don't realize."

"What do you suggest?"

Klaus considered. "I don't know. Get them to come up to the surface. So you can see."

Hendricks brought his transmitter from his belt, raising the antenna. "Let's get started."

Klaus signaled to Tasso. She crawled expertly up the side of the rise to where they were sitting.

"He's going down alone," Klaus said. "We'll cover him from here. As soon as you see him start back, fire past him at once. They come quick."

"You're not very optimistic," Tasso said.

"No, I'm not."

Hendricks opened the breech of his gun, checking it carefully. "Maybe things are all right."

"You didn't see them. Hundreds of them. All the same. Pouring out like ants."

"I should be able to find out without going down all the way." Hendricks locked his gun, gripping it in one hand, the transmitter in the other. "Well, wish me luck."

Klaus put out his hand. "Don't go down until you're sure. Talk to them from up here. Make them show themselves."

Hendricks stood up. He stepped down the side of the rise.

A moment later he was walking slowly toward the pile of bricks and debris beside the dead tree stump. Toward the entrance of the forward command bunker.

Nothing stirred. He raised the transmitter, clicking it on. "Scott? Can you hear me?"

Silence.

"Scott! This is Hendricks. Can you hear me? I'm standing outside the bunker. You should be able to see me in the view sight."

He listened, the transmitter gripped tightly. No sound. Only static. He walked forward. A claw burrowed out of the ash and raced toward him. It halted a few feet away and then slunk off. A second claw appeared, one of the big ones with feelers. It moved toward him, studied him intently, and then fell in behind him, dogging respectfully after him, a few paces away. A moment later a second big claw joined it. Silently, the claws trailed him as he walked slowly toward the bunker.

Hendricks stopped, and behind him, the claws came to a halt. He was close now. Almost to the bunker steps.

"Scott! Can you hear me? I'm standing right above you. Outside. On the surface. Are you picking me up?"

He waited, holding his gun against his side, the transmitter tightly to his ear. Time passed. He strained to hear, but there was only silence. Silence, and faint static.

Then, distantly, metallically—

"This is Scott."

The voice was neutral. Cold. He could not identify it. But the earphone was minute.

"Scott! Listen. I'm standing right above you. I'm on the surface, looking down into the bunker entrance."

"Yes."

"Can you see me?"

"Yes."

"Through the view sight? You have the sight trained on me?"

"Yes."

Hendricks pondered. A circle of claws waited quietly around him, gray-metal bodies on all sides of him. "Is everything all right in the bunker? Nothing unusual has happened?"

"Everything is all right."

"Will you come up to the surface? I want to see you for a moment." Hendricks took a deep breath. "Come up here with me. I want to talk to you."

"Come down."

"I'm giving you an order."

Silence.

"Are you coming?" Hendricks listened. There was no response. "I order you to come to the surface."

"Come down."

Hendricks set his jaw. "Let me talk to Leone."

There was a long pause. He listened to the static. Then a voice came, hard, thin, metallic. The same as the other. "This is Leone."

"Hendricks. I'm on the surface. At the bunker entrance. I want one of you to come up here."

"Come down."

"Why come down? I'm giving you an order!"

Silence. Hendricks lowered the transmitter. He looked carefully around him. The entrance was just ahead. Almost at his feet. He lowered the antenna and fastened the transmitter to his belt. Carefully, he gripped his gun with both hands. He moved forward, a step at a time. If they could see him they knew he was starting toward the entrance. He closed his eyes a moment.

Then he put his foot on the first step that led downward.

Two Davids came up at him, their faces identical and expressionless. He blasted them into particles. More came rushing silently up, a whole pack of them. All exactly the same.

Hendricks turned and raced back, away from the bunker, back toward the rise.

At the top of the rise Tasso and Klaus were firing down. The small claws were already streaking up toward them, shining metal spheres going fast, racing frantically through the ash. But he had no time to think about that. He knelt down, aiming at the bunker entrance, gun against his cheek. The Davids were coming out in groups, clutching their teddy bears, their thin knobby legs pumping as they ran up the steps to the surface. Hendricks fired into the main body of them. They burst apart, wheels and springs flying in all directions. He fired again, through the mist of particles.

A giant lumbering figure rose up in the bunker entrance, tall and swaying. Hendricks paused, amazed. A man, a soldier. With one leg, supporting himself with a crutch.

"Major!" Tasso's voice came. More firing. The huge figure moved forward, Davids swarming around it. Hendricks broke out of his freeze. The First Variety. The Wounded Soldier. He aimed and fired. The soldier burst into bits, parts and relays flying. Now many Davids were out on the flat ground, away from the bunker. He fired again and again, moving slowly back, half-crouching and aiming.

From the rise, Klaus fired down. The side of the rise was alive with claws making their way up. Hendricks retreated toward the rise, running and crouching. Tasso had left Klaus and was circling slowly to the right, moving away from the rise.

A David slipped up toward him, its small white face expressionless, brown hair hanging down in its eyes. It bent over suddenly, opening its arms. Its teddy bear hurtled down and leaped across the ground, bounding toward him. Hendricks fired. The bear and the David both dissolved. He grinned, blinking. It was like a dream.

"Up here!" Tasso's voice. Hendricks made his way toward her. She was over by some columns of concrete, walls of a ruined building. She was firing past him, with the hand pistol Klaus had given her.

"Thanks." He joined her, gasping for breath. She pulled him back, behind the concrete, fumbling at her belt.

"Close your eyes!" She unfastened a globe from her waist. Rapidly, she unscrewed the cap, locking it into place. "Close your eyes and get down."

She threw the bomb. It sailed in an arc, an expert, rolling and bouncing to the entrance of the bunker. Two Wounded Soldiers stood uncertainly by the brick pile. More Davids poured from behind them, out onto the plain. One of the Wounded Soldiers moved toward the bomb, stooping awkwardly down to pick it up.

The bomb went off. The concussion whirled Hendricks around, throwing him on his face. A hot wind rolled over him. Dimly he saw Tasso standing behind the columns, firing slowly and methodically at the Davids coming out of the raging clouds of white fire.

Back along the rise Klaus struggled with a ring of claws circling around him. He retreated, blasting at them and moving back, trying to break through the ring.

Hendricks struggled to his feet. His head ached. He could hardly see. Everything was licking at him, raging and whirling. His right arm would not move.

Tasso pulled back toward him. "Come on. Let's go."

"Klaus—he's still up there."

"Come on!" Tasso dragged Hendricks back, away from the columns. Hendricks shook his head, trying to clear it. Tasso led him rapidly away, her eyes intense and bright, watching for claws that had escaped the blast.

One David came out of the rolling clouds of flame. Tasso blasted it. No more appeared.

"But Klaus. What about him?" Hendricks stopped, standing unsteadily. "He—"

"Come on!"

They retreated, moving farther and farther away from the bunker. A few small claws followed them for a little while and then gave up, turning back and going off.

At last Tasso stopped. "We can stop here and get our breaths."

Hendricks sat down on some heaps of debris. He wiped his neck, gasping. "We left Klaus back there."

Tasso said nothing. She opened her gun, sliding a fresh round of blast cartridges into place.

Hendricks stared at her, dazed. "You left him back there on purpose."

Tasso snapped the gun together. She studied the heaps of rubble around them, her face expressionless. As if she were watching for something.

"What is it?" Hendricks demanded. "What are you looking for? Is something coming?" He shook his head, trying to understand. What was she doing? What was she waiting for? He could see nothing. Ash lay all around them, ash and ruins. Occasional stark tree trunks, without leaves or branches. "What—"

Tasso cut him off. "Be still." Her eyes narrowed. Suddenly her gun came up. Hendricks turned, following her gaze.

Back the way they had come a figure appeared. The figure walked unsteadily toward them. Its clothes were torn. It limped as it made its way along, going very slowly and carefully. Stopping now and then, resting and getting its strength. Once it almost fell. It stood for a moment, trying to steady itself. Then it came on.

Klaus.

Hendricks stood up. "Klaus!" He started toward him. "How the hell did you—"

Tasso fired. Hendricks swung back. She fired again, the blast passing him, a searing line of heat. The beam caught Klaus in the chest. He exploded, gears and wheels flying. For a moment he continued to walk. Then he swayed back and forth. He crashed to the ground, his arms flung out. A few more wheels rolled away.

Silence.

Tasso turned to Hendricks. "Now you understand why he killed Rudi."

Hendricks sat down again slowly. He shook his head. He was numb. He could not think.

"Do you see?" Tasso said. "Do you understand?"

Hendricks said nothing. Everything was slipping away from him, faster and faster. Darkness, rolling and plucking at him.

He closed his eyes.

Hendricks opened his eyes slowly. His body ached all over. He tried to sit up but needles of pain shot through his arm and shoulder. He gasped.

"Don't try to get up," Tasso said. She bent down, putting her cold hand against his forehead.

It was night. A few stars glinted above, shining through the drifting clouds of ash. Hendricks lay back, his teeth locked. Tasso watched him impassively. She had built a fire with some wood and weeds. The fire licked feebly, hissing at a metal cup suspended over it. Everything was silent. Unmoving darkness, beyond the fire.

"So he was the Second Variety," Hendricks murmured.

"I had always thought so."

"Why didn't you destroy him sooner?" He wanted to know.

"You held me back." Tasso crossed to the fire to look into the metal cup, "Coffee. It'll be ready to drink in a while."

She came back and sat down beside him. Presently she opened her pistol and began to disassemble the firing mechanism, studying it intently.

"This is a beautiful gun," Tasso said, half aloud. "The construction is superb."

"What about them? The claws."

"The concussion from the bomb put most of them out of action. They're delicate. Highly organized, I suppose."

"The Davids, too?"

"Yes."

"How did you happen to have a bomb like that?"

Tasso shrugged. "We designed it. You shouldn't underestimate our technology, Major. Without such a bomb you and I would no longer exist."

"Very useful."

Tasso stretched out her legs, warming her feet in the heat of the fire. "It surprised me that you did not seem to understand, after he killed Rudi. Why did you think he—"

"I told you, I thought he was afraid."

"Really? You know, Major, for a little while I suspected you. Because you wouldn't let me kill him. I thought you might be protecting him." She laughed.

"Are we safe here?" Hendricks asked presently.

"For a while. Until they get reinforcements from some other area." Tasso began to clean the interior of the gun with a bit of rag. She finished and pushed the mechanism back into place. She closed the gun, running her finger along the barrel.

"We were lucky," Hendricks murmured.

"Yes. Very lucky."

"Thanks for pulling me away."

Tasso did not answer. She glanced up at him, her eyes bright in the firelight. Hendricks examined his arm. He could not move his fingers. His whole side seemed numb. Down inside him was a dull steady ache.

"How do you feel?" Tasso asked.

"My arm is damaged."

"Anything else?"

"Internal injuries."

"You didn't get down when the bomb went off."

Hendricks said nothing. He watched Tasso pour the coffee from the cup into a flat metal pan. She brought it over to him.

"Thanks." He struggled up enough to drink. It was hard to swallow. His insides turned over and he pushed the pan away. "That's all I can drink now."

Tasso drank the rest. Time passed. The clouds of ash moved across the dark sky above them. Hendricks rested, his mind blank. After a while he became aware that Tasso was standing over him, gazing down at him.

"What is it?" he murmured.

"Do you feel any better?"

"Some."

"You know, Major, if I hadn't dragged you away they would have got you. You would be dead. Like Rudi."

"I know."

"Do you want to know why I brought you out? I could have left you. I could have left you there."

"Why did you bring me out?"

"Because we have to get away from here." Tasso stirred the fire with a stick, peering calmly down into it. "No human being can live here. When their reinforcements come we won't have a chance. I've pondered about it while you were unconscious. We have perhaps three hours before they come."

"And you expect me to get us away?"

"That's right. I expect you to get us out of here."

"Why me?"

"Because I don't know any way." Her eyes shone at him in the half light, bright and steady. "If you can't get us out of here they'll kill us within three hours. I see nothing else ahead. Well, Major? What are you going to do? I've been waiting all night. While you were unconscious I sat here, waiting and listening. It's almost dawn. The night is almost over."

Hendricks considered. "It's curious," he said at last.

"Curious?"

"That you should think I can get us out of here. I wonder what you think I can do."

"Can you get us to the Moon Base?"

"The Moon Base? How?"

"There must be some way."

Hendricks shook his head. "No. There's no way that I know of."

Tasso said nothing. For a moment her steady gaze wavered. She ducked her head, turning abruptly away. She scrambled to her feet. "More coffee?"

"No."

"Suit yourself." Tasso drank silently. He could not see her face. He lay back against the ground, deep in thought, trying to concentrate. It was hard to think. His head still hurt. And the numbing daze still hung over him.

"There might be one way," he said suddenly.

"Oh?"

"How soon is dawn?"

"Two hours. The sun will be coming up shortly."

"There's suppose to be a ship near here. I've never seen it. But I know it exists."

"What kind of a ship?" Her voice was sharp.

"A rocket cruiser."

"Will it take us off? To the Moon Base?"

"It's supposed to. In case of emergency." He rubbed his forehead.

"What's wrong?"

"My head. It's hard to think. I can hardly—hardly concentrate. The bomb."

"Is the ship near here?" Tasso slid over beside him, settling down on her haunches. "How far is it? Where is it?"

"I'm trying to think."

Her fingers dug into his arm. "Nearby?" Her voice was like iron. "Where would it be? Would they store it underground? Hidden underground?"

"Yes. In a storage locker."

"How do we find it? Is it marked? Is there a code marker to identify it?"

Hendricks concentrated. "No. No markings. No code symbol."

"What then?"

"A sign."

"What sort of sign?"

Hendricks did not answer. In the flickering light his eyes were glazed, two sightless orbs. Tasso's fingers dug into his arm.

"What sort of sign? What is it?"

"I—I can't think. Let me rest."

"All right." She let go and stood up. Hendricks lay back against the ground, his eyes closed. Tasso walked away from him, her hands in her pockets. She kicked a rock out of her way and stood staring up at the sky. The night blackness was already beginning to fade into gray. Morning was coming.

Tasso gripped her pistol and walked around the fire in a circle, back and forth. On the ground Major Hendricks lay, his eyes closed, unmoving. The grayness rose in the sky, higher and higher. The landscape became visible, fields of ash stretching out in all directions. Ash and ruins of buildings, a wall here and there, heaps of concrete, the naked trunk of a tree.

The air was cold and sharp. Somewhere a long way off a bird made a few bleak sounds.

Hendricks stirred. He opened his eyes. "Is it dawn? Already?"

"Yes."

Hendricks sat up a little. "You wanted to know something. You were asking me."

"Do you remember now?"

"Yes."

"What is it?" She tensed. "What?" she repeated sharply.

"A well. A ruined well. It's in a storage locker under a well."

"A well." Tasso relaxed. "Then we'll find a well." She looked at her watch. "We have about an hour, Major. Do you think we can find it in an hour?"

"Give me a hand up," Hendricks said.

Tasso put her pistol away and helped him to his feet. "This is going to be difficult."

"Yes it is." Hendricks set his lips tightly. "I don't think we're going to go very far."

They began to walk. The early sun cast a little warmth down on them. The land was flat and barren, stretching out gray and lifeless as far as they could see. A few birds sailed silently, far above them, circling slowly.

"See anything?" Hendricks said. "Any claws?"

"No. Not yet."

They passed through some ruins, upright concrete and bricks. A cement foundation. Rats scuttled away. Tasso jumped back warily.

"This used to be a town," Hendricks said. "A village. Provincial village. This was all grape country, once. Where are we now."

They came onto a ruined street, weeds and cracks criss-crossing it. Over to the right a stone chimney stuck up.

"Be careful," he warned her.

A pit yawned, an open basement. Ragged ends of pipes jutted up, twisted and bent. They passed part of a house, a bathtub turned on its side. A broken chair. A few spoons and bits of china dishes. In the center of the street the ground had sunk away. The depression was filled with weeds and debris and bones.

"Over here," Hendricks murmured.

"This way?"

"To the right."

They passed the remains of a heavy-duty tank. Hendricks's belt counter clicked ominously. The tank had been radiation-blasted. A few feet from the tank a mummified body lay sprawled out, mouth open. Beyond the road was a flat field. Stones and weeds, and bits of broken glass.

"There," Hendricks said.

A stone well jutted up, sagging and broken. A few boards lay across it. Most of the well had sunk into rubble. Hendricks walked unsteadily toward it, Tasso beside him.

"Are you certain about this?" Tasso said. "This doesn't look like anything."

"I'm sure." Hendricks sat down at the edge of the well, his teeth locked. His breath came quickly. He wiped perspiration from his face. "This was arranged so the senior command officer could get away. If anything happened. If the bunker fell."

"That was you?"

"Yes."

"Where is the ship? Is it here?"

"We're standing on it." Hendricks ran his hands over the surface of the well stones. "The eye-lock responds to me, not to anybody else. It's my ship. Or it was supposed to be."

There was a sharp click. Presently they heard a low grating sound from below them.

"Step back," Hendricks said. He and Tasso moved away from the well.

A section of the ground slid back. A metal frame pushed slowly up through the ash, shoving bricks and weeds out of the way. The action ceased as the ship nosed into view.

"There it is," Hendricks said.

The ship was small. It rested quietly, suspended in its mesh frame like a blunt needle. A rain of ash sifted down into the dark cavity from which the ship had been raised. Hendricks made his way over to it. He mounted the mesh and unscrewed the hatch, pulling it back. Inside the ship the control banks and the pressure seat were visible.

Tasso came and stood beside him, gazing into the ship. "I'm not accustomed to rocket piloting," she said after a while.

Hendricks glanced at her. "I'll do the piloting."

"Will you? There's only one seat, Major. I can see it's built to carry only a single person."

Hendricks's breathing changed. He studied the interior of the ship intently. Tasso was right. There was only one seat. The ship was built to carry only one person. "I see," he said slowly. "And the one person is you."

She nodded.

"Of course."

"Why?"

"*You* can't go. You might not live through the trip. You're injured. You probably wouldn't get there."

"An interesting point. But you see, I know where the Moon Base is. And you don't. You might fly around for months and not find it. It's well hidden. Without knowing what to look for—"

"I'll have to take my chances. Maybe I won't find it. Not by myself. But I think you'll give me all the information I need. Your life depends on it."

"How?"

"If I find the Moon Base in time, perhaps I can get them to send a ship back to pick you up. *If* I find the Base in time. If not, then you haven't a chance. I imagine there are supplies on the ship. They will last me long enough—"

Hendricks moved quickly. But his injured arm betrayed him. Tasso ducked, sliding lithely aside. Her hand came up, lightning fast. Hendricks saw the gun butt coming. He tried to ward off the blow, but she was too fast. The metal butt struck against the side of his head, just above his ear. Numbing pain rushed through him. Pain and rolling clouds of blackness. He sank down, sliding to the ground.

Dimly, he was aware that Tasso was standing over him, kicking him with her toe.

"Major! Wake up."

He opened his eyes, groaning.

"Listen to me." She bent down, the gun pointed at his face. "I have to hurry. There isn't much time left. The ship is ready to go, but you must give me the information I need before I leave."

Hendricks shook his head, trying to clear it.

"Hurry up! Where is the Moon Base? How do I find it? What do I look for?"

Hendricks said nothing.

"Answer me!"

"Sorry."

"Major, the ship is loaded with provisions. I can coast for weeks. I'll find the Base eventually. And in a half-hour you'll be dead. Your only chance of survival—" She broke off.

Along the slope, by some crumbling ruins, something moved. Something in the ash. Tasso turned quickly, aiming. She fired. A puff of flame leaped. Something scuttled away, rolling across the ash. She fired again. The claw burst apart, wheels flying.

"See?" Tasso said. "A scout. It won't be long."

"You'll bring them back here to get me?"

"Yes. As soon as possible."

Hendricks looked up at her. He studied her intently. "You're telling the truth?" A strange expression had come over his face, an avid hunger. "You will come back for me? You'll get me to the Moon Base?"

"I'll get you to the Moon Base. But tell me where it is! There's only a little time left."

"All right." Hendricks picked up a piece of rock, pulling himself to a sitting position. "Watch."

Hendricks began to scratch in the ash. Tasso stood by him, watching the motion of the rock. Hendricks was sketching a crude lunar map.

"This is the Appenine range. Here is the Crater of Archimedes. The Moon Base is beyond the end of the Appenine, about two hundred miles. I don't know exactly where. No one on Terra knows. But when you're over the Appenine, signal with one red flare and a green flare, followed by two red flares in quick succession. The Base monitor will record your signal. The Base is under the surface, of course. They'll guide you down with magnetic grapples."

"And the controls? Can I operate them?"

"The controls are virtually automatic. All you have to do is give the right signal at the right time."

"I will."

"The seat absorbs most of the takeoff shock. Air and temperature are automatically controlled. The ship will leave Terra and pass out into free space. It'll line itself up with the Moon, falling into an orbit around it, about a hundred miles above the surface. The orbit will carry you over the Base. When you're in the region of the Appenine, release the signal rockets."

Tasso slid into the ship and lowered herself into the pressure seat. The arm locks folded automatically around her. She fingered the controls. "Too bad you're not going, Major. All this put here for you, and you can't make the trip."

"Leave me the pistol."

Tasso pulled the pistol from her belt. She held it in her hand, weighing it thoughtfully. "Don't go too far from this location. It'll be hard to find you, as it is."

"No. I'll stay here by the well."

Tasso gripped the takeoff switch, running her fingers over the smooth metal. "A beautiful ship, Major. Well built. I admire your workmanship. You people have always done good work. You build fine things. Your work, your creations, are your greatest achievement."

"Give me the pistol," Hendricks said impatiently, holding out his hand. He struggled to his feet.

"Good-bye, Major." Tasso tossed the pistol past Hendricks. The pistol clattered against the ground, bouncing and rolling away. Hendricks hurried after it. He bent down, snatching it up.

The hatch of the ship clanged shut. The bolts fell into place. Hendricks made his way back. The inner door was being sealed. He raised the pistol unsteadily.

There was a shattering roar. The ship burst up from its metal cage, fusing the mesh behind it. Hendricks cringed, pulling back. The ship shot up into the rolling clouds of ash, disappearing into the sky.

Hendricks stood watching a long time, until even the streamer had dissipated. Nothing stirred. The morning air was chill and silent. He began to walk aimlessly back the way they had come. Better to keep moving around. It would be a long time before help came—if it came at all.

He searched his pockets until he found a package of cigarettes. He lit one grimly. They had all wanted cigarettes from him. But cigarettes were scarce.

A lizard slithered by him, through the ash. He halted, rigid. The lizard disappeared. Above, the sun rose higher in the sky. Some flies landed on a flat rock to one side of him. Hendricks kicked at them with his foot.

It was getting hot. Sweat trickled down his face, into his collar. His mouth was dry.

Presently he stopped walking and sat down on some debris. He unfastened his medicine kit and swallowed a few narcotic capsules. He looked around him. Where was he?

Something lay ahead. Stretched out on the ground. Silent and unmoving.

Hendricks drew his gun quickly. It looked like a man. Then he remembered. It was the remains of Klaus. The Second Variety. Where Tasso had blasted him. He could see wheels and relays and metal parts, strewn around on the ash. Glittering and sparkling in the sunlight.

Hendricks got to his feet and walked over. He nudged the inert form with his foot, turning it over a little. He could see the metal hull, the aluminum ribs and struts. More wiring fell out. Like viscera. Heaps of wiring, switches and relays. Endless motors and rods.

He bent down. The brain cage had been smashed by the fall. The artificial brain was visible. He gazed at it. A maze of circuits. Miniature tubes. Wires as fine as hair. He touched the brain cage. It swung aside. The type plate was visible. Hendricks studied the plate.

And blanched.

IV—IV.

For a long time he stared at the plate. Fourth Variety. Not the Second. They had been wrong. There were more types. Not just three. Many more, perhaps. At least four. And Klaus wasn't the Second Variety.

But if Klaus wasn't the Second Variety—

Suddenly he tensed. Something was coming, walking through the ash beyond the hill. What was it? He strained to see. Figures. Figures coming slowly along, making their way through the ash.

Coming toward him.

Hendricks crouched quickly, raising his gun. Sweat dripped down into his eyes. He fought down rising panic, as the figures neared.

The first was a David. The David saw him and increased its pace. The others hurried behind it. A second David. A third. Three Davids, all alike, coming toward him silently, without expression, their thin legs rising and falling. Clutching their teddy bears.

He aimed and fired. The first two Davids dissolved into particles. The third came on. And the figure behind it. Climbing silently toward him across the gray ash. A Wounded Soldier, towering over the David. And—

And behind the Wounded Soldier came two Tassos, walking side by side. Heavy belt, Russian army pants, shirt, long hair. The familiar figure, as he had seen her only a little while before. Sitting in the pressure seat of the ship. Two slim, silent figures, both identical.

They were very near. The David bent down suddenly, dropping its teddy bear. The bear raced across the ground. Automatically, Hendricks's fingers tightened around the trigger. The bear was gone, dissolved into mist. The two Tasso Types moved on, expressionless, walking side by side, through the gray ash.

When they were almost to him, Hendricks raised the pistol waist high and fired.

The two Tassos dissolved. But already a new group was starting up the rise, five or six Tassos, all identical, a line of them coming rapidly toward him.

And he had given her the ship and the signal code. Because of him she was on her way to the moon, to the Moon Base. He had made it possible.

He had been right about the bomb, after all. It had been designed with knowledge of the other types, the David Type and the Wounded Soldier Type. And the Klaus Type. Not designed by human beings. It had been designed by one of the underground factories, apart from all human contact.

The line of Tassos came up to him. Hendricks braced himself, watching them calmly. The familiar face, the belt, the heavy shirt, the bomb carefully in place.

The bomb—

As the Tassos reached for him, a last ironic thought drifted through Hendricks's mind. He felt a little better, thinking about it. The bomb. Made by the Second Variety to destroy the other varieties. Made for that end alone.

They were already beginning to design weapons to use against each other.

THERE IS NO DEFENSE

Theodore Sturgeon

Cursing formality, Belter loosened his tunic and slouched back in his chair. He gazed at each of the members of the Joint Solar Military Council in turn, and rasped: "You might as well be comfortable, because, so help me, if I have to chain you to this table from now until the sun freezes, I'll run off this record over and over again until someone figures an angle. I never heard of anything yet, besides The Death, that couldn't be whipped one way or another. There's a weakness somewhere in this thing. It's got to be on the record. So we'll just keep at the record until we find it. Keep your eyes peeled and the hair out of your eyes. That goes for you too, Leess."

The bottled Jovian shrugged hugely. The infrared sensory organ on its cephalothorax flushed as Belter's words crackled through the translator. Glowering at the creature, Belter quenched a flash of sympathy. The Jovian was a prisoner in other things besides the bottle which supplied its atmosphere and gravity. Leess represented a disgraced and defeated race, and its position at the conference table was a hollow honor—a courtesy backed by heat and steel and The Death. But Belter's glower did not change. There was no time, now, to sympathize with those whose fortunes of war were all bad ones.

Belter turned to the orderly and nodded. A sigh, compounded of worry and weariness, escaped the council as one man. The lights dimmed, and again the record appeared on the only flat wall of the vast chamber.

First the astronomical data from the Plutonian Dome, showing the first traces of the Invader approaching from the direction of the Lyran Ring—Equations, calculations, a sketch, photographs. These were dated three years back, during the closing phases of the Jovian War. The Plutonian Dome was not serviced at the time,

72

due to the emergency. It was a completely automatic observatory, and its information was not needed during the interplanetary trouble. Therefore it was not equipped with instantaneous transmissions, but neatly reeled up its information until it could be visited after the war. There was a perfectly good military observation base on Outpost, the retrograde moon of Neptune, which was regarded as quite adequate to watch the Solar System area. That is, there *had* been a base there—

But, of course, the Invader was well into the System before anyone saw the Pluto records, and by that time—

The wall scene faded into the transcript of the instantaneous message received by Terran HQ, which was rigged to accept any alarm from all of the watch posts.

The transcript showed the interior of the Neptunian military observatory, and cut in apparently just before the Sigmen heard the alarm. One was sprawled in a chair in front of the finder controls; the other, a rangy lieutenant with the burned skin of his Martian Colonial stock, stiffened, looked up at the blinking "General Alarm" light as the muted, insistent note of the "Stations" bell began to thrum from the screen. The sound transmission was very good; the councilmen could distinctly hear the lieutenant's sharp intake of breath, and his voice was quite clear as he rapped:

"Colin! Alarm. Fix!"

"Fix, sir," said the enlisted man, his fingers flying over the segmented controls. "It's deep space, sir," he reported as he worked. "A Jovian, maybe—flanking us."

"I don't think so. If what's left of their navy could make any long passes at all, you can bet it would be at Earth. How big is it?"

"I haven't got . . . oh, here it is, sir," said the e.m. "An object about the size of a Class III-A Heavy."

"Ship?"

"Don't know, sir. No heat radiation from any kind of jets. And the magnetoscope is zero."

"Get a chaser on him."

Belter's hands tightened on the table edge. Every time he saw this part of the record he wanted to get up and yell, *"No, you idiot! It'll walk down your beam!"* The chaserscope would follow anything it was trained on, and bring in a magnified image. But it took a mess of traceable vhf to do it.

Relaxing was a conscious effort. *Must be slipping*, he thought glumly, *wanting to yell at those guys. Those guys are dead.*

In the picture recording, a projection of the chaserscope's screen was flashed on the observatory screen. Staring fearfully at this shadow picture of a shadow picture, the council saw again the familiar terrible lines of the Invader—squat, unlovely, obviously not designed for atmospheric work; slabsided, smug behind what must have been foolproof meteor screens, for the ship boldly presented flat side and bottom plates to anything which might be thrown at her.

"It's a ship, sir!" said the e.m. unnecessarily. "Seems to be turning on its short axis. Still no drive emanations."

"Range!" said the lieutenant into a wall mike. Three lights over it winked on, indicating the batteries were manned and ready for ranging information. The lieutenant, his eyes fixed on the large indicators over the enlisted man's head, hesitated a moment, then said "Automatics! Throw your ranging gear to our chaser."

The three lights blinked, once each. The battery reporters lit up, showing automatic control as the medium and heavy launching tubes bore round to the stranger.

The ship was still on the screen, turning slowly. Now a dark patch on her flank could be seen—an open port. There was a puff of escaping gas, and *something* appeared whirling briefly away from the ship, toward the scanner. They almost saw it clearly—and then it was gone.

"They threw something at us, sir!"

"Track it!"

"Can't, sir!"

"You saw the beginning of that trajectory! It was coming this way."

"Yes sir. But the radar doesn't register it. I don't see it on the screen either. Maybe it's a warper?"

"Warpers are all theory, Colin. You don't bend radar impulses around an object and then restore them to their original direction. If this thing is warping at all, it's warping light. It—"

And then all but the Jovian closed their eyes as the screen repeated that horror—the bursting inward of the observatory's bulkhead, the great jaggered blade of metal that flicked the lieutenant's head straight into the transmission camera.

The scene faded, and the lights went up.

"Slap in the next re—Hold it!" Belter said. "What's the matter with Hereford?"

The Peace delegate was slumped in his chair, his head on his arms, his arms on the table. The Martian Colonial representative touched him, and Hereford raised his seamed, saintly face:

"Sorry."

"You sick?"

Hereford sat back tiredly. "Sick?" he repeated vaguely. He was not a young man. Next to that of the Jovian, his position was the strangest of all. He represented a group, as did each of the others. But not a planetary group. He represented the amalgamation of all organized pacifistic thought in the System. His chair on the Joint Solar Military Council was a compromise measure, the tentative answer to an apparently unanswerable question—can a people do without the military? Many thought people could. Some thought not. To avoid extremism either way, the head of an unprecedented amalgamation of peace organizations was given a chair on the JSMC. He had the same vote as a planetary representative. "Sick?" he repeated in a whispering baritone. "Yes, I rather think so." He waved a hand at the blank wall. "Why did the Invader do it? So pointless . . . so . . . . so stupid." He raised his puzzled eyes, and Belter felt a new kind of sympathy. Hereford's hollow-ground intelligence was famous in four worlds. He was crackling, decisive; but now he could only ask the simplest of questions, like a child too tired to be badly frightened.

"Yeah—why?" asked Belter. "Oh . . . never mind the rest of the record," he added suddenly. "I don't know how the rest of you feel, but at the moment I'm hypnotized by the jet-blasted thing.

"*Why*, Hereford wants to know. If we knew that, maybe we could plan something. Defenses, anyway."

Somebody murmured: "It's not a campaign. It's murder."

"That's it. The Invader reaches out with some sort of a short-range disrupting bomb and wipes out the base on Outpost. Then it wanders into the System, washes out an uninhabited asteroid beacon, drifts down through the shield screening of Titan and kills off half the population with a cyanogen synthesizing catalyst. It captures three different scanner-scouts, holding them with some sort of a tractor beam, whirling them around like a stone on a string, and letting them go straight at the nearest planet. Earth ships, Martian, Jovian—doesn't matter. It can outfly and outfight anything we have so far, except—"

"Except The Death," whispered Hereford. "Go on, Belter. I knew it was coming to this."

"Well, it's true! And then the cities. If it ever drops a disrupter like that"—he waved at the wall, indicating the portion of the record they had just seen—"on a large city, there wouldn't be any point in even looking for it, let alone rebuilding it. We can't communicate with the Invader—if we send out a general signal it ignores us, and if we send out a beam it charges us or sends one of those warping disrupter bombs. We can't even surrender to it! It just wanders through the System, changing course and speed from moment to moment, and every once in a while taking a crack at something."

The Martian member glanced at Hereford, and then away. "I don't see why we've waited so long. I saw Titan, Belter. In another century it'll be dead as Luna." He shook his head. "No pre-Peace agreement can stand in the way of the defense of the System no matter how solemn the agreement was. I voted to outlaw The Death, too. I don't like the idea of it any more than . . . than Hereford there. But circumstances alter cases. Are we going to sacrifice everything the race has built just for an outdated principle? Are we going to sit smugly behind an idealistic scrap of paper while some secret weapon chops us down bit by bit?"

"Scrap of paper," said Hereford. "Son, have you read your ancient history?"

The translator hissed. Through it, Leess spoke. The flat, unaccented words were the barest framework for the anger which those who knew Jovians could detect by the sudden paling of the creature's sensory organ. "Leess object phrase secret weapon. Man from Mars suggest Invader Jovian work."

"Cool down, Leess," Belter said, reaching over and firmly putting the Martian back in his seat. "Hey you—watch your language or you'll go back to the canals to blow the rust off supersoy. Now, Leess; I rather think the delegate from Mars let his emotions get the better of him. No one thinks that the Invader is Jovian. It's from deep space somewhere. It has a drive far superior to anything we've got, and the armament . . . well, if Jupiter had anything like that, you wouldn't have lost the war. And then there was Titan. I don't think Jovians would kill off so many of their own just to camouflage a new secret weapon."

The Martian's eyebrows lifted a trifle. Belter frowned, and the Martian's face went forcibly blank. The Jovian relaxed.

Addressing the Council generally, but looking at the Martian, Belter gritted: "The war is over. We're all Solarians, and the Invader is a menace to our System. After we get rid of the Invader we'll have time to tangle with each other. Not before. Is that clear?"

"No human trust Jupiter. No man trust Leess," sulked the Jovian. "Leess no think. Leess no help. Jupiter better off dead than not trusted."

Belter threw up his hands in disgust. The sensitivity and stubborness of the Jovian were well known. "If there's a clumsy, flat-footed way of doing things, a Martian'll find it," he growled. "Here we need every convolution of every brain here. The Jovian has a way of thinking different enough so he might help us crack this thing, and you have to go and run him out on strike."

The Martian bit his lips. Belter turned to the Jovian. "Leess, please—come off your high horse. Maybe the Solar System is a little crowded these days, but we all have to live in it. Are you going to cooperate?"

"No. Martian man no trust Jupiter. Mars die, Jupiter die, Earth die. Good. Nobody not trust Jupiter." The creature creased inward upon itself a movement as indicative as the thrusting out of a lower lip.

"Leess is in this with the rest of us," said the Martian. "We ought to—"

"That'll do!" barked Belter. "You've said enough chum. Concentrate on the Invader and leave Leess alone. He has a vote on this council and by the same token, he has the right to refrain from voting."

"Whose side are you on?" flashed the Martian, rising.

Belter came up with him, but Hereford's soft, deep voice came between them like a barrier. The Peace delegate said: "He's on the side of the System. All of us must be. We have no choice. You Martians are fighting men. Do you think you can separate yourselves from the rest of us and stop the Invader?"

Flushed, the Martian opened his mouth, closed it again, sat down. Hereford looked at Belter, and he sat down, too. The tension in the chamber lessened, but the matter obviously relegated itself to the "For Further Action" files in at least two men's minds.

Belter gazed at his fingers until they would be still without effort, and then said quietly: "Well, gentlemen, we've tried everything. There is no defense. We've lost ships, and men, and bases. We will lose more. If the Invader can be destroyed, we can be sure of a little time, at least, for preparation."

"Preparation?" asked Hereford.

"Certainly! You don't think for a minute that that ship isn't, or won't soon be, in communication with its own kind? Suppose we can't destroy it. It will be able to go back where it came from, with the news that there's a culture here for the taking, with no weapon powerful enough to touch them. You can't be so naive as to believe that this one ship is the only one they have, or the only one we'll ever see! Our only course is to wipe out this ship and then prepare for a full-scale invasion. If it doesn't come before we're prepared, our only safe course will be to carry the invasion to them, wherever they may be!"

Hereford shook his head sadly. "The old story."

Belter's fist came down with a crash. "Hereford, I *know* that Peace Amalgamated is a great cultural stride forward. I *know* that to de-condition the public on three planets and a hundred colonies from the peaceful way of life is a destructive move. But—can you suggest a way of keeping the peaceful way and saving our System? Can you?"

"Yes . . . if . . . if the Invaders can be persuaded to follow the peaceful way."

"When they won't communicate? When they commit warlike acts for nothing—without plan, without conquest, apparently for the sheer joy of destruction? Hereford—we're not dealing with anything Solarian. This is some life-form that is so different in its aims and its logic that the only thing we can do is reciprocate. Fire with fire! You talk of your ancient history. Wasn't fascism conquered when the democratic nations went all but fascist to fight them?"

"No," said Hereford firmly. "The fruits of fascism were conquered. Fascism itself was conquered only by democracy."

Belter shook his head in puzzlement. "That's irrelevant. I . . . think," he added, because he was an honest man. "To get back to the Invader: we have a weapon with which we can destroy him. We can't use it now because of Peace Amalgamated; because the Solarian peoples have determined to outlaw it forever. The law is specific: The Death is not to be used for any purposes, under any circumstances. We, the military, can say we want it until our arteries harden, but our chances of getting it are negligible unless we have public support in repealing the law. The Invader has been with us for eighteen months or more, and in spite of his depredations, there is still no sign that the public would support repeal. Why?" He stabbed out a stumpy forefinger. "Because they follow *you*, Hereford. They have completely absorbed your quasi-religious attitude of . . . what was your phrase?"

" 'Moral Assay.' "

"Yeah—Moral Assay. The test of cultural stamina. The will power to stand up for a principle in spite of emergencies, in spite of drastic changes in circumstances. A good line, Hereford, but unless you retract it, the public won't. We could bulldoze 'em into it, maybe; and maybe we'd have a revolution on our hands, get a lot of people killed, and wind up with a bunch of dewy-eyed idealists coming out on top, ready to defend the principles of peace with guns if they have to draft every able-bodied Solarian in the System. Meanwhile, the Invader—and perhaps, by that time, his pals—will continue to circulate around, taking a crack at any target he happens to admire. Already the crackpots are beginning to yell about the Invader being sent to test their love of peace, and calling this the second year of the Moral Assay."

"He won't back down," said the Martian suddenly. "Why should he? The way he is, he's set for life."

"You have a lousy way of putting things!" snappled Belter, wondering *How much does personal power mean to the old saint?*

"Why this pressure?" asked Hereford gently. "You, Belter, with your martial rationalizing, and our Martian colleague here, with his personal insults—why not put it to a vote?"

Belter studied him. Was there a chance that the old man would accept the wishes of the majority here? The majority opinion of the Council was not necessarily the majority opinion of the System. And besides—how many of the Council would go along with Hereford if he chose to vote against it?

He took a deep breath. "We've got to know where we stand," he said. "Informally, now—shall we use The Death on the Invader? Let's have a show of hands."

There was a shuffling of feet. All the men looked at Hereford, who sat still with his eyes downcast. The Martian raised his hand defiantly. The Phoebe-Titan Colonial delegate followed suit. Earth. The Belt. Five, six—eight. Nine.

"Nine," said Belter. He looked at the Jovian, who looked back, unblinking. Not voting. Hereford's hands were on the table.

"That's three-quarters," Belter said.

"Not enough," answered Hereford. "The law stipulates *over* three-quarters."

"You know what my vote is."

"Sorry, Belter. You can't vote. As chairman, you are powerless unless all members vote, and then all you can do is establish a tie so that the matter can be referred for further discussion. The regulations purposely keep a deciding vote out of the Chair, and with the membership. I . . . frankly. Belter, I can't be expected to go further than this. I have refrained from voting. I have kept you from voting. If that keeps The Death from being used—"

Belter's knuckles cracked. He thought of the horror at Outpost, and the choking death on Titan, and what had happened to their asteroid. It and its abandoned mine workings had flared up like a baby nova, and what was left wouldn't dirty a handkerchief. It was a fine thing for every Solarian that at long last a terrible instrument of war had been outlawed, this time by the unquestionable wish of the people. It would be a bad thing for civilization if an exception should be made to this great rule. It was conceivable that, once the precedent was established, the long-run effects on civilization would be worse than anything the Invader could do. And yet—all his life Belter had operated under a philosophy which dictated action. Do something. It may be wrong, but—*do* something.

"May I speak with you alone?" he asked Hereford.

"If it is a matter which concerns the Council—"

"It concerns you only. A matter of ideology."

Hereford inclined his head and rose. "This won't take long." said Belter over his shoulder, as he let the peace delegate precede him into an antechamber.

"Beat it, Jerry," he said to the guard. The man saluted and left.

Belter leaned back against a desk, folded his arms and said: "Hereford, I'm going to tear this thing right down to essentials. If I don't, we can spend the rest of our lives arguing about social necessities and cultural evolution and the laws of probability as applied to the intentions of the Invader. I am going to ask you some questions. Simple ones. Please try to keep the answers simple."

"You know I prefer that."

"You do. All right—the whole basis of the Peace movement is to prevent fighting, on the grounds that there is always a better way. Right?"

"That is right."

"And the Peace movement recognizes no need for violence in any form, and no conceivable exception to that idea."

"That is right."

"Hereford—pay close attention. You and I are in here because of the Invader, and because of the refusal of Peace Amalgamated to allow the use of the only known counter-measure."

"Obviously."

"Good. Just one more thing. I hold you in higher regard than any other man I know. And the same goes for the work you have done. Do you believe that?"

Hereford smiled slowly and nodded. "I believe it."

"Well, it's true," said Belter, and with all his strength brought his open hand across Hereford's mouth.

The older man staggered back and stood, his fingers straying up to his face. In his eyes was utter disbelief as he stared at Belter, who stood again with his arms folded, his face impassive. The disbelief was slowly clouded over by puzzlement, and then hurt began to show. "Why—"

But before he could say another word, Belter was on him again. He crossed to Hereford's chest, and when the Peace delegate's hand came down, he struck him twice more on the mouth. Hereford made an inarticulate sound and covered his face. Belter hit him in the stomach.

Hereford moaned, turned, and made for the door. Belter dove, tackled him. They slid into a thrashing heap on the soft carpeting. Belter rolled clear, pulled the other to his feet and hit him again. Hereford shook his head and began to sink down, his arms over his head. Belter lifted him again, waited for just the right opening, and his hand flashed through for still another stinging slap across the mouth. Hereford grunted, and before Belter quite knew what was happening, he came up with one great blasting right that landed half on Belter's dropped chin, half on his collar bone. Belter came up off the floor in a cloud of sparks and fell heavily six feet away. He looked up to see Hereford standing over him, big fists bunched.

"Get up," said the Peace delegate hoarsely.

Belter lay back, put his hands under his head, spat out some blood, and began to laugh.

"*Get up!*"

Belter rolled over and got slowly to his feet. "It's all over, Hereford. No more rough stuff, I promise you."

Hereford backed off, his face working. "Did you think," he spat, "that you could resort to such childish, insane measures to force me into condoning murder?"

"Yup," said Belter.

"You're mad," said Hereford, and went to the door.

"*Stop!*"

There was a note of complete command in Belter's voice. It was that note, and the man behind it which had put Belter where he was. Equally startling was the softness of his voice as he said: "Please come here, Hereford. It isn't like you to leave a thing half understood."

If he had said "Half finished," he would have lost the play. Hereford came slowly back, saying ruefully: "I know you, Belter. I know there's a reason for this. But it better be good."

Belter stood where he had been, leaning against the desk, and he folded his arms. "Hereford," he said, "one more simple question. The Peace movement recognizes no need for violence in any form, and no conceivable exception to that idea." It sounded like a recording of the same words, said a few minutes before, except for his carefully controlled breathing.

Hereford touched his bruised mouth. "Yes."

"Then," Belter grinned, "why did you hit me?"

"Why? Why did you hit *me*?"

"I didn't ask you that. Please keep it simple. Why did you hit me?"

"It was . . . I don't know. It happened. It was the only way to make you stop."

Belter grinned. Hereford stumbled on. "I see what you're doing. You're trying to make some parallel between the Invader and your attack on me. But you attacked me unexpectedly, apparently without reason—"

Belter grinned more widely.

Hereford was frankly floundering now. "But I . . . I had to strike you, or I . . . I—"

"Hereford," said Belter gently, "shall we go back now, and vote before that eye of yours blackens?"

The three Death ships, each with its cover of destroyer escorts, slipped into the Asteroid Belt. *Delta*, the keying unit, was flanked on each side by the opposed twins *Epsilon* and *Sigma*, which maintained a rough thousand-mile separation from the key. Behind them, on Earth, they had left a froth of controversy. Editorial comment on the air and in print, both on facsimile and the distributed press, was pulling and hauling on the age-old question of the actions of duly elected administrators. We are the people. We choose these men to represent us. What must we do when their actions run contrary to our interests?

And—do they run contrary? How much change can there be in a man's attitude, and in the man himself, between the time he is elected and the time he votes on a vital measure? Can we hark back to our original judgment of the man and trust his action as we trusted him at election time?

And again—the old bugaboo of security. When a legislative body makes a decision on a military matter, there must be news restrictions. The Death was the supreme weapon. Despite the will of the majority, there were still those who wanted it for their own purposes; people who felt it had not been used enough in the war; others who felt it should be kept assembled and ready, as the teeth in a dictatorial peace. As of old, the mass of the people had to curb its speech and sometimes its thought, to protect itself against the megalomaniac minorities.

But there was one man who suffered. Elsewhere was anger and intellectual discourse, ethical delvings and even fear. But in one man, supremely, existed the struggle between ethics and expediency. Hereford alone had the power to undo his own work. His following would believe and accept when he asked them to make this exception. Having made it, they would follow no more, and there was no place for him on Earth.

His speech had been simple, delivered without a single flickering of his torture on the fine old face. Once the thing was done, he left Earth in a way foreign to everything he had ever believed, or spoken, or recommended. He, the leader of Peace Amalgamated, who regarded with insistent disfavor the very existence of weapons, left Earth with Belter, and shared the officer's quarters of a warship. Not only was it a warship, but it was the keying unit *Delta*, under the command of "Butcher" Osgood, trigger man of The Death.

For months they tracked the Invader, using their own instruments and information relayed to them by various outposts. Under no circumstances did they use tracers. One observation post and seven warships had been crushed because of that. The Invader's reaction to a tight beam was instant and terrible. Therefore, they were limited to light reflection—what there was of it, even from the bold, bright flanks of the marauder—and the detection of the four types of drive radiations used by the ship at different accelerations.

The body of descriptive matter on the Invader increased, and there were certain irrefutable conclusions. The crew of the Invader were colloidal life, like all known life, and would be subject to

The Death. This was deduced by the fact that the ship was enclosed, pressurized and contained an atmosphere of some sort, which precluded the theoretically suggested "energy" and "crystalline" life-forms. The random nature of the enemy's vicious and casual attacks caused more controversy than almost any other factor; but as time went on, it became obvious that what the ship was doing was calling forth any attack of which the System might be capable. It had been bombed, rayed, and attempts had been made to ram. It was impervious. How long would it stay? When would its commanders conclude that they had seen the worst, and laughing, go back into the depths to bring reinforcements? And was there anything—anything at all—besides The Death that could reach the Invader, or stop him, or destroy him, or even let him know fear?

Right up until D-day—Death-day—the billions who had followed Hereford hoped that some alternative could be found, so that at least their earlier resolutions would be followed in letter if not in spirit. Many of them worked like slaves to this end, and that was the greatest anomaly of all, for all the forces of Peace were engaged in devising deadly methods and engines for use as alternatives to The Death. They failed. Of course they failed.

There came a day when they had to strike. The Invader had all but vanished into the celestial north, only to come hurtling back in a great curve which would pass through the plane of the ecliptic just beyond the orbit of Jupiter. The Invader's trajectory was predictable despite his almost unbelievable maneuverability—even for him there were limits of checking and turning, which was another fact indicating colloidal life. There was no way of knowing whether he was coming back to harass the planets, or whether he was making one last observation before swinging through the System and away from Sol, back to the unknown hell which had spawned him. But whether it was attack or withdrawal, he had to be smashed. There might never be another chance.

The three Death ships moved out from the Belt, where they had lain quiet amongst the other masses floating in that great ring of detritus. Still keeping their formation, they blasted away with a crushing acceleration, their crews dopey with *momentomine*. Their courses were set to intersect that of the Invader, or close enough to bring them well within range of The Death—twelve to twenty thousand miles. Delicate, beamless scanners checked the enemy's course moment by moment, making automatic corrections and maintaining the formation of the three ships.

Delta was Earth-manned, *Epsilon* a Martian ship, and *Sigma* belonged to the Colonials. Originally, the plan had been to scatter Colonials through the three ships, and use a Jovian craft. But Leess, as the Jovian representative, had vetoed any Jovian participation, an action which had brought about a violent reawakening of antipathies toward the major planet. Public feeling was so loaded against the use of The Death that the responsibility must be shared. Jupiter's stubborn and suicidal refusal to share it was inflexible; the Jovian solidarity was as thorough as ever.

Four days out, the master controls dropped the acceleration to 1 G, and the air conditioners blasted out enough superoxygen to counteract the acceleration drug. Personnel came to full life again, and the command gathered on the bridge of *Delta*. Hereford was there too, standing well back, his face misleadingly calm, his eyes flicking from the forward screen to the tactical chart, from Belter's absorbed face to the undershot countenance of Commander Osgood.

Osgood looked over his shoulder at the Peace leader. His voice was gravel in a wire sieve as he said: "I still don't like that guy hanging around here. You sure he won't be better off in his quarters?"

"We've been over that," said Belter tiredly. "Commander, maybe I'm out of order, but would it be too much trouble for you to speak directly to him once in a while?"

"I am satisfied," smiled Hereford. "I quite understand his attitude. I have little to say to him, and much to say about him, which is essentially his position as far as I am concerned. It is no more remarkable that he is unfamiliar with politeness than that I should be ignorant of spatial ballistics."

Belter grinned. "O.K., O.K.—don't mind me I'm just a poor military man trying to make peace. I'll shut up and let you and the Butcher have your inimical *status quo*."

"I'll need a little quiet here for a while, if it's all the same to you, Councilman," said Osgood. He was watching the tactical chart. The red spot representing *Epsilon* was at the far right, the blur of *Sigma* at the left, and down at the bottom was *Delta's* green spark. A golden bar in the center of the chart showed the area on the ecliptical plane at which the Invader could be expected to pass through, and just above it was a white spot showing the Invader himself.

Osgood touched a toggle which added a diagram to the chart—a positioning diagram showing the placement of the three Death ships in relation to the target. *Sigma* and *Epsilon* were exactly in the centers of their white positioning circles; *Delta* was at the lower edge of the third circle. Osgood made a slight adjustment in the drive circuit.

"Positioning is everything," Belter explained to Hereford. "The Death field is a resultant—a violent node of vibrations centering on the contiguous focal points of the opposed fields from *Sigma* and *Epsilon*. The beam from *Delta*—that's us—kicks it off. There's an enormous stress set up at that focal point, and our beam tears into it. The vibration changes frequency at random and with violence. It had been said that the fabric of space itself vibrates. That's learned nonsense. But fluids do, and gases, of course, and colloids worst of all."

"What would happen if the positions were not taken exactly?"

"Nothing. The two focal points of the concentrated fields from *Epsilon* and *Sigma* would not coincide, and *Delta's* beam would be useless. And it *might* have the unhappy result of calling the Invader down on us. Not right away—he's going too fast at right angles to our course—but I'm not crazy about the idea of being hunted down by that executioner."

Hereford listened gravely, watching Osgood, watching the chart. "Just how great is the danger of The Death's spreading like ripples in a pool—out in every direction from the node?"

"Very little, the way it's set up. The node moves outward away from our three ships—again a resultant, strictly according to the parallelogram of force. How long it lasts, how intense it gets, how far it will go—we never know. It changes with what it encounters. Mass intensifies it and slows it down. Energy of almost any kind accelerates and gradually seems to dissipate it. And it varies for other reasons we don't understand yet. Setting it up is a very complicated business, as you have seen. We don't dare kick it off in such a way that it might encounter any of the planets, if it should happen to last long enough. We have to clear space between us and Outside of all shipping."

Hereford shook his head slowly. "The final separation between death and destruction," he mused. "In ancient times, armies met on battlefields and used death alone to determine the winner. Then, gradually, destruction became the most important factor— how much of the enemy's material could you destroy? And then, with the Atomic Wars, and the Dust, death alone became the end of combat again. Now it has come full circle, and we have found a way to kill, to punish and torture, to dissolve, slowly and insistently, colloidal cells, and still leave machines unharmed. This surpasses the barbarism of jellied gasoline. It takes longer, and—"

"It's complete," Belter finished.

"Stations!"

Osgood's voice sliced raggedly through the quiet bridge. The screen-studded bulkhead beside him winked and flickered with acknowledgements, as tacticians, technicians, astrogators, ballistics men, and crewmen reported in. All three ships were represented, and a master screen collected and summarized the information, automatically framing the laggards' screen with luminous red. There was little of the red showing, and in seconds it disappeared. Osgood stepped back, glanced at the master screen and then at the chart. On it, the ship symbols were centered in their tactical circles.

The commander turned away and for the first time in these weary months he spoke directly to Hereford: "Would you like the honor of triggering?"

Hereford's nostrils dilated, but his voice was controlled. He put his hands behind his back. "Thank you, no."

"I thought not," said the Butcher, and there was a world of insult in his scraping voice.

Before him was a triangular housing from which projected three small levers with round grips. One was red, one blue. The third was set between and in front of the others, and was green. He pulled the two nearest him. Immediately a red line appeared on the chart, running from *Epsilon's* symbol to the golden patch, and a blue line raced out from *Sigma* to meet it. Just above the gold hovered the white spot representing the Invader. Osgood watched it narrowly as it dipped toward the gold and the junction of the red and blue lines. He rested his hand on the green lever, made one last check of the screens, and snatched it back. Obediently, a thick, bright green line appeared on the chart. A purple haze clouded the gold.

"That's it!" breathed Belter. "The purple, there—The Death!"

Hereford, shaking, leaned back against the bulkhead. He folded his arms, holding tightly to his elbows, obviously trying to get a grip on much more.

"Scan him!" spat Osgood. "This I've got to see!"

Belter leapt forward. "Commander! You don't . . . you *can't* beam him! Remember what happened at Outpost?"

Osgood swore. "We've got so much stuff between here and

there already that a scanning beam isn't going to make that much difference. He's done, anyway!" he added exultantly.

The large scanning screen flicked into colors which swirled and fused into the sharp image of the Invader. Since the beam tracked him exactly, there was no sign of motion. "Get me a diagrammatic!" bellowed Osgood. His small eyes were wide, his cheeks puffed out, his lips wet.

The lower quarter of the screen faded, went black, then suddenly bore a reduced image of the Invader. Apparently creeping toward him was a faint, ever-brightening purple mist.

"Right on the nose!" gritted Belter. "He's sailing right into it!"

Startlingly, the large actual image showed signs of life. A stream of blue white fire poured out of the ship side.

"What do you know!" whistled Osgood. "He's got jets after all! He knows there's something ahead of him, doesn't know what it is, and is going to duck it if he has to smear his crew all up and down the bulkheads!"

"Look!" cried Belter, pointing at the chart. "Why, he's pulling into a curve that . . . that—Man, oh man, he's killing off all hands! He can't turn like that!"

"Maybe he wants to get it over with quickly. Maybe he's run into The Death somewhere before," crowed Osgood. "Afraid to face it. Hey, Belter, the inside of that ship's going to be a pretty sight. The Death'll make jelly of 'em, and that high-G turn'll lay the jelly like paint out of an airbrush!"

"Ex . . . ex—" was as much as Hereford could say as he turned and tottered out. Belter took a step after him, hesitated, and then went back to stand before the chart.

Purple and gold and white, red and green and blue coruscated together. Slowly, then, the white spot moved toward the edge of the puddle of color.

"Commander! He's still side-jetting!"

"Why not?" said the Butcher gleefully. "That's the way his controls were set when his command got emulsified. He'll blow off his fuel in a while, and we can board him."

There was a soft click from the master communications screen and a face appeared on it. "*Epsilon*," the man said.

"Good work, Hoster," said Osgood, rubbing his hands.

"Thank you, sir," said the captain of the Martian vessel. "Commander, my astrogators report an extrapolation of the derelict's change of course. If he keeps jetting, he's going to come mighty close."

"Watch him then," said Osgood. "If he comes too close, get out of his way. I'll stake my shoulder boards on your safety." He laughed. "He's a dead duck. You'll be able to clear him. I don't care if it's only by fifty meters."

The Martian saluted. Osgood checked him before he could fade. "Hoster!"

"Yes sir."

"I know you Martians. Trigger happy. Whatever happens, Hoster, you are not to bomb or ray that derelict. Understand?"

"Roger, sir," said the Martian stiffly, and faded.

"Those Martians," said Osgood. "Bloodthirsty bunch."

Belter said: "Commander, sometimes I understand how Hereford feels about you."

"I'll take that as a compliment," said the Butcher.

They spent the next two hours watching the tactical chart. The Death generators had long ago been cut out, and The Death itself showed on the chart as a dwindling purple stain, headed straight Outside and already fading. But the derelict was still blasting from its side jets, and coming about in an impossible curve. The Martian astrogator had been uncomfortably right, and Captain Hoster had been instructed to take evasive action.

Closer and closer came the white spot to the red one that was *Epsilon*. Viewers were clamped on both ships: the Martian had begun to decelerate powerfully to get out of that ratiocinated curve.

"Doesn't look so good," said Belter, after a careful study of the derelict's trajectory.

"Nonsense," said Osgood worriedly. "But it'd be more than a little silly to lose a ship after we've whipped the enemy." He turned to the control bulk head. "Get me *Epsilon*."

He had started his famous monotone of profanity before the screen finally lit up. Hoster's face was flushed—blotched, really. "What's the matter?" snapped Osgood. "You take your own sweet time answering. Why haven't you taken any *momentomine?*"

Captain Hoster clutched the rim of his communicator. "Lissen," he said thickly, " 'Nvader out t' get us, see. Nobody push Martian around. 'S dirty Jovian trick."

"Acceleration disease," said Belter quietly. "He must've had some crazy idea of keeping away from the drug so he'd be able to keep on the alert."

"Hoster! You're hopped up. You can't take *momentomine* for as many years as you have and stay sober under deceleration without it. You're relieved. Take a dose and turn in. Put your second on."

"Lissen, Butch, ol' horse," mouthed the Martian. "I know what I'm doin', see? I don't want trouble with *you*. Busy, see? Now, you jus' handle your boat an' I'll handle mine. I'm gonna give that Jovian a case of Titanitis 'f'e gets wise with me." And the screen went blank.

"Hoster!" the commander roared. "Sparks! Put that maniac on again!"

A speaker answered promptly: "Sorry, sir. Can't raise him."

In helpless fury Osgood turned to Belter. "If he so much as throws a dirty look at that derelict, I'll break him to an ammo passer and put him on the sun side of Mercury. We *need* that derelict!"

"What for?" asked Belter, and then wondered why he had asked, for he knew the answer. Hereford's influence, probably. It would be Hereford's question, if he were still here.

"Four drives we don't know anything about. A warp-camouflaged disrupter bomb. A chain-instigating ray, that blew up the asteroid last year. And probably lots more. Man, that's a *warship!*"

"It sure is," said Belter. "It certainly is." *Peace Amalgamated*, he thought. *A great step forward*.

"Get 'em both on a screen," Osgood rapped. "They're close enough—Hey, Belter, look at the way that ship is designed. See how it can check and turn that way?"

"No, I—Oh! I see what you mean. Uses lateral jets—but what laterals!"

"Functional stuff," said Osgood. "We could've had that a hundred years ago, but for naval tradition. We put all our drive back aft. We get a good in-line thrust, sure. But look what he's got! The equivalent of ten or twelve of our sterntube assemblies. What kind of people were they, that could stand that kind of thing?"

Belter shook his head. "If they built it that way, they could stand it." He looked thoughtfully up at the derelict's trajectory. "Commander, you don't suppose—"

Apparently stuck by the same awful thought, Osgood said uneasily, "Certainly not. The Death. They went through The Death."

"Yes," said Belter. He sounded relieved, but he did not feel relieved. He watched the screen, and then clutched Osgood's arm.

Osgood swore and sprang to the control bulkhead. "Get

Epsilon! Tell him to cease fire and then report to me! Blast the hub-forted fun of a plistener! I'll pry him loose from his—"

Belter grunted and threw his arm over his eyes as the screen blazed. The automatic shields went up, and when he could see again, the screen showed him the Invader. *Epsilon* wasn't there at all.

After the excitement had died down a little, Osgood slumped into a chair. "I wish we'd had a Jovian ship out there instead," he rasped. "I don't care what they did to us during the war, or anything else. They could obey orders. When they say they'll do a thing, you can bet on it. What's the score on that business of the Jovian's electing themselves out, anyhow?"

Belter told him how the Jovian delegate had been insulted at the Council.

"Those hot-headed, irresponsible Martians!" said the Butcher. "Why in time did that drunken cretin have to fire on the derelict?"

"What derelict?" Belter asked dryly.

Osgood stared at him. Belter pointed at the chart. The white spot was slowly swinging toward the green—toward *Delta*. On the screen, the Invader still gleamed. It was not blasting any more.

One of the technician's screens flashed. "Detection reporting, sir."

"Report."

"Invader's Type Two drive radiation showing strong, sir."

"R-Roger."

The screen winked out. Commander Osgood opened his mouth, held it open silently for an unbearably long moment, and then carefully closed it again. Belter bit the insides of his cheeks to keep from roaring with hysterical laughter. He knew that the Butcher was trying to swear, and that he had met a situation for which no swearing would be adequate. He had shot his vituperative bolt. Finally, weakly, he said the worst thing he could think of—a thing that until then had been unthinkable.

He said: "They're not dead."

Belter did not feel like laughing any more. He said: "They went though The Death, and they're not dead."

"There is no defense against The Death," said the commander authoritatively. Belter nodded.

One of the screens flashed, and a voice said impersonally: "Mathematics."

"Go on," said the Butcher.

"The derelict's course will intersect ours, sir, unless—"

"Don't say 'derelict,'" whispered Osgood. "Say 'Invader.'"
He lay back and, closing his eyes, swabbed his face with a tissue.
Then the muscles in his jaw clenched and he rose and stood erect
before the control bulkhead, pulling the wrinkles out of his tunic.
"Batteries. Train around to the Invader. Tech! Put the batteries on
auto. Everything—torpedoes, rays, artillery. Now give me all
hands. All hands! Prepare to abandon ship. *Delta* will engage the
enemy on automatics. Life craft to scatter. Take your direction
from your launching port and maintain it until you observe some
decisive action between *Delta* and the Invader. Fill up with
momentomine and give your craft everything they can take.
Over." He swung to Belter.

"Councilman! Don't argue with me. What I want to do is stay
here and fight. What I *will* do is abandon ship with the rest of you.
My only reason is so I can have another chance to take a poke at
a Martian. Of all the blundering, stupid, childish things for Hoster
to do, taking a pot shot at that killer out there was the most—"

Belter very nearly reminded the commander that Hoster had
been instructed to let the "derelict" pass within fifty meters if
necessary. He swallowed the comment. It didn't matter, anyway.
Hoster and his crew had been good men, and *Epsilon* a good ship.
All dead now, all smashed, all gone to lengthen the list that had
started on Outpost.

"You know your abandon-ship station, don't you, Belter? Go to
your quarters and haul out that white-livered old pantywaist and
take him with you. I'll join you as soon as everyone else is off the
ship. Jump!"

Belter jumped. Things were happening too fast for him, and he
found it almost pleasant to use someone else's intelligence rather
than hunt for his own.

Hereford was sitting on the edge of his bunk. "What's the
matter, Belter?"

"Abandon ship!"

"I know that," said the older man patiently. "When they have
an 'all hands' call on one of these ships there's no mistaking it. I
want to know what's the matter."

"We're under attack. Invader."

"Ah," Hereford was very calm. "It didn't work."

"No," said Belter. "It didn't."

"I'll stay here, I think."

"You'll *what*?"

Hereford shrugged. "What's the use? What do you think will

happen to the peaceful philosophy when news gets out that there is a defense against The Death? Even if a thousand or a million Invader ships come, nothing will keep us from fighting each other. I'm—tired."

"Hereford." He waited until the old man lifted his head, met his eyes. "Remember that day in the anteroom? Do we have to go through that again?"

Hereford smiled slowly. "Don't bother, friend. You are going to have trouble enough after you leave. As for me—well, the most useful thing I can be now is a martyr."

Belter went to the bulkhead and pressed into his personal storage. He got his papers and a bottle of viski. "All right," he said, "let's have a quick one before I go." Hereford smiled and accepted. Belter put all the *momentomine* in Hereford's drink, so that when they left the ship he, Belter, passed out cold. From what he heard later he missed quite a show. *Delta* slugged it out with the Invader. She fought until there was nothing but a top turret left, and it kept spitting away at the enemy until a disrupter big enough for half a planet wiped it out. She was a good ship too. The Invader went screaming up into the celestial north again, leaving the terrified *Sigma* alone. Belter regained consciousness in the life craft along with the commander and Hereford. Hereford looked like an illustration in the Old Testament which Belter had seen when he was a child. It was captioned "And Moses Threw Down and Broke the Two Tablets of Stone."

Sigma picked them up. She was a huge old Logistics vessel, twice reconverted—once from the Colonial Trade, once as the negative plant of The Death. She had a main hold in her like a convention hall, and a third of it was still empty in spite of the vast pile plant she carried. Her cargo port was open, and *Delta's* life craft were being warped in and stacked inside, along with what wreckage could be salvaged for study.

The place was a hive. Spacesuited crews floated the boats in, handling them with telescoping rods equipped with a magnetic grapple at each end. One end would be placed on the hull of a boat, the other on the deck or bulkhead or on a stanchion; and then by contracting or expanding the rod by means of its self-contained power unit, the boat would be pushed or pulled to its stack.

The boats had completed their rendezvous after two days of signaling and careful jetting. All were accounted for but two, which had probably tangled with debris. The escape of so many was largely due to the fact that there was very little wreckage large enough to do any damage after the last explosion.

Osgood's boat hovered outside until the last, and by the time it was warped in all the others had unloaded and their crews were inboard, getting refreshment and treatment. By the time the little "Blister" had been racked, the cargo port was sealed and the compartment refilled with air. *Sigma's* captain opened the boat's hatch with his own hands, and Osgood crawled out, followed by a dazed Belter and a sullen Hereford.

"Your ship, sir," said the captain of *Sigma*, formally, in the traditional presentation of a ship and its facilities to a superior.

"Yeah. I need one at the moment," said the Butcher wryly. He stretched, looked around. "Get any parts of the Martian?"

"No, sir," said the captain. He was a worried-looking, gangly specimen from the Venusian Dome. His name had so many syllables that only the first three were used. They were Holovik. "And little enough from *Delta*, I'm sorry to say. Wh . . . what happened?"

"You saw it, didn't you? What do you think?"

"I'll say it, if you can't get it out," said Osgood bluntly. "He has a defense against The Death. Isn't that fine?"

"Yes sir." The horizontal lines across Captain Holovik's forehead deepened, and the corners of his mouth turned down. "Fine."

"Don't burst into tears!" snapped the commander. He looked around taking stock of the salvage. "Get all available techs on that scrap. Find out if any of it is radioactive, and if so how much of what type. What's that?"

"That" was a thirty-foot tapered cylinder with three short mast antennae projecting at right angles to the long axis, near each rounded end.

"I don't know for sure, sir." said Holovik. "I knew that there were . . . ah . . . weapons, new ones. We don't get information the way we used to during the war—"

"Stop mumbling, man! If that's a secret weapon, it isn't from *Delta*."

Belter put in, "It isn't from *Epsilon* either. I went over the specs of everything aboard all of these vessels."

"Then where did—Oh!" His "Oh!" was echoed by Belter and two junior officers who had overheard the conversation. It was a most respectful sound. Also respectful was the unconscious retreat all hands took to the inboard bulkhead.

Hereford, who had not spoken a word for nearly a day, asked: "What's the matter? What is it?"

"Don't know," breathed Belter. "But I'd like to see it out of here. Way out. It's the Invader's."

"G-get it out of here. *Jump*!"

They piled into the inboard section and sealed the cargo inspection hatch behind them, leaving three spacesuited e.m. and an officer to worry the object tenderly out of the port.

"You're a cretin," Osgood told the captain. "You're a drooling incompetent. Whatever possessed you to bring in an unidentified object?"

"I . . . it was . . . I don't know," stammered Holovik. Belter marveled at the degree of the worriment the man's face could register.

A junior officer with communication pips spoke up. "That was the object which didn't register on the detectors until it was within a mile, sir," he reminded. "I still can't understand it, commander. Our detectors—all of 'em—are sensitive to fifty thousand at the very least. I'm ready to swear our equipment was in order, and yet we had no sign of this thing until it was right on top of us."

"Somebody in Detection is asleep," growled the Butcher.

"Wait, commander," Belter turned toward the young sigman. "How was this thing bearing?"

"Right on the ship, sir. An intersection course from down left forrad, as I remember. We deflected it and then brought it about with the short tractors."

"It just appeared out of nowhere, eh?" rasped Osgood. "And so you invited it in."

"There was a good deal of debris in that sector, commander," said Holovik faintly. "We were busy . . . tracers sometimes give resultant indications when they pick up two separated objects simultaneously—"

"Yeah, and then they indicate something where nothing is. They *don't* indicate nothing where there is something. Why, I'll break you to—"

"It seems to me," said Belter, who had been pursuing his own line of reasoning, "that what we have here is mighty similar to what hit Outpost. Remember? They put a tracer on it as they saw it leave the Invader. It blanked out. They got no radiation or radar reflection at all. But it came in and wiped out the base."

"The nonexistent, hypothetical 'warper,'" said Hereford, with a wisp of his old smile.

Osgood glanced at him coldly. "If you're trying to tell me that the Invader used a warper to protect himself from The Death, you're showing your ignorance. The Death is a vibration, *not* a radiation. It's a physical effect, not an energy phenomenon."

"Blast The Death!" spat Belter. "Don't you see what we've got here? It's one of their disrupters. Short range—always short range. Don't you see? It *is* a warper, and for some reason it can only carry a limited amount of power. The Invader started popping away at *Delta*, and when she fought back, he let loose with everything he had. This must've been one of his disrupters which was launched while *Delta* was in one piece and arrived after she'd been blasted. Then it went right on seeking, but ran out of fuel before it reached *Sigma*. That's why it suddenly appeared to the detectors."

"Now, that makes sense," said the Butcher, looking at Belter as if he were seeing him for the first time. He creased his lower lip sharply with his thumb and forefinger. "Warp camouflage, eh? H-m-m-m. I wonder if we could get a look at that unit. Maybe we could build something like it and get close enough to that devil to do some good." He turned to the fretful Holovik. "Captain! See if you can get a couple of techs to volunteer to defuse that thing. If you can't get volunteers—"

"I'll get them, sir," said Holovik, for the first time looking a little happier. It made him appear wistful instead of mournful.

It was easier to count those not volunteering, once the proposition went out over the intercom. In a few minutes *Sigma* lay off a couple of hundred miles to stand by while a crack squad worked over the drifting bomb. They carried three viewers, and the control bridge of The Death ship was mobbed with experts. Every move was carefully discussed; every possibility was carefully explored before a move was made.

They did it. It was slow, and suspense reached an agonized pitch; but once it was done and could be reviewed, it was unbelievably simple. The warhead was clamped to the main hull of the bomb. The activators were in the head, controlled simply by a couple of rods. The seeking gear, proximity circuits, power source, drive, and what was apparently the camouflage unit were all packed into the hull.

A torch was clamped to the warhead, which was cast adrift. The precious hull was towed a few miles with reaction-pistols and picked up by the ship, which then got clear and rayed the virulent little warhead into shocking, flaring extinction.

• • •

In shops and laboratories throughout the System, feverish work was carried on over plans and mock-ups of the alien weapon. One of the first things discovered about it was that the highly theoretical and very popular term "warper" was a misnomer. The camouflage was an ingenious complexity of wiring in concentric "skins" in the hull. Each impinging radiation caused the dielectric constant of the hull to change so that it reradiated that exact frequency, at the same intensity as received, but a hundred and eighty degrees out of phase. The heart of the device was what might have been the thousandth generation descended from a TR tube. It hunted so constantly, and triggered radiations with so little lag, that the device could handle several frequencies almost simultaneously.

What used most of the power was the drive. It involved a magnetic generator and a coil which carried magnetic flux. Induced in this was an extremely intense gravitic field, self-canceling forward and on all sides. The intensified "reverse" gravity pressure was, therefore, at the stern. Maneuvering was accomplished by variations in field strength by inductance-coupling of the mag-flux coils.

The hull was a totally absorbent black, and the missile was made of an alloy which was transparent to hard radiation.

All information was pooled, and sub-projects were constantly assigned from Science Center. Etherfac transmission was full of last-minute reports on phases of the problem, interspersed with frequent communiqués on the last known position of the Invader. He had indulged in an apparently aimless series of convolutions for several weeks following D-Day, evidently to assess his damage. After that he had maintained a great circular course, parallel in plane to the Solar ecliptic, and the assumption was that he was undergoing repairs and engaging in reconnaissance. Both were certainly indicated, for he must have undergone an incredible strain in that wild curve on D-Day. And as before, he was the symbol of terror. If he struck, where would he strike? If not, he would leave. Then, would he be back? Alone, or with a fleet?

Belter's life was a continuous flurry of detail, but he found time to wonder about several things. The Jovians, for example. They had been a great help in the duplication of the camouflage device, particularly in their modification of the fission power plant it carried. The Jovian improvement was a disruption motor using boron, an element which appeared nowhere in the original. It gave vastly more range to the Solarian device. And yet—there was something about the Jovian willingness that was not quite in harmony with their established behavior patterns. The slight which Leess had suffered from the Martian was not, after all, a large thing in itself, but the fact that Leess had led his planet into a policy of noncooperation made it large. The sudden reversal of this policy since D-Day was more than puzzling. A hundred times Belter shrugged the question off, grunting "Jovians are funny people," and a hundred times it returned to him.

There was another unprecedented worry. The Martian delegate called Belter aside one afternoon and presented it to him. "It's that Hereford," the man said, scratching his sunburned neck. "He's too quiet. I know he lost a mess of 'face' over his vote on The Death, but he still has a following. More than I like to think about."

"So?"

"Well, when the big day comes, when we send a formation of the new camouflaged boats out there, what's to keep him from opening his trap and making trouble for us?"

"Why should he?"

"You know what the pacifists are after. If we fitted out a bunch of these new gadgets with disrupters and wiped the Invader out, they'd have no kick. They don't want the Death-defense to get back to the System. You know that."

"Hm-m-m. And how would you handle this on Mars?"

The Martian grinned. "Why, I reckon Brother Hereford would have a little accident. Enough to keep him quiet, anyhow—maybe for a little while, maybe for—"

"I thought as much." Belter let himself burn for a luxurious second before replying. "Forget it. Supposing what you say is true—and I don't grant that it is—what else can you think of?"

"Well now, I think it would be a bright idea to send a camouflage force out without consulting the Council. That way, if Hereford is waiting for the psychological moment to blow his mouth off, we'll get what we're after before he knows what's happening. *If* we can keep the lid on it, that is."

Belter shook his head. "Sorry friend. No can do. We can stretch a point of security and take a military action without informing the people, but there's no loophole in the charter which will let any of us take military action without the knowledge of the Council. Sorry. Anyway, thanks for the tip."

This, like the Jovian matter, was a thing he shrugged off and forgot—five or six times a day. He knew the case-hardened character which lived behind Hereford's dignified mien, and he respected it for what it was and for what it could do.

There was a solution to these problems. He laughed when it occurred to him, smiled when it recurred; but he frowned when he realized that he had already decided. He must have, for he found himself slipping Addison's report into a private drawer of his desk. Addison was the Tech in charge of the local camouflage project. It was top secret and had been delivered, sealed, by an orderly. It invited him to inspect a two-place craft which had been finished and tested, fueled and equipped. The report should have gone to the Agenda.

He called Hereford, and when they were alone he asked, without preliminary: "Are you interested in heading off a war?"

"A rhetorical question, certainly."

"Nope. Question two. Have you anything special to do the next few weeks?"

"Why I—nothing out of the ordinary," said Hereford, sadly. Since his historic "Exception" speech, he had had little enough to do.

"Well, clear your social calendar, then. No, I'm not kidding. This is hot. How soon can you be ready for a little trip?"

Hereford studied him. "In about thirty minutes. I can tell by the way you act that you'd want it that soon."

"You're psychic. Right here, then, in thirty minutes."

Within two hours they were in space, aboard a swift scoutship. Behind him Belter left a bewildered deputy-chairman with a brief authorization in his hands, and an equally astonished MasterTech, both of whom were sworn to silence. In the scoutship were a sworn-in crew and the black hulk of the camouflaged lifeboat.

For the first two days out he left Hereford to twiddle his thumbs in the cramped recreation room of the ship, while he closeted himself with the skipper to work out an approach course. It took him half of the first day to convince the young man that he was in his right mind and that he wanted to board the Invader—two facts that had been regarded, during the past three years, as mutual incompatibilities.

The approach was plotted to permit the boat to overtake the Invader using a minimum of power. The little craft was to be launched from the scout at high speed on a course which would put it in an elliptical orbit in respect to the sun. This ellipse was at right angles to the plane of the circular course the Invader had been maintaining for the past few weeks. The ellipse intersected this circle in two places, and the launching time was set to synchronize these points of intersection with the predicted position of the Invader on its own course. The big *if*, naturally, was whether or not the Invader would maintain course and speed. He might. He had, twice before, once for nine months and once for over a year. If Belter watched his tables, and spent enough time with his tetrant and calculex, it would require only an occasional nudge of power to follow his course, or to correct it for any variations of the Invader's predicted position.

After the matter was settled, and he had slept, he rejoined Hereford. The old man was apparently staring right through the open book on his knee, for his eyes were wide and unmoving. Belter slumped down beside him and expelled an expressive breath. "What a way to make a living!"

Amusement quirked the corners of Hereford's mouth. "What?"

"Finding tough ways to die," grinned the chairman. "I'm ready to tell you about this thing, if you want me to."

Hereford closed his book and put it by.

"It's the Jovians, first of all," said Belter, without preliminary. "Those critters think so well, so fast, and so differently that it scares me. It's tough . . . no, it's downright foolish to try to judge their actions on a human basis. However, they pulled one stunt that was so very human that it completely escaped me. If Mars had tried it, I'd have been on to it instantly. It's taken a long time for it to percolate, since it concerns the Jovians. Do you remember how ready they were to help out after D-Day? Why do you suppose that was?"

"I would judge," said Hereford thoughtfully, "that they had awakened to their responsibility as members of the System. The Invader had a defense against the ultimate weapon, the emergency was intensified, and they pitched in to help for the common good."

"That's what I thought, too. Has it occurred to you at all what would probably happen if Jupiter—and only Jupiter—had a defense against The Death?"

"Why, I don't think they would—"

Belter broke in roughly. "Never mind what you would like to believe. What would happen?"

"I see what you mean," said Hereford. His face was white. "We came up from almost certain defeat and won the war when we developed The Death. If Jupiter had a defense, we would be no match for them."

"That's way understated," said Belter.

"But . . . but they signed a peace treaty! They're disarming! They won't break their word!" cried Hereford.

"Of course they won't! If they get their hands on that defense, they'll calmly announce the fact, give us time to prepare, even, and then declare war and wipe us out. There's a great deal of pride involved, of course. I'll venture to say that they'd even help us arm if we'd let them, to make the struggle equal to begin with. They're bugs for that kind of fairness. But the whole System knows that machine for machine, unit for unit, Jovian for man, there is no equality. They're too much for us. It is only our crazy, ingrained ability to manufacture suicidal weapons which gives us the upper hand. The Jovians are too wise to try to conquer a race which insists on introducing murder-machines without any due regard for their future significance. Remember what Leess said when the Martian insulted him? 'Earth dead, Jupiter dead, Mars dead. Good.' They know that unless we as a race are let alone, we will certainly find a way to kill off our neighbors, because as a race we don't care if we get killed in the process."

Hereford shuddered. "I'd hate to think you were right. It makes Peace Amalgamated look so very useless, for all its billions of members."

Belter cracked his knuckles. "I'm not trying to tell you that humans are basically rotten, or that they are fated to be what they always have been. Humanity has come very close to extinction at least four times that I know of, through some such kind of mass suicide. But the existence of Peace Amalgamated does indicate that it believes there is a way out, although I can't help thinking that it'll be a long haul to get us 'cured.'"

"Thank you," said Hereford sincerely. "Sometimes I think you might be a more effective peace worker than I can ever hope to be. Tell me—what made you suspect that the Jovians might be after the defense device for themselves?"

"A very recent development. You must know that the one thing which makes our use of the camouflage unit practicable is the new power plant. With it we can run up to the Invader and get inside his detectors, starting from far out of his range. Now, that was a Jovian design. They built it, ergo they had it first.

"In other words, between the time of its invention and the time they turned it over to us, they had the edge on us. That being the case, there would be only one reason why, in their supreme self-confidence, they would turn it over to us; namely, they didn't need that edge any more!"

"It fits," said Hereford sorrowfully.

"Good. Now, knowing Jovians—and learning more every day, by the way—I conclude that they gave us the drive, not because they had something better, but because it had already served its purpose for them. I am convinced that Jovian camouflage boats are on the way to the Invader now—and perhaps they have even . . . but I'd rather not think about that." He spread his arms, dropped them. "Hence our little jaunt. We've got to get there first. If we're not first, we have to do what we can when we get there."

The boat, lightless, undriven, drifted toward the Invader. At this arc of the chosen ellipse, its velocity was low, and suspense was as ubiquitous a thing as the susurrus of the camouflage unit which whispered away back aft. Hereford and Belter found themselves talking in whispers too, as if their tense voices could carry through those insulated bulkheads, across the dim void to the mysterious crew of the metal murderer which hung before them.

"We're well inside his meteor deflectors," gritted Belter. "I don't know what to think. Are we really going to be able to get to him, or is he playing with us?"

"He doesn't play," said Hereford grimly. "You will excuse the layman's question, but I don't understand how there can be a possibility of his having no detector for just this kind of approach. Since he uses bombs camouflaged the way we are, he must have some defense against them."

"His defense seems to be in the range of his deflectors," answered the chairman. "Those bombs were hunters. That is, they followed the target wherever it moved. The defense would be to stall off the bomb by maneuvering until it ran out of fuel, like the one we picked up. Then his meteor-repellers would take care of it."

"It was obviously the most effective weapon in his arsenal," said Hereford hopefully.

"As far as we know," said Belter from the other end of the emotional spectrum. Then, "I can't stand this, I'm going to try a little drive. I feel as if we'd been hanging here since nuclear power was discovered."

Hereford tensed, then nodded in the dark. The boat was hardly the last word in comfort. The two men could lie prone, or get up

to a cramped all-four position. Sitting was possible if the
cheekbones were kept between the knees and the occipital bones
tight against the overhead. They had been in that prison for more
days than they cared to recall.

Belter palmed the drive control and moved it forward. There
was no additional sound from the power unit, but the slight
accelerative surge was distinctly felt.

"I'm going to circle him. No point being too careful. If he
hasn't taken a crack at us by this time, I don't think he's going to."
He took the steering lever in his other hand and the boat's nose
pulled "up" in relation to the Invader's keel-plane. There was no
fear of momentum-damage; the controls would not respond to
anything greater than a 5-G turn without a special adjustment.

Within four hours the craft was "over" the alien. The ugly,
blind-looking shape, portless and jetless, was infuriating. It went
its way completely unheeding, completely confident. Belter had a
mad flashback to a childish romance. She hadn't been a very
pretty girl, but to have her near him drove him nearly insane. It
was because of her perfect poise, her mask. He did not want her.
He wanted only to break that calm, to smash his way into the
citadel of her *savoir faire*. He had felt like that, and she was not
evil. This ship, now—it was completely so. There was something
unalive, implacable, inescapable about this great murderous
vessel.

Something clutched his arm. He started violently, bumped his
head on the overhead, his hand closing on the velocity control.
The craft checked itself and he bumped his head again on the
forward port. He swore more violently than Hereford's grip on his
arm called for, and said in irritation: "What?"

"A—hole. A hatch or something. Look."

It was a black shadow on the curve of the grayshadowed hull.
"Yes . . . yes. Shall we—" Belter swallowed and tried again.
"Shall we walk into his parlor?"

"Yes. Ah . . . Belter—"

"Hm-m-m?"

"Before we do—you might as well tell me. Why did you want
me to come?"

"Because you're a fighting man."

"That's an odd joke."

"It is not. You have had to fight every inch of the way,
Hereford."

"Perhaps so. But don't tell me you brought me along for the potential use of my mislaid pugnacities."

"Not *for* them, friend. Because of them. You want the Invader destroyed, for the good of the System. I want it saved, for the good of the System, as I see it. You could achieve your end in one of two ways. You could do it through Peace Amalgamated, back at Central. It would only need a few words to obstruct this whole program. *Or*, you could achieve it yourself, here. I brought you to keep you from speaking to Peace Amalgamated. I think having you here where I can watch you is less of a risk to the procurement of The Death defense."

"You're a calculating devil," said Hereford, his voice registering something between anger and admiration. "And suppose I try to destroy the ship—given, of course, the chance?"

"I'd kill you first," said Belter with utter sincerity.

"Has it occurred to you that I might try the same thing, with the same amount of conviction?"

"It has," Belter replied promptly. "Only you wouldn't do it. You could not be driven to killing. Hereford, you pick the oddest times to indulge in dialectics."

"Not at all," said Hereford good-humoredly. "One likes to know where one stands."

Belter gave himself over to his controls. In the back of his mind was a whirling ball of panic. Suppose the power plant should fail, for example. Or suppose the Invader should send out a questing beam of a frequency which the camouflage unit could not handle. How about the meteor deflector? Would they be crushed if the ship located them and hurled them away with a repeller? He thought with sudden horror of the close-set wiring in the boat. Shorts do happen, and sometimes oxidation and vibration play strange tricks with wiring. Do *something*, his inner voice shouted. *Right or wrong, do something*.

They drifted up to the great silver hull, and the hole seemed to open hungrily to them as they neared it. Belter all but stopped the craft in relation to the ship, and nosed it forward with a view to entering the hatch without touching the sides.

"In the visirecord, didn't the camouflage disrupter at Outpost show up for a moment on the screen as it left the ship?" Hereford whispered.

"Yeah. So what? Oh! You mean the cam unit was shut off until the bomb was clear of the ship. You have something there, Hereford. Maybe we'd better shut it off before we go in. I can see where it would act like something less than camouflage, enclosed in a metal chamber and reradiating all the stray stuff in there plus the reflections of its own output." He put his hand out to the camouflage control. "But I'm going to wait until we're practically inside. I don't relish the idea of being flung off like a meteorite."

Handling the controls with infinite care, touching them briefly and swiftly with his fingertips, Belter tooled the boat through the hatch. He switched off the camouflage effect and had the boat fully inboard of the Invader before he realized he was biting his tongue.

Surprisingly, the chamber they entered was illuminated. The light was dim, shadowless, and a sickly green. The overhead and bulkheads themselves, or a coating on them, accounted for the light. There was a large rack on the forward partition containing row on row of the disruption bombs, minus their warheads. Above each ended a monorail device which ran to a track ending in a solid-looking square door—obviously the storage space for the warheads. Another hoist and monorail system connected the hulls themselves with the open hatch. This trackage, and the fact that the chamber was otherwise untenanted, indicated that the bomb assembly, fuse setting, and dispatching were completely automatic.

"Camouflage again," gritted Belter. "This boat is enough like those bombs to fit sort of cozily in one of those racks. In this crazy light no one would notice it."

"This light is probably not crazy to those on board," said Hereford.

"We'll worry about that later. Slip into your suit."

From the aft locker they drew the light pressure suits around themselves and secured them. Belter demonstrated the few controls—oxygen, humidity, temperature, magnetism, and gravity, to be quite sure the old man was familiar with them all. "And this is the radio. I think it will be safe to use the receivers. But don't transmit unless it's absolutely necessary. If we stick close together we can talk by conduction—touching our helmets."

It was the work of only a few minutes to grapple the weightless craft into the rack. It was a fair fit. When they had finished, Belter reached in and took out two blasters. He secured the escape hatch and turned to Hereford, handing him one of the guns. Hereford took it, but leaned forward to touch his transparent helmet to Belter's. His voice came through hollowly but clearly.

"What's this for?"

"Morale," said Belter briefly. "You don't have to use it. If we're watched, 'Two armed men' sounds better than 'Two men, one armed.'"

They groped to the inboard partition and followed it cautiously aft. The touch of the metal under his gloves brought a shocking realization to Belter of where he actually was, and for a moment his knees threatened to give way. Deep inside him, his objective self watched, shaking its figment of a head in amazement. Because he had secured a lifeboat equipped for the job, he had come. Because he had gotten inside the Invader's screens, he had approached the ship itself. Because he was close enough and a hatch was open, he had come in. *Just the way I got into the Army, and the way I got into politics*, he grinned.

They found a ladder. It led upward through a diamond-shaped opening in the overhead. The rungs were welded to the bulkhead. They were too narrow and too close together. There were dragging scuffmarks on each side, about eighteen or twenty centimeters on each side of the rungs. What manner of creature ambulated on its centerline, dragging its sides?

A Jovian.

He looked at Hereford, who was pointing at the marks, so he knew that Hereford understood, too. He shrugged and pointed upward, beckoning. They went up, Belter leading.

They found themselves in a corridor, too low to allow them to stand upright. It was triangular in cross-section, with the point down and widened to a narrow catwalk. A wear-plate was set into each side and bore the same smooth scuffs. The deck, what there was of it between the sharply sloping sides, was composed of transverse rods. A creature which could grip with claws and steady itself with the sides of a carapace could move quite freely in such a corridor regardless of gravitic or accelerative effects, within reason.

"*Damn!*"

Belter jumped as if stabbed. Hereford tottered on his magna-grips and clutched at the slanted bulkhead for support. The single syllable had roared at them from inside their helmets. The effect was such that Belter all but swallowed his tongue. He pointed at himself in the dim green light and shook his head. Hereford weakly followed suit. Neither of them had spoken.

"*Lousy Jovians—*"

Belter, following a sudden hunch, laid his hand on Hereford's shoulder to suggest that he stay put, and crept back to the bomb bay opening. He lay down, and cautiously put his head over the lip.

A long, impossibly black *something* was edging across the deck down there. Belter squeezed his eyes tightly closed and opened them wide, trying to see through the foggy green radiance. At last he discerned a small figure pulling and hauling at the shadow, the bomb, the . . . the lifeboat.

A human figure. A man. A man who must have come through the Invader's defenses, even as he had. A man with a camouflaged boat.

But no one except a few Techs even knew that the boats had been completed. And the Council, of course.

The man below reached inside his boat and touched a control. It sank down to the deck next to the bomb rack as its magnetic anchors were activated. The man shut the escape hatch and shuffled toward the inboard partition, his blaster in hand, his head turning as he came.

Belter watched him until he discovered the ladder. Then he scrambled to his feet and, as fast as the peculiar footing would allow him, he scurried back to Hereford. His helmet receiver registered an angry gust of breath as the man below saw the short-paced ladder and the scuff-marks.

Belter slammed his helmet against Hereford's. "It's a Martian," he gritted. "You might know it'd be a blasted Martian. Only a Martian'd be stupid enough to try to climb aboard this wagon."

He saw Hereford's eyebrow go up at this, but the peaceman did not make the obvious comment. He was silent as he followed Belter forward to the nearest turn in the corridor. They slipped around it, Belter conning its extension carefully. There was still, incredibly, no sign of life.

Just around the turn there was a triangular door, set flush into the slanted wall. Belter hesitated, then pressed it. It did not yield. He scrabbled frantically over its surface, found no control of any kind. Hereford grasped his arm, checked him, and when Belter stepped back, the old man went to his knees and began feeling around on the catwalk floor. The door slid silently back.

Belter slipped in, glanced around. But for a huddled, unmoving mass of some tattered matter in the corridor, there was nothing in the room, which was small. Belter waved the old man in. Hereford hopped over the sill, felt on the floor again, and the panel slid shut.

"How did you know how to open that door?" Belter asked when their helmets touched.

"Their feet . . . claws . . . what-have-you . . . are obviously prehensile, or they wouldn't have floors that are nothing more than close-set rungs. Obviously their door handles would be in the floor."

Belter shook his head admiringly. "See what happens when a man thinks for a living?" He turned to the door, set his head against it. Very faintly, he could hear the cautious steps of the Martian. He turned back to Hereford. "I suppose I ought to go out there and pin his ears back. Martians have nothing in their heads but muscles. He'll walk right up to the skipper of this ship if he has to wade through the crew to do it. But I'm mighty interested in just what he's up to. We couldn't be much worse off than we are. Do you suppose we could follow him closely enough to keep him out of trouble?"

"There is no need for caution," said Hereford, and his voice, distorted by the helmets, was like a distant tolling bell.

"What do you mean?"

Hereford pointed to the huddled mass in the corner. Belter crossed to it, knelt, and put out a hand. Frozen substance crumbled under his touch in a way which was familiar to him. He shrank back in horror.

"It's—dead," he whispered.

Hereford touched helmets. "What?"

"It's dead," said Belter dully. "It's—homogenized, and frozen."

"I know. Remember the three Jovian capital ships?"

"They couldn't stand The Death," Belter murmured. "They opened all the locks."

He stood up. "Let's go get that fool of a Martian."

They left the room and followed the corridor to its end. There was another ladder there. They climbed it, and at the top Belter paused. "I think we'd better try for the control central. That'll be the first thing he'll go after."

They found it, eventually, before the Martian did, possibly because they were not being as cautious. They must have passed him en route, but such was the maze of corridors and connecting rooms that that was not surprising. They still eschewed the use of their transmitters, since Belter preferred to find out exactly what the Martian was up to.

They had just opened a sliding door at the end of a passageway, and Belter was half through it when he stopped so suddenly that Hereford collided with him.

The room which spread before them was unexpectedly large. The bulkheads were studded with diamond-shaped indicators, and above them and over the ceiling were softly colored murals. They glowed and shimmered, and since they were the first departure from the ubiquitous dim green, their immediate effect was shocking.

In the center of the chamber was a pair of control desks, a V pointing forward and a V pointing aft, forming another of the repeated diamond forms. There was a passage space, however, between the two V's. In their enclosure was a creature, crouching over the controls.

It was alive.

It stirred, heaving itself up off the raised portion of the deck on which it lay. It was completely enclosed in a transparent, obviously pressurized garment. As it rose, Belter and Hereford shrank back out of sight. Belter drew his blaster.

But the creature was apparently not aware of them. It turned slowly to face the opposite corner of the room, and the sensory organ on its cephalothorax blushed pink.

There was a bold clanking from the corner of the room, which Belter felt through his shoes. Then the wall began to glow. A small section of it shone red which paled into white. It bellied momentarily, and then sagged molten. The Martian, blaster in hand, leapt through the opening. *And he could have opened that door*, thought Belter disgustedly. *Why does a Martian always have to do it the hard way?*

The Martian stopped dead when he was clear of the simmering entrance. He visibly recoiled from the sudden apparition of color, and stood awed before those magnificent murals. His gaze dropped to the center of the room.

"So there is a defense," he snarled. His transmitter was still blatantly operating. "Come on, Jupiter. I was wise to this whole stunt. Who did you think you fooled by poisoning your own forces on Titan? Invader, huh? Some stuff! Get out of there. Move now! I know you can understand me. I want to see that Death defense and the controls. And there's no sense trying to call your buddies. I've seen them all over the ship. All dead. Something saved you, and I mean to find out what it is."

He raised his blaster. The Jovian quivered. Belter crossed his left arm across his body and grasped the edge of the door. He rested his blaster across his left forearm and squinted down the barrel. Hereford reached over his shoulder and drew the muzzle upward.

Belter turned furiously to him, but the old man shook his head and, astonishingly, smiled. His hand went to his belt. He threw his transmitter switch and said in his deep, quiet voice:

"Drop that blaster, son."

The effect on the Martian was absolutely devastating. He went rod stiff, dropping his weapon so quickly that he all but threw it. Then he staggered backward, and they could hear his frightened gasping as he tried to regain his breath.

Belter strode out into the room and backed to the left bulkhead, stopping where he could cover both the Martian and the Jovian. Hereford shuffled over and picked up the blaster.

"P-peace Amalgamated!" puffed the Martian. "What in time are *you* doing here?"

Belter answered. "Keeping you from using your muscles instead of your brains. What do you think you're doing?"

"Recon," said the Martian sullenly.

"For whom?"

"What do you think?"

"I think you're doing it for Mars," said Belter bluntly. "It would be just dandy if Mars had The Death defense now, wouldn't it? You guys have been chafing at the bit for a long time."

"We're not crazy," flashed the Martian. "We never did make peace with Jupiter, remember? We knew better. And now look." He gestured at the Jovian. "What a pretty way to knock slices out of all the Solarian defenses. Just play Invader for a few years and scare the bedizens out of humanity. Wipe out what looks tough, and take advantage of the panic. Heh! Treaties with Jupiter! Why in blazes didn't you exterminate them when you had the chance? Now, if Mars gets the Defense, we'll handle the thing right. And maybe when the smoke clears away we'll be magnanimous enough to let Earth and the Colonies work for us."

"All blast and brawn," marveled Belter. "The famous Martian mouth."

"Don't you brag about brains. I know for a fact that our councilman tipped off that camouflage boats were being made in secret. If you didn't act on it, it's your hard luck."

"In a way he did," said Belter. "Enough I imagine, to keep his little conscience clear. I'm here, for all that."

"Not for long," snapped the Martian, making a long sliding step.

"*Look out, Hereford*!"

Belter snapped a fine-focus shot at the Martian but he was late. The Martian was behind Hereford, grappling for the blaster which the Peace delegate still held in his hand. Hereford tried to spin away but was unsure of his footing in the gravitic shoes and succeeded only in floundering. The Martian suddenly shifted his attack to the blaster at Hereford's hip. He got it and danced clear. "I know the pantywaist won't shoot," he said, and laughed. "So it's you first, Belter, and then old 'Peace-in-our-Time.' Then I'll get The Death defense with or without the aid of the spider yonder."

He swung the weapon on Belter, and the chairman knew that this was it. He closed his eyes. The blaster-flash beat on the lids. He felt nothing. He tried to open his eyes again and was astounded to discover that he could. He stood there staring at Hereford, who had just shot the Martian through the head. The man's magnagrips held him upright as the air in his suit whiffed out, to hang in a mist like a frozen soul over his tattered head.

"I killed him, didn't I?" asked Hereford plaintively.

"To keep the peace," said Belter in a shaking voice. He skated over to the old man and took the blaster, which was still held stiffly out toward the dead man. "Killing's a comparative crime, Hereford. You've saved lives."

He went to the control table and put his hands on it, steadying himself against the broken sounds Hereford was making. He stared across the table at the great jelly-and-bone mass that was a Jovian. He would have given a lot for a translator, but such a machine had never yet been made portable.

"You. Jovian. Will you communicate? Spread that membrane for 'yes.' Contract it for 'no.' "

Yes. The creature was perfectly telepathic, but with humans it had to be one way. A translator could convert its emanations into minute electronic impulses and arrange them into idea-patterns for which words were selected.

"Is there anything on this ship which can resist The Death?"

Yes.

"You understand it?"

Yes.

"Will you share your knowledge with the Council?"

Yes.

"Can you deactivate all automatics on this ship?"

In answer the Jovian extended one of its fourth pseudo-claws, and placed it next to a control on the table. It was a small square housing, set so as to repeat the diamond motif. An orange pilot light glowed in its center, and next to it was a toggle. On the forward side of the toggle was an extremely simple symbol—two dots connected by two lines, each two-thirds of the distance between the dots, so that for the middle third they lay parallel, contiguous. On the after side of the toggle, the symbol differed. The dots were the same, but the lines were separated. It was obviously an indication of "open" and "closed" positions. The toggle slanted forward. Belter put his hand on it, looked at the Jovian.

The membrane spread affirmatively. Jovians did not lie. He pulled the toggle back and the pilot went out.

"This General Assembly has been called," Belter said quietly into the mike, "to clear up, once and for all, the matter of the Invader and the contingent wild and conflicting rumors about a defense against The Death, about interstellar drives, about potential war between members of the Solar Federation, and a number of other fantasies." He spoke carefully, conscious of the transmission of his voice and image to government gatherings on all the worlds, in all the domes, and on ships.

"You know the story of my arrival, with Hereford, aboard the Invader, and the later arrival of the Martian, and his"—Belter cleared his throat—"his accidental death. Let me make it clear right now that there is no evidence that this man was representing the Martian General Government or any part of it. We have concluded that he was acting as an individual, probably because of what might be termed an excess of patriotism.

"Now, as to the presence of the Jovian on the ship—that is a perfectly understandable episode. Jupiter is a defeated nation. I venture to say that any group of us in the same situation would commit acts similar to that of this Jovian. I can say here, too, that there is no evidence of its representing any part of the Jovian Government. What it might have done with, say, a Death defense had it found one aboard is conjecture, and need not enter into this discussion.

"I have before me a transcript of this Jovian's statement. You may rest assured that all facts have been checked; that fatigue and crystalline tests and examinations have been made of metallic samples taken from the vessel; that the half-lives of radioactive by-products in certain fission and disruption machinery have been checked and substantiate this statement. This is the transcript:

"'For reasons consistent with Jovian philosophy, I took a Jovian-built camouflaged boat and departed with it before the improved drive had been submitted to Joint Solar Military Council. I approached the Invader cautiously and found the camouflage successful. I boarded him. I put my boat in the Invader's bomb rack, where it was well hidden in plain sight, being the same size and general shape as the Invader's bombs. I went inboard, expecting a great deal of trouble. There was none. Every port and hatch was open to space except the warhead storage, which was naturally no hiding place due to radioactivity. I proceeded to the control chamber. I found the master control to all the ship's armament.

"'But my most important discovery was a thought record. The Invaders were, like Jovians, of an arthropodal type, and their image patterns were quite understandable after a little concentration. I shall quote from that record:

"'*We are of Sygon, greater of the two planets of Sykor, a star in Symak. The smaller planet, known to us as Gith, is peopled by a mad race, a mistake of nature—a race which fights and kills itself and wars on its neighbors; a race which aspires to conquer purely for the sake of conquest, which hunts for hunting's sake and kills for pleasure. While it progresses, while it cooperates, it bites itself and fights itself and is never done with its viciousness.*

"'*Its planet was large enough to support it, but it was not satisfied. Sygon was no place for these vicious animals, for they had to bring their atmosphere in bubbles for breathing, and Sygon's mass crushed them and made them sicken. Not needing Sygon still they were willing to fight us for it.*

"'*We killed them by the hundreds of thousands, and still they kept coming. They devised incredible weapons to use against us, and we improved on them and hurled them back. They improved on these, completely ignoring the inevitability of their end.*

"'*The ultimate weapon was theirs—a terrible thing which emulsified the very cells of our bodies, and there was no defense against it. The first time it was used it killed off most of our race. The rest of us threw all our resources into this, the Eternal Vengeance—this ship. It is designed to attack anything which radiates, as long as the radiations exhibit the characteristics of those produced by intelligent life. It will stay in Sykor's system, and it will attack anything which might be Gith or of Gith. Gith will strike back with its terrible weapon, and all of us on the ship will die. But the ship will go on. Gith will loose its horror and agony on Sygon, and our race will be dead. But the ship will go on. It will attack and attack, and ultimately will destroy Gith.*

" '*And if Gith should die and be born again and evolve a new race, and if that race shall reach a stage of culture approaching that of its cursed forebears, the ship will attack again until it has destroyed them. It will attack all the more powerfully for having rested, for between attacks it will circle Sykor, drinking and storing its energy.*

" '*Perhaps there will come a time when Sykor will cool, or flare up and explode, or become subject to the influence of a wandering star. Perhaps then the ship will cease to be, but it is possible that it will go wandering off into the dark, never to be active again. But if it should wander into a similar system to that which bore it, then it will bring death and horror to that system's inhabitants. If this should be, it will be unjust; but it will be only an extension of the illimitable evil of Gith.' "*

Belter raised his head. "That is what we were up against. What passed in that Jovian's mind when we burst in on it, with our quarreling and our blasters and our death-dealing, I can only imagine. It made no move to harm us, though it was armed. I think that it may have been leaving us to the same inevitable end which overcame Gith. Apparently a Jovian is capable of thinking beyond immediate advantage.

"I have one more thing to tell you. According to star photographs found in a huge file on the Invader, and the tests and examinations I mentioned, the Invader is slightly over fourteen million years old.

"There is a defense against The Death. You can't kill a dead man. Now, in more ways than one, I give you over to Hereford."

SMASHER

Fred Saberhagen

Claus Slovensko was coming to the conclusion that the battle in nearby space was going to be invisible to anyone on the planet Waterfall—assuming that there was really going to be a battle at all.

Claus stood alone atop a forty-meter dune, studying a night sky that flamed with the stars of the alien Busog cluster, mostly blue-white giants which were ordinarily a sight worth watching in themselves. Against that background, the greatest energies released by interstellar warships could, he supposed, be missed as a barely visible twinkling. Unless, of course, the fighting should come very close indeed.

In the direction he was facing, an ocean made invisible by night stretched from near the foot of the barren dune to a horizon marked only by the cessation of the stars. Claus turned now to scan once more the sky in the other direction. That way, toward planetary north, the starry profusion went on and on. In the northeast a silvery half-moon, some antique stage designer's concept of what Earth's own moon should be, hung low behind thin clouds. Below those clouds extended an entire continent of lifeless sand and rock. The land masses of Waterfall were bound in a silence that Earth ears found uncanny, stillness marred only by the wind, by murmurings of sterile streams, and by occasional deep rumblings in the rock itself.

Claus continued turning slowly, till he faced south again. Below him the night sea lapped with lulling false familiarity. He sniffed the air, and shrugged, and gave up squinting at the stars, and began to feel his way, one cautious foot after another, down the shifting slope of the dune's flank. A small complex of buildings, labs and living quarters bunched as if for companionship, the only human habitation on the world of Waterfall, lay a

115

hundred meters before him and below. Tonight as usual the windows were all cheerfully alight. Ino Vacroux had decided, and none of the other three people on the planet had seen any reason to dispute him, that any attempt at blackout would be pointless. If a berserker force was going to descend on Waterfall, the chance of four defenseless humans avoiding discovery by the unliving killers would be nil.

Just beyond the foot of the dune, Claus passed through a gate in the high fence of fused rock designed to keep out drifting sand—with no land vegetation of any kind to hold the dunes in place, they tended sometimes to get pushy.

A few steps past the fence, he opened the lockless door of the main entrance to the comfortable living quarters. The large common room just inside was cluttered with casual furniture, books, amateur art, and small and middle-sized aquariums. The three other people who completed the population of the planet were all in this room at the moment, and all looked up to see if Claus brought news.

Jenny Surya, his wife, was seated at the small computer terminal in the far corner, wearing shorts and sweater, dark hair tied up somewhat carelessly, long elegant legs crossed. She was frowning as she looked up, but abstractedly, as if the worse news Claus might be bringing them would be of some potential distraction from their work.

Closer to Claus, in a big chair pulled up to the big communicator cabinet, slouched Ino Vacroux, senior scientist of the base. Claus surmised that Ino had been a magnificent physical specimen a few decades ago, before being nearly killed in a berserker attack upon another planet. The medics had restored function but not fineness to his body. The gnarled, hairy thighs below his shorts were not much thicker than a child's; his ravaged torso was draped now in a flamboyant shirt. In a chair near him sat Glenna Reyes, his wife, in her usual work garb of clean white coveralls. She was just a little younger than Vacroux, but wore the years with considerably more ease.

"Nothing to see," Claus informed them all, with a loose wave meant to describe the lack of visible action in the sky.

"Or to hear, either," Vacroux grated. His face was grim as he nodded toward the communicator. The screens of the device sparkled, and its speakers hissed a little, with noise that wandered in from the stars and stranger things than stars nature had set in this corner of the Galaxy.

Only a few hours earlier, in the middle of Waterfall's short autumn afternoon, there had been plenty to hear indeed. Driven by a priority code coming in advance of a vitally important message, the communicator had boomed itself to life, then roared the message through the house and across the entire base, in a voice that the four people heard plainly even four hundred meters distant where they were gathered to watch dolphins.

"Sea Mother, this is Brass Trumpet. Predators here, and we're going to try to turn them. Hold your place. Repeating. . . ."

One repetition of the substance came through, as the four were already hurrying back to the house. As soon as they got in they had played back the automatically recorded signal; and then when Glenna had at last located the code book somewhere, and they could verify the worst, they had played it back once more.

Sea Mother was the code name for any humans who might happen to be on Waterfall. It had been assigned by the military years ago, as part of their precautionary routine, and had probably never been used before today. Brass Trumpet, according to the book, was a name conveying a warning of deadly peril—it was to be used only by a human battle force when there were thought to be berserkers already in the Waterfall system or on their way to it. And "predators here" could hardly mean anything but berserkers—unliving and unmanned war machines, programmed to destroy whatever life they found. The first of them had been built in ages past, during the madness of some interstellar war between races now long-since vanished. Between berserkers and starfaring Earthhumans, war had now been chronic for a thousand standard years.

That Brass Trumpet's warning should be so brief and vague was understandable. The enemy would doubtless pick it up as soon as its intended hearers, and might well be able to decode it. But for all the message content revealed, Sea Mother might be another powerful human force, toward which Brass Trumpet sought to turn them. Or it would have been conceivable for such a message to be sent to no one, a planned deception to make the enemy waste computer capacity and detection instruments. And even if the berserker's deadly electronic brains should somehow compute correctly that Sea Mother was a small and helpless target, it was still possible to hope that the berserkers would be too intent on fatter targets elsewhere, too hard-pressed by human forces, or both, to turn aside and snap up such a minor morsel.

During the hours since that first warning, there had come nothing but noise from the communicator. Glenna sighed, and reached out to pat her man on the arm below the sleeve of his loud shirt. "Busy day with the crustaceans tomorrow," she reminded him.

"So we'd better get some rest. I know." Ino looked and sounded worn. He was the only one of the four who had ever seen berserkers before, at anything like close range; and it was not exactly reassuring to see how grimly and intensely he reacted to the warning of their possible approach.

"You can connect the small alarm," Glenna went on, "so it'll be sure to wake us if another priority message comes in."

That, thought Claus, would be easier on the nerves than being blasted out of sleep by that God-voice shouting again, this time only a few meters from the head of their bed.

"Yes, I'll do that," Ino thought, then slapped his chair-arms. He made his voice a little brighter. "You're right about tomorrow. And over in Twenty-three we're going to have to start feeding the mantis shrimp." He glanced round at the wall near his chair, where a long chart showed ponds, bays, lagoons and tidal pools, all strung out in a kilometers-long array, most of it natural, along this part of the coast. This array was a chief reason why the Sea Mother base had been located where it was.

From its sun and moon to its gravity and atmosphere, Waterfall was remarkably Earthlike in almost every measurable attribute save one—this world was congenitally lifeless. About forty standard years past, during a lull in the seemingly interminable berserker-war, it had appeared that the peaceful advancement of interstellar humanization might get in an inning or two, and work had begun toward altering this lifelessness. Great ships had settled upon Waterfall with massive inoculations of Earthly life, in a program very carefully orchestrated to produce eventually a twin-Earth circling one of the few Sol-type suns in this part of the Galaxy.

The enormously complex task had been interrupted when war flowed again. The first recrudescence of fighting was far away, but it drew off people and resources. A man-wife team of scientists were selected to stay alone on Waterfall for the duration of the emergency. They were to keep the program going along planned lines, even though at a slow pace. Ino and Glenna had been here for two years now. A supply ship from Atlantis called at intervals of a few standard months; and the last to call, eight local days ago, had brought along another husband-and-wife team for a visit. Claus and Jenny were both psychologists, interested in the study of couples living in isolation; and they were to stay at least until the next supply ship came.

So far the young guests had been welcome. Glenna, her own children long grown and independent on other worlds, approached motherliness sometimes in her attitude. Ino, more of a born competitor, swam races with Claus and gambled—lightly—with him. With Jenny he alternated between half-serious gallantry and teasing.

"I almost forgot," he said now, getting up from his chair before the communicator, and racking his arms and shoulders with an intense stretch. "I've got a little present for you, Jen."

"Oh?" She was bright, interested, imperturbable. It was her usual working attitude, which he persisted in trying to break through.

Ino went out briefly, and came back to join the others in the kitchen. A small snack before retiring had become a daily ritual for the group.

"For you," he said, presenting Jen with a small bag of clear plastic. There was water inside, and something else.

"Oh, my goodness." It was still her usual nurse-like business tone, which evidently struck Ino as a challenge. "What do I do with it?"

"Keep him in that last aquarium in the parlor," Ino advised. "It's untenanted right now."

Claus, looking at the bag from halfway across the kitchen, made out in it one of those non-human, non-mammalian shapes that are apt to give Earth people the impression of the intensely alien, even when the organism sighted comes from their own planet. It was no bigger than an adult human finger, but replete with waving appendages. There came to mind something written by Lafcadio Hearn about a centipede: *The blur of its moving legs . . . toward which one would no more advance one's hand . . . than toward the spinning blade of a power saw . . .*

Or some words close to those. Jen, Claus knew, cared for the shapes of non-mammalian life even less than he did. But she would grit her teeth and struggle not to let the teasing old man see it.

"Just slit the bag and let it drain into the tank," Ino was advising, for once sounding pretty serious. "They don't like handling . . . okay? He's a bit groggy right now, but tomorrow, if he's not satisfied with you as his new owner, he may try to get away."

Glenna, in the background, was rolling her eyes in the general direction of Brass Trumpet, miming: What is the old fool up to now? When is he going to grow up?

"Get away?" Jen inquired sweetly. "You told me the other day that even a snail couldn't climb that glass—"

The house was filled with the insistent droning of the alarm that Ino had just connected. He's running some kind of test, Claus thought at once. Then he saw the other man's face and knew that Ino wasn't.

Already the new priority message was coming in: *"Sea Mother, the fight's over here. Predators departing Waterfall System. Repeating . . ."*

Claus started to obey an impulse to run out and look at the sky again, then realized that there would certainly be nothing to be seen of the battle now. Radio waves, no faster than the light, had just announced that it was over. Instead he joined the others in voicing their mutual relief. They had a minute or so of totally unselfconscious cheering.

Ino, his face much relieved, broke out a bottle of something and four glasses. In a little while, all of them drifted noisily outside, unable to keep from looking up, though knowing they would find nothing but the stars to see.

"What," asked Claus, "were berserkers doing here in the first place? We're hardly a big enough target to be interesting to a fleet of them. Are we?"

"Not when they have bigger game in sight." Ino gestured upward with his drink. "Oh, any living target interests them, once they get it in their sights. But I'd guess that if a sizable force was here they were on the way to attack Atlantis. See, sometimes in space you can use a planet or a whole system as a kind of cover. Sneak up behind its solar wind, as it were, its gravitational vortex, as someone fighting a land war might take advantage of a mountain or a hill." Atlantis was a long-colonized system less than a dozen parsecs distant, heavily populated and heavily defended. The three habitable Atlantean planets were surfaced mostly with water, and the populace lived almost as much below the waves as on the shaky continents.

It was hours later when Glenna roused and stirred in darkness, pulling away for a moment from Ino's familiar angularity nested beside her.

She blinked. "What was that?" she asked her husband, in a low voice barely cleared of sleep.

Ino scarcely moved. "What was what?"

"A flash, I thought. Some kind of bright flash, outside. Maybe in the distance."

There came no sound of thunder, or of rain. And no more flashes, either, in the short time Glenna remained awake.

Shortly after sunrise next morning, Claus and Jen went out for an early swim. Their beach, pointed out by their hosts as the place where swimmers would be safest and least likely to damage the new ecology, lay a few hundred meters along the shoreline to the west, with several tall dunes between it and the building complex.

As they rounded the first of these dunes, following the pebbly shoreline, Claus stopped. "Look at that." A continuous track, suggesting the passage of some small, belly-dragging creature, had been drawn in the sand. Its lower extremity lay somewhere under water, its upper was concealed amid the humps of sterile sand somewhere inland.

"Something," said Jenny, "crawled up out of the water. I haven't seen that before on Waterfall."

"Or came down into it." Claus squatted beside the tiny trail. He was anything but a skilled tracker, and could see no way of determining which way it led. "I haven't seen anything like this before either. Glenna said certain species—I forget which—were starting to try the land. I expect this will interest them when we get back."

When Claus and Jenny had rounded the next dune, there came into view on its flank two more sets of tracks, looking very much like the first, and like the first either going up from the water or coming down.

"Maybe," Claus offered, "it's the same one little animal going back and forth. Do crabs make tracks like that?"

Jen couldn't tell him. "Anyway, let's hope they don't pinch swimmers." She slipped off her short robe and took a running dive into the cool water, whose salt content made it a good match for the seas of Earth. Half a minute later, she and her husband came to the surface together, ten meters or so out from shore. From here they could see west past the next dune. There, a hundred meters distant, underscored by the slanting shadows of the early sun, a whole tangled skein of narrow, fresh-looking tracks connected someplace inland with the sea.

A toss of Jen's head shook water from her long, dark hair. "I wonder if it's some kind of seasonal migration?"

"They certainly weren't there yesterday. I think I've had enough. This water's colder than a bureaucrat's heart."

Walking briskly, they had just re-entered the compound when Jenny touched Claus on the arm. "There's Glenna, at the tractor shed. I'm going to trot over and tell her what we saw."

"All right. I'll fix some coffee."

Glenna, coming out of the shed a little distance inland from the main house, forestalled Jenny's announcement about the tracks with a vaguely worried question of her own.

"Did you or Claus see or hear anything strange last night, Jenny?"

"Strange? No, I don't think so."

Glenna looked toward a small cluster of more distant outbuildings. "We've just been out there taking a scheduled seismograph reading. It had recorded something rather violent and unusual, at about oh-two-hundred this morning. The thing is, you see, it must have been just about that time that something woke me up. I had the distinct impression that there had been a brilliant flash, somewhere outside."

Ino, also dressed in coveralls this morning, appeared among the distant sheds, trudging toward them. When he arrived, he provided more detail on the seismic event. "Quite sharp and apparently quite localized, not more than ten kilometers from here. Our system triangulated it well. I don't know when we've registered another event quite like it."

"What do you suppose it was?" Jen asked.

Ino hesitated minimally. "It could have been a very small spaceship crashing; or maybe a fairly large aircraft. But the only aircraft on Waterfall are the two little ones we have out in that far shed."

"A meteor, maybe?"

"I rather hope so. Otherwise a spacecraft just might be our most likely answer. And if it were a spacecraft from Brass Trumpet's force coming down here—crippled in the fighting, perhaps—we'd have heard from him on the subject, I should think."

The remaining alternative hung in the air unvoiced. Jenny bit her lip. By now, Brass Trumpet must be long gone from the system, and impossible of recall, his ships outspacing light and radio waves alike in pursuit of the enemy force.

In a voice more worried than before, Glenna was saying: "Of

course if it was some enemy unit, damaged in the battle, then I suppose the crash is likely to have completed its destruction."

"I'd better tell you," Jenny blurted in. And in a couple of sentences she described the peculiar tracks.

Ino stared at her with frank dismay. "I was going to roll out an aircraft . . . but let me take a look at those tracks first."

The quickest way to reach them was undoubtedly on foot, and the gnarled man trotted off along the beach path at such a pace that Jenny had difficulty keeping up. Glenna remained behind, saying she would let Claus know what was going on.

Moving with flashes of former athletic grace, Ino reached the nearest of the tracks and dropped to one knee beside it, just as Claus had done. "Do the others look just like this?"

"As nearly as I could tell. We didn't get close to all of them."

"That's no animal I ever saw." He was up again already, trotting back toward the base. "I don't like it. Let's get airborne, all of us."

"I always pictured berserkers as huge things."

"Most of 'em are. Some are small machines, for specialized purposes."

"I'll run into the house and tell the others to get ready to take off," Jenny volunteered as they sped into the compound.

"Do that. Glenna will know what to bring, I expect. I'll get a flyer rolled out of the shed."

Running, Jen thought as she hurried into the house, gave substance to a danger that might otherwise have existed only in the mind. Could it be that Ino, with the horrors in his memory, was somewhat too easily alarmed where berserkers were concerned?

Glenna and Claus, who had just changed into coveralls, met her in the common room. She was telling them of Ino's decision to take to the air, and thinking to herself that she had better change out of her beach garb also, when the first outcry sounded from somewhere outside. It was less a scream than a baffled-sounded, hysterical laugh.

Glenna pushed past her at once, and in a moment was out the door and running. Exchanging a glance with her husband, Jenny turned and followed, Claus right at her heels.

The strange cry came again. Far ahead, past Glenna's running figure, the door of the aircraft shed had been slid back, and in its opening a white figure appeared outlined. A figure that reeled drunkenly and waved its arms.

Glenna turned aside at the tractor shed, where one of the small ground vehicles stood ready. They were used for riding, hauling, pushing sand, to sculpt a pond into a better shape or slice away part of a too-obtrusive dune. It'll be faster than running, Jenny thought, as she saw the older woman spring into the driver's seat, and heard the motor *whoosh* quietly to life. She leaped aboard too. Claus shoved strongly at her back to make sure she was safely on, before he used both hands for his own grip. A grip was necessary because they were already rolling, and accelerating quickly.

Ino's figure, now just outside the shed, came hurtling closer with their own speed. He shook his arms at them again and staggered. Upon his chest he wore a brownish thing the size of a small plate, like some great medallion that was so heavy it almost pulled him down. He clawed at the brown plate with both hands, and suddenly his coveralls in front were splashed with scarlet. He bellowed words which Jenny could not make out.

Claus gripped Glenna's shoulders and pointed. A dozen or more brown plates were scuttling on the brown, packed sand, between the aircraft shed and the onrushing tractor. The tracks they drew were faint replicas of those that had lined the softer sand along the beach. Beneath each saucerlike body, small legs blurred, reminding Claus of something recently seen, something he could not stop to think of now.

The things had nothing like the tractor's speed but still they were in position to cut it off. Glenna swerved no more than slightly, if at all, and one limbed plate disappeared beneath a wheel. It came up at once with the wheel's rapid turning, a brown blur seemingly embedded in the soft, fat tire, resisting somehow the centrifugal force that might have thrown it off.

Ino had gone down with, as Claus now saw, three of the things fastened on his body, but he somehow fought back to his feet just as the tractor jerked to a halt beside him. If Claus could have stopped to analyze his own mental state, he might have said he lacked the time to be afraid. With a blow of his fist he knocked one of the attacking things away from Ino, and felt the surprising weight and hardness of it as a sharp pang up through his wrist.

All three dragging together, they pulled Ino aboard; Glenna was back in the driver's seat at once. Claus kicked another attacker off, then threw open the lid of the tractor's toolbox. He grabbed the longest, heaviest metal tool displayed inside.

A swarm of attackers were between them and the aircraft shed; and the shadowed shape of a flyer, just inside, was spotted with them too. As Glenna gunned the engine, she turned the tractor at the same time, heading back toward the main building and the sea beyond. In the rear seat, Jenny held Ino. He bled on everything, and his eyes were fixed on the sky while his mouth worked in terror. In the front, Claus fought to protect the driver and himself.

A brown plate scuttled onto the cowling, moving for Glenna's hands on the controls. Claus swung, a baseball batter, bright metal blurring at the end of his extended arms. There was a hard, satisfying crunch, as of hard plastic or ceramic cracking through. The brown thing fell to the floor, and he caught a glimpse of dull limbs still in motion before he caught it with a foot and kicked it out onto the flying ground.

Another of the enemy popped out from somewhere onto the dash. He pounded at it, missed when it seemed to dodge his blows. He cracked its body finally; but still it clung on under the steering column, hard to get at, inching toward Glenna's fingers. Claus grabbed it with his left hand, felt a lance. Not until he had thrown the thing clear of the tractor did he look at his hand and see two fingers nearly severed.

At the same moment, the tractor engine died, and they were rolling to a silent stop, with the sea and the small dock Glenna had been steering for only a few meters ahead. Under the edge of the engine cowling another of the enemy appeared, thrusting forward a limb that looked like a pair of ceramic pliers, shredded electrical connectors dangling in its grip.

The humans abandoned the tractor in a wordless rush. Claus, one hand helpless and dripping blood, aided the women with Ino as best he could. Together they half-dragged, half-carried him across the dock and rolled him into a small, open boat, the only craft at once available. In moments Glenna had freed them from the dock and started the motor, and they were headed out away from shore.

Away from shore, but not into the sea. They were separated from deep-blue and choppy ocean by a barrier reef or causeway, one of the features that had made this coast desirable for life-seeding base. The reef, a basically natural structure of sand and rock deposited by waves and currents, was about a hundred meters from the shore, and stretched in either direction as far as vision carried. Running from beach to reef, artificial walls or low causeways of fused rock separated ponds of various sizes.

"We're in a kind of square lagoon here," Glenna told Jenny, motioning for her to take over the job of steering. "Head for that far corner. If we can get there ahead of them, we may be able to lift the boat over the reef and get out."

Jen nodded, taking the controls. Glenna slid back to a place beside her husband, snapped open the boat's small first-aid kit, and began applying pressure bandages.

Claus started to try to help, saw the world beginning to turn gray around him, and slumped back against the gunwale; no use to anyone if he passed out. Ino looked as if he had been attacked, not by teeth or claws or knives, but by several sets of nail-pullers and wire-cutters. His chest still rose and fell, but his eyes were closed now and he was gray with shock. Glenna draped a thermal blanket over him.

Jen was steering around the rounded structure, not much bigger than a phone booth, protruding above the water in the middle of the pond. Most of the ponds and bays had similar observation stations. Claus had looked into one or two and he thought now that there was nothing in them likely to be of any help. More first-aid kits, perhaps—but what Ino needed was the big medirobot back at the house.

And he was not going to get it. By now the building complex must be overrun by the attackers. Berserkers . . .

"Where can we find weapons?" Claus croaked at Glenna.

"Let's see that hand. I can't do any more for Ino now . . . I'll bandage this. If you mean guns, there are a couple at the house, somewhere in storage. We can't go back there now."

"I know."

Glenna had just let go his hand when from the front seat there came a scream. Claws and a brown saucer-shape were climbing in over the gunwale at Jenny's side. Had the damned thing come aboard somehow with them, from the tractor? Or was this pond infested with them too?

In his effort to help drag Ino to the boat, Claus had abandoned his trusty wrench beside the tractor. He grabbed now for the best substitute at hand, a small anchor at the end of a chain. His overhand swing missed Jenny's head by less than he had planned, but struck the monster like a mace. It fell into the bottom of the boat, vibrating its limbs, as Claus thought, uselessly; then he realized that it was making a neat hole.

His second desperation-swing came down upon it squarely. One sharp prong of the anchor broke a segment of the brown casing clean away, and something sparked and sizzled when the sea came rushing in—

—seawater rushing—

—into the bottom of the boat—

The striking anchor had enlarged the hole that the enemy had begun. The bottom was split, the boat was taking water fast.

Someone grabbed up the sparking berserker, inert now save for internal fireworks, and hurled it over the side. Glenna threw herself forward, taking back the wheel, and Jenny scrambled aft, to help one-handed Claus with bailing.

The boat limped, staggered, gulped water and wallowed on toward the landbar. It might get them that far, but forget the tantalizing freedom of blue surf beyond . . .

Jenny started to say something to her husband, then almost shrieked again, as Ino's hand, resurgently alive, came up to catch her wrist. The old man's eyes were fixed on hers with tremendous purpose. He gasped out words, and then fell back unable to do more.

The words first registered with Jenny as: ". . . need them . . . do the splashers . . ." It made no sense.

Glenna looked back briefly, then had to concentrate on boathandling. In another moment the fractured bottom was grating over rock. Claus scrambled out and held the prow against the above-water portion of the reef. The women followed, got their footing established outside the boat, then turned to lift at Ino's inert form.

Jenny paused. "Glenna, I'm afraid he's gone."

"No!" Denial was fierce and absolute. "Help me!"

Jen almost started to argue, then gave in. They got Ino up into a fireman's-carry position on Claus's shoulders; even with a bad hand he was considerably stronger than either of the women. Then the three began to walk west along the reef. At high tide, as now, it was a strip of land no more than three or four meters wide, its low crest half a meter above the water. Waves of any size broke over it. Fortunately today the surf was almost calm.

Claus could feel the back of his coverall and neck wetting with Ino's blood. He shifted the dead weight on his shoulders. All right, so far. But his free hand, mutilated, throbbed.

He asked: "How far are we going, Glenna?"

"I don't know." The woman paced ahead—afraid to look at her husband now?—staring into the distance. "There isn't any place. Keep going."

Jenny and Claus exchanged looks. For want of any better plan at the moment, they kept going. Jen took a look back. "They're on the reef, and on the shore too, following us. A good distance back."

Claus looked, and looked again a minute later. Brown speckles by the dozens followed, but were not catching up. Not yet.

Now they were passing the barrier of fused rock separating the pond in which they had abandoned the boat from its neighbor. The enemy moving along the shore would intercept them, or very nearly, if they tried to walk the barrier back to land.

Ahead, the reef still stretched interminably into a sun-dazzled nothingness.

"What's in this next pond, Glenna?" Claus asked, and knew a measure of relief when the gray-haired woman gave a little shake of her head and answered sensibly.

"Grouper. Some other fish as food stock for them. Why?"

"Just wondering. What'll we run into if we keep on going in this direction?"

"This just goes on. Kilometer after kilometer. Ponds, and bays, and observations stations—I say keep going because otherwise they'll catch us. What do you think we ought to do?"

Claus abruptly stopped walking, startling the women. He let the dead man slide down gently from his shoulders. Jen looked at her husband, examined Ino, shook her head.

Claus said: "I think we've got to leave him."

Glenna looked down at Ino's body once, could not keep looking at him. She nodded fiercely, and once more led the way.

A time of silent walking passed before Jenny at Claus's side began: "If they're berserkers . . ."

"What else?"

"Well, why aren't we all dead already? They don't seem very . . . efficiently designed for killing."

"They must be specialists," Claus mused. "Only a small part of a large force, a part Brass Trumpet missed when the rest moved on or was destroyed. Remember, we were wondering if Atlantis was their real target? These are special machines, built for . . . underwater work, maybe. Their ship must have been wrecked in the fighting and had to come down. When they found themselves on this planet they must have come down to the sea for a reconnaissance, and then decided to attack first by land. Probably they saw the lights of the base before they crash-landed. They know which life-form they have to deal with first, on any planet. Not very efficient, as you say. But they'll keep coming at us till they're all smashed or we're all dead."

Glenna had slowed her pace a little and was looking toward the small observation post rising in the midst of the pond that they were passing. "I don't think there's anything in any of these stations that can help us. But I can't think of anywhere else to turn."

Claus asked: "What's in the next pond after this?"

"Sharks . . . ah. That might be worth a try. Sometimes they'll snap at anything that moves. They're small ones, so I think our risk will be relatively small if we wade out to the middle."

Claus thought to himself that he would rather end in the belly of a live shark than be torn to pieces by an impersonal device. Jen was willing also to take the chance.

They did not pause again till they were on the brink of the shark pond. Then Glenna said: "The water will be no more than three or four feet deep the way we're going. Stay together and keep splashing as we go. Claus, hold that bad hand up; mustn't drip a taste of blood into the water."

And in they went. Only when they were already splashing waist-deep did Claus recall Ino's blood wetting the back of his coverall. But he was not going to stop just now to take it off.

The pond was not very large; a minute of industrious wading, and they were climbing unmolested over the low, solid railing of the observation post rising near its middle. Here was space for two people to sit comfortably, sheltered from weather by a transparent dome and movable side panels. In the central console were instruments that continually monitored the life in the surrounding pond. Usually, of course, the readings from all ponds would be monitored in the more convenient central station attached to the house.

The three of them squeezed in, and Glenna promptly opened a small storage locker. It contained a writing instrument that looked broken, a cap perhaps left behind by some construction worker, and a small spider—another immigrant from Earth, of course—who might have been blown out here by the wind. That was all.

She slammed the locker shut again. "No help. So now it's a matter of waiting. They'll obviously come after us through the water. The sharks may snap up some of them before they reach us. Then we must be ready to move on before we are surrounded. It's doubtful, and risky, but I can't think of anything else to try."

Claus frowned. "Eventually we'll have to circle around, get back to the buildings."

Jen frowned at him. "The berserkers are there, too."

"I don't think they will be, now. You see—"

Glenna broke in: "Here they come."

The sun had climbed, and was starting to get noticeably hot. It came to Claus's mind, not for the first time since their flight had started, that there was no water for them to drink. He held his left arm up with his right, trying to ease the throbbing.

Along the reef where they had walked, along the parallel shore—and coming now over the barrier from the grouper pond—plate-sized specks of brown death were flowing. There were several dozen of them, moving more slowly than hurried humans could move, almost invisible in the shimmer of sun and sea. Some plopped into the water of the shark pond as Claus watched.

"I can't pick them up underwater," Glenna announced. She was twiddling the controls of the station's instruments, trying to catch the enemy on one of the screens meant for observing marine life. "Sonar . . . motion detectors . . . water's too murky for simple video."

Understanding dawned for Claus. "That's why they're not metal! Why they're comparatively fragile. They're designed for avoiding detection by underwater defenses, on Atlantis I suppose, for infiltrating and disabling them."

Jen was standing. "We'd better get moving before we're cut off."

"In another minute." Glenna was still switching from one video pickup to another around the pond. "I'm sure we have at least that much to spare . . . ah."

One of the enemy had appeared on screen, sculling toward the camera at a modest pace. It looked less lifelike than it had in earlier moments of arm's-length combat.

Now, entering the picture from the rear, a shark.

Claus was not especially good on distinguishing marine species. But this portentous and somehow familiar shape was identifiable at once, not to be confused even by the non-expert, it seemed, with that of any other kind of fish.

Claus started to say, He's going right past. But the shark was not. Giving the impression of afterthought, the torpedo-shape swerved back. Its mouth opened and the berserker device was gone.

The people watching made wordless sounds. But Jen took the others by an arm apiece. "We can't bet all of them will be eaten—let's get moving."

Claus already had one leg over the station's low railing when the still surface of the pond west of the observation post exploded. Leaping clear of the water, the premiere killer of Earth's oceans twisted in mid-air, as if trying to snap at its own belly. It fell back, vanishing in a hill of lashed-up foam. A moment later it jumped again, still thrashing.

In the fraction of a second when the animal was clearly visible, Claus watched the dark line come into being across its white belly as if traced there by an invisible pen. It was a short line that a moment later broadened and evolved in blood. As the fish rolled on its back something dark and pointed came into sight, spreading the edges of the hole. Then the convulsing body of the shark had vanished, in an eruption of water turned opaque with its blood.

The women were wading quickly away from the platform in the opposite direction, calling him to follow, hoping aloud that the remaining sharks would be drawn to the dying one. But for one moment longer Claus lingered, staring at the screen. It showed the roiling bloody turmoil of killer fish converging, and out of this cloud the little berserker emerged, unfazed by shark's teeth or digestion, resuming its methodical progress toward the humans, the life-units that could be really dangerous to the cause of death.

Jen tugged at her husband, got him moving with them. In her exhausted brain a nonsense-rhyme was being generated: *Bloody water hides the slasher, seed them, heed them, sue the splashers* . . .

No!

As the three completed their water-plowing dash to the east edge of the pond, and climbed out, Jenny took Glenna by the arm. "Something just came to me. When I was tending Ino—he said something before he died."

They were walking east along the barrier reef again. "He said smashers," Jen continued. "That was it. Lead them or feed them, to the smashers. But I still don't understand—"

Glenna stared at her for a moment, an almost frightening gaze. Then she stepped between the young couple and pushed them forward.

Two ponds down she turned aside, wading through water that splashed no higher than their calves, directly toward another observation post that looked just like the last.

"We won't be bothered in here," she assured them. "We're too big. Of course, of course. Oh, Ino. I should have thought of this myself. Unless we should happen to step right on one, but there's very little chance of that. They wait in ambush most of the time, in holes or under rocks."

"They?" Injury and effort were taking toll on Claus. He leaned on Jenny's shoulder now.

Glenna glanced back impatiently. "Mantis shrimp is the common name. They're stomatopods, actually."

"Shrimp?" The dazed query was so soft that she may not have heard it.

A minute later they were squeezed aboard the station and could rest again. Above, clean morning clouds were building to enormous height, clouds that might have formed in the unbreathed air of Earth five hundred million years before.

"Claus," Jen asked, when both of them had caught their breath a little, "what were you saying a while ago, about circling back to the house?"

"It's this way," he said, and paused to organize his thoughts. "We've been running to nowhere, because there's nowhere on this world we can get help. *But the berserkers can't know that.* I'm assuming they haven't scouted the whole planet, but just crash-landed on it. For all they know, there's another colony of humans just down the coast. Maybe a town, with lots of people, aircraft, weapons . . . so for them it's an absolute priority to cut us off before we can give a warning. Therefore every one of their units must be committed to the chase. And if we can once get through them or around them, we can outrun them home, to vehicles and guns and food and water. How we get through them or around I haven't figured out yet. But I don't see any other way."

"We'll see," said Glenna. Jen held his hand, and looked at him as if his idea might be reasonable. A distracting raindrop hit him on the face, and suddenly a shower was spattering the pond. With open mouths the three survivors caught what drops they could. They tried spreading Jenny's robe out to catch more, but the rain stopped before the cloth was wet.

"Here they come," Glenna informed them, shadowing her eyes from re-emergent sun. She started tuning up the observing gear aboard the station.

Claus counted brown saucer-shapes dropping into the pond. Only nineteen, after all.

"Again, I can't find them with the sonar," Glenna muttered. "We'll try the television—there."

A berserker unit—for all the watching humans could tell, it was the same one that the shark had swallowed—was centimetering its tireless way toward them, walking the bottom in shallow, sunlit water. Death was walking. A living thing might run more quickly, for a time, but life would tire. Or let life oppose it, if life would. Already it had walked through a shark, as easily as traversing a mass of seaweed.

"There," Glenna breathed again. The advancing enemy had detoured slightly around a rock, and a moment later a dancing ripple of movement had emerged from hiding somewhere to follow in its path. The pursuer's score or so of tiny legs supported in flowing motion a soft-looking, roughly segmented tubular body. Its sinuous length was about the same as the enemy machine's diameter, but in contrast the follower was aglow with life, gold marked in detail with red and green and brown, like banners carried forward above an advancing column. Long antennae waved as if for balance above bulbous, short-stalked eyes. And underneath the eyes a coil of heavy forelimbs rested, not used for locomotion.

"Odonodactylus syllarus," Glenna murmured. "Not the biggest species—but maybe big enough."

"What are they?" Jen's voice was a prayerful whisper.

"Well, predators . . ."

The berserker, intent on its own prey, ignored the animate ripple that was overtaking it, until the smasher had closed almost to contact range. The machine paused then, and started to turn.

Before it had rotated itself more than halfway its brown body was visibly jerked forward, under some striking impetus from the smasher too fast for human eyes to follow. The *krak!* of it came clearly through the audio pickup. Even before the berserker had regained its balance, it put forth a tearing-claw like that which had opened the shark's gut from inside.

Again the invisible impact flicked from a finger-length away. At each spot where one of the berserker's feet touched bottom, a tiny spurt of sand jumped up with the transmitted shock. Its tearing claw now dangled uselessly, hard ceramic cracked clean across.

"I've never measured a faster movement by anything that lives. They strike with special dactyls—well, with their elbows, you might say. They feed primarily on hard-shelled crabs and clams and snails. That was just a little one, that Ino gave you as a joke. One as long as my hand can hit something like a four-millimeter bullet—and some of these are longer."

Another hungry smasher was now coming swift upon the track

of the brown, shelled thing that looked so like a crab. The second smasher's eyes moved on their stalks, calculating distance. It was evidently of a different species than the first, being somewhat larger and of a variant coloration. Even as the berserker, which had just put out another tool, sharp and wiry, and cut its first assailant neatly in half, turned back, Claus saw—or almost saw or imagined that he saw—the newcomer's longest pair of forelimbs unfold and return. Again grains of sand beneath the two bodies, living and unliving, jumped from the bottom. With the concussion white radii of fracture sprang out across a hard, brown surface . . .

Four minutes later the three humans were still watching, in near-perfect silence. A steady barrage of *kraks,* from every region of the pond, were echoing through the audio pickups. The video screen still showed the progress of the first individual combat.

"People sometimes talk about sharks as being aggressive, as terrible killing machines. Gram for gram, I don't think they're at all in the same class."

The smashing stomatopod, incongruously shrimp-like, gripping with its six barb-studded smaller forelimbs the ruined casing of its victim—from which a single ceramic walking-limb still thrashed—began to drag it back to the rock from where its ambush had been launched. Once there, it propped the interstellar terror in place, a Lilliputian monster blacksmith arranging metal against anvil. At the next strike, imaginable if not visible as a double backhand snap from the fists of a karate master, fragments of tough casing literally flew through the water, mixed now with a spill of delicate components. What, no soft, delicious meat in sight as yet? The *smash* again . . .

An hour after the audio pickups had reported their last *krak,* the three humans walked toward home, unmolested through the shallows and along a shore where no brown saucers moved.

When Ino had been brought home, and Claus's hand seen to, the house was searched for enemy survivors. Guns were got out, and the great gates in the sand-walls closed to be on the safe side. Then the two young people sent Glenna to a sedated rest.

Her voice was dazed, and softly, infinitely tired. "Tomorrow we'll feed them, something real."

"This afternoon," said Claus. "When you wake up. Show me what to do."

"Look at this," called Jen a minute later, from the common room.

One wall of the smallest aquarium had been shattered outward. Its tough glass lay sharded on the carpet, along with a large stain of water and the soft body of a small creature, escaped and dead.

Jen picked it up. It was much smaller than its cousins out in the pond, but now she could not mistake the shape, even curled loosely in her palm.

Her husband came in and looked over her shoulder. "Glenna's still muttering. She just told me they can stab, too, if they sense soft meat in contact. Spear-tips on their smashers when they unfold them all the way. So you couldn't hold him like that if he was still alive." Claus's voice broke suddenly, in a delayed reaction.

"Oh, yes I could." Jen's voice too. "Oh, yes I could indeed."

FLESH AND THE IRON

Larry S. Todd

Marigold stepped cautiously along the ledge, one hand tightly gripping his great shol-wood bow, the other holding his three gaily-painted trophy skulls away from his chest plates. The skulls tockled hollowly against one another but made no other sound.

He stopped and stared out across the scrub-jungle, straining his telescopic lenses and infrared pickups for a glance of Flesh, but none of the elusive creatures were to be seen, which was not to say that none were watching him. Slowly Marigold began inching along the limestone ledge again, but paid little attention to the pebbles rolling beneath his plastic feet till he nearly slipped and fell.

Raucous colors dancing across the semaphore in his face and motors whining nervously, he jerked himself back to safety. Cautiously looking over the ledge, he reflected ruefully upon his unparalleled ability to stand himself out on high, narrow ledges. Then, shrugging to adjust the quiver of arrows on his back, he took out along the ledge again.

It dropped rapidly, then, and Marigold had a difficult time retaining his balance. Finally he decided to be safe rather than dead and took the remaining hundred feet very slowly, avoiding any large rocks which could scratch his armor. The Mill was always very touchy about scratched plating.

Attaining the ground safely, Marigold gave the landscape another quick scan to assure himself that no Flesh lurked nearby. Small and soft as they were, they could still be very fast and very nasty. The first Flesh whose skull Marigold had taken had chosen to vent his pleasure at being captured by swinging a heavy club at Marigold's right leg and relieving him of the responsibility thereof. The Mill had been so displeased about having to replace the leg that she demanded he hunt down a skull for her in payment, to be kept in her private treasury. So, though three skulls hung on Marigold's chest, he had actually slain four Flesh.

The vista seemed harmless, so the robot cast off into the bushes, heading for a distant blue ridge where a team of Flesh had been reported.

Marigold was on the hunt.

He was uncertain whether it would prove to be a fruitful hunt, for his past three had been blanks. He had not so much as even seen a Flesh. Nor had many of his Mill-brethren; their hunts were bringing in sparse returns, too. For a while there had been quite a few Flesh about; not only the number of new skulls but the amount of Mill-Brethren who never returned indicated this. But the days were getting lean, and more and more hunters returned without skulls and even without scratches to show they had met or seen a Flesh.

It was hard to say whether the Mill was pleased or not by this. The great metal and plastic behemoth, a large dark cube with dozens of little stalls and incomprehensible machinery inside, had been uncommunicative recently, and if she spoke at all, it was usually petulant nagging about inconsequential subjects. As often as not, her anger was directed at Marigold. The replacement leg had caused her to label him as careless.

At first, all she had ever given him was a scolding, but every time he returned with scratches, she cut into him anew, till extreme embarrassment had caused him to take longer and longer hunting trips. These week-long forays never amounted to anything, but at least they kept the critical speakers of the Mill at a comfortable distance. He dreaded the day when she would take to complaining about their length.

As he strolled through the gorse, mirror-bright armor flickering in the sun, he became nervously aware of how late in the afternoon it was. Late afternoon was not a good time to be abroad, for Flesh could lurk behind sun-warmed rocks and never have their body heat give them away, and the gentle breezes that blew across the plain rattled the bushes much more than any smart Flesh would. Even their beige-pink bodies matched the color of the dried grasses and bushes, and Marigold knew all too well that one could be behind him at that very moment, club held high . . .

He checked, and finding nothing there, decided to make sure it stayed that way. He increased his pace till he was moving at a rapid walk, almost a jog.

But not for long; for he was over eight feet tall and clearly visible for miles, and his heavy tread made him think uncomfortably about Flesh putting their ears to the ground and hearing him come.

The brush got thicker and Marigold became painfully cognizant of the tremendous rustling and scraping he made as he forced himself through the dry bushes. A quick look back showed him a trail a blind Flesh could follow with a walking-stick, to beat him to extinction with the stick. He looked around him, motors whining high and shrill, and all his relays on the verge of tripping. He forgot about the ridge and just ran off, feeling the eyes of all the Flesh in creation on his back, casting lots for his radar antenna and listening to the music of his newly-squeaking hip and his violent crashing through the furze. Almost on the verge of panic, he dashed through the thickets and nearly fell into a small stream. With a sudden internal *splap* all his systems shut down to clear his brain for dealing with this new obstacle. All of this took less than a second but was enough time for the Flesh sitting across the stream to leap into frantic activity.

The Iron had crept up on him so silently, yet so fast, that Locker Bannock was almost caught dead. But the thing stood there dumbly, so he grabbed his hook-club and raced in on the machine, screaming at it to confuse it.

The Iron jerked convulsively as Bannock cleared the stream; moving with stupid slowness, it tried to strike him with a great rubber hand. The hook-spike on Bannock's club tore into the hand and cut through it, but caught. The arm followed through with its swing and tore the club from his grasp. Howling in terror, he dove for it and caught it just as the Iron reached out for and gripped his ankle.

The Flesh and the Iron were both stretched out along the ground, both somewhat stunned and both ultimately captured.

Bannock twisted himself about for a better look at his captive captor, who tightened the grip on his ankle till the man hissed and turned red in the face. Marigold recognized a red semaphore signal as meaning annoyance, so he loosened his grip. Bannock looked at him and thought furiously.

So the Iron could break his leg. The creature was stretched out along the ground as he was, so at least it couldn't bang him around against anything. If he sacrificed his ankle he could stave in its head.

Marigold stared thoughtfully at the Flesh, wholly aware of this possibility and not wanting to tempt fate. He recalled that his first Flesh had fought very creditably with a broken arm and leg. Flesh and Iron watched each other for a long time.

Finally the Flesh shrugged and began to pull himself erect. With a crackle of alarm from his speaker, Marigold gripped the ankle tighter, and the Flesh's face twisted and contorted.

"Stop!" he cried. "I'm only sitting up!" Marigold hesitantly relaxed his grip, but did not release the Flesh. "You sit up, too," said the Flesh, and Marigold obliged him, since the order seemed as good an idea as any.

II

For five minutes more they sat that way, silently musing one another and considering the ridiculous situation they now found themselves in. The Flesh could swing his club and crush Marigold's good arm before it could squeeze his ankle, but the lame left arm was still a formidable bludgeon.

"Well, shall we sit here all afternoon or shall we be about our business and try to kill one another?" asked the Flesh, and he spat into the dust.

Being at a loss for words, Marigold did not reply.

The Flesh spoke again. "I see you're a three-skull iron. I'm a four tenna man myself." He swung a necklace out of his tunic and displayed the four reception cones strung on a leather thong. Marigold could think of only one way that the Flesh could have gotten those antennae.

"You have . . . stopped . . . four Mill-brethren?"

"That what you call each other? Yeh. I have. Five, actually, but I never did claim that fifth tenna 'cause a few of your Mill brethren were coming up fast. Discretion is better than valor."

"I have stopped four Flesh, but I paid one skull to the Mill for a new leg."

Bannock suddenly grinned, his fancy struck by the way in which he and his mortal enemy were comparing hunting records. Then he scowled, for his present situation held little possibility for humor and levity. He examined the broken arm of Marigold, then plucked a small leather pouch from his bandolier and began to eat something. "You interrupted my dinner, Iron," he accused.

Marigold watched the Flesh stuff the crumbly brown cakes into the large aperture in his head, and felt obliged to say something. He winced inside, for this was an extremely embarrassing position to be in. If the Mill ever heard of it . . .

"What are you doing, Flesh?"

"The name's Locker Bannock . . . call me Bannock. I'm eating."

"You're . . . eating?"

"Yeah." He looked sharply at Marigold's impassive features searching for expression. "Doing my equivalent to what you do when you fill yourself up with water. Only I have to do it a lot oftener than you. I haven't any fusion plant inside of me."

"What is a fusion plant?"

"You, Iron, have carried a fusion plant around inside of you since you . . . all your so-called life, and you don't know what it is?"

"I have never even heard of a fusion plant. I do not know what is inside of me—only the Mill knows."

"The Mill! You Iron are like little ants," Bannock muttered, for the edification of nobody in particular. "You even have a Queen. Ah, fist." He finished eating, wiped his mouth with the back of his hand and rolled over toward the robot. "Okay. I'll explain what's inside of you."

He took a sharp stone and began scratching little diagrams on the surface of a flat rock, expounding upon the contents of Marigold's chest, head and limbs. As he spoke, the Iron absent-mindedly let go his leg, but he quickly vetoed breaking away and trying to ambush Iron the next day. It could still strike out with that arm, catch him with the other. He finished the lecture.

"I don't think it will make any difference, though."

Marigold did not know what to make of that statement. He said so.

"What I meant," explained Bannock, "was that even if you know how you work inside, you won't really understand it. You're not equipped with enough mental machinery. For example, do you know why the gears in your arm work?"

"They go around and around?"

"You're guessing and you're wrong. That's how they turn. Why do they turn? Because force is applied to them and they are anchored in a particular way. It sounds pretty obvious, but I don't think you could really understand."

Marigold thought this over for a while, and agreed. But he added that only the Mill had to know, anyway.

"Yeah," murmured Bannock, and fell back to appraising his enemy.

It was getting quite late, and neither had moved from where they were. The sun was sinking low to the western horizon, and the night insects were beginning to make their rounds. Bannock swatted one and broke into the customary cursing. Marigold flashed green upon his semaphore, and Bannock held up the corpse of the offending neocop.

"Little Flesh, Iron. Pests." He tossed the insect away and looked up at the robot again.

"Iron, do you have a name or a serial number or something I can call you? You call me Bannock, I may as well call you something other than Iron."

"Yes. Marigold." He tapped a small brass flower inset in the ID disk at the base of his neck.

"Okay, Marigold, I'm getting cold — an unpleasant response to dropping temperature — and these bugs are eating me. Hadn't we better go someplace where I can rest?"

"Isn't this place as good as any?"

"No. For the reasons I outlined to you and others. Look, if you're worried I'm going to kill you by attacking your legs, I'm quite sure you could kill me while I did it to you. And I don't know how fast and accurate you are with that bow and arrow and I've no desire to find out. So come on . . ."

Marigold did not move.

"Come on, damn you!"

Marigold remained motionless.

"I'll clobber you . . ."

Marigold jerked to his feet and poised to strike Bannock, but the human danced back at little and motioned for peace. The robot made no other move, other than to nock the arrow. Bannock looked at him.

"Put that thing away," he said. He was aware that he was as good as dead, but he poised his club.

"I want your skull."

"That's reasonable. I want your tenna."

"If you dove into the water and walked along under it, I could not see you to stop you."

"It's not deep enough anyway. Put that thing away, will you? I don't want to wreck your legs."

Bannock knew too clearly that if the Iron did not put away the bow and arrow, he would have very little chance indeed of even coming near him, but the Iron was either none too smart or quite careless and did not see this. The robot slowly loosed the tension on the bowstring and replaced the arrow. "We have captured each other, Bannock. So that neither should escape from the other, let us bind each other to one another, and then go to your place to retire."

"I'm game. You have rope?"

Marigold snapped open a little cabinet in his metal belly and brought forth a long nylon cable. Bannock eyed it cautiously.

"I'll bet you can break it."

"I can't, and you would know it if I tried, anyway." Marigold hooked the clip at one end into a buckle on his hook and tossed the other end to Bannock.

Hand on club, the human tied it about his wrist, using a one-handed knot. "I'll walk to one side of you—the left side, so you can't grab the rope and rip off my right arm." He pointed with the club at a nearby tumble of rocks. "There's a cave over there. We'll go to it."

Marigold didn't care where they went, so long as it wasn't into a trap. As they walked, he kept his radar antenna pointed at Bannock, for he didn't want the Flesh to come at him suddenly, swinging the club and howling. But the Flesh kept its distance, whether aware of the surveillance or not.

Marigold reflected upon the Mill's calling him careless and unobservant and not very alert. He could easily agree that he was not very alert, for he knew that the Flesh had exposed himself to dangerous situations quite frequently, and quite willingly.

As he ran through his sensory memories, he located parts where the Flesh's heartbeat had sped up tremendously, as though it was taking a terrible risk. And these times coincided with the times Marigold had not paid careful attention to what he was doing. But the Flesh had not made any dangerous moves. But granting that it recognized its chances and seemed aware that they came quite often, it was apparently playing a game with Marigold. *You trust me and I'll trust you.* Marigold cautioned himself to watch for this; it could be some kind of a blind for future sneak attacks.

Bannock saw the antenna swing to cover him, and knew that the Iron was not entirely as dumb as it had been trying to make him think it was. He would have to keep this act up for a couple of days to provide any positive results.

III

They climbed a black tumble of basalt and granite and came to the cave, a fissure in the ground which widened into a chamber at the end. Bannock, after announcing that he was untying himself, retreated to a dark corner of the cave, talking all the while.

"Marigold, shall we forget this rope business tomorrow? It's a needless precaution, since I couldn't get very far from you and that bow. If you tried to break and run, I wouldn't have much luck in stopping you. You weigh over a ton, which implies a lot."

"Very well, we will not use it." Though Marigold recognized that he had given up a very good chance to catch the Flesh, simply by suddenly running over rough terrain, he determined that two could play at the game of simulated honesty.

Bannock came forth from the depths of the cave and dropped a load of dry wood on the floor. He lit it aflame and roasted his supper, a few chunks of meat from a leather pouch, and Marigold watched him dully.

After a while, he stood and said, "We Flesh sleep—like recharging our capacitors or something. You know? Anyway while I'm sleeping you could kill me, so I'm going to climb down into that little hole over there, where you can't reach me, and I'll sleep there."

As he dropped down into the small-mouthed pit, Bannock watched the Iron. He wouldn't leave during the night, unfortunately. He wanted his skull too much.

The following morning Bannock lit his fire again and roasted his breakfast. Marigold sat impassively on a rock, lit by golden radiance from the morning sun.

"Well, Marigold. It's about time we determined what we're going to do about each other. Any ideas?"

"I thought about it all last night. I could think of but one thing. Since neither of us wants to let the other go, for the risk of ambush, all we can reasonably do is have our fight and let that decide who gets what."

Bannock's heart leaped sickeningly. This was all he needed, since the broken arm could still kill him and the other was twice as deadly. He adopted a scorning manner.

"Won't work. I have an unfair advantage. You got a busted arm."

"I can use it as a club."

Bannock closed his eyes painfully, then sat on a rock and glared at Marigold. "All right, all right. We're both thinking the same thing. How do I get this guy to trust me enough for his guard to come down? No show-down, Marigold. Think again."

"We shall go to your settlement, and I will set you free."

"Huh?"

"I will take you to your settlement, and bind you with the rope so you will not try to bushwhack me, and I will depart."

"You came on that idea mighty fast. Sure, you'll escape, with my skull under your arm. The moment I drop my club you will swing that cleverly concealed knife — yes, I see it — and I'll be dead. No dice."

Marigold's semaphore filled with murkiness, and he strode silently out into the daylight to scan the morning landscape. He was silent.

"Marigold, try this adaptation of your plan. There's this big plain; we will walk to the middle; you will give me your arrows, and I will carry them to one side; you will carry yourself to the other. When I get to my side I'll put the arrows down and hightail it away. You can get them and not get bushwhacked. Follow me?"

"No. What if you do not return my arrows?"

Bannock spat into the dust. "Dumb Iron. How far do you think I could carry those arrows with you after me, and not expect to get caught? I don't need them. I don't have a bow, and if I put them down I could be a mile away before you got near."

Marigold grumbled blue on his semaphore, then asked, "Where is this plain you speak of?"

"See that ridge way off that way?" Bannock pointed. "Behind that. My settlement is a dozen or so kilometers from it." The last was untrue; his settlement was a good forty miles from the ridge, along it to the west, but there was no need in risking an armored attack of Iron against the town of Werser.

They set out.

Later in the day, Marigold's fractured arm began squeaking loudly and was becoming difficult for the Iron to move up as far as the shoulder joint. He showed numerous signs of dismay but Bannock did not seem to notice anything until the squeaking got quite loud.

"What's the trouble?"

"The arm." Marigold indicated the afflicted member. "It's hard to move."

"Oh, fist," swore Bannock. "I should have expected that. Still I'm surprised it wasn't a helluva lot worse. Or sooner."

"What is the matter?"

"Lubrication. You Iron have a built-in lube system, like my blood vessels, except they're not for lube. It keeps your joints moving smooth and silent."

Bannock fell behind the robot.

"What can I do about it?" Marigold asked.

"Nothing . . . except maybe hold that stump high in the air so you won't lose any more lube."

Marigold lifted the broken limb, finding that it moved very stubbornly. He heard Bannock snicker with subdued laughter. A rather humiliating thing, Marigold decided, if the Flesh thought it was so funny — unless the laughter was only a trick to distract him or put him off guard. Several times he considered swinging it down upon Bannock, but it firmly resisted all efforts to move it quickly; besides, the Flesh was smart and could be useful.

Marigold endured the humiliation.

"Marigold, what's that up ahead?" Bannock pointed toward a hill, at the crown of which the scrub grew thinner. In the tawny grass and dry brown bushes something gleamed brightly.

"A Mill-brother."

Bannock jerked uncomfortably, but Marigold was oblivious of this and went on describing what he saw. "He is — dead — that is the word, dead? He moves no more; in fact, I'd say he hasn't done any moving for a good many sunnycycles now."

"You're getting a wry, dry wit, Marigold. So he's dead, eh? That solves two problems in one stroke."

"Eh? I can see that in his current state, he won't come to my aid, but what is the other advantage?"

"Fist, can't you guess? It's to your advantage. Head this way."

The dead robot lay on the ground, parts of its stainless-steel plate worn off by weather to show the dusty yellow plastic beneath. There were lichens straggling up the side of its chest and head, and the reception core of the antenna had been twisted off. The legs were crumpled, but aside from that, there seemed to be little damage. Bannock crouched next to the corpse and tapped it lightly with a pebble, listening to the clicks. Marigold began getting impatient and shifted about on his feet, till Bannock suddenly jerked.

"Stop shifting about like that. I don't know if you've got ideas on my head or not, but stop it, damnit!"

"I wasn't . . ."

Bannock cut Marigold's defense short with a noncommittal grunt and returned to tapping on the hulk.

"What are you doing?"

"Getting a new arm for you." Bannock pried a panel from the back of the hulk, reached in, and tugged a little black box free from its position beneath the power plant. He undid a few snaps, opened it, and removed a handful of tools.

"It sure is a shame you Iron don't know about all the goodies you have stashed away inside of you. A little fooling around with his insides would have had this fellow still alive today." He paused to laugh sarcastically. "I'll bet your Mill doesn't even know she puts them inside of you. Siddown."

Marigold sat, and Bannock critically eyed the ruin of his arm. After cautioning the Iron against any sudden moves, he attached the elbow joint of the corpse with several of the tools. It fell away, and Bannock began performing the same operation on Marigold. The Iron twisted nervously and received a reverberating slam against his side with the wrench. "Stay still, damn your hide," growled Bannock. Marigold's arm fell off, and Bannock took the other and wrestled it into place. A few left motions with his wrench, a snap connection of some of the little tubes, pressure splices applied to the cables; and the arm was on.

"Try it out."

"It squeaks."

"Your lube system will take care of that pretty soon. It's in perfectly good condition itself. That hulk might have been dead, but all his parts were still sealed tight away. Everything above his hip-joint was in top-flight condition."

Marigold grunted with his semaphore, then stood up.

"Very good, Marigold," Bannock commented. "You didn't try to kill me right off or anything. Shall we go on our way?"

"It's getting late. You may want to sleep soon, am I wrong? And make your fire and cook your food?"

"You may be right," Bannock agreed, and began to gather dry wood. He brought it to a small hollow which was surrounded by tall trees, and there he cooked his supper.

IV

Marigold watched disconsolately, unable to direct his thoughts upon any one subject. He tried to think of new ways in which he could kill Bannock, but none came to his mind. The Flesh just seemed to *know* so damn much.

"Bannock?"

"Grnnnch?"

"How is it that you know so much about Iron?"

"I'm a junkman, if that means anything to you. No? Well, suppose some hunter comes in with a dead Iron, pulling it on a little cart or something, and he wants to use it for a servant or a farm laborer or sell it. Someone has to fix the Iron, and since most hunters are rather unremarkable as brains go, it won't be the hunter who does it. I do. Remember that dead Iron we saw today? Given a few weeks I could have him running again. I studied your anatomy for six years and I'm pretty sure I could make one of you from scrap parts alone. And hell . . . I think it's pretty obvious that I know more about you than your Mill does."

"I doubt it," Marigold replied stuffily.

"Doubt it if you want."

"If you know so much about us, why are you out hunting us like those stupid hunters?"

Bannock broke out laughing, rocking back and forth, and gasped, "If you're so smart why ain't you rich?" He stifled the chuckling. "Never expected to get that from an Iron."

Marigold blinked his semaphore in puzzlement.

"Well, Marigold, I'm out here hunting because I need spare parts. I don't come out here to hunt for Iron like you, still up and kicking. I look for ones like your benefactor back there. Use them in my shop." Marigold sat on his tree-stump. Bannock disturbed him a great deal, for he knew the man was smarter than he was, and quite a bit more self-confident, seeming to know an infinity of facts. The self-confidence disturbed him especially, for the Flesh could be leading him right into a trap and wouldn't let loose a peep. Still, there had been plenty of times when Bannock could have dispatched Marigold, and he had not taken advantage of them. Marigold wasn't so sure any more that this trustworthiness was so much a game on Bannock's part. It seemed to come so naturally to the Flesh. Still . . . Marigold squelched his thoughts and watched the fire burn. Bannock slept through the night high in a thick-trunked tree.

The first sunbeams of dawn sent the bugs fleeing over his face, and seeking refuge in his ears and nose, so Bannock spluttered awake, climbed back down the tree, and saw Marigold exactly as he had left him—hunched over on the stump looking at the ashes of the burnt-out fire. The Iron turned when Bannock landed in the shadowed turf.

"You slept all night."

"Right you are. Help me gather some firewood?" Presently a small fire was roasting Bannock's breakfast, and Marigold watched, as disconsolate as ever. As the human ate, he spoke to the machine. "Have you decided to let me carry your arrows across the clearing?"

"Yes. You may as well."

"Good." Bannock opened a case from his bandolier and began shaving and trimming his sandy mustache. As he did, he asked, "Marigold, why do you Iron hunt men?"

"Men?"

"Flesh, then. Why?"

"Oh. Because you hunt us."

"Well, then, why do you wear our skulls as ornaments?"

"Prestige, of course. To show we have adequately defended the home Mill."

"Reasonable. That's why we wear the receptors of your tennas—to show we've kept the Iron away from our settlements. The more we wear around our necks, the bigger and hairier and stronger we look in the eyes of the girls. It's good for social relations to be able to be dangerous." He swore when he cut a nick out of his lower lip. "Anyway, we could probably wipe a lot of you Iron out, if you weren't so useful."

Marigold didn't like that statement and let Bannock know.

"I don't care if you don't like it, Marigold. It happens to be true. If I know so almighty much about your insides, doesn't it indicate to you that I can pull a few wires in you and make your fusion plant cut loose all over the countryside? No. Of course you don't know. Anyway forget it. We don't wipe you all out because there aren't enough of us to do the job right and there are still too damn many of you."

"You threw a few words at me I don't know. Girls?"

"You've got a lot of questions, Marigold." Bannock gnawed at a fingernail. "But then you've got a helluva lot to learn. All right. What is there to life, for one of you Iron?"

"Why . . . uh . . . hunting, and seeing that the Mill . . ."

"Has a lot of metal-bearing rocks in her belly so she can make more Iron, right? Well, get this. What does *she* mean?"

"The Mill . . ."

"Of course, the Mill. It's always the Mill. *She* is also a word referring to the procreative aspect of something living, or semiliving, as you. You refer to another Iron as *he*, indicating the provider aspect. I've oversimplified it, but do you know where those words came from? They weren't invented by the Mill."

"No."

"Well. Does the Mill ever tell you where *she* comes from?" Marigold signalled negatively. "Okay. I'll tell you:

"Thousands of suncycles ago, this whole world was covered with a beautiful culture of wise and erudite people, all Flesh. There were great cities which extended miles into the air and miles underground, and you may have seen some of their ruins. It's from those that you get so much rusty metal. These Flesh originally came from some star high in the sky, and they communicated with the Flesh living on that star, just as I talk with you. Men had houses that could fly, provided with all possible comforts, and you Iron were the servants of men in those days.

"But something happened. I don't know what and none of the books explain what. Anyway, the great settlements toppled to the ground and millions of men were killed."

Marigold stopped him with a blue-green flash and a honk of derision. "Millions?" he asked. "Why there are hardly a million of you Flesh in the whole world."

"A million and a half within a thousand miles of here. But don't interrupt." Bannock resumed his explanation. "The remaining Flesh had to learn to live off the land, while all that you Iron had to do was throw assorted old junk into your Mills. And I guess the Mills forgot all about the Flesh having built them in the beginning. Anyway, when we started to need metal, we used you Iron, and then you began to fight back. So, here we are. Probably matched in strength, though I doubt there are as many of you as there are of us.

"Anyway, to get back to the subject—he and she. Any idea where the words came from?"

"From *Flesh?*"

"Yes indeed. From male and female Flesh." Bannock began to explain the facts of life.

Surprisingly, in the end, Marigold understood and believed most of it. The idea upset him no small amount, and he wandered off to think. He was too abstracted to bother watching the man, even.

Finally, Bannock called him to suggest they get going.

The robot jerked to his feet and flashed assent. He buckled his quiver back on, took his bow, and followed Bannock off toward the ridge. They hiked through a wide expanse of toss-furz, and Bannock swatted at the clouds of little spider-gnats that rose to sting him. Marigold did not pay any attention to the vehement cursing and slapping; and when they had passed the insects, Bannock noticed that the robot was wandering in a rather contemplative state, probably only following him and not watching him at all. He could easily be brained, then, and marked for future recovery, but Bannock decided to wait, since it seemed rather impolite to cut into someone's thoughts so suddenly and literally.

As the day began to get late, Marigold started to quiver with his late-afternoon apprehension.

Bannock stopped him and said, "Look, you're starting to get all nervous again. Cut it out. When you get nervous, you get careless, and that happened once too often already, from what you've told me. I caught you. So for fistsake, calm down. Nobody is going to brain you while you're able to kill me. Look—wouldn't you keep another Iron away from me, because I could kill you before he could do anything?"

Marigold flashed agreement, and his spirits began to improve. He had not noticed the fallacy of Bannock's reasoning that two Irons could not easily deal with one Flesh, but neither had Bannock.

The ridge was quite close now, and they could see a gash through it, where Bannock said a river flowed.

"The plain is just on the other side of the ridge. If we follow this ledge that leads along the side of that cliff, we can cut two days off our time."

"A ledge," Marigold mused doubtfully, but when Bannock threw him a questioning glance, he flashed accord and set out toward it. His ability to home in on ledges and cliffs had struck again.

V

As they walked along the edge of the river, Bannock began to realize what a position he was in. As leader, he was vulnerable to anything the Iron decided to do, such as putting an arrow through his back. But occasional backward glances showed him that the Iron held a clear conscience and was planning no such action.

The ground was rough with granite boulders scattered through the sere brown grass and rustling scratch-bushes, and the ridge was quite near, its base hidden by a huddle of dark crawberry trees. They reached it as the sun was nearing the horizon. Marigold felt the loose gravel footing of the path and raised a doubt.

"Hadn't we better leave the crossing till tomorrow? We might not be so sure of our footing in the dark. Even with all my machinery, I don't like trying it now."

Bannock shook his head. "Why bother? The crossing is less than a mile; it shouldn't take us more than twenty minutes. If it gets too dark for your tastes, just turn on that headlight of yours. We might as well get it over with."

Marigold hesitated to agree, but finally followed Bannock.

As they strode out onto the ledge, the last rays of daylight stained the cliff a flaming orange, bright enough to see clearly, and Marigold felt temporarily secure. But he kept going faster and tagging at the heels of Bannock. The man warned him several times against going so fast. But he did not really slow down until a rattling shower of dislodged pebbles nearly sent him flying into the rapids a hundred feet below. He sobered up fast and proceeded at a more leisurely pace.

Bannock turned a corner, then stuck his head back around.

"Slow down, Marigold. We've come to a bit of shaky footing." There was a dull stony creaking as Bannock moved. When Marigold rounded the corner, he saw the ledge here consisted of narrow slabs of horizontal rock, thrust out from the cliffside. They were unsupported beneath, and not very wide. The Iron eyed the tossing current below, which now made a tight curve around the base of the ridge, and the boulders upon which he would fall if he were incautious. He slowed as he crossed the indicated shelves of rock, but not enough. There was a sinister creaking, and the rock upon which Marigold stood shuddered. He stopped still.

"What's the trouble?" Bannock called. Then he turned back.

Marigold did not move other than to carefully, slowly, extend his bow to Bannock, who took it and put it aside. "The arrows," he whispered, as though the very weight of his breath would cause the rocks to fall.

The rock did not creak. Bannock looked uncomfortably at the Iron, thinking fast. Then he said, "Take your rope out of your belly and toss it to me, and for fistsake don't be careless as you usually are. Don't get panicky."

Marigold tightened all his motors and slowly reached for the rope. He buckled one end to a clip in his front, then flipped the other end to Bannock. The human caught it and quickly tied it to a projecting rock which looked capable of supporting the robot's weight, then turned back.

"All right, now. Be as careful as hell. Take one step. If you feel the rock twitch, stop still."

Marigold's motors whined, and his cables tensed as he lifted his foot and moved it gently forward. The rock creaked, and suddenly he panicked. His foot slapped heavily against the rock, which shuddered and fell away. Marigold spun free on the rope and slammed loudly against the side of the cliff, suspended above a two-hundred-foot fall by a thin nylon thread.

Bannock looked uneasily over the ledge.

"How the hell am I going to get you up here, anyway? You weigh a good ton, and I sure as hell can't lift that."

Marigold stopped the frightened turgid flow of colors on his semaphore and blazed forth a red so hot and angry that it seemed to bypass Bannock's eyes and burn directly into his brain.

"Why should *you* care, *Flesh*? You might as well cut the rope and let me fall, so I won't take your skull!"

Bannock looked at the Iron for a moment, then turned away, saying something foul and commonplace, and could be heard fidgetting with the rope. Marigold winced and expected a sudden fall, but the Flesh peered over the edge.

"The rope'll take you. Now what you must do is try and pull yourself up the wall. Prop your legs against it and try to walk up."

The Three Hunters had been out of Werser for five days and had not had noticeable success. They had seen four funny-looking Iron on a distant hillside, but when they got there, armor-piercing rockets ready in their wooden launchers, the Iron had gone. There was no spoor.

Tom Bigboy decided that they must have been the new Sky Iron that could fly, which some Mill away east had been experimenting with, if one could believe what the New Romans said. Red Williams agreed. Dall Fingal, disappointed at not having been able to show how good a marksman he was, made no comment.

They were coming to the Werser River for a drink, before they camped for the night, when there came a loud and sudden clang, a burst of surprised static, and the rumble of falling rocks.

"Clumsy Iron gone hung himself up," laughed Red Williams grimly, and the three headed for the sound.

High on a cliff, lit by the last rays of the sun, was a small human figure struggling with a rope, and on the other end was an Iron, struggling to climb onto the ledge.

"Goddamnit! It's Bannock! He was out looking for parts, and I guess they found him?"

Dall Fingal dourly stuffed a small rocket into the launcher, one lit the fuse with his electric lighter. The breech slammed shut, he aimed carefully, and the little projectile arced its fiery trail across the river and exploded against the rock holding the rope. The nylon cable parted, and the Iron scratched static through the silent dusk and fell bouncing and chunking from rock to rock.

To get where the Iron lay was a somewhat more difficult matter than the three had thought, for they had to go downstream a bit to ford the river. When they approached the Iron's corpse, they saw Bannock huddled over it.

"Uh-oh," mumbled Fingal. "He'll probably try to claim it."

"Look, man, you shot the damn thing, and he'd be dead if you hadn't done it. You tell him *that*!"

Thus resolved, the three hunters went up to the corpse and faced Bannock. But Bannock was not trying to wrest the tenna from the machine, as they had expected. His face was white and streaked with wetness, and his eyes were red and angry.

"Well, Bannock . . ."

The semaphore flickered a few last times, then died out. The Iron shuddered and settled to stillness.

"You bastards . . ." Locker Bannock said thickly. He glared at them with futile raging hatred.

A RELIC OF WAR

Keith Laumer

The old war machine sat in the village square, its impotent guns pointing aimlessly along the dusty street. Shoulder-high weeds grew rankly about it, poking up through the gaps in the two-yard-wide treads; vines crawled over the high, rust- and guano-streaked flanks. A row of tarnished enameled battle honors gleamed dully across the prow, reflecting the late sun.

A group of men lounged near the machine; they were dressed in heavy work clothes and boots; their hands were large and calloused, their faces weatherburned. They passed a jug from hand to hand, drinking deep. It was the end of a long workday and they were relaxed, good-humored.

"Hey, we're forgetting old Bobby," one said. He strolled over and sloshed a little of the raw whiskey over the soot-blackened muzzle of the blast cannon slanting sharply down from the forward turret. The other men laughed.

"How's it going, Bobby?" the man called.

Deep inside the machine there was a soft chirring sound.

"Very well, thank you," a faint, whispery voice scraped from a grill below the turret.

"You keeping an eye on things, Bobby?" another man called.

"All clear," the answer came: a bird-chirp from a dinosaur.

"Bobby, you ever get tired just setting here?"

"Hell, Bobby don't get tired," the man with the jug said. "He's got a job to do, old Bobby has."

"Hey, Bobby, what kind o'boy are you?" a plump, lazy-eyed man called.

"I am a good boy," Bobby replied obediently.

"Sure Bobby's a good boy." The man with the jug reached up

to pat the age-darkened curve of chromalloy above him. "Bobby's looking out for us."

Heads turned at a sound from across the square: the distant whine of a turbocar, approaching along the forest road.

"Huh! Ain't the day for the mail," a man said. They stood in silence, watching as a small, dusty cushion-car emerged from deep shadow into the yellow light of the street. It came slowly along to the plaza, swung left, pulled to a stop beside the boardwalk before a corrugated metal store front lettered BLAU-VELT PROVISION COMPANY. The canopy popped open and a man stepped down. He was of medium height, dressed in a plain city-type black coverall. He studied the store front, the street, then turned to look across at the men. He came across toward them.

"Which of you men is Blauvelt?" he asked as he came up. His voice was unhurried, cool. His eyes flicked over the men.

A big, youngish man with a square face and sunbleached hair lifted his chin.

"Right here," he said. "Who're you?"

"Crewe is the name. Disposal Officer, War Materiel Commission." The newcomer looked up at the great machine looming over them. "Bolo *Stupendous*, Mark XXV," he said. He glanced at the men's faces, fixed on Blauvelt. "We had a report that there was a live Bolo out here. I wonder if you realize what you're playing with?"

"Hell, that's just Bobby," a man said.

"He's town mascot," someone else said.

"This machine could blow your town off the map," Crewe said. "And a good-sized piece of jungle along with it."

Blauvelt grinned; the squint lines around his eyes gave him a quizzical look.

"Don't go getting upset, Mr. Crewe," he said. "Bobby's harmless—"

"A Bolo's never harmless, Mr. Blauvelt. They're fighting machines, nothing else."

Blauvelt sauntered over and kicked at a corroded treadplate. "Eighty-five years out in this jungle is kind of tough on machinery, Crewe. The sap and stuff from the trees eats chromalloy like it was sugar candy. The rains are acid, eat up equipment damn near as fast as we can ship it in here. Bobby can still talk a little, but that's about all."

"Certainly it's deteriorated; that's what makes it dangerous.

Anything could trigger its battle reflex circuitry. Now, if you'll clear everyone out of the area, I'll take care of it."

"You move kind of fast for a man that just hit town," Blauvelt said, frowning. "Just what you got in mind doing?"

"I'm going to fire a pulse at it that will neutralize what's left of its computing center. Don't worry; there's no danger—"

"Hey," a man in the rear rank blurted. "That mean he can't talk any more?"

"That's right," Crewe said. "Also, he can't open fire on you."

"Not so fast, Crewe," Blauvelt said. "You're not messing with Bobby. We like him like he is." The other men were moving forward, forming up in a threatening circle around Crewe.

"Don't talk like a fool," Crewe said. "What do you think a salvo from a Continental Siege Unit would do to your town?"

Blauvelt chuckled and took a long cigar from his vest pocket. He sniffed it, called out: "All right, Bobby—fire one!"

There was a muted clatter, a sharp *click*! from deep inside the vast bulk of the machine. A tongue of pale flame licked from the cannon's soot-rimmed bore. The big man leaned quickly forward, puffed the cigar alight. The audience whooped with laughter.

"Bobby does what he's told, that's all," Blauvelt said. "And not much of that." He showed white teeth in a humorless smile.

Crewe flipped over the lapel of his jacket; a small, highly polished badge glinted there. "You know better than to interfere with a Concordiat officer," he said.

"Not so fast, Crewe," a dark-haired, narrow-faced fellow spoke up. "You're out of line. I heard about you Disposal men. Your job is locating old ammo dumps, abandoned equipment, stuff like that. Bobby's not abandoned. He's town property. Has been for near thirty years."

"Nonsense. This is battle equipment, the property of the Space Arm—"

Blauvelt was smiling lopsidedly. "Uh-uh. We've got salvage rights. No title, but we can make one up in a hurry. Official. I'm the Mayor here, and District Governor."

"This thing is a menace to every man, woman, and child in the settlement," Crewe snapped. "My job is to prevent tragedy—"

"Forget Bobby," Blauvelt cut in. He waved a hand at the jungle wall beyond the tilled fields. "There's a hundred million square miles of virgin territory out there," he said. "You can do what you like out there. I'll even sell you provisions. But just leave our mascot be, understand?"

Crewe looked at him, looked around at the other men.

"You're a fool," he said. "You're all fools." He turned and walked away, stiff-backed.

In the room he had rented in the town's lone boardinghouse, Crewe opened his baggage and took out a small, gray-plastic-cased instrument. The three children of the landlord who were watching from the latchless door edged closer.

"Gee, is that a real star radio?" the eldest, a skinny, long-necked lad of twelve asked.

"No," Crewe said shortly. The boy blushed and hung his head.

"It's a command transmitter," Crewe said, relenting. "It's designed for talking to fighting machines, giving them orders. They'll only respond to the special shaped-wave signal this puts out." He flicked a switch, and an indicator light glowed on the side of the case.

"You mean like Bobby?" the boy asked.

"Like Bobby used to be." Crewe switched off the transmitter.

"Bobby's swell," another child said. "He tells us stories about when he was in the war."

"He's got medals," the first boy said. "Were you in the war, mister?"

"I'm not quite that old," Crewe said.

"Bobby's older'n grandad."

"You boys had better run along," Crewe said. "I have to . . ." He broke off, cocked his head, listening. There were shouts outside; someone was calling his name.

Crewe pushed through the boys and went quickly along the hall, stepped through the door onto the boardwalk. He felt rather than heard a slow, heavy thudding, a chorus of shrill squeaks, a metallic groaning. A red-faced man was running toward him from the square.

"It's Bobby!" he shouted. "He's moving! What'd you do to him, Crewe?"

Crewe brushed past the man, ran toward the plaza. The Bolo appeared at the end of the street, moving ponderously forward, trailing uprooted weeds and vines.

"He's headed straight for Spivac's warehouse!" someone yelled.

"Bobby! Stop there!" Blauvelt came into view, running in the machine's wake. The big machine rumbled onward, executed a half-left as Crewe reached the plaza, clearing the corner of a building by inches. It crushed a section of boardwalk to splinters, advanced across a storage yard. A stack of rough-cut lumber toppled, spilled across the dusty ground. The Bolo trampled a board fence, headed out across a tilled field. Blauvelt whirled on Crewe.

"This is your doing! We never had trouble before—"

"Never mind that! Have you got a field car?"

"We—" Blauvelt checked himself. "What if we have?"

"I can stop it—but I have to be close. It will be into the jungle in another minute. My car can't navigate there."

"Let him go," a man said, breathing hard from his run. "He can't do no harm out there."

"Who'd of thought it?" another man said. "Setting there all them years—who'd of thought he could travel like that?"

"Your so-called mascot might have more surprises in store for you," Crewe snapped. "Get me a car, fast! This is an official requisition, Blauvelt!"

There was a silence, broken only by the distant crashing of timber as the Bolo moved into the edge of the forest. Hundred-foot trees leaned and went down before its advance.

"Let him go," Blauvelt said. "Like Stinzi says, he can't hurt anything."

"What if he turns back?"

"Hell," a man muttered. "Old Bobby wouldn't hurt *us* . . ."

"That car," Crewe snarled. "You're wasting valuable time."

Blauvelt frowned. "All right—but you don't make a move unless it looks like he's going to come back and hit the town. Clear?"

"Let's go."

Blauvelt led the way at a trot toward the town garage.

The Bolo's trail was a twenty-five foot wide swath cut through the virgin jungle; the tread-prints were pressed eighteen inches into the black loam, where it showed among the jumble of fallen branches.

"It's moving at about twenty miles an hour, faster than we can go," Crewe said. "If it holds its present track, the curve will bring it back to your town in about five hours."

"He'll sheer off," Blauvelt said.

"Maybe. But we won't risk it. Pick up a heading of 270°, Blauvelt. We'll try an intercept by cutting across the circle."

Blauvelt complied wordlessly. The car moved ahead in the deep green gloom under the huge shaggy-barked trees. Oversized insects buzzed and thumped against the canopy. Small and medium lizards hopped, darted, flapped. Fern leaves as big as awnings scraped along the car as it clambered over loops and coils of tough root, leaving streaks of plant juice across the clear plastic. Once they grated against an exposed ridge of crumbling brown rock; flakes as big as saucers scaled off, exposing dull metal.

"Dorsal fin of a scout-boat," Crewe said. "That's what's left of what was supposed to be a corrosion resistant alloy."

They passed more evidences of a long-ago battle: the massive, shattered breech mechanism of a platform-mounted Hellbore, the gutted chassis of what might have been a bomb car, portions of a downed aircraft, fragments of shattered armor. Many of the relics were of Terran design, but often it was the curiously curved, spidery lines of a rusted Axorc microgun or implosion projector that poked through the greenery.

"It must have been a heavy action," Crewe said. "One of the ones toward the end that didn't get much notice at the time. There's stuff here I've never seen before, experimental types, I imagine, rushed in by the enemy for a last-ditch stand."

Blauvelt grunted.

"Contact in another minute or so," Crewe said.

As Blauvelt opened his mouth to reply, there was a blinding flash, a violent impact, and the jungle erupted in their faces.

The seat webbing was cutting into Crewe's ribs. His ears were filled with a high, steady ringing; there was a taste of brass in his mouth. His head throbbed in time with the thudding of his heart.

The car was on its side, the interior a jumble of loose objects, torn wiring, broken plastic. Blauvelt was half under him, groaning. He slid off him, saw that he was groggy but conscious.

"Changed your mind yet about your harmless pet?" he asked, wiping a trickle of blood from his right eye. "Let's get clear before he fires those empty guns again. Can you walk?"

Blauvelt mumbled, crawled out through the broken canopy. Crewe groped through debris for the command transmitter—

"Good God," Blauvelt croaked. Crewe twisted, saw the high, narrow, iodine-dark shape of the alien machine perched on jointed crawler-legs fifty feet away, framed by blast-scorched foliage. Its multiple-barreled micro-gun battery was aimed dead at the overturned car.

"Don't move a muscle," Crewe whispered. Sweat trickled down his face. An insect, like a stub-winged four-inch dragonfly, came and buzzed about them, moved on. Hot metal pinged, contracting. Instantly, the alien hunter-killer moved forward another six feet, depressing its gun muzzles.

"Run for it!" Blauvelt cried. He came to his feet in a scrabbling lunge; the enemy machine swung to track him . . .

A giant tree leaned, snapped, was tossed aside. The great green-streaked prow of the Bolo forged into view, interposing itself between the smaller machine and the men. It turned to face the enemy; fire flashed, reflecting against the surrounding trees; the ground jumped once, twice, to hard, racking shocks. Sound boomed dully in Crewe's blast-numbed ears. Bright sparks fountained above the Bolo as it advanced. Crewe felt the massive impact as the two fighting machines came together; he saw the Bolo hesitate, then forge ahead, rearing up, pushing the lighter machine aside, grinding over it, passing on, to leave a crumpled mass of wreckage in its wake.

"Did you see that, Crewe?" Blauvelt shouted in his ear. "Did you see what Bobby did? He walked right into its guns and smashed it flatter'n crockbrewed beer!"

The Bolo halted, turned ponderously, sat facing the men. Bright streaks of molten metal ran down its armored flanks, fell spattering and smoking into crushed greenery.

"He saved our necks," Blauvelt said. He staggered to his feet, picked his way past the Bolo to stare at the smoking ruins of the smashed adversary.

"Unit Nine five four of the Line, reporting contact with hostile force," the mechanical voice of the Bolo spoke suddenly. *"Enemy unit destroyed. I have sustained extensive damage, but am still operational at nine point six percent base capability, awaiting further orders."*

"Hey," Blauvelt said. "That doesn't sound like . . ."

"Now maybe you understand that this is a Bolo combat unit, not the village idiot," Crewe snapped. He picked his way across the churned-up ground, stood before the great machine.

"Mission accomplished, Unit Nine five four," he called. "Enemy forces neutralized. Close out Battle Reflex and revert to low alert status." He turned to Blauvelt.

"Let's go back to town," he said, "and tell them what their mascot just did."

Blauvelt stared up at the grim and ancient machine; his square, tanned face looked yellowish and drawn. "Let's do that," he said.

The ten-piece town band was drawn up in a double rank before the newly mown village square. The entire population of the settlement—some three hundred and forty-two men, women and children—were present, dressed in their best. Pennants fluttered from strung wires. The sun glistened from the armored sides of the newly-cleaned and polished Bolo. A vast bouquet of wild flowers poked from the no-longer-sooty muzzle of the Hellbore.

Crewe stepped forward.

"As a representative of the Concordiat government I've been asked to make this presentation," he said. "You people have seen fit to design a medal and award it to Unit Nine five four in appreciation for services rendered in defense of the community above and beyond the call of duty." He paused, looked across the faces of his audience.

"Many more elaborate honors have been awarded for a great deal less," he said. He turned to the machine; two men came forward, one with a stepladder, the other with a portable welding rig. Crewe climbed up, fixed the newly struck decoration in place beside the row of century-old battle honors. The technician quickly spotted it in position. The crowd cheered, then dispersed, chattering, to the picnic tables set up in the village street.

It was late twilight. The last of the sandwiches and stuffed eggs had been eaten, the last speeches declaimed, the last keg broached. Crewe sat with a few of the men in the town's lone public house.

"To Bobby," a man raised his glass.

"Correction," Crewe said. "To Unit Nine five four of the Line." The men laughed and drank.

"Well, time to go, I guess," a man said. The others chimed in, rose, clattering chairs. As the last of them left, Blauvelt came in. He sat down across from Crewe.

"You, ah, staying the night?" he asked.

"I thought I'd drive back," Crewe said. "My business here is finished."

"Is it?" Blauvelt said tensely.

Crewe looked at him, waiting.

"You know what you've got to do, Crewe."

"Do I?" Crewe took a sip from his glass.

"Damn it, have I got to spell it out? As long as that machine was just an oversized half-wit, it was all right. Kind of a monument to the war, and all. But now I've seen what it can do . . . Crewe, we can't have a live killer sitting in the middle of our town—never knowing when it might take a notion to start shooting again!"

"Finished?" Crew asked.

"It's not that we're not grateful—"

"Get out," Crewe said.

"Now, look here, Crewe—"

"Get out. And keep everyone away from Bobby, understand?"

"Does that mean—?"

"I'll take care of it."

Blauvelt got to his feet. "Yeah," he said. "Sure."

After Blauvelt left, Crewe rose and dropped a bill on the table; he picked the command transmitter from the floor, went out into the street. Faint cries came from the far end of the town, where the crowd had gathered for fireworks. A yellow rocket arced up, burst in a spray of golden light, falling, fading . . . .

Crewe walked toward the plaza. The Bolo loomed up, a vast, black shadow against the star-thick sky. Crewe stood before it, looking up at the already draggled pennants, the wilted nosegay drooping from the gun muzzle.

"Unit Nine five four, you know why I'm here?" he said softly.

"I compute that my usefulness as an engine of war is ended," the soft rasping voice said.

"That's right," Crewe said. "I checked the area in a thousand-mile radius with sensitive instruments. There's no enemy machine left alive. The one you killed was the last."

"It was true to its duty," the machine said.

"It was my fault," Crewe said. "It was designed to detect our command carrier and home on it. When I switched on my transmitter, it went into action. Naturally, you sensed that, and went to meet it."

The machine sat silent.

"You could still save yourself," Crewe said. "If you trampled me under and made for the jungle it might be centuries before . . ."

"Before another man comes to do what must be done? Better that I cease now, at the hands of a friend."

"Good-bye, Bobby."

"Correction: Unit Nine five four of the Line."

Crewe pressed the key. A sense of darkness fell across the machine.

At the edge of the square, Crewe looked back. He raised a hand in a ghostly salute; then he walked away along the dusty street, white in the light of the rising moon.

THE DUKES OF DESIRE

Christopher Anvil

Vaughan Roberts glanced from the viewscreen to the landing display, and dropped the salvaged Interstellar Patrol ship into the clearing, between a gnarled tree with thorns as big as a man's forearm, and a battered space yacht whose big hatch was just swinging open.

Roberts pushed forward a toggle-switch on the left side of the control panel, and with a faint whir the stabilizer feet telescoped out, to steady the ship on its smoothly-curved underside. Roberts switched off the gravitors and unbuckled his safety harness, then slipped out of the control seat, ducked under the long shiny cylinder that ran the length of the ship, and went up several steps in the cramped aft section, to release the clamp on the small outer hatch. He spun the lockwheel counterclockwise, pulled the hatch-lever down and slammed it forward, and the hatch swung up and back. A shaft of sunlight shone in, casting shadows of large sharp thorns partly hidden by leaves.

Roberts looked warily all around, loosened his fusion gun in its holster, and pulled himself out the hatch. He sucked in a breath of fresh planetary air, glanced around at the rustling leaves and gently blowing grass, looked up at a white puffy cloud drifting across the clear blue sky, and abruptly snapped his gun out of its holster as brush moved in a rippling motion at the edge of the clearing.

A thing much bigger than a tiger, mottled gray in color, silently blurred out of the brush to bound straight for Roberts, forepaws outstretched.

Roberts fired, fired again, jumped down the hatchway, grabbed the lever and heaved.

Clang! The hatch slammed shut.

WHOOM! There was a noise like an enormous gas burner, gone almost as soon as it began. The ship quivered. Then there was a thud somewhere aft.

Roberts crouched in the cramped space under the hatch, gripping the fusion gun, and listened intently. He heard nothing more. Very cautiously, he raised the hatch.

In the slit of sunlight revealed, he could see, farther aft, the number two reaction-drive nozzle slowly settle back into position. A wisp of smoke was rising from a small gun turret a few feet from the hatch. A long shiny metal stalk, not quite as thick as a man's wrist, arced out from another turret forward, extruded a set of metal fingers, picked up a riddled and smoldering furry head and dropped it over the side. Roberts looked around, but if the rest of the body was anywhere nearby, he couldn't see it.

He thought a moment, went back and put on a bulky suit of battle armor, and decided to try again.

He shoved open the hatch, and climbed out to look at the ship. Wherever he turned, guns bristled. Small turrets, meant for short-range defense, dotted the smooth armored surface. Amidships, a movable belt of fusion turrets faced aft, so that he was looking down their muzzles. Farther forward, two large turrets, one behind and above the other, mounted fusion cannon big enough for a man to put his arm into. The sight of all these gun turrets, and of the snap-beam transceptor head steadily rotating atop its mast, gave Roberts a warm pleasant sensation, far different from what he'd felt the last time he'd been on this planet.

From above, where to one side the big hatch of the battered space yacht was now wide open, a rough masculine voice called down.

"The place hasn't changed much, has it?"

Roberts looked up, to see a strongly-built figure, somewhat foreshortened by his angle of vision, grinning down at him. This was Hammell, who'd been stranded here with him the last time.

"No," said Roberts, automatically glancing around the clearing, and taking a quick look overhead. "Not out here, at least. Where's Morrissey?"

"Up above. He just got through setting up the gear. Come on up, if you can stand to leave that flying fort of yours."

Roberts grunted, took another quick look around, studied the ground below the curve of the patrol-ship's hull, walked aft along one of the horizontal fins, and dropped off. The moment he was clear of the ship, there was a clang, and Roberts turned to see that the patrol-ship's hatch had shut.

From overhead, Hammell laughed, and called, "You've got that thing trained."

Roberts gave a second grunt, but no reply. The patrol ship was a sore point between them. Marooned on the planet earlier because of gravitor trouble, the three men had promised themselves to come back under better conditions, bringing with them an improved version of the device that had made their escape possible. One of the little details they hadn't settled beforehand was what they would come back in. Hammell and Morrissey wanted something roomy, comfortable—if possible, luxurious. Roberts wanted plenty of firepower, and as much armor between himself and the planet as possible. Hammell and Morrissey duly selected a large roomy yacht with a solitary energy-cannon mounted in the bow, but otherwise equipped like a luxury hotel. Roberts selected the much smaller patrol ship, cramped and functional perhaps, but armed to the teeth, and fitted with a powerful drive-unit. Neither side had compromised, and the argument was still going on.

Roberts, climbing the ladderlike recessed holds up to the space yacht's big hatch, reminded himself that he, Hammell, and Morrissey were all equals in rank for the duration of their leave. At work, Roberts was captain of the fast interstellar transport *Orion*, Hammell was cargo-control officer, and Morrissey was communications officer. Possibly for this reason, there was a little extra friction now and then. Roberts was determined not to add to it if he could help it. But he didn't intend to lean over backwards so far that he fell on his head, either.

He reached the top of the ladder, and Hammell reached down to help him up.

"It would be better if we were all in the same ship," said Hammell. "You wouldn't have to go around looking like a gorilla in an iron suit every time we have to get together. It would be a *lot* more convenient."

"You take the convenience," said Roberts, "and I'll take the guns. Where's Morrissey?"

"Up on the sixth level."

Roberts thought a moment, and remembered that on the yacht, which set down upright on its tail, the horizontal levels started with the drive-unit and storage compartment at the base, below where they now stood. The sixth level would be the control room.

"Wouldn't there be more room down one level?"

Hammell nodded. "That's where he's got the spy screen set up. But right now I think he's back up in the control room checking the communicator again."

"Good," said Roberts. "We can get an idea whether things have changed much."

Hammell touched a button beside the hatch, and the hatch swung silently shut. He and Roberts walked towards a softly-glowing oval on the deck. The right half of this oval was green, and left half red. Roberts stepped carefully onto the green, and at once the walls of the ship dropped downward, and with a soft murmur an oval section of the next level overhead slid back. One-by-one, the levels dropped past, disclosing entrances to a succession of medium-sized rooms with curving walls, designed for entertainment, eating, sleeping, and then they passed the level where Morrissey had set up the equipment, and reached the control room, which seemed comparatively small because of the inward-curving sides near the nose of the ship. Roberts caught a polished silvery bar, and stepped out of the lift. He nodded to the lean sandy-haired individual who glanced up with worried electric-blue eyes from the communicator.

"Hello, Morrissey," said Roberts.

Morrissey blinked in momentary alarm at the battle armor.

"Sir," he said automatically, then added. "Something's changed since we were here before."

"What?"

"The screen no longer gives continuous news broadcasts from the city."

"That doesn't sound good."

"It sure doesn't. So we can see what's happening, I've let go the spy-system pickups, set to tap onto the city's surveillance network. I hope *that* works."

"Yes," said Roberts, remembering that this had been Morrissey's big worry. "When will we find out?"

"If nothing's wrong, we ought to be able to pick up the relayed signals any time now. I came back up here because I didn't want to sit down below chewing my nails."

"Let's go take a look now. If we can't get that spy screen to work, we're in a mess right at the beginning."

They dropped down to the next lower level, to see with relief that the big spy screen, though still unfocused, was already lit up. As Roberts and Hammell dragged over some chairs, Roberts climbed out of the battle armor.

• • •

They sat down in the three chairs, in front of the wide improvised control panel, and Roberts, in the center, adjusted the focus of the spy screen. At once, he had a sharply-detailed view of a potholed street strewn with trash. To the left was a large building with the windows knocked out. To the right was a park where rats scurried amidst the leafless dead trees and smoldering heaps of garbage. Straight ahead, in the center of the street, two small boys stood menacingly with short lengths of iron pipe, their legs wide apart, their clothes ragged and dirty save for armbands marked with triple lightning-bolt insignia. Just rolling onto the screen were a pair of roboid policemen, their whip antennas swaying, the sunlight flashing on the spokes of their high bicycle-type wheels.

Morrissey, to Roberts' right, gave a surprised grunt.

Roberts said, "If this is typical, no wonder they aren't broadcasting."

Hammell nodded. "There's nothing like disorder and violence to get people worked up. And there's nothing like having people worked up to bring on disorder and violence."

"And this is just the spot for it," said Roberts. He was thinking of the gigantic slum-city, built by a beneficent foundation and peopled from the slums of half-a-dozen older worlds. But it struck him suddenly that it applied to the whole planet as well.

He glanced out one of the space yacht's portholes at the small bristling Interstellar Patrol ship below. Roberts had located the patrol ship in a salvage cluster, and the salvage operator had been only too happy to trade it for most of Roberts' accumulated savings. There were quite a number of special devices on the patrol ship, any one of which was worth far more than the purchase price. But this didn't affect the salvage operator's delight in getting rid of the ship.

In the first place, his sharpest tools and hottest torches wouldn't cut the patrol ship's armor. In the second place, the patrol ship's large and numerous weapons were controlled by a combat computer, which came on automatically whenever anyone tried anything that promised to blast off a chunk of high-grade metal. In the third place, worst of all, the ship was partially controlled by what was sometimes called a "symbiotic computer." This computer had apparently existed in a special relationship with the former crewmen, and now it passed judgment on prospective purchasers, applying roughly the same standards that were necessary to enlist in the Interstellar Patrol. If the prospective purchaser wasn't up to par—mentally, physically, or morally—the computer disdained him. As a result, nothing on the ship would work for him.

Roberts had barely squeezed by the computer's forbidding scrutiny. But that was all he needed to do. The ship flew for him. Roberts soon found himself with a ship equipped with an armament fit to dent a planet. The salvage operator, for his part, relievedly blew a kiss after the dwindling speck in the distance, and resolved never again to touch anything like that unless he had a private dreadnought to break it up with.

Now, on the planet, Roberts looked out with pleasure at the ship, but at the same time got a view of the trees that surrounded the clearing. Just what was hidden back in those trees, perhaps only fifty feet from the clearing, would have been hard to say. But the space yacht, while coming down to land, had run into some kind of monster with the bad judgment to jump up and take a snap at one of the big fins that would steady the yacht as it stood on its tail. The fin, with the weight of the yacht behind it, crushed the animal. The smell of blood having already apparently spread the promise of a free meal, Roberts could see that other creatures were now prospecting around. There was a flap of big wings overhead, and the rustle of leaves at the edge of the clearing. Just what would pop out when was hard to say, but Roberts took a quick glance at his suit of battle armor, fixing its location in mind so he could get into it with no wasted time if he had to. Then he reluctantly placed his trust in the space yacht's energy-cannon, and turned back to the spy screen.

Hammell was leaning forward tensely, "Something's getting ready to blow in that city. Otherwise the police just wouldn't be this heavily reinforced."

On the screen, two more roboid policemen had swung into view behind the first pair, and these were followed in turn by a flying wedge of roboid police.

Straight ahead, the two boys in the middle of the street stayed where they were and jeered.

Roberts glanced at the locator screen in front of Morrissey. This screen was marked off in city blocks, like a big elongated chessboard with oval edges. A strip of street, running through an intersection and about a fourth of a block farther in both directions, was lit up whitely, showing the section now in view on the spy screen.

As Roberts glanced from one screen to the other, suddenly the two boys snapped their arms forward, the lengths of pipe arced out, to slam into the roboid police, and twin flashes of dazzling light outlined a tangle of ripped and torn metal housings, shredded insulation, bent tubing, and bare gears, shafts, and axles. The first pair of roboid police smashed to a stop.

The two boys were already sprinting toward opposite sides of the street.

The second pair of roboid police rolled unswervingly past the wreckage of the first.

Roberts, Hammell, and Morrissey stared at the screen, their expressions perfectly blank.

From behind a heap of garbage at the edge of the park, two more boys raced out, clutching short lengths of pipe.

As Morrissey snapped a switch, twin speakers to either side of the spy screen came on, relaying sounds from the scene. An amplified voice spoke out:

"Clear the street. This warning will not be repeated. Clear the street. Further violence against your Law-Enforcement Officers will be met with maximum force. Clear the street."

The two boys sprinted directly toward the approaching roboid police. Their right arms swung back. Their faces twisted in hatred and contempt, and their arms swung sharply forward. The short lengths of pipe streaked out, slammed into the fronts of the pair of oncoming machines. There were two dazzling flashes.

The roar of the explosions drowned out all other sounds. The boys had already separated, to sprint, off-balance from the force of the explosions, toward opposite sides of the street.

Two more roboid policemen smashed to a stop in a whirl of flame, smoke, and showers of sparks.

Behind them, the V of the flying wedge rushed forward. Unlike the others, which had been light-blue, these roboid police were painted black with silver markings.

In the building to the left of the street, the doors now swung open, and small groups of boys sprinted out to form a line completely across the street. The ends of the line rushed forward, then the center, forming a rough inverted U that raced toward the oncoming V. The V opened briefly to pass the wrecked police machines, then closed again in precise alignment.

For a moment there was a silence broken only by the hiss of

tires on pavement, the pound of feet, and the panting of breath. Then there was a concerted yell, *"Kill the mechs!"* The boys' arms swung back in unison.

At the fronts of the police machines, small doors snapped up and back. From behind each door came a bright spurting flash.

The boys' arms flew out, their knees buckled, and their lengths of pipe dropped free as they fell sprawling to the pavement amidst sudden dazzling flashes of light.

The flying wedge of roboid police swept steadily forward with no change of speed or direction. Their narrow tires, heavily-loaded, crossed the torn inert bodies, cut, ground, and slashed them. The tires and rims turned red, to lay down narrow red strips in absolutely straight lines on the pavement.

Hammell, Roberts, and Morrissey, momentarily unable to move, sat with their hands gripping the edge of the control panel.

A pretty woman, a baby bundle in her arms, rushed from a door down the street, screaming, "My boys! My boys!" and ran toward a pair of the inert, mangled bodies, herself coming into the path of the flying wedge.

In the fronts of the onrushing police robots, the little doors snapped open.

Hammell gave an inarticulate sound of horror.

Roberts, his mind a whirling maze of calculations, came to his feet. His patrol ship was heavily enough armed to handle any concentration of police robots. If he took the ship to the edge of this section of the city . . .

On the screen, directly in the path of the flying wedge, the woman screamed, and raised her bundle high overhead, as if to lift her baby out of danger.

From behind the little doors, bright flashes spurted out.

Roberts had already started to turn away, his hand reaching out for the battle armor he had to wear to cross the clearing.

On the screen there was a huge, brilliantly dazzling flash as the "baby" blew up.

Roberts, blank-faced, one hand on the battle armor, stared at the screen.

Beside him, Morrissey stood motionless with a perfectly blank expression.

Hammell grunted in disgust, and settled back into his seat.

Roberts tilted the battle armor back against the wall of the ship and sat down.

• • •

On the screen, the wedge of roboid police swept by, followed by two long columns of roboid police firing as they passed at the building and into the dump on opposite sides of the street.

Down the street at the end of the building, a flash of movement left Roberts with a brief afterimage of something vaguely shaped like a camera, that had apparently recorded what had happened so far, and was now pulled inside as the roboid police came dangerously close.

The long double column of roboid police was now slowing to a halt, the point of the wedge extending exactly to the center of the intersection beyond the far end of the building. From the left, a second wedge followed by another two columns appeared from behind the building, moving along the intersecting street, and joined up with the first wedge. The individual roboid police now had turned ninety degrees, to face the building and the adjoining parks, and the lines of police themselves moved farther apart, to open up a wide protected strip of avenue between the lines.

Down this protected roadway came something long, low, and broad, with jointed body sections running on many wheels, with turrets on top slowly swinging large muzzled uptilted guns toward the building.

From the building came shots and small bundles that arced out and down. Up and down the street, more small bundles flew out from the cellar windows. With bright flashes, gaps began to appear in the lines of roboid police.

The long many-wheeled device now slowed to a stop. Its upward-pointing barrels moved slowly, methodically. At the mouth of each barrel there was a blur, then another blur, then another blur.

From the windows of the building came a flash, then from the next window another flash, then from the next window another flash.

Another long low many-wheeled device rolled past the first and stopped farther down the street, to heave its explosive shells through the next section of windows.

The repeated short blast of a whistle cut through the roar of explosives. The tossing of bundles from the windows abruptly stopped.

Down the street came a chunky vehicle with several big hemispherical bulges at the top. It stopped at a thing in the street like a manhole cover, flipped the cover off with two pronged levers, eased forward and dropped something round and bellows-like over the hole. Wisps of yellowish smoke began to escape around the edges.

"Sealing off the sewer system," said Hammell. "No one will get out of the building that way."

"They'd better get out *some* way pretty quick," said Morrissey, "or they aren't going to. Look there."

A low blocky object, like a huge metal brick, heavily mounted the sidewalk, and moved massively forward on concealed wheels or rollers. The door of the building snapped back before it like a matchstick, there was a bright flash from underneath, with no visible effect, then the device was inside. It backed up, taking half the doorframe and part of the adjoining wall with it, and rolled forward again. In the silence now that the shooting had died away, there was a dull heavy *crunch*. The massive device then reappeared, and rumbled down the sidewalk toward the next door. Behind it, there now moved forward a host of spidery devices, varying from about one to four feet tall, that moved methodically into the building, followed by low long broad things with many short legs, like metal centipedes. These crawled off of a steady procession of low broad-roofed carriers with open sides, that rolled up the street, discharged their cargo, and moved on to vanish around the corner.

Time passed, and spidery many-legged metal forms appeared on successively higher floors of the building, and finally on the roof. But only two humans were carried out, and both of them were plainly dead.

Meanwhile, a small crowd of people had gathered, apparently from neighboring buildings, to watch raptly from the far side of the double line of roboid police. As the metal devices appeared on successively higher floors, the people pointed and shouted in pleasure. As the dead bodies were carried out, they cheered.

Roberts sat back and looked blankly at Hammell. Hammell shook his head. Roberts glanced at Morrissey. Morrissey ran his hand over his face.

"Well," said Roberts finally, "before we can decide what to do this time, it looks like we're going to have to figure out what's developed out of what we did the last time."

Morrissey nodded. Hammell looked moodily out at the clearing.

From behind them came the bland voice of Holcombe, the life-like roboid butler that had come with the space yacht, and added a special touch of luxury that had enabled the manufacturers to charge what they had for this deluxe version of the ship when it was new.

Holcombe was saying deferently: "A little light refreshment, my lords?"

Morrissey said wearily, "Just a pitcher of water, Holcombe. Plus three glasses and a large bottle of aspirin."

"Yes, my lord." Holcombe bowed and retired.

The three men stared moodily at the screen.

It took them most of the day, methodically working with the spy screen to get a rough idea what was going on in the city. Once they had it, they sat back in exasperated bafflement.

From one end of the city to the other, barring only the region around the Planetary Control Center itself, a highly-organized gang of fanatics seemed to be at work, operating from a network of their own tunnels. These tunnels were independent of the city's network of steam lines, cables, pipes, and underground maintenance tunnels, though the two connected at a number of points. Except at these points, the city's surveillance devices showed nothing of what went on inside the newly-dug tunnels. Hence the spy screen, which operated from taps on the city's surveillance system, also showed nothing, except at these points. But from watching the movement of maintenance and combat devices inside the city's tunnels, it became obvious that a continuous skirmishing and probing was going on, with the computer trying to isolate and clean out sections of the fanatics' tunnels, while the fanatics calculatedly sabotaged water pipes, steam lines, and power cables, to keep the computer distracted with maintenance problems, and its tunnels clogged with maintenance devices. Meanwhile, above ground, gangs of fanatics, wearing triple-lightning-bolt insignia, burst out to seize able-bodied protesting citizens for work in the shovel gangs. The general bulk of the populace, if anything, looked more rundown and put upon than before. Now they had two sets of rulers instead of one, and the rulers were at war with each other.

"This network of tunnels," said Hammell finally, "makes it a mess. How do we know what effect we're having on them if we can't see them?"

"We can try," said Morrissey, "to figure it out from what happens afterward."

"That's nice. We can figure out whether a bottle had nitroglycerine in it by 'what happened afterward' when we jarred the bottle."

Roberts studied the screen. "Suppose we bring them all to the surface, then?"

"How?"

"Have we got anything on that list that will serve the purpose of claustrophobia?"

Morrissey blinked. "That's a thought." He ran his finger down a paper tacked by the locator screen, flipped the paper up, and ran down a second list underneath.

"Here we are. 'Desire for light and air.' 'Desire to escape confinement.'" He flipped up the next page. "'Desire for room, space.'"

"Just what we need. How would you like to be down in a tunnel and suddenly start to feel one of *those* desires?"

"I wouldn't. But if I were a fanatic, maybe I'd be able to resist it."

"Could we work it so that a *blend* of all those desires would be generated? After all, with this synchronous rotor setup you worked out, we can hit different sections with different settings at the same time. Why not the same section with several settings at once?"

Morrissey blinked, and looked wary. "But not throughout the whole city?"

"*No*, of course not," said Roberts. "Who knows what would happen? No, just try one place at a time. A good spot to start might be near that building where all the fighting was earlier. There should still be some people in tunnels under there. Then we can see how this works."

Morrissey nodded. "Good idea. We'll try it."

They switched the spy screen back to a view of the building, and of the garbage-filled park beside the building, and Morrissey set up the want-generator to hit just that section of the city with "desire for light and air," "desire to escape confinement," and "desire for room, space."

Then they watched the screen.

Somewhere underground, there should be some fanatical humans, lurking in tunnels, and suddenly stricken with an urgent desire for light, air, and unconfined space.

Very soon, these humans should come to the surface somewhere.

For a long time, they waited.

But for a long time, nothing happened.

Roberts, frowning, studied first the building, then the park, to make out finally, in the center of the park amidst the enormous heaps of garbage, the remains of what appeared to be a bandstand. He was frowning at this structure, when a wild-looking individual with improvised gun in one hand suddenly burst out a trapdoor in the center, and plunged out into the heaped-up garbage. Right behind him came two more, their faces frantic and chests pumping desperately for air. After the first three came a flood of humanity, each carrying a club, a length of pipe, and gun apparently taken from a wrecked roboid policeman, and fitted with a stock, or some other weapon. There was no room for them all on the bandstand, and in any case they didn't try to stay there, but immediately sprang off into the heaped garbage, to plunge and heave desperately, as if trying to climb up into the open air itself.

Last out of the hole came a man about five feet ten inches tall, strongly built, neatly-dressed in coveralls with triple-lightning-bolt armband, carrying a rifle in his right hand, and plainly boiling mad. He gestured angrily toward the trapdoor, shook his fist, and threatened the others with his gun. His voice came out in a flow of words so rapid that all Roberts could make out was the sense of urgency and the tone of command. Meanwhile, the scores of armed men ceased their struggles and lay flat, face-down in the garbage, or stared up dazedly at the open sky overhead, and tried to act as if they didn't hear.

At the same time, around the edges of the park, roboid police began to pour in from eight different directions, coming both ways along the four wide streets that intersected to form the boundaries of the park.

It dawned on Roberts that this scene must have appeared on some panel in the Planetary Control Center, or otherwise have come to the attention of the planetary computer. And the computer was losing no time in taking advantage of the windfall.

A new urgency came into the voice of the man on the bandstand.

Around the sides of the park, the rapidly accumulating roboid police milled, searching for some route through the heaps of garbage. Here and there, one or two eased in, went forward a little distance, lost headway, came to a stop, backed up, and slammed forward again, to bog down once more in towering piles of decaying trash and garbage.

Down one of the intersecting streets came a long snakelike wheeled carrier, that pulled alongside the edge of the dump and slowed to a stop. The arched armored roof tilted up and back in sections, the first sections swinging far back to brace the carrier from tipping off-balance as, successively, other heavy sections swung up and over. Out of the carrier crept a long device like a metal centipede, with flanged underside instead of legs. The device inched its way forward as successive waves of expansion and contraction moved along its length. The headlike appendage at the front, fitted with multiple visual receptors behind thick glass plates, and two groups of four large gun muzzles on a side, selected a low place between two heaps of garbage, and pushed forward steadily, thrust ahead by the metallic bulk following along behind in steady successive waves of expansion and contraction; the flanges lifting, tilting, flowing forward, dipping down, and thrusting steadily back.

Now an amplified voice boomed out:

"You are surrounded. Surrender peacefully and you will be remanded for psychiatric examination to the Central Medical Computer. You will not be harmed. Resist, and you will be destroyed at once. You have no choice. Surrender. Throw your weapons toward the—"

Atop the bandstand, the man who'd been arguing with the others had dropped to one knee, his gun resting on a half-rotted rail at the edge of the platform.

There was a solitary bang, and the voice demanding surrender went silent.

Morrissey said, "They aren't throwing their guns out, and they aren't fighting, either. That metal snake is going to get to them in about a minute-and-a-half and blow them to bits. Isn't there something we can—"

Roberts thought fast, and said, "Reset the generator. Hit them with 'Desire to obey the law.' "

Morrissey flipped quickly through the list, glancing nervously back at the screen as the enormous metal centipede crawled steadily through the piles of trash.

"Do we *have* 'Desire to obey the law'?"

Roberts tore his gaze from the screen. "It's halfway down the list. 'Obedience to authority' or something like that."

"That's it," said Morrissey. Quickly, he reset the want-generator.

On the screen, the leader of the humans, on the bandstand, was talking in a low urgent voice, lying flat on the stand as a metallic head started up over a mound of trash, and suddenly every other human stood up. Every single individual either threw a length of pipe, or threw a padded bundle, or fired a gun, or lunged right or left through the garbage to get a clean shot or throw around the side of the stand.

Everyone's aim was good.

In a terrific series of flashes, the head end of the huge metal centipede blew apart.

In one spontaneous surge, the humans then plunged through the garbage to the stand and, in a line that moved like clockwork, dropped one-by-one through the trapdoor into the interior.

All save for the leader, who was now on his knees, hands clasped and head uplifted, lips moving, his expression earnest.

"Shut it off," said Roberts exasperatedly.

On the screen, the leader suddenly bowed his head, opened his eyes, and jumped down the hole.

The trapdoor slammed shut.

A plume of dirty smoke climbed up from the wrecked front end of the metal centipede.

"*Now* what?" said Morrissey, glancing from the controls to the screen. "Did I somehow get the wrong setting?"

"No," said Roberts. "As usual, it was the right setting, but they just interpreted it their own way. To them, 'desire to obey authority' meant desire to *obey their leader*. And to their leader, it apparently meant desire *to obey God*. None of them had the slightest impulse to do what *we* intended, and obey the *city* authority—the computer and the roboid police."

"Well," said Morrissey, "all I have to say is, this little incident opens up sweeping vistas of trouble ahead. *Other* groups of people in that city *would* have obeyed the city authorities."

Roberts nodded. "Their reactions are more diverse than they were the last time. It's as if they were somehow splitting up into fractions that respond differently to the same desire."

Hammell cleared his throat. "And there's one minor fraction that apparently can resist the desire-field when it conflicts with his purpose—the leader of that gang. To hit *him* with the effects we want might take an intensity that would send the others into shock."

Roberts considered that in silence.

"You've got to admit we're getting nowhere," said Morrissey.

"We've just started," said Roberts stubbornly.

Hammell said sourly, "Yeah. We're finding out the things that *don't* work."

Outside in the forest, where darkness was starting to gather, something gave a bellowing roar that the yacht's thin hull hardly seemed to muffle.

The roboid Holcombe appeared at the entrance to the gravity lift, and bowed.

"Dinner is served, my lords."

Dinner was a sumptuous meal, but halfway through the dessert the curving wall of the space yacht's dining saloon lit up in a reflected pinkish glow. There was a bellow of pain and rage from outside. From overhead came a metallic rattle, then a muffled booming voice:

"Your attention, please. This vessel is fully protected by appropriate devices of the Advanced Synodic Products Corporation. It will retaliate automatically against any aggressive or hostile action."

There was a second glare of pink light, the deck shook underfoot; there was a bellow that traveled around in a large circle outside; then abruptly there was a dazzling white glare, followed by a sizzle as if ten tons of meat had been dropped into a monster frying pan.

Roberts quickly understood that sound. It meant that some gigantic beast, singed by the space yacht, had galloped around and got too close to the patrol ship. Which of the patrol ship's big fusion guns had done the business was a good question, but it was all the same to whatever got in their way. Roberts finished his dessert quickly, anxious to get back to something with a hull that wouldn't fold up if some irritable monster took a crack at it.

Hammell said nervously, "The stinking fifth-rate computer on this tub must not be able to distinguish between dead behemoths lying around, and live ones sneaking in. Otherwise, how did *that* thing get so close?"

"Yes," said Roberts, getting up and reaching for his suit of battle armor. He tilted it off-base, lugged it over to the table, reached inside and turned a valve that relaxed the hydraulic columns inside. The suit slumped facedown on the table, which creaked under it, then Roberts heaved the back panel open and climbed in. Without a sling to hold the suit upright, getting into it was a fairly ridiculous procedure, but neither Hammell nor

Morrissey had anything to say about that. They were too busy staring out into the dark clearing, and worrying about ways to get a little more protection out of the energy cannon and the pure-routine computer that operated it. Hammell finally shook his head, glanced absently toward Roberts, and suddenly jumped back.

Roberts had straightened up, and was just swinging the back panel shut. He grinned.

"What's the matter? Don't I look nice in this thing?"

Hammell's laugh came to him clearly, through the earphones of the suit. "I've already told you. You look like an overgrown gorilla. I was thinking about those animals outside, and for a second, I thought one had got in. Ye gods, that suit is big! Is it hard to work the arms?"

"A little," said Roberts. "Not too bad."

"Why's the helmet so big?"

"I don't know. It's not big inside."

"Well, it must be comforting to be inside that."

"You want one?" said Roberts. "There are three extras just like it on the patrol ship—for three other crew members. In fact, you could sleep there. There are four bunks. I could bring back a couple of extra suits for you to wear across the clearing, and—"

Hammell hesitated, then shook his head.

"No, thanks. Even at used-ship prices, we've got too much invested in this yacht to leave it to the mercies of these beasts, even overnight. And we couldn't work in armored suits, so—thanks anyway."

Reluctantly, Roberts nodded. "O.K. then."

The three men said good night, and Roberts went down the grav-drop, out the hatch and into the night.

Roberts was sound asleep when, sometime during the night, there was a banging noise somewhere outside. It reached him well-muffled and distant, and he merely turned over and pulled the covers more tightly around him.

Several hours went by, broken by very faint distant bellows and screams, and booming far-off public-address-system noises.

Around four in the morning, there came a thundering crash.

Roberts woke up enough to wonder if he had heard something, but quickly fell asleep again.

About 0630, the symbiotic computer gradually turned up the lights, and then woke him with a buzz.

Roberts slid out of the bunk, performed a series of exercises to the computer's satisfaction, shaved, showered, dressed, ate an A-ration bar, drank two glasses of water, swung the suit of battle armor out on its sling, got into it, and headed for the hatch.

Roberts had the hatch up, and had already pulled himself halfway out, before he saw what was going on outside.

Three huge mottled-gray cats were working on the remains of several gigantic bony-snouted creatures, tearing the meat off the bones in chunks, and wrestling with sheets of tough fibrous membrane that apparently separated one huge bundle of muscle fiber from another.

Creeping in on the cats, apparently for a quick grab at a chunk of the meat, was a long many-legged segmented green creature with jaws about three feet long.

Overhead, light-blue against a sky that was a darker blue with drifting white clouds, huge birds circled, the dark green of their upper feathers showing from time to time as they dipped, eyeing a behemoth with suggestively flickering sledgehammer tail, that was upright on two pillarlike hind legs beside the space yacht. The head and shoulders of this beast were inside the yacht, the big door of the space yacht being buckled outward, and the side inward, to make room.

Studying the other animals with cold calculating gaze from the foliage of a nearby thorn tree, was a large snaky head.

Roberts dropped back inside the patrol ship, and slammed the hatch.

The voice of the symbiotic computer spoke from the helmet's earphones.

"For an armored member of the Interstellar Patrol to retreat in the face of mere beasts, with onlookers watching from another ship, is unacceptable."

"To do anything else would be nuts. And as I've explained at least a dozen times, I'm *not* a member of the Interstellar Patrol."

"Evidently you've neglected to study your 'Model A-6 Battle-Suit Dynamics.' A demonstration is in order. Press down the chin-lever in the left side of the helmet."

Roberts, not wanting to pointlessly antagonize the computer, pressed down the lever. He immediately found himself walking toward the hatch. Before he knew what had happened, he'd thrown the hatch open, and was climbing out.

The three gigantic cats looked up from their meal and bared their teeth. The green many-legged creature swung its yard-long jaws around and hissed. In the thorn tree, the snaky eyes looked on with cold calculation.

Roberts dropped off the curving side of the ship, his feet sinking deeper into the soil at every step, as if the suit were acquiring mass as it moved forward. He was headed straight for the green many-legged creature.

After a moment's startled hesitation, this beast opened up its yard-long, four-foot-wide jaws, and lunged for Roberts.

Roberts' right foot came up in a kick that left a ten-inch-wide groove in the soil, hit the creature's lower jaw and shut it with a *CLACK!* that echoed around the clearing.

His right hand then reached out, seized the top of the creature's snout, and yanked it down, cracking its nose into the ground.

The three huge cats began edging back toward the forest.

All the many legs of the green creature now began to kick, but Roberts set his feet, turned the whole head over sidewise, pinned the upper swell of the head under the right arm of his suit, and gripping the forward curve of the snout with his left arm, heaved the head of the monster along with him as he started for the space yacht. Behind him, the rest of the beast lifted clear of the ground, like one cable of a suspension bridge, the far end anchored out of sight somewhere back in the forest.

Roberts kept going for the space yacht, his feet sinking as if he were in soft muck.

Behind him, there was a heavy rending, a loud creak, successive cracking straining noises, then the rustling, and swishing of uncounted leafy branches, followed by the ground-shaking crash of a big tree.

The far end of the many-legged creature suddenly was trotting along, stumbling and lurching as it crossed ground not selected by the head end, so that some of its feet went down into holes while others banged into rotting logs and low hillocks, but the creature did its best, and stopped instantaneously when Roberts stopped, beside the gray pillarlike leg of the behemoth that had its shoulders and snout inside the space yacht, and its huge sledgehammer-like tail swishing threateningly behind it.

Roberts unhesitatingly reached up, gripped one of the tail's muscular cords, that stood out like tree roots, and yanked on it.

The upper end of the creature froze. There was a menacing rumble. The tail wrenched, twisted, and couldn't get free. The head and shoulders of the behemoth jerked back and out of the space yacht. Roberts gripped the tail. The animal tried without success to step back to get its balance, but Roberts held the tail while his body blocked the right rear leg.

Ponderously, stamping hard with its left leg to try to right itself, the creature tipped over, to land full-length with a shock that jarred the earth.

Overhead, in the thorn tree, a little flutter of leaves marked the departure of the snake.

The behemoth lay still for a moment, in shock, then sucked in a huge breath of air, let out a ringing high-pitched bellow, rolled over, twisting its tail loose at the expense of a large chunk of skin, and staggered to its feet.

Roberts took a few steps, bent, shoved his armored left hand through the dirt under the behemoth's left hind foot, and heaved it up.

Roberts himself sank into the soil as if it were quicksand, but the behemoth's left hind leg shot high up into the air, and the whole creature went up and over on its back with a jar that made the trees sway.

The many-legged creature again had its nose pinned to the earth, this time because Roberts was down inside a form-fitting foxhole in the soil, but was still absently holding onto the many-legged creature with his right hand. For its part, it kept its eyes shut, its mouth closed, and just waited to see what Roberts wanted it to do next.

Roberts pulled himself up out of the ground.

The behemoth staggered to its feet, gave a pitiful bleat, and bolted for the forest.

Roberts let go the head of the many-legged creature, its eyes came warily half-open, and with steadily gathering speed, it headed for the forest.

Roberts looked around, saw that the clearing was deserted, and climbed up the handholds into the space yacht.

Inside, Hammell and Morrissey stared at him as he climbed out of the battle armor. The suit having done practically all the work, Roberts was just slightly damp with perspiration.

Hammell and Morrissey, on the other hand, looked like they'd spent the night being bounced around in an oversize tin can. Which, Roberts thought, was probably exactly what had happened.

"Well," he said, "are you guys *sure* you don't want to come over to the patrol ship?"

Hammell stared at the armor, and said hesitantly, "Ah— No offense, but— Look, was it *your* idea to just go out there and kick those monsters around?"

"No," said Roberts frankly, "the symbiotic computer on the patrol ship got the idea, and it . . . well . . . made the initial suggestion."

"Ah. And so you—"

"Naturally," said Roberts, standing the battle armor against a bulkhead, "when the symbiotic computer is unhappy, the ship isn't worth living in. I have to extend myself a little now and then to keep the symbiotic computer happy."

Morrissey glanced out into the clearing where the huge dead carcasses were lying around, swallowed hard, and said nothing.

"We'll stay here," said Hammell firmly.

Roberts shrugged exasperatedly. "Suit yourself."

They went up to the spy screen, and as they turned it on, a dazzling flash loomed out through an unfocused scene of grayness and blowing smoke, and when Roberts adjusted the focus, a nightmarish barren landscape came into view, with running figures briefly glimpsed in the distance.

Roberts glanced at the locator screen, and realized that he had a view of the dump they'd watched earlier. He frowned at it for a moment, then said, "Let's see the streets adjoining this."

Morrissey changed the setting, and in quick succession Roberts saw views of four different streets. On all of them, there were overturned roboid policemen, being taken apart by humans using tools apparently improvised from the axles, shafts, and cover plates of other roboid policemen.

On the streets, leading toward the center of the city, little groups of men and boys went past, alternately running and walking, carrying guns, short lengths of pipe, and heavy axles sharpened on one end to a needle point. Other groups of men carried buckets and still others carried garbage cans slung on pairs of long pipes.

"Ye gods," said Hammell. "It looks like that first time we tried to do something, and they had a revolution going before the day was over."

Roberts said, "The want-generator hasn't been on overnight, has it?"

Morrissey shook his head. "We couldn't even have started to figure out what to do. We left it turned off."

"Then we don't have that to worry about, at least. Let's follow one of these avenues toward the center of the city."

The scene shifted, up one of the long avenues, to show, at first, scattered gangs of men moving forward out in the open, then men moving single file next to the buildings, then men sprinting across intersections to file through narrow lanes through the trash-filled parks, to emerge opposite the center of the next block, cross the street at a run and disappear through doorways guarded by armed men who stayed flat against the wall and peered warily toward the nearest intersection.

As the scene shifted still farther forward, the alternating checkerboard pattern of buildings and garbage-dump-filled parks was suddenly interrupted. Two-thirds of the way down the next block, the buildings were smashed to rubble, and the dumps were burnt black. A tangled confusion of barbed wire and tetrahedral clusters of razor-sharp needle-pointed blades was shrouded in a foamy mass of solidified translucent bubbles, through which could be dimly seen the glitter of other, finer, wires, of narrow sharp-edged metal strips, and the looming shapes of dark spheres, ovoids, and platelike objects suggestive of explosive mines.

In the street bordering this barrier, armored turrets mounting four guns apiece, in two opposite pairs, were thrust up out of manhole-like openings in the street. Mobile guns were clustered at the corners of the parks. In the avenues farther back long, low, many-wheeled devices waited.

With growing amazement, Roberts, Hammell, and Morrissey watched as they shifted the scene, and the length of this barrier became clear. It stretched on far across the city from west to east, then swung far to the south, then finally west again, with massively fortified squares at the corners.

Hammell said in astonishment, "Two-thirds of the city is outside that barrier."

"At least," said Roberts. As the scene changed, they could see, at the high windows of the smashed buildings outside the barrier, triple-lightning-bolt banners hung out. In the dumps, pipes torn out of buildings were thrust deep in the heaps of garbage, with triple-lightning-bolt flags flying from them. Along the edges of the barrier itself, there were flashes of occasional explosions as small parties of men tried to force their way through. Then, apparently, some new command was given. Along the whole length of the enormous barrier, the attempt to break through gradually died out.

• • •

After a lengthy silence, Hammell said, "Trying to make something out of this place is like trying to build a house out of hand grenades."

Morrissey nodded. "It was easy to see what they needed before: They were too sunk in the backwash of all the slums they'd been taken from before they were put here. But what do they need *now?*"

Roberts stared off into the distance.

Hammell shook his head. "Where do we even start? Last time, we had an inert mass to work with. This time, we've got something that explodes from one crisis to the next. How did this mess ever come about anyway? I thought we'd improved things— not set up a powder keg."

Roberts, who at least had been sleeping at night, began to dimly see a possible cause of the trouble.

After a moment, he said tentatively, "Every time we've used the want-generator, except at very low power on just the three of us, there's been an *inertia*. Once started, the effect seems to go on, even though we turn off the want-generator itself. We've accepted this as a fact, but we haven't tried to find any mechanism to explain it. What if each individual has, in effect, a slight *want-generator capacity* himself? Suppose that once his desire is aroused, it energizes a *field*, similar to an electric field around a wire. This hypothetical desire-field, once energized, would create, in effect, a force tending to maintain the desire, because any lessening of the desire would cause a flow of energy from the collapsing field to reinforce the desire. The result would be an *inertia of the desire*, once created."

Morrissey blinked. "In that case, there should be induction effects. Once a strong desire is created, it will tend to induce a corresponding desire in others, and there will be something similar to attraction and repulsion, based on these interacting desire-fields."

There was a moment's silence as they thought it over, then Roberts said, "To begin with, to all intents and purposes, these people were *desireless*, or rather, their desires were comparatively few, simple, and predictable. It follows that there would be comparatively few of these interacting desire-fields. What *we* apparently did was to *set up more of these interacting fields*."

Hammell said, "Of course, this is just a theory."

"Sure," said Roberts. "But are you under the impression that we were operating without a theory before? We *had* a theory. The theory was that the city, and the people in it, were *passive subjects for the operation of the want-generator*. Granted that when the effect was concentrated on just the three of us, here, it seemed to work that way. But then, the city is much larger, the effect is more widespread and there are far more of what you might call 'natural want-generator units' in the city. Well, we've been acting on the theory that the want-generator operated on a passive object, and the passive object is now running away with the experiment. It looks like time to reconsider the theory."

Hammell thought it over. "You figure we've set up these 'desire-fields' with the want-generator, and now they're in operation, whether we run the want-generator or not?"

"How else do you explain what's going on? It's exactly *as if* such fields were in operation. If so, where do they come from?"

"But look, remember how we hit the whole city with 'desire for achievement'? And how then we discovered that their idea of achievement was to 'kill mechs'? And to stop that, we had to give them a stiff jolt of 'desire to give up'? Then there was an uncontrollable panic, and we gave them a shot of 'desire to fight' to break the panic? That incidentally started a mess of fist fights, and we had to use 'desire to sleep' to end that? Remember?"

"Yes," said Roberts. "I wouldn't be likely to forget that."

"Well, if 'desire to give up' knocked out 'desire for achievement', and if 'desire to fight' knocked out 'desire to give up,' and so on, these hypothetical fields have all been discharged except the last one, which, as I remember, was 'desire to think'. Where's the problem? Where did *this* mess come from?"

"It depends on what you mean when you say the desires were 'knocked out'," said Roberts. "Maybe 'desire to fight' eliminates 'desire to give up'. They're directly opposed to each other. But how does 'desire to think' eliminate 'desire for achievement'? And how do either of them eliminate 'desire to kill mechs', which these people had to start with?"

Hammell was silent for a moment, then his eyes narrowed in thought. "Yes, I see. One desire may just be *set aside* for a while, as when you tune a receiver to pick up one signal instead of another."

Roberts nodded. "And it seems to me that we've added quite a few signals to those that can be picked up in that city. 'Desire to achieve' seems to be operating, and in practice it's still interpreted the same way: 'Kill mechs'. This affects 'desire to learn', which is interpreted as 'desire to learn how to kill mechs'. And then, 'desire to work' seems to be in operation, since, for instance, the improvised tools and weapons take work. But that desire manifests as 'desire to work at killing mechs'. And it's obvious that for all this to happen so fast, 'desire to think' must have been operating, no doubt in the form of 'desire to think how to kill mechs'. Every desire we've added has apparently been brought to serve that one dominating desire that they had before we started, namely, 'Kill the lousy mechs'. Thanks to that, they've got a fair chance to blow up the planetary computer and smash every machine that serves it."

"Yes," said Hammell. "And once they succeed in that, there'll be mass starvation here, because the computer and a few technicians run the mechanized farms through roboid machinery. Once they destroy the computer they land right back in a bare subsistence, dog-eat-dog set-up."

"Speaking of technicians," said Roberts, frowning, "have you noticed these different kinds of specialized machines that weren't here before? Did that computer program itself to make them. Or—"

Morrissey had been experimentally changing the view on the screen, and now cleared his throat. "While you theoreticians have been groping for conclusions by pure deduction, I've got hold of some facts. Take a look at this."

Roberts and Hammell glanced at the screen, to see a tall gray-haired man wearing dark-blue clothing of good material and narrow cut, who was standing before a wall-size screen showing a roughly rectangular section of fortified city, with square bastions at the corners.

Beside him stood a burly giant with bristling red beard, who said angrily, "Damn it, Kelty, they'll tunnel. Right this minute, a dozen teams of shovel-gangs are digging under your fortified line."

Hammell stared at the red-bearded giant. "*That's* one of the technicians!"

Roberts ran his hand over his face. The last time they'd been here, Kelty, second-in-command of the city's huge police force, had told Roberts that the bulk of the technicians had left the city. Moreover, Kelty said, there was an implacable enmity between the bulk of the technicians and the computer, and hence no chance of the technicians returning to the city. So, how—

From somewhere in the ship came an odd creaking gritting noise, but Roberts was too preoccupied to pay any attention to it.

Morrissey said, "I suppose if anything could make that planetary computer give concessions to get the technicians back, this is it."

On the spy screen, Kelty was now saying, ". . . Very true. Right this minute, they're tunneling. But eventually, they'll have to come up, or come out in another tunnel, that *we* control. And when they do—"

"No, they *won't* have to come out. That's the point. They can dig from that fortified line of yours, right under one of the power mains, all the way to Center, and with a little luck they can then blow the computer itself right off the map."

"*If*," said Kelty, "they don't lose their following first."

"How?"

"This tunnel will take a long time to dig. A lot of food will be consumed in that time. They don't have it *to* consume. The stores outside the line have only so much, and no more is going to them. Without food, the fanatics will lose their grip on the populace. They'll be forced to give up."

The red-bearded giant shook his head. "Maybe we can starve the *other* eighty or ninety percent of the populace into submission, but not that crew. They're a bunch of fanatics, led by a fanatic to end all fanatics. They'll dig till they don't have the strength to lift a pick. And all they need to do to maintain their strength is to take the lion's share of the food for themselves."

"The point," said Kelty, "is in this other eighty or ninety percent of the populace you speak of. What will they do *when they don't get food?*"

The giant snorted. "Raid the remaining food stores, steal from each other, run around screaming till they're out of strength. Don't kid yourself that they'll attack the fanatics' Leader. *He's* got ninety percent of the men with weapons. The best the rest of them will do is to knock off a few stragglers and isolated guards here and there to relieve their feelings. Meanwhile, the fanatics and their work-gangs will tunnel. When the computer blows up, you and I and the rest of us will have no choice but to get out somewhere beyond the forest, and I can tell you from experience that that's no fun. But it's better than starving, which is what will happen to us if we're back here once the computer is gone."

Kelty's face had the look of a man forcing himself to consider unwelcome facts. He turned away, then suddenly turned back again.

"What's your idea?"

"We're producing some items of machinery I haven't mentioned before."

"Namely?"

"I've got three oversize trenchers in process, and the largest is almost finished. These are step-trenchers. The first makes a trench big enough for a canal. The second rides in the bottom of that and sends its dirt up on a conveyor. The third rides in the bottom of *that* trench and makes a deep cleft like a glacial crevasse. Let the fanatics try to tunnel across *that*. For good insurance, we can drop projectors of some good heavy gas in there, and when their tunnel comes through the wall of the trench down below, the gas will go to work on them."

Kelty looked horrified. "That's too hor . . ."

"It will *work*."

Kelty shook his head. "A trench like that would cut every power and water main from Center out."

"We can stop the flow from the cut mains. We've . . ."

"I don't mean that. This will cut off their water supply."

"Let it. We'll still be alive afterward, and we'll have the wherewithal to put the whole place back together again."

"Do you have some way to put millions of dead men back together? The minute you cut those mains, you sign the death-warrant for three-quarters of the human population of this planet."

"The minute you let the Great Leader blow up the computer, you sign the death-warrant for ninety-nine percent of the human population of this planet."

Kelty hesitated. "Suppose we cut off the water in the mains from here? Just shut the main valves?"

"Now you're grasping at straws. Their leader thought of that before we did. He's already got gangs of men doing nothing but carrying up buckets and waterproofed trash cans filled with water. A deep trench is what we need, to cut their tunnels. Shutting off the water from here won't do it."

Kelty shook his head wearily. "These trenchers of yours *will* cut through the mains? Won't they break down?"

"They'll chew right through them. *That* part's no problem. What we need is your approval, so we don't waste any time. When you're dealing with fanatics, you can't afford to give them any advantage, and we don't want them to get a minute's lead on us."

"But it's my job in a situation like this to *restore order with a minimum loss of life.*"

"That's exactly what I'm talking about. You spend a winter out with us in that forest, and you'll run into situations that make this seem easy by contrast. All *you* have to do is *stop those fanatics,* and the best-skilled, most cooperative section of the populace *lives.* This is horrible in its way"—the giant shrugged—"but what do you expect? This way, you get to save the sources of power, the skills, and the organization, to hold back what you might call the wild forces of this planet. Do you know what it's like to fight the elements and the beasts and insects of this so-called Paradise *with no technology? That's* the problem, Kelty. To save *humanity plus technology.*"

Kelty, his face pale and shaken, said, "How long before this first big trencher of yours is ready?"

"Not long. About three hours."

"I'll think it over."

"The sooner we get started with it, the better."

"All right. I'll think it over."

Roberts glanced at Morrissey. "Is there any way we can possibly find this chief fanatic they call the Great Leader?"

Morrissey shook his head. "So far as I can see, only by pure luck. He's almost sure to be in one of those tunnels, and since the city's surveillance system doesn't cover the tunnels, the screen won't either. How do we find him?"

"Yes. That's no solution."

From somewhere in the ship came a creaking noise that momentarily caught Roberts' attention, but then he saw what was happening on the screen. The red-bearded technician had left the room, and Kelty had crossed to a kind of typewriter keyboard set out from the wall. His hands flashed over it in a blur. After only a moment's delay, the wall lit up in several lines of green letters:

PLAN FEASIBLE.

LONG-RANGE COST ACCEPTABLE.

PLAN IS APPROVED.

Now that it was too late, it suddenly came to Roberts that the crisis might have been delayed by using the want-generator on Kelty; but now the computer had accepted the plan, and the want-generator could no more influence the computer than a bee could intimidate a sledgehammer.

Hammell said, "Wait—Why not hit the whole city with an

overpowering jolt of 'desire for peace'? Just pour it on, and *end* this!"

Morrissey's face cleared. "Why didn't we think of that sooner?" He set up "desire for peace" on the want-generator, and turned it on.

Roberts, Hammell, and Morrissey waited tensely to see what would happen.

Somewhere, there was a grinding crunching noise.

Roberts looked around curiously, then a flash of movement on the screen caught his attention.

A number of hard-looking individuals were walking out of doorways and climbing out of trenches in the garbage dumps. They tossed their guns aside, and waving their hands over their head, shouted "Let's be friends!" and walked out toward the burnt bare no-man's-land and its wire barrier.

The roboid police devices waited until the men were well out in the open. Then they opened fire, and shot the men down.

More men came forward behind them, shouting, "We want peace!"

The roboid devices cut them down with automatic efficiency.

Still more came forward.

"Shut it off!" said Roberts.

The roboid devices waited for a better shot, and suddenly the target vanished in flying dives into the nearest gutter, through cellar windows, and behind heaps of trash.

The three men stared at the screen and the unmoving bodies.

"Well," said Morrissey in a dull voice, "*that* sure didn't work."

Hammell said shakily, "Suppose we hit Kelty with an extra-strong dose of 'desire for peace'? He could call off the police, couldn't he?"

Roberts thought a moment, then shook his head. "If the computer is in its right mind, so to speak, it will sack Kelty if he tries that. The fanatics have apparently booby-trapped the roboid police so many times that any call for peace will ring false to it—like the woman with her 'baby', but on a larger scale."

"Damn it," said Hammell, "we can't influence the *computer*. The thing has no emotions *to* influence."

Roberts was frowning. "There's a thought."

"What do you mean?" said Hammell.

Roberts glanced out the porthole, which was nearer Hammell than himself, at the patrol ship. "It just occurred to me that if the want-generator won't influence the computer, maybe we've got something else here that *will*."

"We have?" Hammell turned around, looked out, and froze.

"There are advantages," said Roberts, "to having something a little stronger than a space yacht. We . . . what's the matter?"

Hammell drew in a slow deep breath.

"Have you been hearing a funny gritting noise lately?"

"Now that you mention it," said Roberts, "I have. But every time I've heard it, something else has come up. Why?"

"Ease over here a little, and look outside from a different angle. Don't make any fast move, or the thing may jerk back and hurt the ship."

Frowning, Roberts carefully eased over toward Hammell—to look directly into the cold calculating gaze of a pair of snaky eyes as big as his fists. The thing had a pointed head large enough at the thickest to wrap both arms around and just clasp hands. Roberts at once recognized the creature. This was the thing that had been looking down at him earlier from the trees. Apparently it had coiled itself around the ship to climb up this high, and the pressure of its coils had created the creaking noise.

Roberts carefully glanced aside, at his battle armor. Probably the best thing to do was to get into that, go out, and—

Hammell sitting as if paralyzed, murmured. "Oh, oh. Look—"

CRACK!

The porthole, transparent plate, frame, gasket, rims, and all smashed inward and clattered and bounced on the deck.

The big head was right there in the ship beside them, looking at them and the want-generator coldly.

Somewhere there was a creaking grating noise. The head flowed in farther on its dark-green muscular neck.

Roberts, half-paralyzed, began to have the illusion that he was dreaming. This *couldn't* be real. With an effort, he forced his mind to face the facts.

For him to try to quickly reach the battle armor now would only get the snake's attention. *Any* sudden motion was a form of suicide. Yet, to stay still promised the same result after a slight delay.

Very gradually, he began to ease toward the armor. Then he began to wonder, how was he going to go through the awkward process of getting into the armor with the snake looking on?

Meanwhile, the snake was feeding another length of coil in steadily; but abruptly it froze, looking back past Roberts.

It dawned on Roberts that the snake had just spotted the battle armor standing against the wall. Its attention intensely riveted, the snake hung motionless.

Roberts barely murmured.

"Morrissey."

"Sir?"

"Turn on 'desire for peace'. Focus it on the yacht here."

Morrissey, moving with slow careful motions, refocused the want-generator.

Roberts warily turned, very slowly, to look around.

A sleepy film suddenly seemed to come down over the snake's eyes.

At the same moment, Roberts felt an intense yearning for peace and quiet. *Enough* of conflict. "For heaven's sake," the thought went through his mind, "why can't everyone get along together?"

The snake was moving carefully, its huge head lowered and somehow suggestive of a dog expecting a kick. With increasing speed, the length of neck went out the hole in the ship, followed by the head.

There was a grating, grinding, scraping noise, and Roberts cautiously put his head out, to see the creature drop free at the base of the ship and rapidly head for cover.

Roberts sucked in a deep breath, and glanced around.

"Morrissey?"

"Sir?"

"Is there a timer in that circuit?"

"Yes, sir."

"Set it for a minute, and give us a stiff jolt of 'desire for sleep'."

Morrissey bent briefly at the controls.

Roberts suddenly realized that he was worn out, dazed. The room spun around him, and he sat down, cradled his head on his arms, sagged against the control panel . . .

. . . Somewhere, tinnily, a bell was ringing, and Roberts dazedly sat up. He felt as if he had been dredged up from a hundred fathoms down, but he was amazed at the way his desire for sleep evaporated. Now he felt rested, refreshed, and—

Suddenly he remembered something, and sprang to the porthole.

Outside, the huge snake lay motionless, half in and half out of the forest.

Hammell and Morrissey were both face down on the control panel. As the timer's bell rang on, only Morrissey was even beginning to stir.

The alarm kept ringing, and now Morrissey groped around dazedly but couldn't seem to connect with it.

Naturally, Roberts thought. He glanced around sourly. After a night spent in this bucket, who *wouldn't* be worn out? Every time you turned around, some monster was coming in after you. Why not just live in a cheesecloth tent, and get it over with quick?

Morrissey finally found the timer, shut it off, and passed out again.

So far, Hammell hadn't even moved.

Roberts grunted in disgust, looked back out into the clearing, and decided the snake mustn't have spent a very restful night, either. It lay on the ground like a felled tree.

Roberts leaned out farther, to see what damage it might have done to the yacht in climbing up it, and at once he heard a rustle overhead, and felt the heat of the sun, shining down on his neck, abruptly cut off.

There was a dazzle of light.

WHAP!

Roberts was inside so fast that he knocked Hammell half out of his chair, and himself landed in a sprawl over the edge of the want-generator's control panel.

The air outside the porthole was suddenly filled with huge blue and green feathers. There was a sizzling noise, a smell of cooked meat and burnt pinfeathers, a kind of low popping sound, and a burnt-paint smell.

Cautiously, Roberts looked out, to see one of the smaller turrets on the patrol ship swinging back into position.

Just what caused it, Roberts didn't know, but there was something about the patrol ship as he looked at it that suggested reproach.

Roberts eased farther back and looked around. Morrissey and Hammell—despite the fact that he'd almost been knocked flat—were still asleep. Roberts glanced at the patrol ship. How had it—

That thought was drowned out as it began by a crackling noise, and the boom of a loudspeaker close by:

"YOUR FULL ATTENTION, PLEASE. THIS VESSEL IS FULLY PROTECTED BY APPROPRIATE DEVICES OF THE ADVANCED SYNODICS PRODUCTS CORPORATION. IT WILL RETALIATE AUTOMATICALLY AGAINST ANY AGGRESSIVE OR HOSTILE ACTION."

• • •

Hammell was immediately on his feet. Morrissey lurched out of his chair and looked stuporously around.

"The *snake!*" said Hammell. "Where—"

"It's right down below," said Roberts, "and it's just started to move. This warning system you've got here just *woke it up.*"

Morrisey looked blankly at the want-generator.

"Then—"

"Then," said Roberts, "it follows that the snake, at least, is affected by the want-generator. The last time we were here, we used a 'desire to help out' field to persuade the technicians to trade with us on a fair basis. The instant that field was shut off, there was an uproar out in the forest. It occurred to me at the time that there might be a bunch of predators out there being obliging to their prey."

Hammell glanced at the hole in the side of the ship. "That knowledge may just get us some sleep tonight. But we're *still* stuck with the problem of what to do about this city. The want-generator may affect the wild animals, but it still doesn't affect that computer."

"No," said Roberts, "but something we can do *may* affect the computer. I was thinking of doing it with the patrol ship alone, but this snake suggests new possibilities."

Hammell glanced uneasily out into the clearing. "What were you thinking of?"

"Well," said Roberts, "the immediate problem here is that the fanatics and the computer are opposed. Either one, if successful, can destroy the other. The enmity has to be gotten around somehow inside of three hours or so, or we are right on the edge of a crisis that can mean the death of millions of people."

"Yes," said Hammell, "I see the *problem*. But where's the *solution?*"

Roberts said, "Why do we get unexpected reactions from the people in the city when we beam desires at them? Isn't it because *their thought processes are different?*"

"Sure," said Hammell exasperatedly. "But how do we—"

"We have to affect, not only the emotions, but the thought processes, too. The want-generator affects only the emotions. *We've got to reach their minds.*"

Morrissey looked puzzled.

Hammell said, "I can see, with the guns on that patrol ship of yours, that you can reach their *bodies*. But how you get at their *minds*—"

"When you and your brother," said Roberts, "are about to shoot each other, it really breaks up the family quarrel fast if you find some outsider waiting around to shoot the survivor."

"Yeah," said Hammell, frowning, "that's a point. You mean, we make ourselves the villains, in order to unite them?"

"Once we're the villains, will they listen to us?"

Hammell looked momentarily foolish. "Then how *do* we do it?"

"Obviously, somebody *else* has to be the villain."

"*Who*? There are only the three of us."

Roberts thought a moment. "How's 'Oggbad' sound?"

Morrissey said blankly, "Who in space is Oggbad?"

"If we're going to have a villain," said Roberts, "I fail to see why any of *us* has to be stuck with the job. Let Oggbad do it."

"Who's Oggbad?" said Morrissey.

"Do *what?*" said Hammell.

Roberts said, "Amongst other things, attack the city. Can you think of any better way to get our advice listened to than by a demonstration of what the fiend Oggbad is up to?"

Morrissey looked at Hammell. "Have we missed this much sleep?"

Hammell shook his head. "We can follow it this far: a) The city is divided into two warring factions. b) We've got to unite them to straighten out the mess. c) An outside menace is the best way to unite them. d) *We* don't want to play the part of this outside menace ourselves, because that would debar us from taking any direct part in the situation. e) Therefore, somebody *else* should do it—I suppose Oggbad is as good as anybody; but, in the first place, where do we get Oggbad? And how do we provide Oggbad with an army to attack the city? And, just incidentally, that computer may be stupid in dealing with people, but that doesn't mean it can't check facts. We've got to convince *both* sides. How do we outwit the computer? And best of all, how do we do all this in three hours or less?"

Roberts said patiently, "With a decent night's sleep, all this should be obvious. Who says we've got to have a *real* villain? A real villain is likely to get out of hand and complicate the situation when you want to simplify it. Oggbad is strictly a fiction of our imagination."

"*Your* imagination," said Hammell.

"But," said Roberts, "Oggbad is to *appear* real, to the city. This he will accomplish by attacking the city."

Morrissey said earnestly, "How does a figment of your imagination attack the city?"

"Take a look out that porthole," said Roberts. "As we should know, there are beasts out in that forest that can create chaos in nothing flat. Do you mean to tell me you don't see how Oggbad can attack the city?"

"But," said Hammell, "to lead the animals—How does he—"

Morrissey gave a sudden start. "Ye gods. We *must* need sleep. We've already seen that the want-generator affects the animals. If that holds true, *we* can control the animals!"

"I don't *mean* that," said Hammell. "How do we *explain*, so it convinces the computer, among others, that this *Oggbad* can influence the animals?"

"Obviously," said Roberts, "the only conceivable ways are for Oggbad to be either a great animal trainer, a great biologist, or a great sorcerer. And if the story is going to have to stand the computer's scrutiny, I'm in favor of putting in broad claims right at the beginning, so if the computer is going to choke on it, we find it out immediately."

"Hm-m-m," said Morrissey. "How is the computer, based on science, going to judge a *sorcerer?*"

Hammell said thoughtfully, "There *are* rumors of planets run by . . . ah . . . if not sorcery, something just as good."

"Exactly," said Roberts. "That's what I want to take advantage of."

Morrissey shook his head. "This part starts to make sense to me, but there's a catch. Kelty saw you and Hammell when we were here before. So did the computer's surveillance system. The technicians have seen all three of us. How do we explain that a cargo-ship captain, his cargo-control officer, and his communications officer, are tangled up in a fight with this Oggbad?"

"Frankly," said Roberts, "I'm a little sick of being a cargo-ship captain. I don't think a cargo-ship captain is going to have much impact on them, anyway. If we're going to deal with the city, let's deal with them on nothing less than an equal basis. I'm not interested in going through another dose of what we got the last time."

Hammell nodded, but Morrissey still shook his head. "They've got records of our last visit."

"That won't do them much good," said Roberts, "if every time they see us, we're *inside a suit of battle armor.*"

For the first time, Morrissey smiled. "Yes, that's a point. But how do we explain—"

"If we get things on the right basis to start with, I don't think they're going to *ask* for too many explanations."

Hammell said, "Are you going to say we're investigative officers of some kind?"

"No, because then we have to say what bureau we're working for, and so on. I'm in favor of our appropriating so much rank, right at the start, that it jars them back on their heels, makes them listen when we talk, and makes them hesitate before asking *any* questions. If we're going to get them out of this mess, I fail to see why we have to do it on bended knee. The last time we were here, the animals tried to eat us, the plants tried to smother us, the people threw bottles and chunks of cement at us, and the roboids slapped us in prison. This time, let *them* accommodate themselves to *us*. I don't know what you guys intend to be, but as far as I'm concerned, I aim to get a little satisfaction out of this mess. I'm going to be Vaughan the Terrible, Duke of Trasimere, and I'm on the trail of the evil prince and sorcerer Oggbad the Foul, and if anyone disbelieves or doubts my word, I'll punish his impertinence with a couple of blasts from my fusion guns, *which are real.*"

Hammell grinned. "Between the fantastic story, and the real power, it would be possible for the computer to get tied in knots."

Morrissey said, "And there's nothing to prevent our beaming 'desire to believe' at the people. The computer won't be affected, but we should be able to so tie up the computer that it doesn't know what to accept and what to reject."

"That's it," said Roberts.

Hammell said, "Time's passing. This seems to hang together. Let's try it and see what happens."

Morrissey nodded. "Let's get started."

"O.K.," said Roberts.

He got into the battle armor to go back to the patrol ship.

Roberts had intended to make a few slapdash preparations, such as smearing some fresh paint over the Interstellar Patrol identification of the ship—which always showed through any covering he put over it, but the symbiotic computer immediately took a hand.

"Effacing the patrol ship designation without good reason is prohibited."

"I *have* good reason," said Roberts promptly.

"What?" demanded the computer.

Roberts, stupefied at this last-minute delay, gave a quick explanation, and waited angrily for the next piece of obstruction.

"Excellent," said the symbiotic computer. "The plan shows admirable insight into the nature of the problem. However, you evidently have neglected to study your 'Patrol Ship Special Board Number Three—Typical Ship and Equipment Disguises and Physical Aspects of Stratagems.' A demonstration is in order. Press down the blue lever numbered '3' at the left of the control panel."

Roberts hesitated. Beads of sweat popped out on his brow. Then he got control of himself, stopped thinking what the last demonstration had been like, and pushed down blue lever number "3" at the left of the control panel.

At once, there was a hum, and a clank from the weapons lockers where, among other things, the suits of battle armor were stored. From outside came a low whirring noise and a faint sliding sound. Then there was a continuous low rumble, followed by an odd noise Roberts couldn't place. Then the ship lifted.

Roberts waited a moment, then snapped on the outside viewscreen, to see in astonishment that the space yacht was already painted jet black with silver markings, and was now acquiring a set of weird symbols—oddly distorted silver cats, skulls with one red and one blue eye, silver snakes with their gold-colored insides apparently pulled out through their mouths. The sight gave Roberts a nauseous sensation, but he watched as the slender arms with their batteries of nozzles moved over the space yacht while the patrol ship circled it.

There was a clank and rumble from inside the weapons lockers, then the patrol ship set down again.

Roberts quickly climbed out the hatch, and was startled to see that his whole ship was now gold with a kind of platinum trim. Some kind of dark purple marking was evident farther forward, and Roberts glanced around, walked aft along a horizontal fin, dropped off, and took a look at the ship.

From a short distance, the impression of wealth and power set Roberts back on his heels. No detail of trim had been overlooked, and on the sides of the ship were three complete coats of arms, the center one placed slightly higher than the other two, and surrounded by a kind of bright golden sunburst.

Roberts shook his head, and glanced up at the big hatch of the space yacht, where Hammell was leaning out to stare at the lurid designs on the space yacht.

The two men looked at each other blankly, then Roberts grinned, and called, "Ready?"

Hammell nodded. "How many passes?"

"Two should do it, especially if there's some time in between."

"O.K."

They got back in their ships, lifted off, flew low and fast away from the direction of the city, and then rose high into the sky on the far side of the planet. From very high up, Hammell and Morrissey dove on the city, the speed of their passage creating a crack and rumble that brought people into the streets on both sides of the barrier. A few moments later, Roberts flashed low over the city, the sound of his passage creating an even sharper crack and louder rumble.

The communicator buzzed, and there was a faint click, as if someone had just snapped it on. An authoritative voice said, "Planetary Control Center, Paradise City, Paradise. No flights are authorized, and no landings permit—"

A harsh voice snarled, "Be damned with your authorization. This is the Imperial light cruiser *Droit de Main*, flagship of Search Force IX. Vice Admiral Sir Ian Cudleigh is aboard this ship, in direct service to their Imperial Highnesses, the Dukes of Malafont and Greme, who accompany His Royal and Imperial Highness, Vaughan, Duke of Trasimere, surnamed The Terrible, Prince Contestant to the Throne. You seek to bar our way at your own immediate and deadly peril. Submit at once, or we destroy you and every inhabitant of this place. We are on a business of holy vengeance, and you stand warned. Master of the Ordnance! Give them a taste of our steel!"

Roberts sat wide-eyed and half-paralyzed. As thick as he had intended to lay it on, this beat anything he'd had in mind.

There was a faint clicking from somewhere forward, and on the outside viewscreen, two buildings, one inside and one outside the foam-covered barrier of wire and mines, erupted in sheets of flame and smoke.

The harsh voice wasted scarcely a second. "Enough! Stand ready if this place lies servile to the fiend . . . All right, you, which is it? Oggbad, or Vaughan?"

There was a brief buzz from the receiver, then, "Vaughan."

"So be it. Now, know you that their Imperial Highnesses are

locked in mortal combat with Oggbad the Traitor. Know you that Oggbad, though shorn of his material power, still sways mighty forces in the realms of sorcery. Only if his soul be cleaved from his body, and chained for its ten million years of punishment in the nether regions, will the blight be ended. Know, then, that as this condition is as yet unmet, and as you serve the Duke Vaughan, Oggbad may seek to smite you. Now, listen closely. If, under fear of the traitor's evil power, you recant to Oggbad, Duke Vaughan with fire and sword will smite you to the death. If, mayhap, under influence of the fiend's sorcery, you are bound over mindless into his evil cause, Duke Vaughan will then faithfully seek to cleanse your soul by agony here, before sending you to your reward. These are— *There goes the fiend! Give chase!*"

The scene on the viewscreen flashed backwards, whirled, and for the second time, the patrol ship streaked after the space yacht.

The communicator clicked off. The voice of the symbiotic computer said, "The instruments in the city are now picking up all the signs and indications of a formidable fleet passing the planet."

"Good."

Roberts, streaking along the curve of the planet after the space yacht, was starting to wonder what a patrol ship with fully-trained crew would be like. What had happened so far was apparently mere routine, as far as the symbiotic computer was concerned.

Then he was swinging the patrol ship low over the forest, and following the space yacht in a wide curve to a landing in the clearing. He extended the stabilizer feet, snapped off the gravitors, and got up.

He yanked open the weapons locker, to get out the battle armor, and a glittering suit of armor with helmet curving up into a slender spire came out on its sling. The breastplate of this suit was covered with a dazzling coat of arms. The big fusion gun that hung on the right side was matched on the left by a broadsword. Tied to the top of the helmet's spire was a thing like a pink silk handkerchief.

Looking closely, Roberts could see that his armor was essentially the same as what he'd been wearing before. But the effect was very different.

He wasted a moment asking himself how that had been done. Was there some kind of metal-working equipment recessed into the hull behind the weapons locker? How—

The voice of the symbiotic computer spoke dryly: "In a crisis, each minute is a precious jewel."

Roberts swore, got into the armor hurriedly, and started for the hatch. On the way, the sword banged around and got crosswise of his legs. He'd barely recovered his balance when he straightened up and rammed the helmet's spire into the ceiling. There was a sarcastic throat-clearing noise in the earphones, but the symbiotic computer didn't actually say anything; the cause of this trouble was its own fault.

Roberts finally managed to get the hatch open despite the spire, heaved himself out, and crossed to the space yacht, where Morrissey and Hammell looked up from the spy screen to stare at him in amazement.

"Not my idea," said Roberts, getting out of the armor. "This idea belongs to the computer. What's going on in the city?"

Morrissey said, "I've been watching this screen since we started, and as nearly as I can tell, the people generally are scared, and subject to all kinds of rumors. The general impression seems to be that the planetary computer got a spaceship up, and the Great Leader is up there fighting it in one of his own. As for the fanatics themselves, the more rank they have, the more uncertain they seem to be; but again, so far as I've been able to find out, the top ones are still out of sight."

"That makes it nice," said Roberts, trying to tilt the armor against the wall. The needlelike tip of the spire, even though it rested at a shallow angle against the wall, looked as if it just might push a hole through the hull. Exasperated, Roberts tilted the armor away from the wall, and tried to ease it down on the deck. At the last moment, it got away from him, and hit with a heavy thud.

Hammell and Morrissey jumped and looked around. Roberts straightened up carefully, "This thing sure isn't made of feathers. And watch out for the spike on the helmet. I don't know what kind of metal it is, but it doesn't give, and it's got a point like a needle."

Hammell and Morrissey acknowledged the warning with bare grunts, and immediately turned back to the screen. Roberts, uneasily conscious what ship he was in, looked around at the porthole to find it temporarily repaired with an airtight double-plate-and-gasket screwtight seal. Satisfied that nothing was going to come in there, Roberts slid into his chair, and immediately saw, on the screen, Kelty and the red-bearded technician.

"Nuts," the technician was saying. "There isn't any such place. You've been sold a bill of goods. The whole—"

"Shut up for a minute," said Kelty, "and see for yourself. We got the whole thing down as it happened. Look at this." He tapped one of several buttons on the edge of his desk, and the far wall of the room suddenly was like blue sky, across which a black-and-silver ship, weirdly decorated, streaked erratically into view, followed a moment later by a dazzling golden ship that unleashed searing bolts of energy that missed the black-and-silver ship by the narrowest of margins. The golden ship was suddenly enormously magnified, to fill the wall. The details of its trim and armament stood out clearly, the coat of arms thoroughly detailed and distinct, the center coat of arms raised above the others and set off in a blaze of bright gold trim.

Kelty said, "A bill of goods, huh? Are you going to tell me the Great Leader dreamed this up?"

The technician looked dazzled. "Still, I never heard of—"

"Wait," said Kelty. "The computer's air-traffic-control circuit ordered the ship off. Here's what happened." He touched a second button. The wall blanked.

A voice said authoritatively, "Planetary Control Center, Paradise City, Paradise. No flights are authorized, and no landing permit has—"

The wall flared with color, and a hard face, eyes narrowed, scarred below the left eye and across the bridge of the nose, appeared against an unfocused background, to snarl, "Be damned with your authorization. This is the Imperial light cruiser *Droit de Main*, flagship of Search Force IX. Vice Admiral Sir Ian Cudleigh is aboard this ship . . ."

The red-bearded technician stared at the screen, where the tough figure suddenly turned aside:

"Master of the Ordnance! Give them a taste of our steel!"

Kelty hit another button, and the wall lit with a view of buildings exploding in sheets of flame and smoke.

At the end, Kelty turned to the technician. "Then the first ship showed again, and the two ships went out of view, and the long-range pickups started feeding in more data. *There's a fleet out there.*"

The technician, obviously shaken, stared at the blank wall. "Where does this leave us?"

"You tell me. The computer had to make a quick choice which side to be on, and it must have only taken one-tenth of one percent of its circuits to decide that. There wasn't much choice, if you know what I mean."

"But where in space did these—"

There was a jarring buzz. A voice said urgently, "Now receiving."

The wall lit up again. A very pale face, marked by dissipation but with intense dark eyes, looked out under a narrow golden crown.

"I see you not. To whom do I speak?"

"This is the Planetary Control Center, Paradise City, Para—"

"Listen closely. It is I, Oggbad, Prince of the Empire, Premier Peer of the Kingdom, High Master of the Unseen Realms. I require your immediate aid to repulse the treasonous assaults of the low villains, Vaughan, Percy, and Ewald. Yield at once to my command or come under ban of the most hideous punishment. How say you?"

There were several buzzing sounds of varying pitch, then the words, "Owing to a lack of sufficient data—"

"Bah! These are the words of poltroons, or traitors! I am Oggbad! *Yield!*"

There was a total silence, then, "Very well! You think the material power of the traitor Vaughan will protect you. I say it will not! Nay, if the fools hound me throughout the length of the universe, and drive me from sun to sun, and destroy the last remnant of my worldly power, still, I am Oggbad! In the unseen realms, guns count for naught. All is unchanged, and I am still High Master of the Unseen Realms. As an earnest of my intent, and a warning to those who believe matter can of a right rule the universe, I shall inspirit the very animals with a hate of your treason, and hurl the might of the forest against you. Nay, I say, yield, or face the most dread powers of the Unseen Realms!"

The computer could manage nothing but a buzz.

"So be it," said the pale dissipated face looking at them from the wall, its dark eyes blazing. "You anger me. And though I be shorn of material power you will soon learn the might of my dominion. I *will* regain a footing for my power! And as I am here, *you* will serve, or I will destroy you. Bear my words closely in mind."

The wall went blank. Kelty stared at it dazedly. The technician passed a hand across his eyes.

Finally, Kelty said, "All right. But we're on the right side, at least. That last business was lunacy. That's—"

There was another jarring buzz. "Now receiving."

Kelty and the technician winced and turned back toward the

wall. The wall lit up with a view of the same scarred tough face they'd seen first. This face now had a thoughtful exasperated look. .

"The fiend has slipped away. No cloak of invisibility could hide so large a ship from our instruments, but there it is. He is gone. Trouble is on foot again. But he'll not leave this world alive. Well, so be it. I speak now to the Earldom—Designate of Paradise, so-called. *Answer!*"

The computer gave another buzz. "We are listening."

"Why have you a voice but no face?"

"Owing to technical difficulties."

"Be damned with technical difficulties! On all we know, Oggbad is still alive! Listen closely. As you have yielded to His Royal and Imperial Highness, Vaughan, Duke of Trasimere, Prince Contestant to the Throne, on the truth of whose cause the light of Heaven shines, so are you in duty bound to obey him. You are now a part of the Empire, in immediate fiefdom to Duke Vaughan himself. Whosoever denies this, does so on instantaneous peril of his life. Now then, the cursed Oggbad is loose on the planet. You must set your defenses in order. Mischief is afoot, and on such a scale as you may never have seen before. But fear not. Duke Vaughan is here. His material power is no small weight against the invisible might of Oggbad. Oggbad must first ensheathe his strength in material form to act in the visible realms. The Duke Vaughan's power is already on rein to act. And we are quick, ready, and hold our minds to the task—we will come through the storm. Oggbad's first onset is the worst. Prepare to meet the Duke Vaughan himself within the hour. There is no time to waste."

The wall went blank.

Like two punchdrunk fighters, Kelty and the red-bearded technician stared at the wall.

Roberts, himself half-dazed, suddenly realized that Kelty and the technician, probably the two most important humans in the computer-run part of the city, were now stuck on dead center. The slightest push would move them in either direction.

"Quick!" said Roberts. "Hit Kelty with 'desire to inform, explain, and expound'! Easy at first, then if he does what he should, step it up. We want the rest of the city to know what's going on."

On the screen, Kelty was saying dazedly. "Are we dreaming? How do we *handle* a thing like this?"

The red-bearded technician was starting to grin. "They don't waste any time, do they? Well, well. What does the computer say to *this*?"

"That's a point," said Kelty. He crossed to the keyboard set out from the wall. Almost immediately, the wall lit up in yellow letters:

INSUFFICIENT DATA

Kelty stepped back as if he'd been struck.

The technician nodded. "That's about all we can expect from it. After the crisis is over, *then* it will have the data and the answers."

"Damn it," said Kelty, "we've got to do *something*!" His face cleared. "Yes, we'll let the people know what's going on!"

"What good will that do?"

"Maybe it will give that collection of fanatics something to think about beside blowing up the computer."

"Yes. That's an idea."

Roberts glanced at Morrissey. "O.K. So far so good. But now we have the little problem of providing Oggbad with an army."

Morrissey said, "I've been thinking about that. It strikes me we're making big promises, and don't know whether we can actually come through with any results."

"If not, they're no worse off in that city than before. And as for us, we can always explain it away by 'capturing' Oggbad, and then having him escape by sorcery as soon as we figure out what to do next. After all, when you've only got three hours to save the lives of millions of people, you can't expect perfection."

"Well, no—" said Morrissey.

"What *might* work," said Roberts, "is to make a kind of large U-shaped pattern of 'desire to escape', and move it slowly forward, from the forest across the cultivated belt toward the city. Can we do that?"

Morissey nodded. "That's about what I'd planned. What I don't know is whether it will *work*."

"Let's try it. If we can get those behemoths really moving, they should be able to cover that distance pretty fast. Then there's the problem of the city. Unless that symbiotic computer puts its oar in again, what I think we ought to do is for Hammell and me to land near the border between the two parts of the city, while you move the animals along . . ."

"If they move," said Morrissey.

". . . And also pour 'desire to cooperate' at the city's populace. Once we get them into the right frame of mind, we'll wait till the animals arrive, and then there'll be a common enemy. After that, anytime the people start to break into factions, Oggbad will bash them over the head. Meanwhile, we can use the want-generator to pour the right desires at the city, while the situation itself tends to make it certain that these desires are *interpreted the right way*. Once we really get that setup going, we can probably shut off the want-generator entirely, except for emergencies."

"We don't know yet," said Morrissey stubbornly, "if those animals will *move*. I'm going to have to use different intensities of U-shaped regions of 'desire to escape', one region inside the other, to create a kind of fear-gradient, if you know what I mean. The desire to escape has to be strongest at the outermost region, so that the animals will move forward in the right direction, toward the center-line of the U."

"Good." Roberts glanced at Hammell. "Now, unless this Duke Vaughan is going to turn up all alone, probably you'd better come with me."

Hammell nodded without enthusiasm. "I guess so."

"Great," said Morrissey. "And what happens if some tree-sized animal with eight-foot jaws goes after the ship? What do I do then? It takes concentration to work this want-generator and watch the screen to be sure things aren't getting out of hand. I can't do that and fight off a horde of monsters, too."

"Hm-m-m," said Roberts. "Why not hit them with 'desire to sleep'? It certainly worked on that snake."

Morrissey called: *"Holcombe!"*

"Yes, my lord?"

"The tranquilizers."

"At once, my lord."

"O.K.," said Roberts, heaving the battle armor over on its face so he could get the back plate open, "then *that's* settled. Watch out for the point on this helmet when I get up."

"Listen," said Morrissey, "I keep trying to tell you, these animals *may not move*. Or they may mill around, fight each other, and generally be slow as mud."

"Use 'desire to cooperate' on them in the center of the U. Do the best you can. Just pour on the power and hope for the best. It will be quite a coup for Oggbad if you *can* manage it."

Morrissey said something Roberts didn't quite catch, but then he was inside the armor, and the rest of the comment came across clearly in the earphones: ". . . To be quite an experience. Who got this bright idea, anyway?"

Hammell's voice, somewhat hollow, replied, "*We* did."

"Yeah. Then I guess we're stuck with it. Well, stay healthy."

"I'll try. Watch out for the gangbats. Don't let Oggbad get you."

Roberts, inside the armor, swung shut the back plate, listened critically to the multiple click of the latch, and shoved home the lock lever.

"O.K., let's go. Stick close to me crossing the clearing."

"I sure will," said Hammell.

"And look out for the spike on this helmet."

A few minutes later, Roberts and Hammell were aboard the ship.

And a few minutes after that, they were sweeping out in a wide curve, in order to come back toward the city high up, and from a different direction.

Kelty was apparently acting fast under the influence of "desire to inform, explain, and expound." The patrol ship's symbiotic computer, in the guise of a tough no-nonsense Imperial officer, made arrangements to land, and immediately the buildings nearby were crowded with nervous onlookers.

Roberts and Hammell, taking care not to run each other through with their helmet-spikes, squeezed out the patrol ship's hatch, to face an uneasy-looking Kelty, who was accompanied by a nondescript individual with triple lightning-bolts on his armband, on the sash across his chest, and on the visor of his floppy cap. The place was surrounded with roboid police, who with apparent uneasiness faced the gap blasted in the barrier that last time Roberts had gone by. Through this gap, a number of armed toughs were seeping forward, but the roboid police apparently hesitated to stop them lest they provoke an uproar in the midst of the ceremonies.

Roberts decided there was no point fooling around. His voice came out amplified into a close resemblance to thunder:

"I am Vaughan of Trasimere. Let all who would serve me kneel. Let all who would serve the traitor Oggbad stand."

Kelty wasted no time kneeling. About fifty percent of the toughs with armbands took a quick glance at the guns on the patrol ship, and at the ruined buildings nearby, and either kneeled or dove for cover. The remaining fifty percent remained upright. The nearest tough, with the largest number of lightning-bolt insignia, gave a peculiar laugh, and a sidewise flick of his right hand. His followers snapped up their guns. One heaved a sharpened axle straight at Roberts.

There was a brief crisscrossing dazzle of white lines from the patrol ship's fusion cannon.

The wind blew away a few puffs of smoke, and all that was left of the immediate opposition was a smoldering armband here, a red-hot piece of metal there, and a scattering of grisly trophies that Roberts tried not to look at.

Giving no time for the stunned silence to turn into a new show of opposition, this time from under cover, Roberts demanded in a voice of thunder, "Who else serves Oggbad the fiend? Know you not that each man of this city will serve his true liege-lord or die? What manner of treachery is this?"

To give emphasis to his words, and because he sensed he might look silly just standing there after this speech, Roberts whipped out his sword. The sword came out with a menacing hiss that carried a long way in the silence. Then, since it would have been ridiculous to threaten the whole city, he took a quick step toward Kelty.

A roboid policeman immediately blocked his way.

Roberts' sword flashed out, sliced the machine in two with one blow, and a hard kick of his right foot knocked the pieces twenty feet away. He gripped Kelty by the shirt front.

"Serve you Oggbad?"

"No! But this has all been so fast. And we have a . . . ah . . . a *rebellion* going on here—"

"A rebellion? *Against me?*"

"No. No. Against the machines." Hastily, Kelty gave an explanation of the situation in the city, at the end of which Roberts shrugged.

"This is no matter. It is of the past. What concerns us now is Oggbad. I accept the submission of that part of the city ruled by the thinking-machine. And by grace of the power invested in me as suzerain create the thinking-machine a Baron of the Duchy of Trasimere. So, too, do I create you, Kelty, a Baron of the Duchy of Trasimere. Let no man raise his hand against your joint authority in the Inner City, by which I so designate that portion of land within this barrier of fanged wire and subtle entrapments, upwards to the limits of the aery realm, and downwards to the center of the world. Now, so much for that. We have still this Outer City to deal with. Who rules there? Every minute the power of Oggbad ensheathes itself in matter, and we waste time on this foolery! *Who rules?* Come forward now, or I destroy your power root and branch, thorn, twig, seed, and fruit! Come forth, I say!"

Roberts was becoming aware of an urgent desire to cooperate. If everyone else was feeling it as strongly as he was, the factions in the city wouldn't last long. But how could he cooperate with somebody who didn't show up?

Just then, as he was wondering what to do next, and wishing the symbiotic computer was handling this instead of him, a strongly-built figure about five-feet ten, carrying a rifle in his left hand, strode forward, handed the rifle to one of a small group of followers, and walked toward Roberts unarmed. This man had a look of intelligence and intense self-discipline. When he was directly in front of Roberts, he dropped on one knee.

Roberts said. "You rule in the Outer City?"

"I have five to ten percent of the people behind me. My men are armed. The others aren't."

"Good enough. Do you yield to me, Vaughan of Trasimere—or would you serve the foul traitor Oggbad?"

"I'm for you."

"Then by grace of the power vested in me as suzerain, I create you a Baron of the Duchy of Trasimere, and ruler of the Outer City, by which I designate that portion of the presently-existing city outside this barrier of entrapments and fanged wire, upwards to the limits of the aery realm, and downwards to the center of the world. Let no man raise his hand against you in the Outer City. Rise, Baron. Now, we have no time for the pleasures which should attend these ceremonies, or for their proper form. Each minute spent here the foul cause of Oggbad advances that much further. Dissension within our ranks must be healed at once, as it serves Oggbad's cause. Now then, you, Baron Kelty, and you, the thinking-machine with rank of Baron, and you, Baron of the Outer City, listen close.

"What Oggbad will do, we know not. But he vanished to the west, and from the west will his attack almost certainly come. Therefore, so far as is possible, post your main strength to the west, with but light forces toward the other quarters. And your strength permit it, hold strong reserves in hand. Fight by craft and cunning, from hidden places. Oppose stone walls and empty space to Oggbad's attack, so far as it be possible. Fight him not by main strength. That I will do, as my strength surpasses his. Seek to pin him, entangle him. Chisel at his power. When confronted, run, hide, and appear again at his flank. Let his arms fight stone and air, while your sword seeks his belly.

"Oggbad fights by—"

Hammell's voice interrupted. "Your Grace! Look overhead!"

Roberts looked up, to see three huge birds, their feathers blue underneath, winging past. He glanced at Kelty. "Do these birds often fly over the city?"

"Sometimes one alone. I never saw three together before."

Roberts turned toward the ship. "Master of the Ordnance! Bring down those birds!" Roberts turned to his two wide-eyed human Barons. "Their form is but a physical envelope for Oggbad's purpose. Now it begins."

From the ship, a voice called, "Your Highness, this planet must have crystal on it, and Oggbad has found it! The guns are enwrangled!"

Roberts grappled blankly with the word "enwrangled," then turned around, to see the big fusion guns aimed generally toward the birds, but apparently unable to aim precisely. The guns were moving in small circles around their true point of aim, and not one pointed directly at any of the birds.

"Then," said Roberts, thinking fast, "it *is* Oggbad! Well, gentlemen, get your men quickly in hand. Remember, Oggbad's first onset is the worst. I will shield you as best I may, and in the end we will win, because our cause is just. Now, get to cover! *Quick!*"

A terrific desire to fight was building up in Roberts, and, no doubt, in everyone else around. But only Roberts and Hammell knew that the same angry desire they felt was, in all likelihood, shared by the huge birds.

Suddenly, there was a fierce scream from overhead. Roberts looked up, to see the birds draw in their wings. At that same instant, he realized that their camouflage was far better than it seemed. He had seen three birds. But when they began to dive, their green upper feathers came into view, and there were nearly a dozen of them. At once a voice, so like Roberts' own amplified voice that he thought it must be his, roared:

"*Guards!* We'll fight on foot!"

This sounded valiant. It sounded heroic. It just suited the situation, except for one little detail:

There was no one left in the patrol ship.

Hammell already had his sword in one hand and his gun in the other. The patrol ship was already letting off futile bolts at the birds, its "enwrangled" guns doing no damage. So far as Roberts knew, there was nothing left in the ship but a couple of empty suits of battle armor. Meanwhile, from windows and doors, people were looking at him, the birds, and the patrol ship to see what would happen next.

Roberts cursing himself, turned back toward the patrol ship, and braced himself to shout another order.

The patrol ship, somehow sunk deeply as it were digging its way into the cracking concrete, disgorged from its hatch an armed man-sized figure in silver armor. Then another, and another, until there were half-a-dozen of them outside. Since they couldn't be human, they must be roboid, controlled by the symbiotic computer. But where in the cramped interior, with so much space already taken up by guns and missile storage, was there room for the fabricating machinery and the stocks of materials? Was the ship so much more advanced than it seemed? Roberts looked around, hastily gave up trying to find the answer, and roared, *"Have at the fiend!"*

A huge shadow was sweeping over the ground, and now gigantic claws shot toward him. Roberts fired his fusion gun, sheared off one of the clawed feet with a savage stroke of his sword, was grappled and knocked backwards by the other, beheaded the bird, and landed in a tangled bloody mass of bone, sinew, and feathers. He pulled himself free, to find the air suddenly thick with birds of every description, fighting the people and each other. A moment later, carnivorous bats began to arrive, to dive at Roberts' faceplate, bounce off, then cling to his armor, and squeak their teeth grittily over every bump and joint, in the hope of getting through into the flesh underneath.

The city's loudspeaker system was booming, "Take cover! Get to the tunnels! The city is under attack! Get to the tunnels!"

Flying insects were all over the place now. The air was like fog. The screams of the people told of the attacks of every kind of flying pest known to the planet. It dawned on Roberts that Morrissey had been successful beyond their wildest dreams. If they weren't careful, they might exterminate the very population they were trying to save.

Then the onslaught of another gigantic bird knocked Roberts back into the foam-covered entanglement of wires, mines, and sharp-edged strips of metal. Something seemed to snap inside him, and in a terrific outburst of anger, he sliced the bird in half, cut the entangling wires, and settled grimly to the work of slaughter.

He had killed half-a-dozen giant birds, and uncounted numbers of smaller birds and carnivorous gang-bats, when Oggbad's main force arrived on the scene.

Huge gray cats, ordinarily daytime creatures, loomed at him out of the gathering dusk. The computer's roboid police, firing from windows and doorways, were suddenly confronted with gigantic beasts with armored bony snouts and tails like giant sledgehammers. Many-legged segmented creatures crawled up the sides of buildings, groped around out in the air, vanished within, and reappeared in the tunnels. Enormous snakes grappled with equally enormous armored metal caterpillars, and, as often as not, the snakes crushed or smashed some vital part before the guns of the metal caterpillars could kill the snakes. The street lights came on to light a scene out of a nightmare, a war amongst animals and machines, with no humans in sight but Roberts and Hammell, dripping blood, the golden coating of their armor chipped and dented, but swords and guns in hand and hewing to the task with such savage energy that they seemed to be everywhere at once.

Toward dawn, a powerful amplified voice boomed out:

"The power of the fiend yields to the Duke! The usurper weakens!"

As daylight shone down on the bloody shambles, the same voice roared: "By command of the Duke, clear the tunnels of the enemy! The worst is over!"

By noon, dented roboid maintenance machines were dragging off the bodies of huge creatures in one direction, while towing disabled machines away in the other direction.

Kelty, covered with large and small bandages, beside an equally-bandaged figure with tattered lightning-bolt armband, was in a building along the boundary between the two parts of the city, listening attentively to Roberts, whose armor looked as if it had spent the last thousand years grinding along under a glacier. Roberts wasted no time finishing up the conference with his two subordinates.

"That's how it is," he said. "Now you've experienced it. Oggbad inspirited those beasts, using the arts of the Unseen Realms, and had he been able to calm their mutual distrust, it would have gone ill with us. Next time, he may have learned that lesson. By that time, our strength must encompass a portion of the

forest itself, and all of the fields, lest he destroy the food supply.
No man can rest easy while the fiend's soul still cleaves to his
body. Now, then. My duties do not allow me to oversee the
details. Great affairs are afoot in the Empire, and I must see to
them. But count on me to come back, to reward the diligent,
destroy the faithless, cleanse by agony the souls of those ensnared
by Oggbad—and, if possible, surprise the fiend himself when he
expects it least."

Kelty glanced at the fanatics' leader, who looked back with the
expression of someone tangled up in a legal matter that threatens
to go on forever, but who is determined to find a way to somehow
warp it around to his own advantage. This fit right in with the
atmosphere of the Baron's Council Hall, which was what Roberts
had named the building. In this building, there was a mild, but
nevertheless noticeable, urge to *think*. Since Roberts had been in
here, several patrolling guards had turned away uneasily, while
others had briefly stepped in with an air of interest. Other parts of
the city had other faint, but noticeable, suggestions of a desire to
work, a desire to study, to relax, to worship, or to rest. For each
place, a slight but definite atmosphere had been created, and was
being maintained, by the want-generator. But that didn't mean that
it couldn't readily get out of hand, if a person seriously misinter-
preted the *purpose* of the desire.

"I *hope*," said Roberts, noting the intensely-calculating look on
the faces of his two human companions, "that there will be *no
warring among my vassals*. In the Empire, it is our custom to
submit such affairs to heavenly judgment. This we do by sending
both disputants into the next world. We can get them there, but so
far have found no way to get them back again. Now, gentlemen,
I must leave for a time. Would that Oggbad were destroyed, but
at least his material power and the strength of his coalition are
broken. While you hold him here, we must smash the last of his
confederates." Roberts stood up. "Good-bye for now, gentlemen.
I am sorry to be in such haste. But I'll be back."

Roberts went out to the ship just outside, and, worn-out and
half-dazed, and not knowing if he were the Duke Vaughan, or
whether Oggbad was real, or what *was* going on, Roberts got back
into the patrol ship, managed to get out of his armor without
spearing Hammell with the tapering helmet-spike, and lifted off.

The view screen showed him that, down below, battered and
bandaged tens of thousands were cheering the rising patrol ship.

"Well," said Roberts, sucking in a deep breath, "either they're cheering us, or our departure."

"Our *apparent* departure," said Hammell.

"Correct," said Roberts, starting to feel like himself again.

He swung the ship in a fast steep climb, taking it apparently toward outer space. When he'd gotten up high enough, the symbiotic computer told him that that was enough to enable it to fool the planetary computer into thinking they'd left the planet. Then Roberts came back from a different direction, and headed for the clearing.

"Well," he said, "that gets us past the first crisis, anyway. Now they've got an urgent reason to stick together. The next thing we want to do is to lay down an overall 'desire for order' field in the city, and a 'desire for adventure' field outside. It seems to me there's an interaction between a person's natural desires, and the field impressed by the want-generator. People can only be comfortable when the two are compatible. What we want is for the workers to be in the city, and the warriors and hunters to be in the forest. This business of trying to cram different types into the same mold in the same place won't work. Let's have it so that if a man wants out, he can *get* out. But, after he does get out, survival is his problem."

"What you figure," said Hammell, "is that the ones that want to learn will find it possible to study; the ones that want to fight, to conquer something, will be able to do that; the ones that want to work will be able to. And the desire-fields will keep the warriors from raiding the workers, and the teachers from trying to drag the warriors into the classrooms; while the *individual*, if he outlives one desire, is free to settle in another place with a different outlook, so long as his own desire doesn't so conflict with the desire-field there as to make him acutely uncomfortable?"

"That's the general idea," said Roberts. "And if we can do it, it ought to eliminate a lot of need for external controls, allow a good deal of freedom, and bring this place closer to being a paradise than it would ever be with a computer monotonously doling out food, clothing, lodging, and everything else on a ration system, and then insisting that now everyone should be happy. The computer is great for rationalizing the production and distribution of the necessities of life. But it just naturally gets stuck when it leaves *desire* out of its calculations."

"Which," said Hammell, "it naturally does. Human leaders do

it themselves. There's nothing quite like desire to wreck *anyone's* calculations. Maybe even ours."

Roberts nodded soberly. "Very possible. Well—We'll see."

Their accumulated leave was almost up when the three men took a final look at the city on the spy screen. The change in the place was noticeable not only in the glazed windows and painted buildings, but in the walk of the people who remained in the city. They no longer had to fear being knocked over the head and robbed for daring to make anything. Those of them who best loved a good knock-down drag-out fight, an ambush, or a raid for plunder, were out beyond the roboid-manned barrier line fighting Oggbad's army. Either they had what it took, and came back with a heavy leather sack of fangs and claws, which the computer—on Duke Vaughan's order, relayed from a distance—would redeem at an impressive price in whatever merchandise or service the various warriors might choose—or else they lacked what it took and "went to Oggbad." Those that tended to be warriors mostly with their mouths were in a worse spot yet. The workers invariably asked to see their trophies, while the warriors were becoming adept at spotting them on sight, and would lug them off to the forest just for the fun of it.

"Boy," said Hammell, "what a place! And yet, if anyone should go around there now demanding a revolution, he'd get brained."

Roberts nodded. "They don't want to revolt, because their *real* desires have a legitimate outlet. Not just the desires they *ought* to have, but the desires they *do* have. A man who wants steak can get awfully sick of a steady diet of ice cream—even if it's the best ice cream made, and he can't find any fault with it."

Morrissey said moodily, "I hate to leave this place. And I *still* don't trust the head of those fanatics."

Hammell said, "Just among the three of us, it's going to be a little hard to go back to being a cargo-control officer after being His Imperial Highness, Duke Ewald of Greme."

Roberts said, "The first chance we get, after we stock up on some more parts for the want-generator, I think we'd better come back here."

Hammell and Morrissey at once looked up with enthusiasm.

"After all," said Roberts, "from they way things are going, poor Oggbad is going to need help."

STEEL BROTHER

Gordon R. Dickson

> *"We stand on guard."*
> —Motto of the Frontier Force

". . . Man that is born of woman hath but a short time to live and is full of misery. He cometh up and is cut down, like a flower; he fleeth as it were a shadow and never continueth in one stay—"

The voice of the chaplain was small and sharp in the thin air, intoning the words of the burial service above the temporary lectern set up just inside the transparent wall of the landing field dome. Through the double transparencies of the dome and the plastic cover of the burial rocket the black-clad ranks could see the body of the dead stationman, Ted Waskewicz, lying back comfortably at an angle of forty-five degrees, peaceful in death, waxily perfect from the hands of the embalmers, and immobile. The eyes were closed, the cheerful, heavy features still held their expression of thoughtless dominance, as though death had been a minor incident, easily shrugged off; and the battle star made a single blaze of color on the tunic of the black uniform.

"Amen." The response was a deep bass utterance from the assembled men, like the single note of an organ. In the front rank of the Cadets, Thomas Jordan's lips moved stiffly with the others', his voice joining mechanically in their chorus. For this was the moment of his triumph, but in spite of it, the old, old fear had come back, the old sense of loneliness and loss and terror of his own inadequacy.

He stood at stiff attention, eyes to the front, trying to lose himself in the unanimity of his classmates, to shut out the voice of the chaplain and the memory it evoked of an alien raid on an undefended city and of home and parents swept away from him in a breath. He remembered the mass burial service read over the shattered ruin of the city; and the government agency that had taken him—a ten-year-old orphan—and given him care and training until this day, but could not give him what these others about him had by natural right—the courage of those who had matured in safety.

For he had been lonely and afraid since that day. Untouched by bomb or shell, he had yet been crippled deep inside. He had seen the enemy in his strength and run screaming from his spacesuited gangs. And what could give Thomas Jordan back his soul after that?

But still he stood rigidly at attention, as a Guardsman should; for he was a soldier now, and this was part of his duty.

The chaplain's voice droned to a halt. He closed his prayerbook and stepped back from the lectern. The captain of the training ship took his place.

"In accordance with the conventions of the Frontier Force," he said, crisply, "I now commit the ashes of Station Commandant First Class, Theodore Waskewicz, to the keeping of time and space."

He pressed a button on the lectern. Beyond the dome, white fire blossomed out from the tail of the burial rocket, heating the asteroid rock to temporary incandescence. For a moment it hung there, spewing flame. Then it rose, at first slowly, then quickly, and was gone, sketching a fiery path out and away, until, at almost the limits of human sight, it vanished in a sudden, silent explosion of brilliant light.

Around Jordan, the black-clad ranks relaxed. Not by any physical movement, but with an indefinable breaking of nervous tension, they settled themselves for the more prosaic conclusion of the ceremony. The relaxation reached even to the captain, for he about-faced with a relieved snap and spoke to the ranks.

"Cadet Thomas Jordan. Front and center."

The command struck Jordan with an icy shock. As long as the burial service had been in progress, he had the protection of anonymity among his classmates around him. Now, the captain's voice was a knife, cutting him off, finally and irrevocably from the one security his life had known, leaving him naked and exposed. A despairing numbness seized him. His reflexes took over, moving his body like a robot. One step forward, a right face, down to the end of the row of silent men, a left face, three steps forward. Halt. Salute.

"Cadet Thomas Jordan reporting, sir."

"Cadet Thomas Jordan, I hereby invest you with command of this Frontier Station. You will hold it until relieved. Under no conditions will you enter communications with an enemy or allow any creature or vessel to pass through your sector of space from Outside."

"Yes, sir."

"In consideration of the duties and responsibilities requisite on assuming command of this Station, you are promoted to the rank and title of Station Commandant Third Class."

"Thank you, sir."

From the lectern the captain lifted a cap of silver wire mesh and placed it on his head. It clipped on to the electrodes already buried in his skull, with a snap that sent sound ringing through his skull. For a second, a sheet of lightning flashed in front of his eyes and he seemed to feel the weight of the memory bank already pressing on his mind. Then lightning and pressure vanished together to show him the captain offering his hand.

"My congratulations, Commandant."

"Thank you, sir."

They shook hands, the captain's grip quick, nervous and perfunctory. He took one abrupt step backward and transferred his attention to his second in command.

"Lieutenant! Dismiss the formation!"

It was over. The new rank locked itself around Jordan, sealing up the fear and loneliness inside him. Without listening to the barked commands that no longer concerned him, he turned on his heel and strode over to take up his position by the sally port of the training ship. He stood formally at attention beside it, feeling the weight of his new authority like a heavy cloak on his thin shoulders. At one stroke he had become the ranking officer present. The officers—even the captain—were nominally under his authority, so long as their ship remained grounded at his Station. So rigidly he stood at attention that not even the slightest tremor of the trembling inside him escaped to quiver betrayingly in his body.

They came toward him in a loose, dark mass that resolved itself into a single file just beyond saluting distance. Singly, they went past him and up the ladder into the sally port, each saluting him as they passed. He returned the salutes stiffly, mechanically, walled off from classmates of six years by the barrier of his new command. It was a moment when a smile or a casual handshake would have meant more than a little. But protocol had stripped him of the right to familiarity; and it was a line of black-uniformed strangers that now filed slowly past. His place was already established and theirs was yet to be. They had nothing in common anymore.

The last of the men went past him up the ladder and were lost in view through the black circle of the sally port. The heavy steel plug swung slowly to, behind them. He turned and made his way to the unfamiliar but well-known field control panel in the main control room of the Station. A light glowed redly on the communications board. He thumbed a switch and spoke into a grill set in the panel.

"Station to Ship. Go ahead."

Overhead the loudspeaker answered.

"Ship to Station. Ready for take-off."

His fingers went swiftly over the panel. Outside, the atmosphere of the field was evacuated and the dome slid back. Tractor mechs scurried out from the pit, under remote control, clamped huge magnetic fists on the ship, swung it into launching position, then retreated.

Jordan spoke again into the grill.

"Station clear. Take-off at will."

"Thank you, Station." He recognized the captain's voice. "And good luck."

Outside, the ship lifted, at first slowly, then faster on its pillar of flame, and dwindled away into the darkness of space. Automatically, he closed the dome and pumped the air back in.

He was turning away from the control panel, bracing himself against the moment of finding himself completely isolated, when, with a sudden, curious shock, he noticed that there was another, smaller ship yet on the field.

For a moment he stared at it blankly, uncomprehendingly. Then memory returned and he realized that the ship was a small courier vessel from Intelligence, which had been hidden by the huge bulk of the training ship. Its officer would still be below, cutting a record tape of the former commandant's last memories for the file at Headquarters. The memory lifted him momentarily from the morass of his emotions to attention to duty. He turned from the panel and went below.

In the triply-armored basement of the Station, the man from

Intelligence was half in and half out of the memory bank when he arrived, having cut away a portion of the steel casing around the bank so as to connect his recorder direct to the cells. The sight of the heavy mount of steel with the ragged incision in one side, squatting like a wounded monster, struck Jordan unpleasantly; but he smoothed the emotion from his face and walked firmly to the bank. His footsteps rang on the metal floor; and the man from Intelligence, hearing them, brought his head momentarily outside the bank for a quick look.

"Hi!" he said, shortly, returning to his work. His voice continued from the interior of the bank with a friendly, hollow sound. "Congratulations, Commandant."

"Thanks," answered Jordan, stiffly. He stood, somewhat ill at ease, uncertain of what was expected of him. When he hesitated, the voice from the bank continued.

"How does the cap feel?"

Jordan's hands went up instinctively to the mesh of silver wire on his head. It pushed back unyieldingly at his fingers, held firmly on the electrodes.

"Tight," he said.

The Intelligence man came crawling out of the bank, his recorder in one hand and thick loops of glassy tape in the other.

"They all do at first," he said, squatting down and feeding one end of the tape into a spring rewind spool. "In a couple of days you won't even be able to feel it up there."

"I suppose."

The Intelligence man looked up at him curiously.

"Nothing about it bothering you, is there?" he asked. "You look a little strained."

"Doesn't everybody when they first start out?"

"Sometimes," said the other, noncommittally. "Sometimes not. Don't hear a sort of humming, do you?"

"No."

"Feel any kind of pressure inside your head?"

"No."

"How about your eyes? See any spots or flashes in front of them?"

"No!" snapped Jordan.

"Take it easy," said the man from Intelligence. "This is my business."

"Sorry."

"That's all right. It's just that if there's anything wrong with you or the bank I want to know it." He rose from the rewind spool, which was now industriously gathering in the loose tape; and unclipping a pressure-torch from his belt, began resealing the aperture. "It's just that occasionally new officers have been hearing too many stories about the banks in Training School, and they're inclined to be jumpy."

"Stories?" said Jordan.

"Haven't you heard them?" answered the Intelligence man. "Stories of memory domination—stationmen driven insane by the memories of the men who had the Station before them. Catatonics whose minds have got lost in the past history of the bank, or cases of memory replacement where the stationman has identified himself with the memories and personality of the man who preceded him."

"Oh, those," said Jordan. "I've heard them." He paused, and then, when the other did not go on: "What about them? Are they true?"

The Intelligence man turned from the half-resealed aperture and faced him squarely, torch in hand.

"Some," he said bluntly. "There's been a few cases like that; although there didn't have to be. Nobody's trying to sugarcoat the facts. The memory bank's nothing but a storehouse connected to you through your silver cap—a gadget to enable you not only to remember everything you ever do at the station, but also everything anybody else who ever ran the Station did. But there've been a few impressionable stationmen who've let themselves get the notion that the memory bank's a sort of coffin with living dead men crawling around inside it. When that happens, there's trouble."

He turned away from Jordan, back to his work.

"And that's what you thought was the trouble with me," said Jordan, speaking to his back.

The man from Intelligence chuckled—it was an amazingly human sound.

"In my line, fella," he said, "we check all possibilities." He finished his resealing and turned around.

"No hard feelings?" he said.

Jordan shook his head. "Of course not."

"Then I'll be getting along." He bent over and picked up the spool, which had by now neatly wound up all the tape, straightened up and headed for the ramp that led up from the basement to the landing field. Jordan fell into step beside him.

"You've nothing more to do, then?" he said.

"Just my reports. But I can write those on the way back." They went up the ramp and out through the lock on to the field.

"They did a good job of repairing the battle damage," he went on, looking around the Station.

"I guess they did," said Jordan. The two men paced soberly to the sally port of the Intelligence ship. "Well, so long."

"So long," answered the man from Intelligence, activating the sally port mechanism. The outer lock swung open and he stepped the few feet up to the opening without waiting for the little ladder to wind itself out. "See you in six months."

He turned to Jordan and gave him a casual, offhand salute with the hand holding the wind-up spool. Jordan returned it with training school precision. The port swung closed.

He went back to the master control room and the ritual of seeing the ship off. He stood looking out for a long time after it had vanished, then turned from the panel with a sigh to find himself at last completely alone.

He looked about the Station. For the next six months this would be his home. Then, for another six months he would be free to leave while the Station was rotated out of the line in its regular order for repair, reconditioning, and improvements.

If he lived that long.

The fear, which had been driven a little distance away by his conversation with the man from Intelligence, came back.

If he lived that long. He stood, bemused.

Back of his mind with the letter-perfect recall of the memory bank came the words of the other. Catatonic—cases of memory replacement. Memory domination. Had those others, too, had more than they could bear of fear and anticipation?

And with that thought came a suggestion that coiled like a snake in his mind. That would be a way out. What if they came, the alien invaders, and Thomas Jordan was no longer here to meet them? What if only the catatonic hulk of a man was left? What if they came and a man was here, but that man called himself and knew himself only as—

Waskewicz!

"No!" the cry came involuntarily from his lips; and he came to himself with his face contorted and his hands half extended in front of him in the attitude of one who wards off a ghost. He shook his head to shake the vile suggestion from his brain; and leaned back, panting, against the control panel.

Not that. Not ever that. He had surprised in himself a weakness that turned him sick with horror. Win or lose; live or die. But as Jordan—not as any other.

He lit a cigarette with trembling fingers. So—it was over now and he was safe. He had caught it in time. He had his warning. Unknown to him—all this time—the seeds of memory domination must have been lying waiting within him. But now he knew they were there, he knew what measures to take. The danger lay in Waskewicz's memories. He would shut his mind off from them— would fight the Station without the benefit of their experience. The first stationmen on the line had done without the aid of a memory bank and so could he.

So.

He had settled it. He flicked on the viewing screens and stood opposite them, very straight and correct in the middle of his Station, looking out at the dots that were his forty-five doggie mechs spread out on guard over a million kilometers of space, looking at the controls that would enable him to throw their blunt, terrible, mechanical bodies into battle with the enemy, looking and waiting, waiting, for the courage that comes from having faced squarely a situation, to rise within him and take possession of him, putting an end to all fears and doubtings.

And he waited so for a long time, but it did not come.

The weeks went swiftly by; and that was as it should be. He had been told what to expect, during training; and it was as it should be that these first months should be tense ones, with a part of him always stiff and waiting for the alarm bell that would mean a doggie signaling sight of an enemy. It was as it should be that he should pause, suddenly, in the midst of a meal with his fork halfway to his mouth, waiting and expecting momentarily to be summoned; that he should wake unexpectedly in the nighttime and lie rigid and tense, eyes fixed on the shadowy ceiling and listening. Later—they had said in training—after you have become used to the Station, this constant tension will relax and you will be left at ease, with only one little unobtrusive corner of your mind unnoticed but forever alert. This will come with time, they said.

So he waited for it, waited for the release of the coiled springs inside him and the time when the feel of the Station would be comfortable and friendly about him. When he had first been left alone, he had thought that surely, in his case, the waiting would not be more than a matter of days; then, as the days went by and he still lived in a state of hair-trigger sensitivity, he had given himself, in his own mind, a couple of weeks—then a month.

But now a month and more than a month had gone without relaxation coming to him; and the strain was beginning to show in nervousness of his hands and the dark circles under his eyes. He found it impossible to sit still either to read, or to listen to the music that was available in the Station library. He roamed restlessly, endlessly checking and rechecking the empty space that his doggies' viewers revealed.

For the recollection of Waskewicz as he lay in the burial rocket would not go from him. And that was not as it should be.

He could, and did, refuse to recall the memories of Waskewicz that he had never experienced; but his own personal recollections were not easy to control and slipped into his mind when he was unaware. All else that he could do to lay the ghost, he had done. He had combed the Station carefully, seeking out the little adjustments and conveniences that a lonely man will make about his home, and removed them, even when the removal meant a loss of personal comfort. He had locked his mind securely to the storehouse of the memory bank, striving to hold himself isolated from the other's memories until familiarity and association should bring him to the point where he instinctively felt that the Station was *his* and not the other's. And, whenever thoughts of Waskewicz entered in spite of all these precautions, he had dismissed them sternly, telling himself that his predecessor was not worth the considering.

But the other's ghost remained, intangible and invulnerable, as if locked in the very metal of the walls and floor and ceiling of the Station; and rising to haunt him with the memories of the training school tales and the ominous words of the man from Intelligence. At such times, when the ghost had seized him, he would stand paralyzed, staring in hypnotic fascination at the screens with their silent mechanical sentinels, or at the cold steel of the memory bank, crouching like some brooding monster, fear feeding on his thoughts—until, with a sudden, wrenching effort of the will, he broke free of the mesmerism and flung himself frantically into the duties of the Station, checking and rechecking his instruments and the space they watched, doing anything and everything to drown his wild emotions in the necessity for attention to duty.

And eventually he found himself almost hoping for a raid, for the test that would prove him, would lay the ghost, one way or another, once and for all.

It came at last, as he had known it would, during one of the rare moments when he had forgotten the imminence of danger. He had awakened in his bunk, at the beginning of the arbitrary ten-hour day; and lay there drowsily, comfortably, his thoughts vague and formless, like shadows in the depths of a lazy whirlpool, turning slowly, going no place.

Then—*the alarm!*

Overhead the shouting bell burst into life, jerking him from his bed. Its metal clangor poured out on the air, tumbling from the loudspeakers in every room all over the Station, strident with urgency, pregnant with disaster. It roared, it vibrated, it thundered, until the walls themselves threw it back, seeming to echo in sympathy, acquiring a voice of their own until the room rang—until the Station itself rang like one monster bell, calling him into battle.

He leaped to his feet and ran to the master control room. On the telltale high on the wall above the viewer screens, the red light of number thirty-eight doggie was flashing ominously. He threw himself into the operator's seat before it, slapping one palm down hard on the switch to disconnect the alarm.

The Station is in contact with the enemy.

The sudden silence slapped at him, taking his breath away. He gasped and shook his head like a man who has had a glassful of cold water thrown unexpectedly in his face; then plunged his fingers at the keys on the master control board in front of his seat— Up beams. Up detector screen, established now at forty thousand kilometers distance. Switch on communications to Sector Headquarters.

The transmitter purred. Overhead, the white light flashed as it began to tick off its automatic signal. "Alert! Alert! Further data follows. Will report."

Headquarters has been notified by the Station.

Activate viewing screen on doggie number thirty-eight.

He looked into the activated screen, into the vast arena of space over which the mechanical vision of that doggie mech was ranging. Far and far away at top magnification were five small dots, coming in fast on a course leading ten points below and at an angle of thirty-two degrees to the Station.

He flicked a key, releasing thirty-eight on proximity fuse control and sending it plunging toward the dots. He scanned the Station area map for the positions of his other mechs. Thirty-nine was missing—in the Station for repair. The rest were available. He checked numbers forty through forty-five and thirty-seven through thirty to rendezvous on collision course with enemy at seventy-five thousand kilometers. Numbers twenty to thirty to rendezvous at fifty thousand kilometers.

Primary defense has been inaugurated.

He turned back to the screen. Number thirty-eight, expendable in the interests of gaining information, was plunging toward the ships at top acceleration under strains no living flesh would have been able to endure. But as yet the size and type of the invaders was still hidden by distance. A white light flashed abruptly from the communications panel, announcing that Sector Headquarters was alerted and ready to talk. He cut in audio.

"Contact. Go ahead, Station J-49C3."

"Five ships," he said. "Beyond identification range. Coming in through thirty-eight at ten point thirty-two."

"Acknowledge." The voice of Headquarters was level, precise, emotionless. "Five ships—thirty-eight—ten—thirty-two. Patrol Twenty, passing through your area at thirty-two. Patrol Twenty, passing through your area at four hours distance, has been notified and will proceed to your station at once, arriving in four hours, plus or minus twenty minutes. Further assistance follows. Will stand by here for your future messages."

The white light went out and he turned away from the communications panel. On the screen, the five ships had still not grown to identifiable proportions, but for all practical purposes, the preliminaries were over. He had some fifteen minutes now during which everything that could be done had been done.

Primary defense has been completed.

He turned away from the controls and walked back to the bedroom, where he dressed slowly and meticulously in full black uniform. He straightened his tunic, looked in the mirror and stood gazing at himself for a long moment. Then, hesitantly, almost as if against his will, he reached out with one hand to a small gray box on a shelf beside the mirror, opened it, and took out the silver battle star that the next few hours would entitle him to wear.

It lay in his palm, the bright metal winking softly up at him under the reflection of the room lights and the small movements of his hand. The little cluster of diamonds in its center sparked and ran the whole gamut of their flashing colors. For several minutes he stood looking at it; then slowly, gently, he shut it back up in its box and went out, back to the control room.

On screen, the ships were now large enough to be identified. They were medium-sized vessels, Jordan noticed, of the type used most by the most common species of raiders—that same race which had orphaned him. There could be no doubt about their intentions, as there sometimes was when some odd stranger chanced on the Frontier, to be regretfully destroyed by men whose orders were to take no chances. No these were *the enemy*, the strange, suicidal life form that thrust thousands of attacks yearly against the little human empire, who blew themselves up when captured and wasted a hundred ships for every one that broke through the guarding stations to descend on some unprotected city of an inner planet and loot it of equipment and machinery that the aliens were either unwilling or unable to build for themselves—a contradictory, little understood and savage race. These five ships would make no attempt to parley.

But now, doggie number thirty-eight had been spotted and the white exhausts of guided missiles began to streak toward the viewing screen. For a few seconds, the little mech bucked and tossed, dodging, firing defensively, shooting down the missiles as they approached. But it was a hopeless fight against those odds and suddenly one of the streaks expanded to fill the screen with glaring light.

And the screen went blank. Thirty-eight was gone.

Suddenly realizing that he should have been covering with observation from one of the doggies further back, Jordan jumped to fill his screens. He brought the view from forty in on the one that thirty-eight had vacated and filled the two flanking screens with the view from thirty-seven on his left and twenty on his right. They showed his first line of defense already gathered at the seventy-five kilometer rendezvous and the fifty thousand kilometer rendezvous still forming.

The raiders were decelerating now, and on the wall, the telltale for the enemy's detectors flushed a sudden deep and angry purple as their invisible beams reached out and were baffled by the detector screen he had erected at a distance of forty thousand kilometers in front of the Station. They continued to decelerate, but the blockage of their detector beams had given them the approximate area of this Station; and they corrected course, swinging in until they were no more than two points and ten degrees in error. Jordan, his nervous fingers trembling slightly on the keys, stretched thirty-seven through thirty out in depth and sent forty through forty-five forward on a five-degree sweep to attempt a circling movement.

The five dark ships of the raiders, recognizing his intention, fell out of their single-file approach formation to spread out and take a formation in open echelon. They were already firing on the advancing doggies and tiny streaks of light tattooed the black of space around numbers forty through forty-five.

Jordan drew a deep and ragged breath and leaned back in his control seat. For the moment there was nothing for his busy fingers to do among the control keys. His thirties must wait until the enemy came to them; since, with modern automatic gunnery the body at rest had an advantage over the body in motion. And it would be some minutes before the forties would be in attack position. He fumbled for a cigarette, keeping his eyes on the screens, remembering the caution in the training manuals against relaxation once contact with the enemy has been made.

But reaction was setting in.

From the first wild ringing command of the alarm until the present moment, he had reacted automatically, with perfection and precision, as the drills had schooled him, as the training manuals had impressed upon him. The enemy had appeared. He had taken measures for defense against them. All that could have been done had been done; and he knew he had done it properly. And the enemy had done what he had been told they would do.

He was struck, suddenly, with the deep quivering realization of the truth in the manual's predictions. It was so, then. These inimical others, these alien foes, were also bound by the physical laws. They, as well as he, could move only within the rules of time and space. They were shorn of their mystery and brought down to his level. Different and awful, they might be, but their capabilities were limited, even as his; and in a combat such as the one now shaping up, their inhumanness was of no account, for the inflexible realities of the universe weighed impartially on him and them alike.

And with this realization, for the first time, the old remembered fear began to fall away like a discarded garment. A tingle ran through him and he found himself warming to the fight as his forefathers had warmed before him away back to the days when man was young and the tiger roared in the cool, damp jungle-dawn of long ago. The blood-instinct was in him; that and something of the fierce, vengeful joy with which a hunted creature turns at last on its pursuer. He would win. Of course he would win. And in winning he would at one stroke pay off the debt of blood and fear which the enemy had held against him these fifteen years.

Thinking in this way, he leaned back in his seat and the old memory of the shattered city and of himself running, running, rose up again around him. But this time it was no longer a prelude of terror, but fuel for the kindling of his rage. *These are my fear*, he thought, gazing unseeingly at the five ships in the screens, *and I will destroy them.*

The phantasms of his memory faded like smoke around him. He dropped his cigarette into a disposal slot on the arm of his seat, and leaned forward to inspect the enemy positions.

They had spread out to force his forties to circle wide, and those doggies were now scattered, safe but ineffective, waiting further directions. What had been an open echelon formation of the raiders was now a ragged, widely dispersed line, with far too much space between ships to allow each to cover his neighbor.

For a moment Jordan was puzzled; and a tiny surge of fear of the inexplicable rippled across the calm surface of his mind. Then his brow smoothed out. There was no need to get panicky. The aliens' maneuver was not the mysterious tactic he had half expected it to be; but just what it appeared, a rather obvious and somewhat stupid move to avoid the flanking movement he had been attempting with his forties. Stupid—because the foolish aliens had now rendered themselves vulnerable to interspersal by his thirties.

It was good news, rather than bad, and his spirits leaped another notch.

He ignored the baffled forties, circling automatically on safety control just beyond the ships' effective aiming range; and turned to the thirties, sending them plunging toward the empty areas between ships as you might interlace the fingers of one hand with another. Between any two ships there would be a dead spot—a position where a mech could not be fired on by either vessel without also aiming at its right- or left-hand companion. If two or more doggies could be brought safely to that spot, they could turn and pour down the open lanes on proximity control, their fuses primed, their bomb loads activated, blind bulldogs of destruction.

One third, at least, should in this way get through the defensive shelling of the ships and track their dodging prey to the atomic flare of a grim meeting.

Smiling now in confidence, Jordan watched his mechs approach the ships. There was nothing the enemy could do. They could not now tighten up their formation without merely making themselves a more attractive target; and to disperse still further would negate any chance in the future of regaining a semblance of formation.

Carefully, his fingers played over the keys, gentling his mechs into line so that they would come as close as possible to hitting their dead spots simultaneously. The ships came on.

Closer the raiders came, and closer. And then—bare seconds away from contact with the line of approaching doggies, white fire ravened in unison from their stern tubes, making each ship suddenly a black nugget in the center of a blossom of flame. In unison, they spurted forward, in sudden and unexpected movement, bringing their dead spots to and past the line of seeking doggies, leaving them behind.

Caught for a second in stunned surprise, Jordan sat dumb and motionless, staring at the screen. Then, swift in his anger, his hands flashed out over the keys, blasting his mechs to a cruel, shuddering halt, straining their metal sinews for the quickest and most abrupt about-face and return. This time he would catch them from behind. This time, going in the same direction as the ships, the mechs could not be dodged. For what living thing could endure equal strains with cold metal?

But there was no second attempt on the part of the thirties, for as each bucked to its savage halt, the rear weapons of the ships reached out in unison, and each of the blasting mechs, that had leaped forward so confidently, flared up and died like little candles in the dark.

Numb in the grip of icy failure, Jordan sat still, a ramrod figure staring at the two screens that spoke so eloquently of his disaster—and the one dead screen where the view from thirty-seven had been, that said nothing at all. Like a man in a dream, he reached out his right hand and cut in the final sentinel, the *watchdog*, that mech that circled closest to the Station. In one short breath his strong first line was gone, and the enemy rode their strength undiminished, floating in toward his single line of twenties at fifty thousand with the defensive screen a mere ten thousand kilometers behind them.

Training was strong. Without hesitation his hands went out over the keys and the doggies of the twenties surged forward, trying for contact with the enemy in an area as far from the screen as possible. But, because they were moving in on an opponent relatively at rest, their courses were the more predictable on the enemy's calculators and the disadvantage was theirs. So it was that forty minutes later three ships of the aliens rode clear and unthreatened in an area where two of their mates, the forties and all of the thirties were gone.

The ships were, at this moment, fifteen thousand kilometers from the detector screen.

Jordan looked at his handiwork. The situation was obvious and the alternatives undeniable. He had twenty doggies remaining, but he had neither the time to move them up beyond the screen, nor the room to maneuver them in front of it. The only answer was to pull his screen back. But to pull the screen back would be to indicate, by its shrinkage and the direction of its withdrawal, the position of his Station clearly enough for the guided missiles of the enemy to seek him out; and once the Station was knocked out, the doggies were directionless, impotent.

Yet, if he did nothing, in a few minutes the ships would touch and penetrate the detector screen and his Station, the nerve center the aliens were seeking, would lie naked and revealed in their detectors.

He had lost. The alternatives totaled to the same answer, to defeat. In the inattention of a moment, in the smoke of a cigarette, the first blind surge of self-confidence and the thoughtless halting of his bypassed doggies that had allowed the ships' calculators to find them stationary for a second in a predictable area, he had failed. He had given away, in the error of his pride, the initial advantage. He had lost. Speak it softly, speak it gently, for his fault was the fault of one young and untried. He was defeated.

And in the case of defeat, the action prescribed by the manual was stern and clear. The memory of the instructions tolled in his mind like the unvarying notes of a funeral bell.

"When, in any conflict, the forces of the enemy have obtained a position of advantage such that it is no longer possible to maintain the anonymity of the Station's position, the commandant of the Station is required to perform one final duty. Knowing that the Station will shortly be destroyed and that this will render all

remaining mechs innocuous to enemy forces, the commandant is commanded to relinquish control of these mechs, and to place them with fuses primed on proximity control, in order that, even without the Station, they may be enabled to automatically pursue and attempt to destroy those forces of the enemy that approach within critical range of their proximity fuse."

Jordan looked at his screens. Out at forty thousand kilometers, the detector screen was beginning to luminesce slightly as the detectors of the ships probed it at shorter range. To make the manual's order effective, it would have to be pulled back to at least half that distance; and there, while it would still hide the Station, it would give the enemy his approximate location. They would then fire blindly, but with cunning and increasing knowledge and it would be only a matter of time before they hit. After that—only the blind doggies, quivering, turning and trembling through all points of the stellar compass in their thoughtless hunger for prey. One or two of these might gain a revenge as the ships tried to slip past them and over the Line; but Jordan would not be there to know it.

But there was no alternative—even if duty had left him one. Like strangers, his hands rose from the board and stretched out over the keys that would turn the doggies loose. His fingers dropped and rested upon them—light touch on smooth polished coolness.

But he could not press them down.

He sat with his arms outstretched, as if in supplication, like one of his primitive forebearers before some ancient altar of death. For his will had failed him and there was no denying now his guilt and his failure. For the battle had turned in his short few moments of inattention, and his underestimation of the enemy that had seduced him into halting his thirties without thinking. He knew; and through the memory bank—if that survived—the Force would know. In his neglect, in his refusal to avail himself of the experience of his predecessors, he was guilty.

And yet, he could not press the keys. He could not die properly—*in the execution of his duty*—the cold, correct phrase of the official reports. For a wild rebellion surged through his young body, an instinctive denial of the end that stared him so undeniably in the face. Through vein and sinew and nerve, it raced, opposing and blocking the dictates of training, the logical orders of his upper mind. It was too soon, it was not fair, he had not been given his chance to profit by experience. One more opportunity was all he needed, one more try to redeem himself.

But the rebellion passed and left him shaken, weak. There was no denying reality. And now, a new shame came to press upon him, for he thought of the three alien vessels breaking through, of another city in flaming ruins, and another child that would run screaming from his destroyers. The thought rose up in him, and he writhed internally, torn by his own indecision. Why couldn't he act? It made no difference to him. What would justification and the redeeming of error mean to him after he was dead?

And he moaned a little, softly to himself, holding his hands outstretched above the keys, but could not press them down.

And then hope came. For suddenly, rising up out of the rubble of his mind came the memory of the Intelligence man's words once again, and his own near-pursuit of insanity. He, Jordan, could not bring himself to expose himself to the enemy, not even if the method of exposure meant possible protection for the Inner Worlds. But the man who had held this Station before him, who had died as he was about to die, must have been faced with the same necessity for self-sacrifice. And those last-minute memories of his decision would be in the memory bank, waiting for the evocation of Jordan's mind.

Here was hope at last. He would remember, would embrace the insanity he had shrunk from. He would remember and be Waskewicz, not Jordan. He would be Waskewicz and unafraid; though it was a shameful thing to do. Had there been one person, one memory among all living humans, whose image he could have evoked to place in opposition to the images of the three dark ships, he might have managed by himself. But there had been no one close to him since the day of the city raid.

His mind reached back into the memory bank, reached back to the last of Waskewicz's memories. He remembered.

Of the ten ships attacking, six were down. Their ashes strewed the void and the remaining four rode warily, spread widely apart for maximum safety, sure of victory, but wary of this hornets' nest which might still have some stings yet unexpended. But the detector screen was back to its minimum distance for effective concealment and only five doggies remained poised like blunt arrows behind it. He—Waskewicz—sat hunched before the control board, his thick and hairy hands lying softly on the proximity keys.

"Drift in," he said, speaking to the ships, which were cautiously approaching the screen. "Drift in, you. Drift!"

His lips were skinned back over his teeth in a grin—but he did not mean it. It was an automatic grimace, reflex to the tenseness of his waiting. He would lure them on until the last moment, draw them as close as possible to the automatic pursuit mechanisms of the remaining doggies, before pulling back the screen.

"Drift in," he said.

They drifted in. Behind the screen he aimed his doggies, pointing each one of four at a ship and the remaining one generally at them all. They drifted in.

They touched.

His fingers slapped the keys. The screen snapped back until it barely covered the waiting doggies. And the doggies stirred, on proximity, their pursuit mechs activated, now blind and terribly fully armed, ready to attack in senseless directness anything that came close enough.

And the first shells from the advancing ships began to probe the general area of the Station asteroid.

Waskewicz sighed, pushed himself back from the controls and stood up, turning away from the screens. It was over. Done. All finished. For a moment he stood irresolute; then, walking over to the dispenser on the wall, dialed for coffee and drew it, hot into a disposable cup. He lit a cigarette and stood waiting, smoking and drinking the coffee.

The Station rocked suddenly to the impact of a glancing hit on the asteroid. He staggered and slopped some coffee on his boots, but kept his feet. He took another gulp from the cup, another drag on the cigarette. The Station shook again, and the lights dimmed. He crumpled the cup and dropped it in the disposal slot. He dropped the cigarette on the steel floor, ground it beneath his boot sole; and walked back to the screen and leaned over for it for a final look.

The lights went out. And memory ended.

The present returned to Jordan and he stared about him a trifle wildly. Then he felt hardness beneath his fingers and forced himself to look down.

The keys were depressed. The screen was back. The doggies were on proximity. He stared at his hand as if he had never known it before, shocked at its thinness and the lack of soft down on its back. Then, slowly, fighting reluctant neck muscles, he forced himself to look up and into the viewing screen.

And the ships were there, but the ships were drawing away.

He stared, unable to believe his eyes, and half-ready to believe anything else. For the invaders had turned and the flames from their tails made it evident that they were making away into outer space at their maximum bearable acceleration, leaving him alone and unharmed. He shook his head to clear away the false vision from the screen before him, but it remained, denying its falseness. The miracle for which his instincts had held him in check had come—in the moment in which he had borrowed strength to deny it.

His eyes searched the screens in wonder. And then, far down in one corner of the watchdog's screen and so distant still that they showed only as pips on the wide expanse, he saw the shape of his miracle. Coming up from inside of the Line under maximum bearable acceleration were six gleaming fish-shapes that would dwarf his doggies to minnows—the battleships of Patrol Twenty. And he realized, with the dawning wonder of the reprieved, that the conflict, which had seemed so momentary while he was fighting it had actually lasted the four hours necessary to bring the Patrol up to his aid.

The realization that he was now safe washed over him like a wave and he was conscious of a deep thankfulness swelling up within him. It swelled up and out, pushing aside the lonely fear and desperation of his last few minutes, filling him instead with a relief so all-encompassing and profound that there was no anger left in him and no hate—not even for the enemy. It was like being born again.

Above him on the communications panel, the white message light was blinking. He cut in on the speaker with a steady hand and the dispassionate, official voice of the Patrol sounded over his head.

"Patrol Twenty to Station. Twenty to Station. Come in Station. Are you all right?"

He pressed the transmitter key.

"Station to Twenty. Station to Twenty. No damage to report. The Station is unharmed."

"Glad to hear it, Station. We will not pursue. We are decelerating now and will drop all ships on your field in half an hour. That is all."

His hand fell away from the key and the message light winked out. In unconscious imitation of Waskewicz's memory he pushed himself back from the controls, stood up, turned and walked to the dispenser in the wall, where he dialed for and received a cup of coffee. He lit a cigarette and stood as the other had stood, smoking and drinking. He had won.

And reality came back to him with a rush.

For he looked down at his hand and saw the cup of coffee. He drew in on the cigarette and felt the hot smoothness of it deep in his lungs. And terror took him twisting by the throat.

He had won? He had done nothing. The enemy ships had fled not from him, but from the Patrol; and it was Waskewicz, *Waskewicz*, who had taken the controls from his hands at the crucial moment. It was Waskewicz who had saved the day, not he. It was the memory bank. The memory bank and Waskewicz!

The control room rocked about him. He had been betrayed. Nothing was won. Nothing was conquered. It was no friend that had broken at last through his lonely shell to save him, but the mind-sucking figment of memory-domination sanity. The memory bank and Waskewicz had seized him in their grasp.

He threw the coffee container from him and made himself stand upright. He threw the cigarette down and ground it beneath his boot. White-hot, from the very depths of his being, a wild anger blazed and consumed him. *Puppet*, said the mocking voice of his conscience, whispering in his ear. *Puppet!*

Dance, Puppet! Dance to the tune of the twitching strings!

"No!" he yelled. And, borne on the white-hot tide of his rage, the all-consuming rage that burnt the last trace of fear from his heart like dross from the molten steel, he turned to face his tormentor, hurling his mind backward, back into the life of Waskewicz, prisoned in the memory bank.

Back through the swirling tide of memories he raced, hunting a point of contact, wanting only to come to grips with his predecessor, to stand face to face with Waskewicz. Surely, in all his years at the Station, the other must sometime have devoted a thought to the man who must come after him. Let Jordan just find that point, there where the influence was strongest, and settle the matter, for sanity or insanity, for shame or pride, once and for all.

"Hi Brother!"

The friendly words splashed like cool water on the white blaze of his anger. He—Waskewicz—stood in front of the bedroom mirror and his face looked out at the man who was himself, and who yet was also Jordan.

"Hi, Brother!" he said. "Whoever and wherever you may be. Hi!"

Jordan looked out through the eyes of Waskewicz, at the reflected face of Waskewicz; and it was a friendly face, the face of a man like himself.

"This is what they don't tell you," said Waskewicz. "This is what they don't teach in training—the message that, sooner or later, every stationman leaves for the guy who comes after him.

"This is the creed of the Station. *You are not alone.* No matter what happens, *you are not alone.* Out on the rim of the empire, facing the unknown races and the endless depths of the universe, this is the one thing that will keep you from all harm. As long as you remember it, nothing can affect you, neither attack, nor defeat, nor death. Light a screen on your outer most doggie and turn the magnification up as far as it will go. Away out at the limits of your vision you can see the doggie of another Station, of another man who holds the Line beside you. All along the Frontier, the Outpost Stations stand, forming a link of steel to guard the Inner Worlds and the little people there. They have their lives and you have yours; and yours is to stand on guard.

"It is not easy to stand on guard; and no man can face the universe alone. But—*you are not alone!* All those who at this moment keep the Line, are with you; and all that have ever kept the Line, as well. For this is our new immortality, we who guard the Frontier, that we do not stop with our deaths, but live on in the Station we have kept. We are in its screens, its controls, in its memory bank, in the very bone and sinew of its steel body. *We are the station*, your steel brother that fights and lives and dies with you and welcomes you at last to our kinship when for your personal self the light has gone out forever, and what was individual of you is nothing anymore but cold ashes drifting in the eternity of space. *We are with you and of you, and you are not alone.* I, who was once Waskewicz, and am now part of the Station, leave this message for you, as it was left to me by the man who kept this guard before me, and as you will leave it in your turn to the man who follows you, and so on down the centuries until we have become an elder race and no longer need our shield of brains and steel.

"Hi, Brother! You are not alone!"

• • •

   And so, when the six ships of Patrol Twenty came drifting in to their landing at the Station, the man who waited to greet them had more than the battle star on his chest to show he was a veteran. For he had done more than win a battle. He had found his soul.